PRICELESS

Sass and Steam
Book 2

Catherine Stein

Copyright © 2020 Catherine Stein, LLC.

All rights reserved. No part of this book may be used or reproduced by any means, graphic, electronic, or mechanical, including photocopying, recording, taping or by any information storage retrieval system without the written permission of the author except in the case of brief quotations embodied in critical articles and reviews.

This is a work of fiction. Names, characters, places, and incidents are products of the author's imagination or are used fictitiously. Any resemblance to actual events or persons, living or dead, is entirely coincidental.

ISBN: 978-1-949862-22-5

Book cover and interior design by E. McAuley:
www.impluviumstudios.com

For artists, makers, and creators.
Thank you for all the beauty you add to the world.

PROLOGUE

New York City, 1879

The smack of a hand against a cheek reverberated over the hum of machinery. Evan knew better than to turn and look, or even wince.

"But I don't know how!"

New boys. The foreman slapped the boy again, and he whimpered. He'd learn soon enough. When the owners were here, you did as you were told, and never mind if it wasn't your job. They'd take any excuse to hit you. The bruises and swelling didn't show underneath the grime.

Evan scrubbed the floor harder, in case anyone was looking. The foreman brushed past him.

"Mr. Reynolds, sir, it's such a pleasure to have you here today! Mrs. Reynolds, charmed, ma'am."

Evan scooted behind the nearest machine and grabbed his chalk. He'd be safe here for now, though the adults might eventually circle back around to this area. Best to look like he was working. He scratched a few marks on the floor, then scrubbed them away, to make it appear he was actually cleaning something. He wrote his name. *Scrub.* Some numbers. *Scrub.*

1

His mind began to wander, as it always did when he was bored. *Scratch, scratch, scrub. Scratch, scratch, scrub. Scratch...*

He could fix the mechanical rat. If he rounded off the nose and moved the key...

Numbers began to dance in his head and the world drifted away.

"What's that you're drawing, boy?"

Evan jerked back to reality. The chalk clattered to the floor and he lunged for the rag.

"No, don't wipe it."

Mr. Reynolds loomed over him. Mrs. Reynolds stood nearby, in a pale yellow dress as spotlessly clean as anything Evan had ever seen.

"What is that?" Mr. Reynolds asked. "Tell me about it."

Evan coughed—a horrible, sick, hacking sort of cough. He'd get smacked for sure for coughing in front of the owner, but he couldn't control when the fits came on. Mr. Reynolds waited, staring him down. Maybe he'd do the smacking himself.

"It's a cleaning rat," Evan choked out.

"Not one I've ever seen."

"It's a better one. The ones we got, they get stuck."

And often. The smaller boys, like Evan, crawled under the machines to pull them out. When the owners weren't here, at least.

"This one, it don't gots that pointy nose what gets wedged under stuff. And it gots its key on the end like a tail so's it don't stick up. And you can't see the legs, but they're gonna be tucked up underneath so's they won't get caught."

"Stand up, boy, and let me have a look."

Evan leapt to his feet, his fingers clenching on the rag, bracing for a smack. Mr. Reynolds walked a slow circle around the drawing that marred his factory floor.

Mrs. Reynolds lifted a cloth to Evan's face. He flinched, but the material was a gentle caress against his skin.

"Such a beautiful child under that dirt. How old are you, dear? Six?"

"I'm nine."

"Such a tiny thing. Here, do you like apples?"

She presented him a shiny red fruit from her bag. Evan didn't remember what apples tasted like, but his mouth watered.

"This is brilliant!" Mr. Reynolds exclaimed. "You even have measurements!"

"It gots to have numbers so's people make it right."

"You have talent, boy. Damned brilliant talent. Do you know how to read?"

"Yes."

It was only half a lie. Evan knew all his letters. He could write his name and he'd taught himself every word on every sign in the factory.

"Good. What's your name?"

"Evan Tagget. People call me Mite."

"Tagget. I'll remember that. You're a little young, but train you up a few years and you could make me a fortune. Excellent, excellent. Come, Mrs. Reynolds, let's see what other surprises are in store today."

Evan watched them go, clutching his apple, still trembling in anticipation of the beating that had never occurred. His eyes dropped to the fruit in his hand. He had never seen anything so beautiful. It crunched in his teeth, flooding his mouth with the sweetest taste he had ever experienced.

He chewed slowly, savoring the flavor. With his second bite, he closed his eyes, shutting out everything but the perfection of the apple.

A large hand clamped down on his shoulder.

"What've you got there, brat?" The foreman snagged the apple from Evan's grasp. "You stealing?"

"No!" Evan panicked, clawing at the air in a vain attempt to reclaim his treasure. "Give it!" The blow to his head brought tears to his eyes. "It's mine!"

"Not anymore." He chucked the most precious thing Evan had ever had into the nearest furnace.

Evan howled in rage and despair, slamming his fist into the foreman's meaty thigh.

The man slammed him against a metal press. Pain blossomed throughout his left side, and the tears swelled to a deluge. The foreman smacked him one final time, cursed at him, and shoved him to the floor.

"Get back to work."

Evan crawled across the factory floor, weeping in pain and fury. The moment the coast was clear, he scurried under the loose grating to his nest beneath the steam forge. He hugged Ratty to his chest and curled into a ball. The familiar bumps and angles of the battered old cleaning rat brought only mild relief to the hurt and anger boiling inside him. Mr. Reynolds had called him brilliant. Mrs. Reynolds had called him beautiful. He was smarter, prettier, better than those bullies. He would get out of this hellhole, and he would make it so no one could smack him around or tell him what to do ever again.

Someday, Evan Tagget would have all the power.

1

Paris, June, 1905

THE WARDROBE DUG GREAT GOUGES in the floor planks as Violet hauled it across the apartment. The landlord would be furious. The landlord would never see her again.

Heavy boots thundered up the staircase outside. Vi gave the massive cabinet a final shove and it teetered and fell against the door. It would buy her a moment's time.

She made one last sweep of the room, looking for anything of value she may have missed. A single paint brush lay in the dusty rectangle where the wardrobe had once stood. She snatched it up and shoved it through the knot of hair atop her head. No sense leaving good tools lying around. She cinched her purse at her waist and threw open the window.

Her head swam. Four stories up, and no way down but the rickety metal pipe that had been haphazardly affixed to the building to carry water to the upper floors. She swung one leg over the sill. Voices shouted from the hall and fists pounded at her door. She had no choice. She grabbed hold of the pipe and slid out the window.

Several terrifying seconds later, her feet hit the pavement and she let out a gasp of relief.

"Lovely knickers," the neighbor boy said in French, leering at her.

Violet gave him a contemptuous smile. "Aren't they, though?" she answered in the same language. "I stole them from your mother." She scampered off, leaving him staring, open-mouthed.

Vi wound her way through town, disappearing into the crowd, putting good distance between herself and the now-abandoned apartment. It was time to lay low for a few days. She knew several boarding houses that would take overnighters, no questions asked, but her current pursuers were savvier than usual and might know about them. For tonight, she'd drop into a theater or folies house. She could always blend in with the vibrant colors and carefree ways of professional entertainers.

On the bustling streets of the city, Violet at last began to relax and consider her future beyond the night's accommodations. Perhaps she would travel north for a time. She'd never been as far as London, and she wouldn't be sad to spend some time in an English-speaking country. She could hardly remember the last time she'd had a conversation in her native language. Yes, a few months across the Channel sounded just the thing.

Her mind occupied with plans, she turned to enter the theater and nearly crashed into a familiar face.

"Ah, Mademoiselle d'Aubergine, how nice to see you." Monsieur Berger's blue eyes glinted as the French words rolled smoothly off his tongue. "Might I bother you for a moment of your time?" He took her arm and steered her away from the entrance.

Vi tried to shrug out of his grip, but his fingers were as unyielding as a steel manacle. "What do you want from me?" she demanded. "I thought our business was concluded."

"It pains me to say so, mademoiselle, but *your* business has only begun. These gentlemen here would like a word with you."

A trio of uniformed police marched toward her, closing in from all sides. The same goons who had been chasing her earlier. Damn. She squirmed, but her captor didn't relax his hold until escape was an impossibility.

"Why are you doing this? You… you hired me!"

Berger's smile was gentle. "Under false pretenses, mademoiselle. I'm truly impressed by your work, but I fear your criminal career has come to an end. Running will only make things worse."

"You bastard," she spat out.

"It's been a pleasure meeting you. I know you to be a resourceful woman, and I'm certain you will handle the situation with aplomb." He tipped his hat to her. "Best of luck, Miss Dayton," he said in English. Perfect English, spoken with the crisp accent of an upper-class Londoner. A spy? Damn *and* blast.

"I do believe you will go far," he added. He spun on his heel and departed, leaving her in the clutches of the police.

Violet fumed internally as they ushered her to the station. The betrayal stung. How could she have been so stupid? She had liked Monsieur Berger—if that was even his name. He was shrewd and witty. She'd even thought him rather attractive, though he had to be pushing fifty. Stupid, stupid girl. How could she not have learned after all these years? Intelligent men were her weakness.

She plopped down on the wobbly stool and stared up at her interrogator, meeting his harsh gaze with one of indifference. She wouldn't be cowed by brutes, and she wouldn't confess to anything.

"You are Mademoiselle Violette d'Aubergine, correct?" asked the inspector, a stony-faced man named Crevier. Despite Berger's revelation of her real name, Crevier addressed her in French.

"Oui."

"And you are an artist?"

"I am."

He flipped through a stack of papers. "You have been very busy, it seems, Miss d'Aubergine. Or should I call you Vérité?"

"Call me whatever you wish, but I make no guarantee I will respond."

Crevier's laugh was nasty, condescending. "As you can see, mademoiselle, we have a great deal of information about your career. More than enough to lock you away for decades. At present, however, we have larger concerns than rich fools buying fake masterpieces. You have contacts and connections in the criminal world. You know art, and you know the intersection between art and vice. We would like the assistance of someone like you, Miss d'Aubergine, to sniff out a thief. One who has thus far eluded us all, and whose plunderage and audacity continue to grow. Track him down, bring him to justice, and you can go free."

Vi pursed her lips, weighing her options. The door was too well-guarded to make a run for it, and she couldn't fight her way out, despite the small knife she kept concealed beneath her clothing. She didn't believe for an instant he would truly let her go, even if she did do what he wanted. But if she agreed to Crevier's terms, she could escape the police station and perhaps arrange to skip town.

"What resources will be at my disposal?" she asked. Best to have all the information she could get and imply she was considering the matter seriously.

"Resources?" Crevier snorted. "Mademoiselle, your brain and your connections are your resources. We are not in the habit of giving handouts to reprobates."

Vi glared at him. "Then it's impossible. I can't track down a master thief without money and transportation at the very least."

"I will give you papers with information regarding the thefts. Anything further is your own responsibility." His haughty smile grew wider. "And don't think you can run, Madame Vérité. If you try, I will publish your artist name, your real name, and your criminal name in every major paper from here to your hometown of Melbourne." He waved a hand, and a man behind him lifted a camera and snapped several photos. "Your photograph, will, of course, be included."

"Of course," Violet replied, her jaw clenching. They hadn't even taken a real mugshot of her. This entire "negotiation" was underhanded and probably illegal.

"My offer is generous, considering the circumstances," Crevier continued. "Accept it and you have a chance to walk free. Defy me, and you will never work again unless you're flat on your back. Do we have an agreement?"

Violet had no other option. She forced calm into her voice. "Will you make your offer in writing?" The paper would do no good except to prove he'd blackmailed her, but it was better than nothing.

He gave her a nod, his lips curling in a sneer. "I suppose that can be arranged."

"Good. Bring me the document and you have a deal."

The smell of paint and the *chink, chink* of hammer and chisel in the background would forever conjure up a soothing sensation of home, even though Violet hadn't lived in Sophie Pascal's artists' commune for years. Once Vi, too, had worked in this large, open room. Today, she had only come for a visit.

She stretched out her legs and regarded her friend across the large, oak desk that dominated the corner office area.

"You're certain you won't stay?" Sophie asked again. She wound a hand-painted ribbon around one of her tight braids and studied the result in a hand mirror. Another prototype for her booming business of artistic accessories for Black women. The commune thrived off the profits.

Violet eyed the new ribbons. Good for any number of hair textures and styles. Many women here in the multicultural artists' enclave would be eager to display the new merchandise.

Maybe some of them would carry the products back to their homelands and aid Sophie's dream of taking her company international.

The thought of homelands caused a momentary pang in Violet's chest. She missed Australia.

"Amal and I would love to have you here," Sophie pressed on. She glanced over her shoulder at her husband, who paused in his sculpting to wave. Some twenty years younger than Sophie, he was passionately devoted to only two things in life: his wife and his art.

"I know you would." Vi replied. "But you know me. I prefer to make my own way."

"Oui, oui." Sophie waved a hand breezily. "So independent. Always wanting to do it all yourself. Well, we are here if you need us."

"I only need to store my things until I've planned my next move."

"Of course. There's room for all your paintings in our art storage, and anything else can simply go in a closet."

"Thank you. It won't be for long."

Violet loved the people at the commune, and cherished the memories of the months she'd lived here when she'd first come to Paris. Even so, relying on her friends had felt like living off charity. And that wasn't part of her plan.

Her current troubles with that harassing, corrupt Inspector Crevier had set her timeline back somewhat, but she was still close. A few more commissions and she'd have enough saved up for her dream exhibition. She had ideas. She had visions.

All she needed was someone to fund her search for this art thief. Someone with money to burn, the right knowledge, and nothing better to do.

"Sophie…" Violet stared off into the distance, out past where Amal chipped away at his block of marble. "Do you remember that story several months ago about an unscrupulous

American businessman? Something about telephones and spying?"

"Monsieur Tagget? He enjoys art, I believe. Were you planning to sell him one of your paintings?"

"Not exactly. But if you had an idea of how I might contact him…"

Sophie laughed. "You know the hotel La Belle Maison?"

"Of course." It was a huge, wildly popular, gorgeously decorated hotel. Violet had once spent two solid hours lounging in the sumptuous lobby before someone realized she wasn't a guest and kicked her out.

"He owns it."

Vi's jaw dropped. Well. This would be interesting.

2

"**D**ARLING, WON'T YOU come to bed?"

Evan flicked the half-smoked cigarette over the rail and watched it spiral to the ground and die out in the mud below. The lights and sounds of the city lacked their usual vibrancy tonight. Or perhaps that was only an illusion. Nothing seemed exciting these days.

He stepped in from the balcony, pulling the doors closed behind him. The din of the streets faded to a muffled hum. His lover beckoned to him, but the suggestive smile aroused neither his interest nor his body. Three weeks this had lasted. Better than some. He undressed slowly, while his impatient paramour fidgeted in the bed.

"I will be leaving in the morning," Evan stated coolly. "You're welcome to keep the apartment."

Laurent nodded, his handsome face impassive. He'd seen it coming. They all did. It was why Evan took care never to imply that his romantic relationships were anything but temporary. He wanted simple companionship, not heartbreak. These past months, however, even companionship seemed less than satisfactory.

"I knew you'd be leaving," Laurent replied. "You've

withdrawn, and been so silent these last few visits. But I shall move on."

"Yes. I don't doubt you shall." Evan snaked a finger down his lover's chest. "Tonight, however, I will ensure you enjoy what time we have left."

A short time later, the young Frenchman lay writhing and moaning, his fingers clenched in the bed sheets. No one could ever say Evan Tagget left them unsatisfied.

Too bad he couldn't say the same for himself.

Morning brought no relief from the relentless ennui. Only another day of phone calls and telegrams. Business as usual. Even an escape to the one-time warehouse that now served as his workshop did little to improve his mood. As he'd done all too often these days, he drank a glass of cognac for dinner, and decided to turn in early.

"Mr. Tagget, sir?" a bellhop interrupted him on his way through the hotel lobby to the steam lift. "There's a young lady here to see you. She's been waiting for some time."

Evan flinched. A young lady? His heart hammered. Eden? Impossible. She would never leave her husband. Unless something entirely unforeseen had occurred? Then what? Would she have accepted Evan's invitation to join him overseas? Would she have sought him out?

"I took the liberty of escorting her to your suite and sending up dinner, sir," the boy added.

"Thank you."

Evan bypassed the lift and took the stairs two at a time, his stomach churning with excitement and dread. What would he do if his visitor *was* Eden? He was dying to see her, aching to fling his arms around her and hug her senseless. And… nothing more. Any thoughts of romance were long-since banished. If she were here for such a purpose, he'd need to find a way to tell her he'd come to value their long-distance banter and wasn't willing to risk romantic entanglements. Dammit, her letters were the only thing he ever looked forward to.

By the time he reached the penthouse, Evan was wheezing and cursing himself. He *knew* he couldn't run for any distance. The filters simply weren't strong enough. He leaned on the wall for several seconds, catching his breath. He couldn't greet his guest panting like some totty-one-lung.

Ding!

The steam lift settled into place with a mocking clank. So much for efficiency. Pushing himself back upright and taking a slow, deep breath, Evan slotted his key into the lock. The mechanical door slid open.

The woman lounging on his settee was most definitely not Eden, though she dressed with a similar bohemian style. A sleek black corset covered a lavender blouse, and her fluffy, plum skirt tumbled just to her knees. Black and white striped stockings hugged shapely calves. Her boots were scuffed and practical. She could run in those, or kick a man in the balls.

She set down the pastry she was eating and sat up straight. Intent eyes of a dark amber color assessed him. Rosy lips pursed in a slight frown. Dark brown hair streaked with golden highlights had been twisted into a messy knot atop her head and skewered with a pair of paintbrushes. A few stray wisps dangled loose to caress the skin of her neck. Her complexion was unfashionably tanned from the sun, with a handful of freckles. Evan had to admire a person who wasn't afraid to eschew convention.

"Mr. Tagget, I presume?" the woman asked in French. Her voice was luxurious, her accent unfamiliar.

Evan nodded and replied in the same language. "I am he."

"Thank you for dinner. The food is excellent. I assume you paid for it?"

"In a way. I own the hotel."

"So I've been told," she replied. Her lips arced in a smirk fine enough to match his own. She stretched out her long, lean legs, then rose gracefully from her seat to address him eye-to-eye.

Who was this woman? She was bold, beautiful, and unafraid to seek him out in his own personal quarters. A spark of desire stronger than any he'd felt in ages ignited inside him. Whoever she was, she was worth knowing, inside and out.

"To what do I owe the pleasure of this visit, Mademoiselle...?"

"Violette d'Aubergine."

His brows rose. Odd, too. Even better. She'd make him a perfect mistress. Now all he had to do was convince her that a bored American millionaire was exactly her type.

. . . ~ . . .

"D'Aubergine?" Tagget echoed. A smirk tugged at the corner of his arrogant mouth. Amusement sparkled in his eyes. They were a fascinating color, a mottled green full of lighter and darker flecks that flashed when he smiled. He had a naturally pale complexion, without a hint of exposure to the sun. His pristine suit and slender figure also implied he wasn't a man who spent much time outdoors.

Violet held his gaze. "Do you have a problem with my name?"

It was a silly name. She'd known for years it was a silly name, but it was her professional name, and she refused to be embarrassed by it.

The smirk broadened into a full grin. "Not at all. What can I do for you, Miss d'Aubergine?"

His French was excellent, but with a strong American accent. There was no sense speaking a language foreign to the both of them. She switched to English.

"I have a proposition for you, Mr. Tagget."

His neatly trimmed eyebrows twitched. "Excellent!"

Ack, that smug smile. The man was too handsome for his own good, and he knew it. Vi didn't know whether she'd rather kiss that mouth or punch it.

The grainy magazine photograph she's scrounged up hadn't done him justice. It made him look older, more serious. It didn't show the single stray lock of hair curling across his forehead or the dimples at the corners of his mouth, too prominent to hide beneath his short goatee. It failed entirely to capture that wicked glint in his eye. He wasn't the cold, merciless industrialist she'd imagined. His blood ran hot.

She'd also imagined him to be quite a bit taller. Standing here, staring at him, they looked exactly the same height.

"You and I are going to enter a partnership, Mr. Tagget."

"Oh, are we?" He managed to both leer and sound suspicious.

"You have heard, I assume, of the rash of art thefts over the past few months?"

"That fool who styles himself 'l'Exploiteur'? Is he the mastermind he claims, or just a braggart?"

"I'm told he has stolen near to fifty works of art, mainly from private collections and small galleries. His thefts grow bigger and bolder, and he has begun to taunt major galleries and museums with the promise of the greatest heists ever seen."

"Well, that does sound dire, though I fail to see how it is of relevance to myself." His dark brows quirked again. "Unless *you* are this Exploiter? If so, then I absolutely agree to join you on your next heist. What are we stealing?"

"No!" Vi put both hands on her hips. "Oh, for heaven's sake, I'm not an art thief."

"More's the pity. I could use an interesting challenge."

"I'm an artist," Violet huffed. "I create, I don't destroy. I want my work on display, where it can be enjoyed by all."

Tagget stroked his beard. "Hmm. What, then, is your concern with this pilferer of cultural treasures?"

"I'm trying to learn his identity and put a stop to his crimes."

"How noble," he chuckled. "Standing up for the dead masters who can no longer defend their works?"

Obnoxious ass. She really was going to punch him right

in his pretty mouth, then storm out and find herself a different assistant.

Violet clenched her fingers. Rich businessmen with questionable ethics and worldwide communications networks couldn't be found loitering on any street corner. She was lucky to even have the opportunity to speak with him.

"I was asked to help in this case because of my own connections in the art world," she explained, trying not to glower.

He frowned at her, causing a small furrow in his brow. "Your connections? What sort of connections would a lady artist have that would be of any use in this situation? Unless…" The frown twisted into a smile. "You're involved in illicit dealings yourself, naturally. A forger, perhaps?" He twitched. "Well, I'll be damned. Are you Vérité? But of course you are. 'Beauty is truth, truth beauty.' Though you look rather youthful for someone who they say has been working for fifty years and faked three hundred paintings."

"Ten years, twenty-seven forgeries. Many haven't been discovered, and many works have been incorrectly attributed to me."

With her police file as thick as a Bible, Violet didn't see any need to hide her deeds, and she was proud of the work she had done. Tagget looked momentarily surprised by her admission, then his smile returned.

"Fascinating. You made a deal with the authorities, I presume? But you need assistance. Why me?"

"I heard you were kicked out of the United States for spying."

Tagget's green eyes twinkled. "Now, my lovely blossom, you mustn't believe every rumor you hear. I bent some laws, perhaps, but didn't precisely break them. People did take exception, however, so I thought it best to focus on my European interests until the furor dies down."

Violet turned up her nose at him. "I don't care about the

details. I care that you're a teletics expert. Can you or can you not record information over a telephone or telegraph line?"

"I can. Most of it is irrelevant chatter. Sifting through is usually a waste of time."

"And you're an inventor?" she pressed on. "You can build things, and understand how machines work? You could dismantle them if necessary?"

A smile of a different sort touched his lips. More boyish, maybe even happier. "I could break through that mechanical door behind me with no more than a screwdriver, given enough time."

"Then you're the man I need."

He fixed her with a heated stare. "I'm pleased you think so." The husky timbre of his voice sent a shiver down her spine. "I accept your proposal. When do we begin?"

"Tomorrow." Vi snagged her half-eaten pastry. She tried not to let her gaze linger on the remaining chunk of juicy steak and side of truffade. She'd never had such a meal in her entire life. "I'll return in the morning."

"I'll have your dinner packed up for you."

Drat. He'd noticed. "Thank you."

"I won't be eating it, and I don't like to see good food go to waste. Until tomorrow, then?"

She nodded, and he opened the door for her, stepping aside to let her pass. Their shoulders brushed as she walked by, just for an instant, but it was more than enough to send a flash of heat throughout her body. Violet strode down the hall, keeping her pace measured, refusing to look back at him.

This would be tricky, working with a man she didn't trust who nonetheless intrigued and enticed her. And of course she found his blatant flirtations far preferable to the men who ogled her while pretending not to, or the artists who "only wished to sketch" her. Tagget's directness was oddly refreshing. No matter. She would handle it. Violet Dayton was no quitter.

3

Dearest Eden,

I know it will shock you to hear this, my sweet paradise, but you now have competition for my affections, as I have met a woman as fascinating as yourself. She makes her living as a forger, which I find compelling, and I'm certain she is hiding other secrets I will soon uncover. She is both flirtatious and aloof, a charming combination. I intend to make her my mistress. I will let you know when I have succeeded. Kiss your gorgeous & obnoxious husband for me.

Yours ever,
Evan Tagget

Evan picked at his croissant. Smoke curled from the barely-touched cigarette smoldering in the ashtray. He reread the note that had arrived at his suite early that morning.

"Meeting with recent victim at noon. Will be by at breakfast to discuss."

Miss d'Aubergine's artistic talents were visible in the easy swoops of her letters and her elegant hand, even in the hastily-scrawled note.

He abandoned his breakfast and turned to his notebook. Now might be a good time to redesign his suite door so he couldn't dismantle it with a single screwdriver.

A sudden murmur warned him the moment his paramour-to-be entered the restaurant. His head snapped up. Today's skirt was even shorter than yesterday's, though she'd paired it with leg-hugging trousers and spike-heeled boots, all in black. Her white blouse was topped with a purple brocade corset, and a ridiculous fan of peacock feathers nestled in her hair. A beaded purse hung at her hip, paintbrushes poking from the top. Delightful.

The buzz grew as she crossed the room. The primly-dressed ladies and gentlemen occupying the dining room had their heads together, tittering about the curious woman in their midst.

Evan's jaw clenched. This was the same sort of reaction so many had to his darling Eden, and he didn't like it any better now. He despised people. Foolish sheep clinging desperately to arbitrary rules and a love of uniformity. Anyone different was cast aside and trampled on like dirt.

Miss d'Aubergine swished over to his table and seated herself with no regard for the hostile looks of the crowd. The moment she'd taken her chair, the harsh looks turned on Evan, branding him uncultured for consorting in public with a trouser-wearing bohemian.

Too bad. This was his damn hotel, and he'd consort with whomever he pleased.

He bestowed a winning smile on his companion. "Good morning, my flower. How are you today?"

She dropped several sheets of paper in front of him. "Here are the notes. Everything that has gone missing, when, and from where. A few incidents have information on how the thefts may have occurred, but in most cases, the police are baffled."

"Which is why you have need of my superior intellect."

Her luminous eyes rolled skyward. "The papers neglected to mention how revoltingly arrogant you are."

He smirked at her. "I would disguise it better, but I can tell you enjoy it."

"I'm afraid you're delusional, Mr. Tagget. Read the list. I intend to have some breakfast. What's good here?"

"No idea." He beckoned to a waiter. "Miss d'Aubergine would like some breakfast. Give her whatever is best and a pot of tea."

"And an extra cup of hot water," she added.

The waiter scurried off and Evan pulled the papers into a neat stack. Whoever had compiled the list had done a masterful job. Each stolen work listed a title, artist, date, and estimated value. Most of the items on the first page were by artists unknown to Evan and not worth much, but as the list continued he began to recognize names. The values soared. Several galleries he had patronized had been burglarized, and a few small museums.

By the time the food arrived, he'd seen enough.

"Our thief is enjoying this game, I imagine," he remarked.

Miss d'Aubergine dumped a small packet of herbs into her cup of hot water, stirring slowly. A contraceptive tisane, judging by the look and scent of it. Apparently she came prepared for seduction. How charming.

"You think it's a game?" she asked. "Couldn't the culprit be doing this for the money?"

"Have any stolen works appeared for sale on the black market?"

"Not so far as I've heard."

"There you have it. He's not selling. He's collecting. It's a game."

She pondered the idea a moment, sipping her tea and taking a few bites of her eggy pie.

"I admit, his silly name and pompous threats fit well with

that theory," she said at last. "I work for the money, however, and I have a name."

"And a mark."

A grin tugged at the corner of her mouth. She fought it, but her pride in her work was evident. "Indeed. I love the challenge of hiding the 'V' in every painting. Most of the false attributions are because someone thought an innocent shape to be my signature."

"Your 'V' is really for Violette," Evan guessed. "Or is that another disguise for your real name? It's clear you aren't French."

"Violet," she confessed. "My family calls me Vi, but don't you try it. My father was born in England, but I am Australian."

"Ah. That explains why I didn't recognize your accent. I assume your real surname is not Eggplant?"

She cringed. "I was a girl when I chose that name. I thought 'aubergine' sounded pretty and French and I decided another purple color would go well with Violet. I've never even eaten an eggplant."

"They aren't worth the bother. However, Miss Eggplant, if you should like me to call you by something less... colorful, perhaps you might share your true name?"

"Dayton."

"Excellent. It's a pleasure to at last be properly introduced, Miss Dayton. Now, tell me, which of these unfortunate places are we visiting today?"

Violet took another bite of her quiche, chewing slowly before replying.

"We will be going to the home of a man robbed only a few days ago. He isn't on that list. A Monsieur Armand Gaillard."

Evan's brows arched. "Armand Gaillard the perfumier?"

"The same."

His gaze roved up and down her edgy, artistic clothing. "You'll have to change."

She blinked. "I beg your pardon?"

"Monsieur Gaillard is a notoriously conventional man. I can't envision him receiving you in your current ensemble, beautiful though it may be. Have you something more conservative?"

Her eyes hardened. "No."

"We shall have to purchase something. The fit won't be perfect, but I imagine we can make do. Whenever you are done with that mess of curdled eggs, we can be off."

She studied him from beneath narrowed brows. "You're paying?"

"Naturally. And providing transportation, I assume. Gaillard's mansion is several miles outside the city."

"I know. I heard you have a luxene-powered Mercedes that can go fifty miles an hour."

"That information is out-of-date, I'm afraid. I gave the Mercedes to a friend as a wedding gift several months ago. They're building me a new one, but at present I have a two-seater Peugeot with a dreadfully ordinary steam engine. Perhaps when we have captured your thief we can drive up to Germany and get my new car."

"Whatever makes you think I would accompany you on such a journey?"

"Whoever comes along gets the Peugeot."

Her mouth twitched. "I'll consider it." She would come. Violet Dayton was too savvy to pass up a prime opportunity.

Evan lit another cigarette, leaned back in his chair, and watched her finish her meal. She had a good appetite and made little noises of pleasure when tasting her favorite dishes. He looked forward to causing similar noises in the privacy of his bedroom.

He knew of a suitable dressmaker's shop only a few blocks away, and the moment Violet finished her breakfast he escorted her out the door, leaving instructions for his staff to ready the Peugeot for the drive out-of-town.

Madame Rochette waved Evan inside with flowery words

and playful kisses to the air beside his cheeks. She looked Violet up and down in her studious way, nodding and muttering.

"Oui, oui. Not the usual sort of girl, but pretty enough, if done up right. I can accentuate all the right parts and complement her complexion, and we will do something wonderful with this flamboyant style of hers."

Evan's brows knitted. Pretty enough? Violet was a dream. Madame's judgement was questionable.

"We will give her a wardrobe fit for a queen," he replied, "but on some other day."

"Ah, of course. What do you have in mind?"

Violet jumped in to speak for herself. "I need one dress immediately, for visiting a conservative gentleman. That's all."

Madame glanced at Evan. "The usual fee?"

He nodded.

"Excellent. Colette! Pull out our ready-mades."

The harried assistant rushed to see to their needs, producing a pile of garments near to Violet's size. She selected one and held it up for their approval.

Violet made a noise of displeasure. Her nose crinkled and her mouth twisted into a look of disgust. "That dress looks like it was stitched together from one of my stepmother's tablecloths."

Colette whisked away the frothy confection and offered a simple, white shirtwaist with a slim, modern skirt in a green and red plaid. Many women wore such ensembles as everyday garments, but it would never suit Violet. She made another face and began to poke through the pile on her own.

"This."

She held aloft a black and gray striped dress some years out of fashion.

"Oh, that one has not yet been restyled," Madame Rochette apologized. "So lovely a fabric, but it never sold."

"I will take it as is," Violet declared. "May I try it on?"

The dressmaker looked to Evan for approval. He nodded,

and the ladies hustled Violet from the room. He paced while they handled things, considering the upcoming meeting with Gaillard. The man certainly wasn't ready for the likes of Miss Dayton. She would need to behave in a more subdued fashion if they were to gather some useful data. A tricky proposition. Evan would have to take charge of the meeting before she scared Gaillard off.

"Perfect choice," Evan applauded when she emerged several minutes later. The dress looked classic rather than out-of-date, and it flattered her figure. He gave her a smile of approval as she turned around to show off. "Conservative enough and as unique as yourself."

"Thank you."

He offered his arm to escort her. "Let's be off. The car should be waiting. I'll tell you my plan during the drive."

She jerked her hand from his arm. "*Your* plan? This is my venture, Mr. Tagget. Buying the dress was quite enough, thank you. I'll lead from here."

Evan said nothing, just smiled as she walked on ahead of him. Yes, she was lovely. Vexing. And wrong. But delightful nonetheless.

4

A FOOT-LONG METAL PIG with spikes running down its back tore through the foyer, a panicked servant on its heels.

"Pay no mind to the dragons," the butler said. "Madame has a large collection and some of them are unruly."

He led the way to a parlor and sent for refreshments. Violet ensconced herself in a plush armchair while Tagget paced the room, casting critical glares at the decor. Another metal beast wandered through the space on chicken legs, its decorative, latticework wings flapping.

"Absurd things, personal dragons," Tagget scoffed. "How many of them have any sort of function? Not one in fifty, I imagine.

"I thought I saw a dragon in your suite," Vi replied. "Wasn't there one sitting on your desk?"

"Yes. It belches fire. I light cigarettes with it."

"Of course. Terribly useful. Of great benefit to society." She gave him her most ladylike smile.

The door opened to admit a servant with a tray of snacks and a gray-haired man in a pale yellow suit who could only be Gaillard himself. A young woman trailed after, dragging the pig-dragon on a leash. Her lacy dress looked eerily like the one Vi had compared to a tablecloth.

"Monsieur Evan Tagget and Mademoiselle Violet Dayton of the Société des Arts," the butler intoned.

Gaillard held out a hand to Tagget. "Monsieur Tagget, I have heard of you. I did not realize you were involved in the art scene here in my homeland."

The woman sprang toward Tagget, nearly cutting Gaillard off. "Oh, welcome, Mr. Tagget!" she exclaimed in English. "It's so nice to meet a fellow American. You're from New York, yes? I'm from Pennsylvania. Philadelphia, to be precise. Oh, but I must introduce myself. I'm Armand's wife, Virginia Gaillard."

Tagget made a sweeping bow to the lady of the house. "Mrs. Gaillard, it is my pleasure to meet you here in your beautiful home. Allow me to introduce my fiancée, Miss Dayton."

Violet flinched. The conniving bastard. He would pull something like this. She forced a smile through her gritted teeth.

Virginia Gaillard nodded to Violet, her attention flitting back to the dragon. "Pleased to meet you, mademoiselle. Ergh!" She yanked on the leash to prevent the pig butting a table. "Pardon me, Joubert can be a trial. I want to convert him to the new voice controls, but Armand has thus far balked at the cost. To what do we owe the pleasure of your visit?"

Tagget answered before Violet could open her mouth. "The Société is much concerned with the recent theft of an item from your collection."

"Oh, of course, the *Daphne*," Mrs. Gaillard explained. "Such a tragedy. A lovely piece."

"A bronze statuette," her husband clarified. "Very valuable. I have filed an insurance claim."

"Oh, for Pete's sake, Joubert, turn around! You see, darling, he nearly upset the tea table. This is why we need the voice controls."

"A worthy investment," Tagget replied, as if he meant it. "He is a fine specimen of a miniature dragon."

Mrs. Gaillard beamed. Tagget beamed back. Insincere ass. He'd wasted money buying Violet the dress. Apparently he could flirt his way to information regardless of what she was wearing.

"I have some talent with mechanical things. I would be happy to make a few minor adjustments to tide you over. Perhaps after you show us where the theft occurred?"

"Of course! This way. It happened in my husband's study. The damage is clear. He wanted to summon a contractor at once, but I insisted we wait for a proper police inquest. I believe the piece can be recovered."

"Madame has such an optimistic outlook," her husband explained, sounding resigned to the fact that he'd lost control of the meeting.

Once in the study, Mrs. Gaillard waved a hand at a board that covered a portion of the wainscoting, bouncing with enthusiasm. "Right through the wall! You see we have the ironwork over the lower windows here to guard against theft, but I never would have thought someone would bore through the house itself!"

Tagget placed a hand on the board. "May I?"

"But of course!"

He drew back the wood to reveal a hole almost one foot in diameter, so perfectly round it could only have been cut with a giant drill.

"It must have made a terrible racket," Vi mused aloud. "Was no one home?"

"Oh, we were abed. I woke to a great buzzing and a tremor. I sent Armand to investigate, but by the time he arrived in the study, the statuette was gone and the culprit fled."

"Did you look for tracks outside?"

"Yes. I will show you what's left, but it's since rained. Big wheel marks running out into the gardens, where they simply vanished. Poof! I wonder also how the thieves avoided alerting the guard dragons. They are something fearsome."

Violet didn't recall any guard dragons outside. In all likelihood, the mistress of the house severely overestimated the capabilities of her pets.

Tagget knelt and examined the hole, measuring it with a tape produced from his waistcoat, and running his hands along the edges. His mouth turned down in a thoughtful frown. It became him better than his customary smirk, making him seem younger and less jaded. Vi had no idea how old he actually was.

They paid a brief visit to the tracks outside, but as Mrs. Gaillard had warned, they were badly blurred. Tagget thanked her with more smiles and flatteries, then wasted a good quarter hour fiddling with the dials on the stupid pig-dragon while Violet fought her fidgety tendencies.

On the way to the door, he took up her hand and drew her close. She had no choice but to play along, but she retaliated by digging her elbow into his ribs.

"It has been such a pleasure, Mrs. Gaillard," he simpered. "It's a rare treat to make the acquaintance of so arresting and spirited a lady as yourself. Your husband is a lucky man."

She blushed and tittered. Tagget turned his gaze on Vi.

"Almost as lucky as myself."

Violet clung to her false smile as she bobbed a curtsy and made her adieus. By the time Mr. Gaillard helped her into the Peugeot, her face hurt.

Some half-mile down the road, Tagget glanced at her, showing his slightly crooked, yet pristinely white teeth.

"Well, that was revealing and rather enjoyable, don't you think?"

Violet set her jaw. "I think I might hate you."

He only shrugged.

5

"Concept sketch for the theft."

Evan drew back from the paper Violet had thrust into his face. He plucked it out of her hand for a better look and she spun away and plopped herself back down at his desk with her pencil and the notes. She had spoken hardly a word to him since leaving the Gaillard mansion. He wouldn't push her further until her temper cooled. Sparring with her was the best fun he'd had in months, but it had limits. He didn't want to kill that spark of attraction in her eyes when she looked at him. God, she was passionate, though. She would be something in his bed.

He looked over her sketch. A four-wheeled machine with a drill on one end and an extendable arm on the other, reaching through the hole to seize the statue. Overhead, a dirigible hovered. The contraption was fanciful and could never function the way she had drawn it, but the idea was sound.

"This is rather brilliant," he applauded. "You noted the likely number of wheels on the vehicle and the need for some device to reach through the hole. Naturally the entire thing was brought in and carted away by air. We have reached very similar conclusions."

"Good. Seems I may not need your help after all."

A distinct possibility. She had wits and nerves enough to tackle any chore. Money and high-society connections were all she lacked. Evan would have to use both to make himself indispensable.

Violet turned in her seat to smirk at him. "You are also my prime suspect."

"Is that so?"

"Our thief has a great deal of money and builds wild mechanical devices. He craves a challenge and likes to play games. He is puffed up on his own importance."

"And he has excellent taste in art. Yes, I could certainly be your criminal based on that description. I, however, prefer smaller machines to noisy monstrosities. This l'Exploiteur fellow is too ostentatious for my taste. Simple and efficient would be more my style. I'm afraid you shall have to continue your search. What shall we investigate next?"

"Whatever I decide." She returned to her work. Evan walked up behind her and peered over her shoulder. Beside each note about a crime, Violet had marked the papers with probable means of entry. Door. Window. Over a fence.

"This might also have been done by dirigible," she said, tapping her finger on one of the most recent thefts. "The building was accessed from a window in the courtyard. Do you own a dirigible, Mr. Tagget?"

"I do, though not one equipped to haul a machine that can bore through a wall in a matter of seconds. Mine has only a single room for passengers and the crew areas. No means of carrying cargo larger than personal trunks and shipboard equipment."

"So you say."

"Would you like to see it? It's a top-of-the-line Lasher airship. I only just purchased it this winter. Where shall we sail?"

She gathered the papers into a pile and rose. "Sail wherever you wish. I will contact you if I need you again. Good day, Mr. Tagget."

Violet swished from the room, hampered only briefly by the slow mechanical door. In her long gown, she looked regal. Evan waited a few seconds and then followed her from his suite and out of the hotel. He kept his distance as he trailed her down the street, trying for a modicum of circumspection. No need to be obvious, though he assumed she knew what he was about.

When she entered the police station, he took up a seat on the closest bench and took out his notebook. In an instant, the world contracted to his new door design. Eliminate clanking gears. Pulley and cable system for smooth operation. Luxene-powered to reduce motor size and noise. Recognizer system to replace key.

A hand clamped down on his shoulder. He jerked and looked up into the craggy face of an officer of the law.

"Mr. Tagget, I am Inspector Crevier," the man growled in French. "I should like a word with you."

Evan glanced past the inspector at Violet's grinning face. She gave a little wave. "Yes, do give the man a bit of your time," she said. "Best wishes, my paragon of vanity."

Evan couldn't even scowl at her, enchanting as she was in her revenge. Eyes on her departing backside, he stumbled toward the station, prodded by Crevier's beefy arms.

"I would appreciate it if you would cease to knock about my person," Evan snapped.

That earned him a shove.

"We don't take kindly to thieves here," the inspector snarled.

"Monsieur Crevier, I may be many things, but I'm not an art thief."

"You fit the profile."

"True enough, and I'm happy to answer your questions, provided you keep your hands off me." Evan rued the loss of his bodyguards for the first time since dismissing them last November. Large goons had their uses. He'd taken up fencing as a self-defense measure, but it did little good when one couldn't carry a sword.

The inspector dragged him to a small room and shouted at him for the better part of an hour. Evan answered every question calmly and truthfully. He derived a twisted joy from the multiple admissions that he didn't recall his whereabouts at the time of many of the thefts. Crevier clung to those, repeating his questions in a vain hope of getting a different answer.

"Would you like me to check my telephone records to clear up the matter?" Evan offered cheerfully.

Crevier turned so red Evan wouldn't have been surprised to find smoke billowing from his head.

"Stupid bitch, wasting my time."

Evan grinned. A double revenge, then. Marvelous girl.

His pleasure was short-lived. The inspector called for his minions and Evan found himself seized and flung into a tiny cell. He hit the floor hard and rage flared inside him.

"We'll see what you have to say in the morning," Crevier growled. "You may not be l'Exploiteur, but I'll get you for something, and I'll get him, too. I'll be the man that served justice on a corrupt American millionaire, today's greatest thief, *and* today's greatest forger."

Evan shot to his feet, his anger threatening to spiral out of control. He took a deep breath and tamped it down, dusting off his suit and straightening his shoulders. Crevier had made himself an enemy for life. No one got away with mistreating Evan Tagget, and no one would get away with double-crossing Violet Dayton.

When the inspector left, Evan shrugged out of his jacket and pulled his screwdriver from the concealed pocket. Progress was slow with guards hanging about, but by two in the morning he was out of the cell and on his way back to the hotel.

His emotions fluctuated between triumph at the ease of his escape and fury at his mistreatment. Crevier would hear from his lawyers.

No. Better to wait. Crevier was using Violet to further his own ambitions. They could use him in return. They would discuss it in the morning. Evan expected Violet to be in excellent spirits now that she'd gotten the better of him.

He stopped at the desk in the hotel lobby to leave a note for her, certain she would come by in the morning.

"Mr. Tagget, sir!" The sleepy-eyed concierge jerked to attention. "I was told you would be gone until sometime tomorrow."

Evan's eyes narrowed. "Were I you, I would put less trust in unsubstantiated rumors. I would like to leave a message for Miss Dayton when she arrives tomorrow."

"She is here already, sir. We put her up in your suite. Was that wrong?"

"No. That's quite all right. Thank you."

Evan took the stairs again, though this time at a more moderate pace. He reached his door breathing hard, but without wheezing.

The mechanical door clanked and rattled as it opened. Curse the infernal thing. He would have it replaced with due haste. The auto-door fad had faded anyway. He would start a new trend: quieter, faster, and more secure.

Evan flipped on the light to find his sitting room littered with junk. An enormous, battered trunk blocked the main path, and a studio's worth of art supplies covered the rest of the room. He picked his way around easels and canvases, nearly killing himself when he slipped on an unseen paintbrush. He pushed open the door to the bedroom and turned on the light.

Violet Dayton sat in his bed, attired in an airy lavender nightgown, rubbing sleep from her eyes. Waves of dark hair cascaded around her shoulders. The low neckline and tiny sleeves of her gown revealed a great deal of skin. Evan longed to kiss her everywhere.

"What?" she muttered. "You're back so soon? What time is it?"

He began to undress without a word.

"What are you doing?" The sleep-thickened rasp of her voice was intoxicating. "Why are you here?"

"This is my suite, and I'm going to bed," Evan replied. "It's a ghastly hour for a person to be awake. I'm afraid you'll have to make room. Or go sleep on the couch atop your boxes of paints."

She slid to one side of the bed. "We're leaving for Italy tomorrow."

Stripped to his drawers, he doused the light and lay down beside her. "Italy, you say?"

"Yes. Don't touch me."

He didn't need to touch her. He could feel the heat radiating from her body and smell a trace of lilac perfume. It would tide him over for the night.

"I wouldn't dream of it."

6

VIOLET CLOSED HER EYES and let the scent of perfectly cooked eggs wash over her. Putting up with Tagget might be worthwhile given the quality of his food. This morning's breakfast smelled divine. She basked in the warmth and comfort of his expensive bed until her stomach began to rumble, then forced herself up and padded into the sitting room in her bare feet.

Tagget sat at the desk, measuring a drawing with a protractor, a small crinkle creasing his brow. Her previous assessment had been correct. He was one hundred percent more attractive when he was lost in thought. His plate, with a half-eaten croissant and a half-smoked cigarette, had been pushed aside.

"Don't you ever eat?"

He jumped, the pencil skittering. "Miss Dayton." His chair swiveled. "Good morning. I trust you slept well?"

She wedged herself into the only available space on the sofa, and pulled the tray of food that had been left atop her trunk toward her. He'd even requested the extra cup of hot water. Which meant he knew about her contraceptive brew. He probably counted it as a point in his favor. Violet, though, had no intention of giving in. At the moment. Still, with a man as curiously intriguing as Evan Tagget, it was best to be prepared.

"I did sleep well, thank you. Your bed is comfortable. Though I liked it better when I had it to myself."

"I didn't." His eyes raked over her. "You look ravishing this morning, my floweret. Tumbled from bed. Bare arms and legs on delicious display. Makes a man hungry for a taste." His tongue darted out to moisten his lips.

An unwanted shiver of desire skimmed over her. That tongue was wicked, she had no doubt. She fought for composure.

"If you're so hungry, why haven't you eaten anything?" she challenged.

"I ate." He gestured at the unfinished pastry.

"You'll starve yourself that way."

His expression betrayed little, but his limpid eyes couldn't mask a surge of deep, raw emotion. "I will not."

Vi popped a piece of fruit into her mouth to avoid responding. She had hit a nerve, and it would be cruel to pry. These glimpses of the layers beneath his conceited facade kept her from abandoning her original plan and striking out on her own. True, his money and connections would make the job easier and more comfortable, but those were excuses. Probing the depths of Evan Tagget's soul posed a more compelling challenge than unmasking any criminal.

Tagget peeled off a flakey bit of croissant and ate it, as if to prove a point. "So. Italy?"

"That's right."

"Any reason in particular, or have you simply developed a hankering to visit the Flavian Amphitheatre?"

"The what?"

"The Colosseum."

Violet speared a bit of sausage with her fork. "Oh. No, we're not going to Rome. Florence."

"Ah, Michelangelo's *David*, then? You like your men with large muscles and small genitalia? I'm afraid I will never suit you, if that's the case."

"You will never suit me, regardless. I'm not going

sightseeing. Let me show you." She set her food aside and tugged her papers from beneath a bottle of linseed oil. "While you wasted time with the police yesterday, I plotted all the thefts on a map."

"I spent most of that 'wasted' time compromising my cell door." He plucked a tool from the leather cup that held his writing implements. "You should carry a screwdriver, Miss Dayton. Terribly useful things. Here. I have extras."

Violet twisted up a bit of hair into a knot and skewered it in place with the screwdriver. "Thank you. I'll trade you for a paintbrush."

She spread her map on the desk and they bent over it. Her bare arm brushed against him. His attire today was entirely black, from his shirt, to his waistcoat, to the jet cufflinks. As always, it was tailored to perfection and without a single crease. His hair was slicked back, with even the little curl that fell across his forehead tucked into place. She wondered how long he had been awake to achieve his pristine state.

"As I was marking the thefts, I noticed a pattern," she said. "With the exception of the crimes in Paris, they moved further from the city each time. Not in any sort of line, but in an ever expanding circle. Brussels, London, Marseille, Venice. I started drawing the circles with a compass, and it became even clearer."

"But if there has already been a theft in Vienna, why would you think Florence would be next? It's been passed over."

"Partway through the list, the pattern started over. It corresponded to one of the large jumps in the values of the stolen works. He has started again with larger targets. It was also about that time when he began to send threatening letters. I picked up copies of several of those from the police yesterday."

Tagget drummed a finger on the map, wearing his calculating frown. "Recent incidents: Geneva, Milan, Barcelona. Then two in Paris, counting Gaillard."

"Yes. Paris has been hardest hit, and sporadically. I assume it's his base of operations. As for Florence, it's the right distance for an upcoming heist, and the Galleria dell'Accademia has received a threat."

"So you hope to catch him in the act."

"Yes. Or prevent an intrusion entirely. But we mustn't delay. Could we fly in your dirigible? How soon could we get there?"

"If we leave this afternoon, we'll be there by morning."

"Perfect. You can have the vehicle ready in a matter of hours?"

"My crew is extremely competent. They can leave at a moment's notice. However, if you would like dinner this evening and breakfast in the morning, it will take some time to ensure that the proper foodstuffs are brought onboard. Since we need time to pack for the voyage, I don't imagine that to be problematic. How long do you expect us to be away?"

Violet turned her palms up. "I don't know. We could be days waiting, or he could be there now, and we'll turn right around."

"There's also the possibility that we would move on to another location without returning. I'll plan for at least a week. Shall I call for a girl to assist you with your packing?"

"Assist me? No, thank you. I would prefer no one touch my things but me. It was stressful enough watching the bellhops haul my belongings here."

"Ah, yes. What compelled you to move your personal effects into my sitting room? Have you decided so quickly that you wish to be my mistress?" Those dark eyebrows arched. "I'm happy to have you assume the position."

She jabbed him in the ribs.

"Ow!" He rubbed the sore spot. "Was that really necessary?"

"Yes. If not for the lecherous presumption, then for the punning."

Tagget made an offended gasp. "The pun was the best part!

And you can't deny that you moved yourself into my home and slept in my bed."

"I had no choice. My things needed to go somewhere, and I don't like relying on the charity of my friends."

"So you're relying on my charity instead?"

He was too close to the truth for Violet's liking. She needed a place of her own, but didn't trust most of the places she could afford.

"It won't be for long. When I find a new studio, I'll move everything there. This seemed convenient while we're working together."

"I have room in my warehouse."

She blinked at him. "Your warehouse?"

"Yes. Down by the river. I use a portion of it as a workshop, but it's much larger than I need. The area that used to be the loading bay would suit you, I imagine. The doors can be opened to let in plenty of sunlight. I could have windows installed to make it habitable in any weather."

Vi had to stop herself from leaping to say yes. It unnerved her how frequently he offered her things of value. Fancy meals, clothing, a steam car, and now a studio? Did he have so much money he could throw it around without a thought, or was he trying to buy his way into her bed? A bit of both, perhaps.

"That sounds nice. How much do you charge for rent?"

The question surprised him. "Rent? Nothing. It's my personal property, not a business endeavor."

"Well, Mr. Tagget," she sighed, "I'm afraid we must stick to business, so I will have to decline." Vi took up her map and replaced it with her other notes. "Excuse me, I need to prepare for the day. I will make use of that extra room."

Tagget glanced at the closed door opposite his bedroom. "No one has used that extra room for anything, ever. It's full of empty trunks and obsolete equipment I haven't yet disposed of."

"The remnants of your former lovers? Shall I watch out

for skeletons, or just the goods you reclaimed when you sent them packing?"

He frowned at her. "I can't discern if you take delight in teasing me, or if your opinion of me is truly that low."

"Yes."

"Wonderful."

"Isn't it? Get the airship ready. I should like to leave promptly." She grabbed the carpetbag with her favorite clothes and scurried from the room.

7

The Paris airfield was a riot of color—great crimson, green, and gold balloons bouncing in the breeze, rising to the azure skies, or drifting down to spew their festive travelers into the eager embrace of the city. For a decade Vi had watched the grand ships of the sky, as Paris had grown into the world's foremost hub of dirigible transport, yet she had never before set foot on this field. Up close, the inflated spheres and ovoids were not fanciful, colored clouds floating across the sky, but intricate machines, powered by rumbling steam engines and whirring propellers. She had painted a picture of the airfield years ago, when she'd had a view from her boarding house. When she painted it next, she would take a different perspective, contrasting the stark metal of the frameworks and hulls with the whimsical gaiety of the balloons.

If she ever got out of this airfield, that was.

She took another look around. Where was Tagget? She couldn't climb aboard his dirigible and sail off to Italy without him. Taking up residence in his hotel suite had been brash enough. Flying away in his airship would get her locked away for life.

An image flashed through her mind of him waving a hand in a nonchalant manner and telling her to keep the dirigible.

"Miss Dayton?"

Violet jumped. This new trend of people addressing her by her real name unnerved her. It was freeing not to pretend, but at the same time it left her feeling exposed.

She turned to find herself staring into the chest of an enormous man. He was large in all directions—over six feet tall, wide, and thick-limbed. He looked as though he could lift a motorcar.

"Um, yes, I am she."

Her eyes drifted up to his face, and he smiled down at her, a bashful blush reddening his olive complexion. He was no older than his mid-twenties, she guessed, and a lovable giant rather than a bruising one.

"My name is Walton," he said. "I'm the chef here on Dauntless and I handle most of the general work as well. The passenger cabin is ready for you. Mr. Tagget will be along shortly. May I take your bags?"

Vi smiled back. "Thank you, Walton. Pleased to meet you."

She handed over the two large bags with her clothes, but didn't relinquish the small tote with her art supplies. Her tools were her livelihood, and her budget for replacements was small. Most of her things remained at the hotel, but she couldn't travel without a sketchbook and a few paints.

She'd told Tagget she wasn't sightseeing, but in truth the journey to Italy had her giddy with excitement. She *did* want to go to Rome and see the Colosseum, to walk the Tuscan hills, and tour grand churches and museums. She had fled Australia as a girl for the glamor of Europe, but had seen so little of it during her years here. She knew Paris inside and out, but so many other places still existed for her only in fantasies.

Vi followed Walton up the roll-away staircase to the deck of the dirigible. Tagget's ship was among the smaller craft she'd seen—peculiar, for a millionaire. The upper deck was tidy and unadorned, the oblong balloon above a serviceable gray. Two men and two women stood at the bottom of the steps to the bridge, waiting to welcome her aboard.

Most private ships bore insignia and decoration flaunting the owner's wealth, and boasted large crews in matching uniforms. Tagget's employees wore functional working garb, their trousers and tops of styles and colors as varied as themselves.

A tall man with dark brown skin stepped forward and gave Violet a slight bow. He had a pleasing, round face and a wide smile. A crooked pair of aviator's goggles perched atop his closely-cropped hair.

"Miss Dayton. Welcome aboard. My name is Gabriel Harrison, and I'm pilot and captain of this airship. Her name is Dauntless, and I promise she will live up to that description. She flies smooth and steady, and will give you a pleasant journey."

Violet held out her hand, and they shook.

"The rest of the crew will introduce themselves."

"I'm Flynne," said a pale, red-cheeked young man with a squirrel-shaped dragon perched on his shoulder. "I'm one of the engineers. We handle the engines and keep all the machinery in good repair. If you need anything fixed, we probably have the tools for it. This is Parker." He gestured at a petite, freckled, red-headed woman. "She's head engineer."

Parker waved, and said only, "Hi."

Vi nodded. "Nice to meet you."

She looked to the last crew member, a young brunette woman with a baby strapped to her back. Whatever Violet had expected from an airship crew, this eclectic assortment of people was not it. The only commonality between them all was their American accent. Her belly made a queer little flip-flop. Tagget didn't judge people using society's usual standards. He'd picked his crew for their skills alone.

The woman with the baby stuck out her hand. "Dahlia."

"Violet."

Dahlia grinned. "Nice to meet a fellow flower. I'm navigator here. Technically first mate to Harrison, but in practice we all work like partners around here. Ship functions best when we all pull our own weight and respect each other's skills, right? Let me show you around while Walton stows your things."

Violet followed Dahlia across the deck.

"She's a plain and simple sort of ship," Dahlia explained. "Nothing flashy or unusual, but the best quality money can buy. Engine, propellers to steer us, gauges to keep an eye on pressure, speed, altitude, and so on. Room over here for sitting out and taking in the view, if you're interested. The prospect from the little platform at the bow is especially nice. Mr. Tagget doesn't spend time up top, but we'll pull out a chair if you want us to."

Violet couldn't hold back a little wiggle of excitement. She was on an airship! An honest-to-God flying machine. "I would love that. It's my first time on a dirigible, and I want to be up here when it's flying, at least for a short time."

"Warning. It gets cold and windy. You'll want a jacket and a hat that can tie on tight."

"Thank you."

"Pleasure. You have any questions or need anything, just ask." The baby made a gurgling noise, and Dahlia jerked a thumb toward her. "Fern." Her grin turned sheepish. "We like plants. She doesn't fuss much."

"Are there any places that are off limits?" Violet asked. "I'd like to sketch the ship, but I don't want to cause trouble."

Dahlia shrugged. "Haven't given that much thought before. You're our first passenger besides Mr. Tagget, and like I said, he doesn't come up top."

"Does he fly often?"

"Little jaunts here and there. Gets bored, I think. We've also run small shipments for his business when she would otherwise be idle, but the cargo hold's tiny. She's a pleasure ship. Here's the stairs below. Hall acts as an airlock, but it's all open just now. Passenger cabin'll be straight ahead."

"Thank you. It was nice to meet you."

"And you, Miss Violet." Dahlia waved and headed back to her work.

Violet scurried down the stairs and into the passenger cabin. For an instant she felt as if she had walked right off the ship and into a gentleman's library. The walls were papered in flocked velvet, red with burgundy damask, and punctuated by small stained-glass windows. A complementary carpet covered the floor, the same red color, but with a floral motif of dark blues. The left side of the room was lined with bookcases, so crowded that on every shelf several volumes rested horizontally atop the rest. Opposite, a pair of leather armchairs flanked a drop-leaf table. A liquor cabinet and a sturdy desk much like the one in Tagget's hotel room finished out the space.

Beyond the sitting area was a high four-poster bed, with a quilt to match the rest of the room and mounds of blue and burgundy pillows. A washstand stood in the left corner, and to the right a folded privacy screen leaned against the wall. Curtains to either side could be drawn closed to separate the two halves of the room, but the ties didn't look as though they had ever been undone. Tagget wouldn't be bothered by the idea of sleeping in his library. The bed wasn't as large as the one at the hotel, but it looked luxurious. Vi wanted to burrow into the pillows with a book and a cup of strong tea.

"Does it meet your approval?"

Tagget's sudden appearance startled her, but she played casual. "The bed looks too small for two."

"We shall have to be cozy." Arching eyebrows accompanied his familiar smirk. There was a subtle difference between his flirtatious smile and his contemptuous smile, and it was all in the eyes. When he was angry, scornful, or even bored, they were cool, almost icy. But when he was laughing, teasing, or feeling amorous, they sparkled like gemstones in sunlight.

A natural observation from several days' acquaintance, Violet told herself. *Not at all a reflection of an unhealthy fascination with him. Any trained artist would notice it.*

Tagget closed the space between them. "These dirigibles get chilly, but I will make certain to keep you warm tonight."

A gentleman would have offered to bunk with the crew. At least he was honest about his intentions, and he hadn't touched her last night.

She returned his smirk. "Don't get your hopes up."

The flecks of darker green looked to dance in his eyes. "We'll see what you say this evening in that thin nightgown of yours. Your things have been safely stowed, I assume? The closets are here and here." He gestured to either side of the entrance. "Do you need anything, or shall we be off?"

"I was ready to depart the moment I arrived. You are the latecomer. Where have you been?"

"Making telephone calls."

"Ah. Your business. I forgot I'm dragging you away from your work."

"Not particularly. My European operations have always been rather independent, and the more the company has grown, the more expendable I have become. I don't think they need me. No, I was making calls on your behalf, Miss Dayton."

Her eyebrows lifted. "Oh?"

"You did take me on for my information network, did you not? I'm putting it to use. There can't be many mechanically-minded dirigible owners in Paris. I've arranged to get us a list of names. I imagine it will await us when we arrive in Italy."

"Good, and did you also arrange for a hotel?"

"Why, when we have a perfectly serviceable room here? No sense moving all our things in and out. I outfitted this cabin with such use in mind."

"I see." Violet glanced again at the bed. She would be stuck sharing it with him unless she made her own arrangements.

Tagget pulled a cord dangling from the ceiling. A distant bell chimed.

"I've alerted the crew to take off. You may want to have a seat. Ascent can be choppy if the wind gusts. Would you like a book? The selection here is adequate."

Violet pushed one of the armchairs up against the wall and knelt on it, peering out a window. "Perhaps later. Now I want to see everything."

He shrugged. "If you like." He lounged in the chair beside her. "That wall is dreadfully bare above the bookcases. I think it could use a painting. If you see one you like in Florence, let me know. I will arrange to have it stolen."

"And you say you're not l'Exploiteur."

"No." He chuckled. "L'Opportuniste."

8

Evan spent most of the night in a chair. The constant hum of machinery brought on nightmares, and after waking Violet twice he gave up the bed for a glass of brandy and the most boring book he could find. He grabbed sleep in snatches and roused himself before dawn to dress and shave and tame his hair into some semblance of order.

Violet lay tangled in his sheets, hair loose and a peaceful smile touching her lips. He watched her sleep with amorous thoughts and no small amount of envy. When she woke, she hid herself behind the privacy screen to change, tossing her discarded nightgown out at him. Did she realize how much he liked the way she taunted him? The more she snubbed him, the more he wanted her, and the more certain he became he would have her someday. She had the advantage at this stage of the game, but all that mattered was that she was playing. The rules were in constant flux.

After their usual breakfast—his a croissant, hers a quiche—they made directly for the Galleria dell'Accademia, mingling with other tourists. Violet's delicate artist's fingers rested lightly on his arm, allowing him to lead her through the halls.

They made a picturesque contrast: he paled-skinned and light-eyed, dressed all in black but for the silver brocade waistcoat, and she with her tanned complexion, bright green top, flowered hat, and striped stockings. He was night and she day, opposite and complementary, each finest in the presence of the other.

"He *is* rather poorly endowed," Violet observed, peering up at David's marble form.

"And uncircumcised. David was a Judaic king, but it seems artistic convention trumps historical accuracy."

Violet frowned at him. "You're a peculiar man. Do you critique all art in such a fashion?"

"I'm merely making an observation, and one that ought to be apparent to anyone with knowledge of biblical history."

"You don't strike me as a Bible scholar, Mr. Tagget. Given your lax morals, I'm surprised you've read any of it."

"Cover to cover. A strange book. I didn't care for it."

Her brows knit together. "That's not how one is supposed to read the Bible."

"Oh? You have some expertise on the matter?"

"My father is a minister."

"Ah. That explains why you left Australia. I imagine he's a traditional, moralizing sort?"

"Worse. He doesn't practice what he preaches."

Evan nodded. "You're better off here, I expect, though I can't wholly condemn the man. After all, he is responsible for your presence on this earth, and that is a gift to all mankind and to myself in particular."

She heaved a sigh. "You are so annoying."

"I don't understand your aversion to flattery." Most people of Tagget's acquaintance adored flattery, whether in a flirtatious manner or a more business-minded one. It was a tactic he'd used for years, and one he rather enjoyed. Especially in the flirtatious sense.

"My aversion is to insincere flattery," Violet huffed.

"It's not insincere," Evan protested. "You are the most radiant woman I know."

"Stop trying to talk your way into my bed. We are business associates, nothing more. Now, have you made any observations of note concerning the museum?"

"Aside from the questionable rendering of David's quimstake? Not especially. Their security seems as indifferent as at any such institution."

"Indifferent?" Violet gave him a puzzled look. "The doors are monitored, and I'm certain they have night watchmen."

"Breaking into this museum would be child's play," Evan explained. "Forget the doors, or even the windows. There are openings for ventilation, access for electrical wires and steam heating, and any number of other vulnerable places, unguarded and manipulable with simple tools. I can't imagine this museum posing any sort of challenge for our thief, unless he means to haul off this grotesque marble." He waved a hand at the naked stone man.

"Now that would be something!"

The amusement in her voice made Evan grin. "Wouldn't it? I'd like to see that."

"It would require dropping a machine from a dirigible again."

"Absolutely. Shall we return to our own conveyance? I can instruct the crew to float over the city this evening and alert us to any suspicious ships flying by."

Watching out the window himself was another possibility, if he were to sleep as poorly as he had last night.

"I'm happy to return," Violet agreed. "Perhaps we could stop for lunch along the way. I'm beginning to feel hungry."

Evan took her to a nearby restaurant and, despite his broken Italian, managed to procure two heaping dishes of garlicky pasta. By this time of day he'd worked up an appetite, but the necessity of picking out the mushrooms caused Violet to shake her head in disapproval. He couldn't help it. Mushrooms were tied too closely to rot in his mind, and he would never, ever touch any food that might be even the slightest bit off. Never again.

At least she couldn't complain that he didn't eat. He demolished every other scrap of food on the plate and downed two glasses of wine. Evan adored the way the Italians had decent wine in any little shop he happened across.

The walk to the airfield under the bright skies buoyed his spirits, and he was considering turning around and spending the remainder of the day wandering the town with Violet, when his musings were interrupted by Walton's frantic voice.

"Mr. Tagget, sir! We've been looking for you. Shocking news, sir!"

Evan quirked an eyebrow. "Yes?"

"The Uffizi museum was broken into early this morning. An important painting is missing."

Evan and Violet looked at one another. "Oh, hell," she swore. "His threat to the Accademia was a ruse."

"And he beat us here by a day. Nevertheless, we are on his tail. Let's go to the Uffizi and assess this newest incident."

Violet shook her head. "Do you think they'll let us in? The museum is surely closed and it will be under investigation."

Evan grinned. "Money talks, my blossom, and I have a mess of it."

· · · ·⚒· · ·

"The *Venus of Urbino* is a great work!"

Evan did his best not to wince at the volume of the curator's impassioned cry.

"A masterpiece!" His English was excellent, though his accent was thick. "Titian's finest in my humble opinion, and a treasure of our Italian heritage!" He dabbed at a tear with his handkerchief. "She was my favorite."

"Highly erotic, I've heard," Evan added, a bit disappointed at losing the chance to see the famous artistic beauty.

"She is radiant! Celestial!"

"I didn't say otherwise."

"She must be recovered! You must find her. I will be in agony until she is home safely."

Violet rested a dainty white glove on the curator's arm. "We will do all we can. Perhaps if you show us where she belongs and the probable means of entry, we can learn what we need to catch the thief."

"Yes, yes, of course. Please, follow me." The curator led her on his arm through the museum. "You must understand my despair, signorina, being so lovely a lady yourself, and an artist, too!"

"I do, sir, I do. Mistreatment of any art is a crime against beauty."

Evan rolled his eyes. Utter tripe. And she called *him* insincere.

"Yes! You do understand!" The curator looked as though he might kiss her. He'd regret it if he tried. Evan had seen her bare arms, and she had some muscle. He expected Miss Violet Dayton could throw a punch, and she was once again wearing her ball-kicking boots.

"Look!" the scholar wailed, gesturing at a blank wall where the *Venus* should have been. He blew his nose into his handkerchief, loud enough that Evan flinched. "You must excuse me. I am overcome."

Probably he was in charge of keeping the art safe and in danger of losing his job. Evan couldn't see any other reason to be so attached to a painting, no matter how pretty it was. One could find any number of similar works to stand in for it. Hell, Violet could probably replicate it. A Vérité forgery would look lovely in its stead.

Violet extricated her arm from the curator's and gave the blank wall a closer inspection. "Nothing strange here. It was taken down the usual way, I imagine. How did they get in and out?"

"Let me show you," the curator sniffed.

They followed him to a long hall on the second floor, where an entire window had been sliced out. Evan surveyed the area and ran a finger along the broken edge of the glass, considering what sort of tool might have done the cutting.

"I imagine there were guards on duty?" Violet asked. "Did anyone hear strange noises?"

"There was some chaos in the streets. A fight between several men on the opposite side of the building. I am told one had a steam car and was tooting the horn vigorously. The guards were taken in by this noise, and now my Venus will suffer for it."

"The machine that cut this dangled from a dirigible," Evan theorized. "The slices are all angled down. Reaching up from below, they would have sloped the opposite direction."

"Just as we expected, only the wrong museum," Violet agreed. "This opening is plenty big to get the painting out, and whatever mechanism lowered the cutting machine could have picked up the painting and the men who nabbed it."

"And once the cutting is done, the dirigible is largely silent. It can hover with its engines low, or even off, and in the dark it wouldn't be obvious. It's a daring crime, but a well-executed one." He had to give this thief credit. L'Exploiteur knew how to craft a quality plan.

"It confirms our guesses about him," Violet said. "He's using a dirigible and mechanical devices to commit the crimes. He has a crew to assist him with these things, and also possibly with the actual retrieval of the works."

Evan nodded. "We'll have days, at least, before the next attempt. He'll need time to fly somewhere new and to concoct the next plan. I wonder, has he manufactured these burglary machines ahead of time, or does he build them one at a time?"

"At the very least he must store them somewhere. Machines with such cutting power must be large, and no airship could carry multiples."

Evan pursed his lips. "Perhaps. Or perhaps they are small but powerful. Parker uses a hand-held slicer on the airship. It's about seven inches long, and no more than an inch in diameter at its widest point. It's powered by luxene and needs regular refueling, but it can cut through half-inch steel if you turn it to full power."

Violet rubbed her temple. "I feel as if we've learned nothing. Can we return to Dauntless for tea? I want to add this to my notes and read over your list of dirigible owners."

Evan cringed. "It's lengthy. I hadn't realized quite how much the fad of private air travel had grown in Paris. We'll need to whittle down the list as best we can, then consider the chief suspects and their potential access to machine manufacturing."

The museum scholar ushered them down the stairs toward the exit. "This is excellent. You have suspects and records. You detectives will solve this crime and rescue my Venus!" He pumped Evan's hand with vigor, then kissed Violet on the cheek. Sadly, she neither punched him nor kicked him in the balls.

Instead she smiled at him and thanked him for showing them through the museum. "You will be the first to know when we find her."

"Grazie, grazie, signorina!"

"The first to know?" Evan echoed, the moment they stepped out into the sunlight.

"Oh, it can't hurt to tell him that. You saw how upset he was."

"Over a painting. The man is absurd."

"I thought he was nice. And that painting is priceless."

Evan shook his head. "Everything has a price."

Violet gave him a long, hard look. "I'm sorry you think so."

9

VIOLET ROLLED OVER and tried to will herself back to sleep, but Tagget's whimpering was growing worse. The noise itself wasn't the trouble. It wasn't much louder than the hum of the dirigible's engine. But seeing a self-possessed man trembling in the grip of recurring nightmares wrenched her heart. She wondered what it was he feared so badly.

The obvious guess was a fear of heights, since that would also explain why he didn't go out on the deck, but something about that didn't feel right to her. His fear was deep, emotional. Unless he'd suffered a traumatic fall in the past, she didn't think his problem was with flying.

Violet rolled to face him. He was shaking so hard now she could feel the bed move beneath her. She slid closer, surprised by the amount of space between them in the small bed.

His sleeping habits confounded her. She had expected him to sprawl, staking claim to the bed like a king to his realm. Instead, she had only ever seen him on his side, curled into a tight ball, clutching one of his many pillows. He also didn't bother with a proper nightshirt, merely crawled into bed in his underthings.

"Tagget." She placed a hand on his bare shoulder and shook him. "Tagget, wake up. You're dreaming again."

He pulled away from her touch and mumbled something that might have been a "no."

She shook him again. "Evan!"

He started at the use of his given name and rolled onto his back, blinking. She couldn't discern his expression in the dark room, but the trembling hadn't stopped.

"My apologies." His voice held an edge. Embarrassment? Lingering fear? She couldn't tell. "I didn't mean to disturb your rest."

"I'm fine. You're clearly troubled. Is there anything I can do?"

"Do?" His joyless laugh washed over her like ice. "No. Some nights the sounds of the airship trouble me. I can't predict when it will happen. I'm accustomed to it, but I've never had company aboard before."

"Is it the height? I've heard people try hypnosis to handle it, and various herbs mixed into their drinks."

"The height doesn't bother me. It's the noise of the machinery. I prefer city noise—people, cars, that sort of thing." He tossed back the blankets and climbed out of bed. "You may return to your sleep. I won't bother you any longer."

Vi sat up. "I'm wide awake. Feel free to turn on a lamp."

It was wrong to pry into his life, but the curiosity was gnawing at her. What haunted a man who had everything? Did he suffer guilt from horrible things he'd done in the past? She couldn't imagine him having many regrets. Murder, perhaps? That could torment anyone. But no. Too messy. Too much potential for disaster. His calculating mind wouldn't accept that risk. The fact that he hadn't even so much as groped her suggested any physical attack on a person would be unlikely. Lesser crimes wouldn't bother him. His blasé attitude towards the art thefts had her wondering if he might be making mental notes for his own future misdeeds.

Violet could imagine him arranging to upstage l'Exploiteur. Tagget wouldn't be showy about it. He would be calm, efficient, and stylish. He might never even share what he had done. He would snatch some precious work of art, put it on the wall in his home and stand in front of it with a smug smile, thinking how he was so much better than anyone else he didn't even need to prove it.

Tagget pulled clothes from the closet and began to dress. The lack of lighting didn't seem to deter him. Since everything he owned was black except his waistcoats, he probably could dress in total darkness.

She watched his shadowy form, lit only by the dim bulb that marked the doorway. Three nights she had slept in his bed now, and she had yet to get a good look at him unclothed. Stripping him naked ought to be an easier task than stripping away the layers of his character.

"Do you intend to stare at me all night, Miss Dayton?"

"Yes."

He froze for an instant, and she wished she could see his face. He tossed the shirt in his hands onto an armchair and strode back to the bed.

"Perhaps you would like a closer look?"

His sensuous voice brought warmth to her cheeks. When he crawled up onto the bed, she didn't back away. He straddled her legs, pinning her beneath the blanket, and placed both hands against the headboard to either side of her. Heat radiated from his bare chest. His breath caressed her lips.

"Tell me if I get too close," he murmured.

"I don't think that's possible."

His kiss was a deliberate, silken tease, a whisper against her lips, a delectable morsel, snatched away before she could indulge.

"Close enough?" he breathed.

Vi draped her arms around his shoulders, her fingers tickling the hairs at the nape of his neck. "You know it wasn't. You're so hungry you're trembling."

His mouth caught the corner of hers, his tongue flicking

against her bottom lip before he withdrew again. "You see? My appetite isn't so deficient. It wants only for the right cuisine."

She yanked him against her, smothering his arrogant mouth with greedy kisses, feeling the evidence of his desire pressing into her belly. He burned beneath his cool exterior, a searing passion she wanted to devour. His growl of pleasure spurred her on, thrusting aside any doubts. Yes, he was a conceited jackass. She didn't care. He was delicious and she wanted a thorough taste.

"Would that I were an insect, to live off your sweet nectar," he murmured.

The words were irrelevant. His husky voice liquefied her insides. He could read a grocer's inventory in that voice and she would melt in his embrace.

"Lord, Tagget, I could eat you alive."

"Evan." He nibbled at the sensitive skin of her neck, and her head lolled against the headboard.

"Evan," she moaned.

"That's it, darling. I *will* eat you alive, and you will love every second of it."

A hard bump jostled the bed, snapping Violet from her trance. The dirigible grew still, and the engine wound down. They had landed.

"What's happening?"

"We've arrived. Rome is a short flight from Florence."

"Rome? Why aren't we going back to Paris?"

"I wanted to show you the Colosseum."

Of all the high-handed, egotistical, presumptuous… She pushed him away and untangled herself from the blanket. Of course he would usurp her mission and turn it into his own pleasure jaunt. The man never thought about anything but himself. And here she was, in his bed, panting with desire in his arms, ready to spread for him like some kind of two-penny whore.

What in hell was wrong with her? She was out of her mind to let him seduce her. No, worse, to encourage him to do it.

"I told you," she growled, "I'm not sightseeing."

"Oh, but you want to. When you said that, those liquid amber eyes were so round and wistful. And today, walking about Florence, your face was alive with pleasure, drinking in the sights like a sot guzzles his gin."

Violet grabbed one of the largest pillows and the thick quilt they had kicked to the bottom of the bed.

"It's a beautiful night. I'm going up top to sleep under the stars. Don't follow me."

She strode from the room and slammed the door behind her.

Up on the deck she found Dahlia dozing against the hull, her shirt hanging open, the babe at her breast. Her eyes fluttered and she glanced up at Vi.

"Lovers' spat?"

"We're not lovers." Violet cast about for an excuse. "He snores."

Dahlia snorted. "No, he doesn't. He has these soft, raspy sort of breaths. Put your head on his chest sometime and you can hear it real good. Almost like a hum."

Violet gaped at the other woman. "He's not Fern's father, is he?"

"God, no!" Dahlia recovered herself and laughed. "Nah, he only hired me six months ago. I was real pregnant then. Dunno why he took me on so close to my time. No one else would." She shrugged. "It worked out okay."

Violet made herself a bed and settled down into it. "Of course he screws his employees."

Dahlia overheard the muttering. "Just a fling. Never on the ship. During my time off. It was my idea. Think he was bored. Not by me, I mean. In general."

"He's always bored."

"Hasn't looked bored since you came on."

"Well, I'm the fun new project." Vi yanked the quilt over her head. Damn Evan Tagget, anyhow. She'd let him parade her about Rome in the morning. It was stupid to pass up the chance to see such art and history. But the minute they got back to Paris, she was booting him off the team. She'd dredge up one of the low-lifes that brought commissions to her and insist he take her to the man who paid for them. True, he was a notorious underworld leader, but he might enjoy financing her mission. Criminals loved to bring down other criminals. It lessened the competition.

For now she would sleep. Under the starry Roman sky the world faded into dreams of green eyes and sultry whispers.

· · · ⚔ · · ·

Dauntless had fallen silent, but Evan doubted he would ever sleep. He had a throbbing hard-on, and his bed smelled of Violet's lilac perfume. He stared up at the tin ceiling, trying to fathom what had gone wrong. No one had ever kissed him with such abandon and then simply walked away.

The woman was confounding. One second she was putty in his hands, the next she despised him. Plenty of people hated him, certainly, but usually not the ones he wanted to sleep with.

Her reaction to his gifts puzzled him. He recognized the eager glint in her eyes when he offered something. She wanted to grab all she could and stash it away in case she might have need of it. It was an instinctive reaction to financial insecurity. Evan understood the feeling.

What he didn't understand was her struggle to accept, and her occasional rejections. Why didn't she want a studio in his warehouse? It would be nicer than anything she could rent for herself. Why was she angry he was taking her sightseeing when she longed to see the world?

His former paramours had loved to be showered with baubles. They liked the attention, and they liked the financial perks. The only person to have turned down his offers was

Eden. Evan still didn't understand what she had wanted, only that she'd found it in her husband.

He wasn't going to repeat that mess with Violet. He would scrutinize her every move, her every part, until he figured her out and won her over. It was good to have purpose.

Evan curled up on his side and tucked the blanket around himself. The bed was cold without her. He wouldn't let it stay that way.

10

Evan had struck two-thirds of the names from his list of dirigible owners in a single morning's worth of phone calls.

He shoved the phone to the back corner of the desk and unplugged the wire that connected it to the network. Having a telephone installed in his hotel suite allowed him to conduct business in private, but he disliked the feeling of being available to anyone with a telephone of their own. Evan Tagget would not be at anyone's beck and call.

He poured himself a glass of cognac and reviewed the adjustments he'd made to his list.

This fad of the upper class buying garish ships to flaunt their wealth irked him. He had spared no expense on the purchase of his own ship. Lasher dirigibles were without peer. Dauntless was made to exacting standards from the best materials. His crew were an unusual assortment, but they were experts who flew fast and sure and kept her in flawless condition. She had no need for a bright red balloon or gold leaf decoration. She was the best without a need to preen.

Fortunately, the trend meant that most of the owners weren't suspects. Many showy dirigibles masked dwindling fortunes. Such men would steal for profit, not for pleasure. They'd been the first crossed out.

Others pursued careers such as law or finance and lacked the necessary knowledge of automechanology, regardless of financial standing. Those that could afford to hire engineers and machinists remained distant possibilities and were marked as such, though Evan believed the culprit to be personally involved in the building of the contraptions.

Several men on the list, such as Gaillard, were victims themselves. Evan put them onto a separate list in case the thief might be clever enough to steal from himself.

Satisfied he'd made progress, he turned his attention to Eden's latest letter.

> *I already like this woman you have met. I think she sounds perfect for you, and she will hopefully cause you terrible trouble. It will be good for you. I want to hear all about it!*
>
> *I'm sorry to say that I dinged the Mercedes. I was going a bit much too fast and ran over a feral dragon. I wish people wouldn't turn them loose when they tire of them. Some of them are very efficient and go for weeks or even months before their luxene runs out. I took the crushed creature to my father, who is turning it into a hat rack.*

A fist hammering on the door startled Evan. Annoyed, he rose from the desk and pounded on the button that started up the clockwork. The moment the gap was large enough to admit a person, an unshaven lout of a man squeezed through, looming over Evan with his foul breath and complete lack of personal hygiene. He had two metal teeth and a large knife on his belt. A second reprobate followed behind.

A terrified porter joined the crowd, gasping for breath. "Mr. Tagget, sir. I'm so sorry. We tried to stop them. They punched Claude!"

Evan took a cautious step backward, imagining the room behind him, searching for a potential weapon. Damn it all, he was going to his fencing lesson tomorrow and then buying a sword.

He grabbed the dragon from his desk. It kicked its little legs and opened its mouth, spewing a gout of flame.

"I believe you have the wrong room," he stated in his most commanding tone. "Vacate my suite at once, or I shall summon the management and the police, if necessary."

Goon One shied away from the dragon. "We're here for the lady's things. She said you'd pay us."

Evan would have preferred the man to punch him. A tremor of shock ran through him, followed by a wave of anguish. Violet was truly done with him? He'd thought it an idle threat. She'd been so happy yesterday, goggling at the ancient ruins, enjoying her food and wine. He'd even slept on the floor to avoid waking her on the flight back to Paris—only to sleep nightmare free.

How could she leave him? What had he done wrong? A tremor radiated through his body.

Fucking hell.

Evan loathed the panicked, helpless feeling that burbled inside him every time someone tried to take something that belonged to him. When Eden had rejected him, he'd completely lost control. Never again. He forced himself to take a deep breath.

Violet is not yours, Tagget.

But, damn, did he want her to be.

This was a problem like any other. It had a solution. He would find it.

"I'm to pay you?" The serenity of his voice surprised him. "How much?"

"She said ten francs each for moving all her stuff."

"Ten?" No wonder they had bullied their way in here. These men probably made half that much for a full day's work. "I will give you each fifteen to get out of here and never come back. If you can take me to Miss Dayton, I'll give you each twenty francs."

"Take you to who?" Goon Two asked.

"Mademoiselle d'Aubergine."

"Oh, yeah. We can take you to where she hired us."

"Good enough. Go downstairs and meet me outside the hotel. We'll hire a cab."

"I don't know. She said if we didn't move her things we'd get nothing."

"Twenty francs if you do as I say. Nothing and a phone call to the police if you don't. Do you understand me?" Evan made the dragon belch again to emphasize his point.

Goon One elbowed his companion. "Right. Outside." They shoved their way past the unfortunate porter and thundered down the stairs.

Evan replaced the dragon and downed the rest of his cognac. He was going to miss lunch. He ripped a few pages from his notebook and thrust them at the porter on his way out the door.

"See that these are delivered to Monsieur Roland of the Studio d'Automechanologie. Inform him that Mr. Tagget would like a new door manufactured and installed as soon as possible. Money is no object, only quality should be considered."

"Yes, sir." The boy scampered off.

The goons had failed to hail a cab. In this part of town no respectable driver would stop for a pair of miscreants who looked like they might not have the means to pay. Not with so many fat fares nearby. Evan flagged down the first passing vehicle and ushered his guides inside.

"We are making one stop before we go to see Miss d'Aubergine. You are to wait with the cab. Do as I say and you'll get your money. Fail to comply and I'll throw you out on the street with nothing."

"What's 'comply' mean?" Goon Two asked.

His partner elbowed him again. God, where had Violet

found these buffoons? It would have taken a miracle for them to move her things without either stealing or breaking most of them. She must have known Evan would never let that happen. Perhaps she didn't want to be rid of him after all.

He glared at the goons with the scowl he usually reserved for lazy, negligent, or crooked employees. They were natural underlings, and his commanding attitude kept them in check. He didn't dare back off for even an instant. These men could kill him with their bare hands.

What was he getting himself into, following a pair of lowlifes to God knows where? He would need to use extra caution. His brain was his best tool, and he didn't want it splattered on the pavement.

. . . ⟶ . . .

Hell and damn, Violet cursed silently. He'd found her already. So much for the chance to explore a different path to her art thief. She turned toward Tagget and away from the unpainted wooden door—one of many such doors along the dark, narrow street. In this part of town certain businesses didn't advertise, and outsiders entered by invitation only.

"You look terrible," Tagget said.

And now he was insulting her? She didn't like that any better than the meaningless compliments. It was her makeup, she suspected. She'd rubbed pink powder over her cheeks, painted her lips bright red, and even used kohl to draw attention to her eyes. "Proper" ladies were subtle with their beauty products, and usually claimed not to use them at all. Violet had layered hers on thickly. But she'd intended to look like a prostitute or a serving girl in a cheap bar.

"It's not the cosmetics," Tagget said, as if reading her mind. "It's the clothes. You are appallingly... beige."

Violet glanced down at her neutral dress. Plain, but short, with the edge of her petticoat and several inches of stocking showing. The neckline was high, so she'd padded the bust. She thought she looked the part.

"At least I fit in," she hissed. "You're begging to be beaten and robbed."

Everyone within twenty yards was staring at him. The trim on his military-style jacket and the patterning on his tie were blood red. Everything else was perfect, crisp, clean black. He gleamed like a jewel among the browns and grays of the dirty streets. He usually went without accessories, but today he wore gloves and a top hat and carried a silver-handled cane.

He leaned toward her, anger flashing in his eyes. "I am fully aware of that," he snarled. "Do you have any idea how many people I have had to bribe to track you down?"

Vi crossed her arms and matched his furious expression. "You poor, poor man, having to part with a meager handful of your hard-earned money."

"The expense is irrelevant. What matters is that I have had to carry a significant sum of money on my person. I despise doing so, particularly in such unsavory areas as you have led me to today. I'm one false step away from dying in a puddle of filth, and I'm not pleased about it."

"You didn't have to follow me." Her retort didn't carry the force she'd meant it to. She'd made him vulnerable, and guilt welled up inside her, whether she deserved it or not.

Tagget's eyes softened, then turned to ice. "I wouldn't have you die in a puddle of filth, either."

She turned away. "I don't need your protection."

He stepped close enough that she could feel his breath on the back of her neck. "You have it, nonetheless. Why do you run from me? I can give you the world."

Vi shivered. "I don't want anything you're offering."

His lips brushed her neck. "Then why do you tremble so in my arms?"

"Get off me."

He took a step back. "Come, my reluctant blossom, you

can't deny you desire me. You are no naive innocent to shy away from passion. Why do you fight it?"

She tossed a derisive look over her shoulder. "I take my lovers where I will, Mr. Tagget, but I won't be anyone's kept woman." The door in front of her creaked open. "Excuse me, I have an appointment."

A wiry, squint-eyed man handed back her card and waved her in.

"He will see you, mademoiselle."

Tagget moved to follow, but the man brandished a knife. "Where do you think you're going?"

Tagget hefted his cane. Vi hoped he didn't try to fight his way in. She expected he would lose, even with the longer weapon. "To speak with your boss. I'm with the lady."

"Oh, are you? What's your name, Mr. Fancy-pants?"

"Evan Tagget."

The man flinched and stepped aside. "Monsieur Lacenaire will see you."

"Thank you."

Violet's fingers clenched. A whole day's worth of talking her way up to this meeting, and all he had to do was throw around some money and drop his name.

"Have I mentioned that I hate you?" she hissed.

She refused to look at him, but knew he was smirking anyway. "I believe you have, yes."

"Good. Don't forget it."

The squinty man closed the door behind them. "We'll be checking you for weapons." He eyed Tagget's cane. "You'll have to leave that here."

Tagget leaned it against the wall. "I expect it back undamaged."

Squinty nodded. "Not to worry, sir. Now, if you would, please, lift your arms."

Vi watched in amazement as Tagget allowed the man to pat down his arms, legs, and torso. He looked bored by the whole thing, when she would have sworn he ought to be angry or insulted.

Squinty paused on Tagget's left arm, poking at something. "What's this, then?"

"A screwdriver." He shrugged out of the jacket and pulled the tool from somewhere in his sleeve.

Squinty's mouse-like eyes peered at it a long moment. "You can keep it. You're clean." He turned to Violet. "Mademoiselle, if you please?"

Tagget rested a finger atop his cane. "If you touch her inappropriately you will regret it."

"No worries, sir. I can buy a girl down the street if I'm needing one."

Violet gritted her teeth and held as still as possible for the search. Squinty didn't grope her, but he smelled of sour cheese and his fingers poked uncomfortably. He deprived her of her small knife before stepping away.

"You may go in, now. Right this way."

If Violet had seen Monsieur Lacenaire's office out of context, she would have guessed it to belong to a lawyer or professor. Floor-to-ceiling bookshelves lined two of the four walls, filled with an assortment of books and objets d'art. His desk was of a thick, dark wood, with hefty legs carved in the shape of winged lions. Papers and writing implements littered the surface.

Lacenaire himself was an unassuming man of fifty or sixty years—gray-haired with a careworn face, but showing signs of vigor. His clothes were neat and of good quality, all in gray but for a burgundy waistcoat. He sat quietly, his hands folded, assessing his visitors.

Behind him, on an otherwise blank wall, hung one of Violet's early forgeries. A bubble of joy swelled inside her. She'd thought it had been burned when it was unmasked.

"Beautiful painting," Tagget remarked.

"Isn't it? An early Vérité. I snatched it up when the police were done with it. I wouldn't want good art to go to waste."

"Certainly not." Evan studied the painting, his hand stroking his tidy beard. "A product of great talent and careful work."

A giddy shiver ran over Violet's skin at the praise.

"What can I do for you, Mr. Tagget?" Lacenaire asked.

"I'm in the market for a painting to be hung in my personal dirigible. I believe a Vérité would do nicely. I would like one of the newer works. One that hasn't yet been discovered as a forgery."

Vi elbowed him. He needed to stop interfering with her assignment. She tried to glare at him, but her grin wouldn't fade. Seeing others take pleasure in her art was too rare a satisfaction. Tagget waggled his eyebrows, and in that instant he looked no more than a mischievous little boy.

"Ah." Lacenaire chuckled. "I can do that for you, at a price. There is a wonderful Rembrandt currently on display, or if you prefer an exact copy, I can recommend her exquisite Botticelli. I have the original in my own collection at the moment. Oh, would I love to see the look on Crevier's face when he discovers that his 'recovery' of that work was nothing of the sort."

Violet laughed. "So would I!"

"We are all in agreement on that point," Tagget said. "As regards the painting, however, I don't think that particular piece would suit my tastes."

"Perhaps you would prefer to commission your own," Lacenaire suggested. "Vérité does the Dutch masters especially well. She could make you a nice Vermeer."

Tagget waved a disdainful hand. "Too plebeian. Everyone has a forged Vermeer. No, I would prefer something elegant and eye-catching, but a bit different. A de Heem will do nicely. I'm enamored of the realism in the details of his still-lifes."

Lacenaire nodded approvingly. "In that case, you have no

need of my services. I suggest you draw up a contract with the lady herself."

Vi withdrew her card and presented it. "At your service, Mr. Tagget."

Tagget examined the battered card, marked only with her signature V in dark green ink. He flipped it over a few times and held it up to the light before returning it to her.

"Ah, but how do I know the lady is who she says she is? An artist's mark is much easier to forge than a painting." His eyes twinkled with laughter, his smirk threatening to grow into a true grin.

Lacenaire held out a hand for the card. "Allow me."

He lifted the wings of a mechanical ladybug that rested on his desk, and slid the card underneath. When the wings dropped down, the antennae began to twitch.

Tagget's eyes grew wide. "You mixed luxene in with the ink. Clever trick!" He reached for the ladybug, but Lacenaire pulled it away and tucked it inside his desk, handing the card back to Violet.

"A means of identification among those who work with me. Its existence does not leave this room."

Tagget withdrew his hand. "Of course." His eyes locked on some distant point and his mouth turned in concentration. He intended to engineer his own reader, Vi had no doubt.

"Monsieur Lacenaire," she began, making use of Tagget's distraction, "our true purpose here is to gather information on the art thief who calls himself l'Exploiteur."

"An amateur," Lacenaire scoffed. "Playing a stupid game. As a man of business I cannot condone any such action."

"Do you know anything about him? Any hints to his identity?"

"He is not a direct competitor of mine, nor is he working for any of them. He's a dangerous sort—a loner, a gambler. He thinks himself above the law of the land and above the law of the street. If you seek to be rid of him, I won't stand in your way.

"He has yet to encroach on my territory. Until then, he is yours to handle, but my eyes and ears are noting his capers. He builds his machines here in Paris, I can tell you that much. He stole an engineer from Thibodeaux and left him hopping mad."

"Thibodeaux who builds those carriage-pulling dragons?" Vi asked.

"Just so. An excellent customer. Not the brightest, though. He bought one of your paintings, I believe, for an exorbitant price."

"An exorbitant price that I saw all too little of," she grumbled.

"Such is the way of the world, Mademoiselle Vérité. If you desire money, write up a contract directly with Mr. Tagget. He has millions waiting to be squandered."

Vi nodded. "Thank you, Monsieur Lacenaire. You've been most helpful. I'll let you know what I discover."

"Excellent. If you are successful in this, perhaps I will consider other commissions for you besides art."

Violet grimaced. "I don't hope to make a career out of this."

He nodded. "Very well. Art it is."

Tagget set a slip of paper on the desk. "My head of records here in Paris. You might find him useful."

Lacenaire eyed the paper a moment. When he looked up at Tagget, their gazes locked—blue eyes to green, cold and implacable—two men of power in an uneasy alliance.

"Thank you, Mr. Tagget. You may see yourself out."

Tagget offered his arm and walked Vi to the exit, where Squinty returned Tagget's cane and hat and Vi's knife. He made an awkward bow and held the door for them.

"Did you just give a crime lord the name of your chief spy?" Violet whispered.

"He's in my debt now. We can call on him freely if we have need of him."

She shook her head. "You're playing a dangerous game."

"And you aren't? Going to see him alone, with nothing to bargain with but your artistic talents and your audacity?" His voice carried a note of pride, not scorn. Violet refused to be swayed by it.

"You're manipulating a notorious gang leader. Perhaps the most notorious in the city! I expected to beg for his assistance and promise him a favor."

Tagget sniffed. "My way is better."

"The man is said to have murdered a dozen people himself."

"I quite liked him. He's a man of reason. He knows the value of my connections."

"I hope you're right. I didn't take on this job with the intent of winding up dead."

"We all wind up dead someday, Miss Dayton. It's what we do on the path to death that determines whether we live on afterward."

Their conversation had carried them to a busier street, where an empty cab zipped up the moment Tagget lifted his cane.

"Everything comes easy for you, doesn't it?"

His brows shot up. His words were brusque. "Easy? No, Miss Dayton, it does not, but you seem determined to think ill of me."

"You've given me little reason to think otherwise."

Only once the words were spoken did she realize the lie behind them. He'd surprised her with a multitude of good qualities. He was quick-witted, intelligent, and thoughtful. He valued skill, hard work, and loyalty, and he looked for those things in his employees. He judged people by their abilities, with little regard for the social divides of class, race, or gender. He was oddly generous. Some of his offers were too spontaneous to be calculated attempts to buy her.

It was these things that drew her to him and made her want to overlook his self-centered facade to dig for the real

Evan Tagget underneath. Her one worry was that he might prove to be self-centered all the way down.

He certainly didn't lack for feelings, despite his often cool demeanor, and she seldom took that into consideration. Her words to him just now had stung, and they rode in silence to the hotel, he petulant, she guilty.

Tagget had recovered himself enough to adopt his customary smile when he helped her from the carriage. "These capers of yours caused me to miss lunch today. What would you say to an early dinner?"

"As long as you're paying, I'm all for it. I'll have to change. I look like a cheap whore, and we wouldn't want anyone to think you'd lowered your standards."

"I should think you would be more concerned for yourself."

"Myself? Why? I clearly don't have any standards or I wouldn't be consorting with you."

His answering smile was one of genuine amusement, so lacking in cynicism that Vi's breath hitched.

"Now you are teasing me. I think you like me, Miss Dayton, despite yourself. And I think we are more similar than you care to admit."

"Ha!" she scampered into the hotel and up the stairs to his room. She hadn't stopped to ask someone to let her in, and she didn't have a key of her own, so she stood there, tapping her foot impatiently as she waited for the steam lift. Better, though, to have a moment to compose herself. He was altogether too intriguing, and she needed to keep her mind on what mattered.

Catch the thief. Sell a few more paintings.

That was it. That was all she needed. Even one sale, or one commission, if it were large enough. If Tagget really wanted a Vérité forgery, her dream would be within reach. All her scraping by would be worth it. She would have the money to hold the exhibition she'd dreamed of for ten years.

When Tagget at last arrived, he slotted his key into the monstrosity of a door and pulled it open, holding it and waving

Violet in. "I'm having a new door installed soon. I'll make certain we tune the recognizer to admit you."

She started through the entranceway. "That would be nice. I…" She stumbled to a halt. "Where are all my things?"

"I took the liberty of having them moved, since that seemed to be your desire. I'm afraid your two ruffians weren't up to the task, so I had to pick the location myself."

Violet spoke through clenched teeth. "Where are my things?"

"All your art supplies have been relocated to your new studio in my warehouse. It's a sizeable space and will have plentiful natural lighting. I promise you will like it. Your personal effects are in our bedroom, naturally."

She raised her hand to slap him, but froze mid-swing at the look on his face. Some savage emotion between rage and terror seethed in the depths of his eyes. Her hand dropped and she stumbled backward, not certain if she was terrified of him or for him.

"I'm so sorry," she blurted. "I shouldn't hit you, regardless of what you've done."

Tagget only stared, as if not quite hearing her. He'd been hit before, Vi realized. And not a childhood swat on the bum, but a blow meant to inflict pain.

"I'm sorry," she repeated.

His lashes fluttered, and the haunted expression vanished. In an instant he was his usual self, cool and confident. "I appreciate your restraint, Miss Dayton. Perhaps now that your rage has cooled you will also be able to see the logic in relocating your possessions."

Despite the casual tone, his body language revealed a continuing inner turmoil. He leaned slightly away from her, instead of toward her as he usually did. Vi wanted to hug him, even while anger at his actions still burned inside her. Who was this man, and why was he so blasted complicated?

She shook off the feeling and stalked toward the bedroom,

needing time and space to sift through her muddled reactions to him. "You presume too much, Mr. Tagget. Stop trying to control my life."

"I control everything, mademoiselle. Perhaps you should have done your research before you involved yourself in *my* life."

Violet shut his own bedroom door in his face, firmly, but carefully enough not to let the door strike him.

"Dinner will be in half an hour," he called after her.

11

FINISHED. Evan paused to wipe his goggles clean, then adjusted one of the leather straps of the tool holder wrapped snuggly around his left arm. Covered in clips and rings, the brass armpiece allowed him to keep an array of small tools on his person as he worked. He slotted a small wrench back into place, then made a quick perusal of his completed project.

The new copper tip on his cane didn't match the silver handle, but it was a small price to pay for a successful installation of the recognizer technology. The mechanism felt good in Evan's hands and made a satisfying click when it engaged. Pleased with the results, he set the cane aside and moved on to his next task: replicating Lacenaire's card reader. The concept was simple enough he could throw together a prototype using spare parts. And his device wouldn't look like a ladybug.

Evan didn't bother with a schematic, instead working from the picture in his head and making mental calculations. This was freedom and joy. In his own space, on his own time, the world outside evaporated, leaving only the numbers dancing in his mind, begging to flow out into the metal in his hands.

A few minutes into the project, he scrapped his original concept and pulled his cigarette case from his vest pocket. He dumped the cigarettes onto the table and held the case up for examination. Perfect.

Time flew by unheeded. Soon enough the card reader needed only a thin brass plate for completion. Evan had seen a properly sized piece in the scrap bin earlier. He reached behind him to feel for it.

A hand touched his.

His yelp echoed off the high ceiling of the open warehouse space and he toppled from his stool. Violet stood above him, cringing.

"Sorry. I was poking through your bucket of bits. They're pretty."

Evan dusted himself off, his heart still pounding. He'd forgotten she was nearby. It had been years since he'd worked anywhere but a locked room.

"Pretty?"

"Yes. They would make lovely jewelry if they could be shaped and shined."

He climbed to his feet. "How long have you been here?"

"Oh, ten minutes, maybe fifteen? You work more intently than anyone I've seen. I found it rather fascinating."

"I see." Evan pushed his goggles up and wiped the sweat and grime from his face.

Violet frowned at him. Her cheek was smeared with red paint and several other colors decorated her hands. "Why don't you do this for a living?"

"I do. How do you think I got started? I built things and sold them. When I had sold enough, I began to hire others to help me make more."

He wondered if she would let him wipe away that paint. He toyed with his handkerchief, weighing the consequences.

"But now you're a businessman. Your work is letters and telephone calls. Investments, meetings, ordering about your underlings. You do it well, but why? For the money?"

In part. Two decades after escaping Reynolds Manufacturing

for good, the echoes of his time there still haunted Evan. Distractions helped: art, music, books, new projects in his workshop. But even now, he needed the knowledge that he'd never be out on the streets. Never lack for food or shelter. Money provided only a portion of that security.

"Money is a yardstick and a means of bargaining," he replied. "Nothing more."

He held Violet's gaze, trying to think of anything other than his nagging need for *more*. If he reached for her, would she shy away? She'd spent hours last evening dragging everything from the spare room in order to move her own things into it. His sitting room was a disaster again. Today, though, she was relaxed and they were having a real conversation. Damn, he wanted to kiss her.

"So, if not for the money, then what?"

Since she wouldn't relent, he answered her truthfully. "To be the most powerful man in the world."

Her nose crinkled up. "Power." She sniffed in disdain. "Well. I'm sure that will bring you great happiness."

"It brings me whatever I want," Evan snapped.

It protects me.

The conversation had pushed him too far down this path. Old memories blazed in his mind, vivid even after all these years. The smack of a palm against his cheek. The smell of burning apple. The sickening helplessness. The boy shivered and wept and swore no one would ever hurt him again.

"Go back to your art," Evan said, forcing his voice into a more measured tone. "I need to finish this."

She regarded him in silence, her gaze sharp, studious. Then she gave her head a small shake. "We need to leave, if we want to speak with Monsieur Thibodeaux."

"What?" Evan consulted his watch. "Damn. Well, all I need to do is cut down the plate and rivet it in place. We can leave directly after."

"You don't need time to wash up and change clothes?"

"No. I thought I would go like this."

Her dark eyebrows arched. "Like that? You would leave the building looking anything but perfect?"

"Thibodeaux will respond better to a mechanic than to a man of business. You, however, might want to wipe the paint from your face." He held out the handkerchief.

"I'll change." Violet spun around and disappeared through the door that connected their two studios.

Evan finished the contraption in minutes. He wiped it down, shined it up, and gave it a quick examination. Simple and elegant, just how he liked. He tossed a bit of scrap into the bucket, watching it land atop the others.

Pretty. He'd never thought of his creations that way, but they did have their own sort of beauty. He made things with purpose, but there was nothing to stop him from building for purely aesthetic reasons. He pulled a few nice pieces from the bucket, an idea forming in his mind.

"Ahem."

Evan set the project aside. "I'm ready." He pulled off his goggles and unstrapped his armpiece. He hung both in their customary location, ready for next time.

On the way out he paused to look himself over in the mirror. His left sleeve was wrinkled from the tool holder, both his shirt and vest were stained, and his hair was mussed. He'd left off his jacket, so his screwdriver jutted from a vest pocket. He looked terrible, but he expected Thibodeaux to look much the same.

Violet, on the other hand, was a picture of loveliness. A purple riding jacket buttoned over a red dress that fell just to the top of black, knee-high boots. The red top hat decorated with black and purple feathers pulled it all together. She had tidied her hair and wiped away all streaks of paint. Anything left on her hands would be hidden beneath elegant embroidered gloves. A refined lady artist.

With her three-inch heels and her tall hat, she towered

above Evan. When he offered his arm, she smiled down at him, a more affectionate expression than her usual smirk. She definitely liked him, at times. He needed those times to come more often if he wanted to win her. He thought he might start taking notes.

"We're walking?" Violet asked when they bypassed the Peugeot.

"Arriving at the manufactory in a motorcar may appear to be a snub, and we must be friendly for this interview. Otherwise I would gladly do it. I find carriage dragons appallingly absurd."

"They're popular, though."

"Yes, with the same fools who gild their dirigibles. Thibodeaux sells hundreds of the things to British aristocrats who think fripperies from Paris can make up for their dying titles and flagging fortunes."

"His creations are fashionable all over Europe, as I understand it."

"They are, though I fail to see why. I like motorcars much better."

Violet's laugh floated on the air like music. "Of course you do. You're a man of technology. You carry a screwdriver the way a soldier carries a weapon."

Evan didn't know if she meant it to be a compliment, but it made him smile nonetheless. He tossed a coin at a girl selling flowers, and she presented Violet with a fragrant purple bouquet.

"I don't know if you are aware, Miss Dayton," he said, "but there is a production of *Carmen* playing at the opera house. It's my favorite opera, and I haven't yet seen it performed by this cast. Would you do me the honor of accompanying me tonight? I have excellent seats. After we meet with Thibodeaux we can visit Madame Rochette's shop to find you a dress. She should have several things made to your measurements by now."

Violet's usually brisk pace slowed. "I'll consider it."

"I will, of course, buy you dinner as well."

She rolled her eyes and resumed her customary speed. "I said I would consider it. Stop trying to bribe me, Tagget."

"It's not a bribe. It's an offer of a pleasant evening for a woman whom I admire."

"It's a bribe to lure me into your bed."

Evan flexed his fingers. It wasn't a bribe. It was a gift. And he wanted her to have it whether she came to his bed or not. "Believe what you like. I'm going to the damned opera with or without you."

They spent the remainder of the walk in sullen silence.

Thibodeaux himself opened the door for them when they arrived. A stout man of forty-some years, he was dressed much like Evan was, with goggles perched atop his head and a fully-laden tool belt around his waist.

The entrance hall to his building was hung all over with photographs of his work. Two carriage dragons flanked the door to the manufactory, one a winged horse, the other a half-sized elephant with horns on its head and spikes protruding from its sides. The addition of pointy bits where they didn't belong was yet another fad Evan hated.

"Monsieur Thibodeaux, so lovely to meet you," Violet simpered in flawless French. "It's such a pleasure to see your beautiful art up close. I am Violette d'Aubergine of the Société des Arts, and this is my associate, Mr. Tagget, an automechanologist like yourself."

Thibodeaux bowed. "I am pleased to meet you, mademoiselle, monsieur."

"The Société is working diligently to unmask the thief who calls himself l'Exploiteur," Violet continued. "We have been led to believe you might have information that could be of use to us. In particular, I understand an engineer has left you in recent days in some mysterious manner? I would be so grateful for any information you could offer us."

Thibodeaux crooked his arm, and Violet rested her

fingertips atop it. "A sad affair, mademoiselle, very sad, indeed. Come, let us walk. I am happy to tell you what I know."

"Thank you, monsieur. We artists must band together to protect our treasures."

"Just so." He led the way into his manufactory, grinning at Violet, while Evan trailed after, scowling.

He may as well have cleaned himself up. Thibodeaux hardly spared a glance in his direction. Now Evan was stuck standing around in filthy clothes with unwashed hands and uncombed hair while a man who built giant toys made eyes at the woman he wanted.

He needed a cigarette. He patted down all his pockets before remembering he'd upended his case onto his workbench and left everything there. Damn. He would have to suffer until he returned to the workshop.

Evan distracted himself by scrutinizing the dragons under construction. In some places, workers surrounded the machines, busily attaching parts or making adjustments. In other spots, dragons stood like metal statues, awaiting inspections or parts. Evan lingered near these, peering closely to assess the quality. The materials Thibodeaux used were good, but the welding was inconsistent, and Evan spotted several weak rivets. In one instance, he found a loose screw and fixed it himself. Thibodeaux needed to vet his employees better.

Thibodeaux was a chatterer, and Evan and Violet were forced to endure the entire life history of the disloyal engineer—some relative of Thibodeaux's. The boy had vanished one day, leaving only a note saying he'd taken a higher paying job.

"What was his salary here?" Evan asked.

"I pay a fair wage," Thibodeaux insisted, and turned back to Violet.

No matter. Evan would ask Durand to pull some of Thibodeaux's phone and telegraph records.

"He was a good boy, and I worried something might be wrong, but his parents tell me he comes home every night and is satisfied with the work. He will not say who he works for. I do not understand why he wasn't happy here."

"Perhaps only the vagaries of youth," Violet soothed him. Evan loathed the familiar way she touched Thibodeaux's arm. "I'm certain he'll return when the novelty wears off."

"I hope you are right, ma chère."

"Is there anything else you can tell us about his new situation?"

"Only that his mother thinks he has taken the job because it is closer to their home. It is out past the airfield, she says."

Evan looked up from his critique of a serpentine beast weighed down by worthless glass gems. "There are no manufactories past the airfield."

Thibodeaux held up his hands in a gesture of helplessness. "I know only what they tell me. He will not speak to me himself."

"You have been most helpful," Violet assured him. "We will look into the matter. If we find anything unsavory, we'll notify you and contact the police. They will ensure no harm comes to your cousin."

"Thank you, sweet lady, you are too kind. Would you like a full tour of the factory before you depart?"

"That would be wonderful, thank you."

Evan groaned.

By the time the tour finished, he had tightened half a dozen more loose bolts and had begun to think he ought to have been dismantling the dragons instead of mending them.

Thibodeaux bent low over Violet's hand and kissed it. "It has been a true pleasure, mademoiselle." He straightened. "I know I must look a mess now, but when I leave my factory I become a gentleman again, and I am a devotee of all the arts. Do you enjoy opera, Mademoiselle d'Aubergine?"

Violet's eyes widened. "Er, yes, I do. In fact—"

"*Carmen* is playing tonight. I would love to have the

company of so pleasant a woman as yourself, if you are available."

Evan's knuckles tightened around his screwdriver. If she accepted this yammering bore just to spite him, he was going to throw all her possessions out of his suite and never speak to her again. Or more likely he would just get drunk and sulk all night.

"Actually, Mr. Tagget has already invited me to the performance."

Evan's heart leapt. He fought to keep his grin of elation under control.

Thibodeaux frowned at Evan as if seeing him for the first time. "Oh? Young fellows have all the luck. Enjoy your evening, mademoiselle."

Violet thanked him again and all but shoved Evan out the door.

He turned his grin on her, no longer able to hold it back. "So, you accept then?"

"Yes, yes. I will go with you. Lord, I can't believe he asked me to the opera!"

"Your charms are irresistible, my flower. I suppose I shall have to accustom myself to the seething jealousy I feel when another man pays court to you and take solace in the knowledge that you are more fond of me than any of them."

She scowled at him. "Don't make me change my mind."

"You won't." She could taunt him all she wanted. She liked him. Nothing else mattered.

12

THE DRESS WAS INCREDIBLE. The sleeveless underdress of pale green silk slid over Violet like a second skin, and the fitted lace overlay looked nothing like her stepmother's tablecloths. The plunging neckline accentuated her bosom, while the low back showed off a generous amount of skin. Daring, without being entirely scandalous.

Violet pulled her hair up into a bun and tugged a few curls loose to dangle behind her ears. Green teardrop earrings were her only jewels. The stones were glass, but they were pretty enough. She looked as elegant as any fine lady she might meet tonight.

She stepped into the sitting room to find Tagget pacing, smoking a cigarette. He looked gorgeous in his customary black, the subtle gold pattern in his waistcoat echoed by his cufflinks and watch fob. A haircut and shave had tamed his wavy locks and left his short beard neatly trimmed. Only the unruly curl licking at his forehead spared him from an inhuman perfection.

He froze when he saw her and stabbed the cigarette into an ashtray.

"Royalty pales in comparison, my resplendent blossom. Would that I might play the Antony to your Cleopatra."

"Look where they ended up," Violet countered.

"What great lovers have any other ending? Lancelot and Guinevere? Tristan and Isolde? Romeo and Juliet?"

"I prefer Beatrice and Benedick."

Tagget smirked. "Petruchio and Kate?"

"Ha! Don't you wish."

He held out a hand to her and scooped up his cane. "Come, my evening blossom, the car is waiting and I'm prepared to fight off a multitude of rivals."

She eyed the copper cladding on the tip of his cane. "What did you do to that? Electrify it?"

"An interesting idea! But, no. Just a bit of personalization. Do you need anything else before we depart?"

Vi flipped her fan up into her hand and snapped it open. It was a sturdy piece, with metal ribs that could do some damage if she needed to strike someone with it. Spread open, it became a dainty green companion to her dress. "No. I am armed and dangerous."

Tagget grinned at her. "Do you have your screwdriver?"

"No, but one of my hair sticks is actually a paintbrush." She seized his hand. "Let's go."

Her excitement swelled as they neared the opera house. In all her years in Paris she had never been inside. She'd walked past many a time, imagining what it must be like inside, seeing paintings and photographs, hearing talk about the shows.

She hadn't truly needed time to consider Tagget's offer. The instant he'd asked, she'd known she would join him. It could be a once-in-a-lifetime opportunity.

Vi was feeling more charitable toward him after seeing the portion of the warehouse he'd given her for a studio. It really was a perfect space. Temporary, for certain, but not to be wasted. And a day focused on her art had given her a renewed energy and sense of purpose. She could handle a night out with Tagget without succumbing to his schemes.

Are you sure about that? her inner voice warned.

She ignored it.

The Palais Garnier was as beautiful inside as she had dreamed. Violet clung to Tagget's arm, hoping he would steer her in the right direction, because she couldn't stop her head from swiveling every which way, trying to take it all in.

Everywhere was art and gold and glamor. She ran her hand over the marble balustrade of the grand staircase, goggled at the gleaming chandeliers and ornate columns of the grand foyer, and nearly fell over her own feet half a dozen times as she craned her neck to look at some bit of the ceiling that caught her eye.

She paused in her contemplations only when Tagget stopped to introduce her to someone. Tagget glittered as much as the building, charming men and women both with smiles and handshakes and a dizzying knowledge of everyone's business. The opera was no mere entertainment to him. It was a critical part of his work—a display of his connections and a means of extending them.

Despite her earlier pleasure with her dress and Tagget's compliments, the sense that she was an impostor began to prickle across Violet's skin. The women she met dripped with diamonds, gold, and pearls. They spoke of gowns from the House of Worth and other high-fashion names. Vi was outside her usual sphere, and she didn't doubt everyone could tell.

Several ladies cast pitying looks in her direction. Others took a more condescending approach, turning up their noses or giving backhanded compliments. Vi clenched her fan and put on her best fake smile.

Tagget noticed her distress and drew her aside. "You are the loveliest woman here. Don't fret if some of these ladies are intimidated."

"It's not wholly unexpected. I've dealt with their sort plenty of times. Some snub me for the way I dress, some for the way I act, some for daring to be a woman making my own way in the world. They aren't worth my time."

Which didn't mean it didn't sting. But Vi wasn't about to let it hold her back.

Tagget stared at her a long, silent moment, his expression thoughtful. "The reasons they snub you are the reasons I like you." He withdrew a necklace from his pocket and dangled it in front of her. "But I can offer this, if you think it will help."

She caught the jewel in her hand, her jaw dropping. The single, square cut emerald hung from an unadorned gold chain. It would have been a modest addition to her ensemble were it not for the size of the thing. One part of her wanted to fling it at him and tell him to take it back to where he'd gotten it from. Another part wanted to stuff it down her bodice to hide it. It could pay rent for months. Even better, it could make her exhibition a reality.

"It's yours to keep regardless of whether you wish to wear it," Tagget said, sounding entirely sincere.

The idea of achieving both financial security and her dream won out over her dislike of accepting his gifts. "I'll wear it, though I imagine everyone will think it's glass like my earrings." Everyone would also probably think she was his mistress, but since they likely thought that already and she'd never see any of them again, she didn't greatly care.

Tagget fastened the chain behind her neck and let the stone trickle through his fingers and drop onto her chest. It fell to a point just above her breasts, drawing attention to her décolletage. His eyes lingered there a second longer than was proper.

"No, my sweet, they will think the earrings are real like the necklace."

Violet touched the emerald with a hesitant finger. Between the gem and the dress, she guessed she was wearing more than she earned in a typical year.

Tagget took her arm and led her back into the crowd, wending his way expertly to his box. "We will have this space to ourselves and can leave off the socializing until intermission."

The note of relief in his voice surprised Violet. He chatted with such a natural ease that she'd had no idea he wasn't enjoying it.

"You seem well-practiced at mingling. You do this often?"

"All the time. Chiefly in New York and here in Paris, but I've also been to operas in London, Vienna, Berlin, Prague, and Milan. I'm probably forgetting a few. So, yes, I've had a lot of practice. It's been good for business. Fortunately, I can escape into the music when the presence of people wears on me. That's why I do it here and not at a restaurant or horse race or what-have-you. I enjoy all types of theater and concerts, but their melding in opera is my favorite."

"I hope I can enjoy it as much as you do. This is my first opera."

"Is it? You will be enchanted, I assure you. I snuck into a performance of this show when it first played in New York. I was thirteen. I was discovered and thrown out halfway through Act Three, but I have since seen it in its entirety many a time."

Violet arched her brows at him. "And how many of those times did you actually pay for your seats?"

His lips twitched in his mischievous-boy smile. "Oh, two or three at least."

The moment the music began, Violet forgot about the crowds and the opulence of her surroundings, and even the enormous emerald around her neck. The only thing that seemed to exist outside the stage was the man sitting beside her.

Tagget leaned forward in his seat, tilted toward her just enough to bring a bit of heat to her skin. He barely moved, barely even breathed. The performance sucked him in, and he dragged her along with him. The voices rang in her ears and pierced her heart. At times she felt transformed into Carmen, teasing and seducing her chosen man.

When the lights brightened at intermission, she straightened, fanning herself.

"Enchanting, isn't it?" His silky baritone voice made her

shiver in the warm room. She was alone in a box with an operatic villain.

"Yes." She fanned more vigorously. "Though it's very warm in here."

"Have you need of refreshments? I can fetch you some water or some wine."

"No, I'm well. Don't make the trip on my account. Unless you need to mingle again?"

"I should." He shifted very slightly toward her. "But I wouldn't complain if you gave me an excuse to remain here."

"In that case, I feel too overcome to walk about just now and in terrible need of company. Does that sound convincing?"

"I shall use those exact words if anyone asks. Now, tell me how you like the performance."

"The singing is incredible. I'm astounded at the talents of the performers. The quality of the acting doesn't reach that same level, however. The Don José, in particular, seems a bit stilted."

Tagget chuckled. "Yes, poor Laurent struggles with that."

"You know him?"

"Edouard Laurent. Brilliant up-and-coming tenor. Voice of an angel. Alas, he has difficulty feigning passion for his co-stars."

"Ah." Violet nodded. "Prefers the company of men, does he?"

Tagget pulled back abruptly. "It's not my place to speculate."

Violet regarded him with raised brows, puzzled by his sudden change in demeanor. He'd become stiff and somber. And had he actually said, "It's not my place"? That wasn't a phrase she'd ever expected to hear cross his lips. Not from a man who spent much of his time prying into other people's business.

"I would never hold it against him," Violet said. "I've met several men of that persuasion. The Paris art scene is quite open to unconventional individuals. Much more so than most communities, in my experience."

"That may be true." Tagget's voice was tight. "Regardless, I shouldn't have said anything." He turned his gaze on the auditorium. "Good crowd tonight. Shall we take a closer look?" He reached into a pocket and withdrew a pretty pair of opera glasses—black, of course, and accented with mother-of-pearl.

Thinking it best to move on, Violet made her own brief perusal of the crowd. It certainly wasn't *her* place to pry. Stopping herself from speculating, though, was more difficult. Was Tagget truly concerned for his friend the opera singer? He wasn't entirely heartless, clearly.

A pair of opera glasses trained on her made her shiver. Hundreds of eyes could be watching them at any moment. Many of the people they had met tonight would be interested in what Tagget was doing with a strange woman. Her eyes darted around, looking for other faces who might be spying on her.

Tagget handed over his opera glasses. "Try these. Flip that dial on the side and it will double the magnification."

Violet lifted the glasses to her eyes. With the dial turned, she could make out details on clothing and almost read the numbers on the pocket watch of a man directly across from them.

"Incredible."

"My own modification."

She flipped the dial back with a shake of her head. "Don't be so modest."

For a minute Violet swept the opera glasses across the auditorium, never lingering on one spot long enough to be considered rude. Even with many seats empty, dozens of eyes without such restraint were turned her direction.

She leaned back in her chair, lowering the glasses. "On second thought, perhaps I could use a glass of wine. It's unnerving how many people are staring at us."

Tagget chuckled softly. "One learns to ignore the scrutiny. After all, what have I to hide?" He rose and gave her a hand up. "They are extra curious today. It has been quite some time since I had a companion at the opera."

Their second foray into the mob was much like the first. Violet nodded at those she'd met earlier and was introduced to many more, always in her guise as "accomplished artist" Violette d'Aubergine. With wine in hand and no longer dazzled by her surroundings, she paid closer attention to the people watching her. Most, it seemed, considered her not as herself but as an extension of Tagget, some new aspect of his business. The critical eyes now looked less judgmental and more calculating.

"How many people ever see Tagget the man and not Tagget the industrialist?" she asked when they retook their seats.

"There's a difference?"

"I think so. But I think the man rarely shows himself." She picked up the opera glasses for a good look at the performers taking the stage. "Let's see how your friend sings this next act."

"Friend?" Tagget sounded almost confused. "Oh, Laurent? We're not really friends. I'll likely never speak to him again."

Violet frowned down at the stage, unable now to focus on the performance. Tagget's peculiar statements turned over in her mind as she watched Laurent. He was a handsome man, in a burly, barrel-chested way, with porcelain-white skin and reddish-blond hair. And definitely not quite as entranced by Carmen as his character was supposed to be. Not a friend, Tagget had claimed. But enough of one to worry about exposing his private life?

"Oh!" she blurted, putting the pieces together at last.

Tagget gave her a confused frown, then turned back to his rapt observation of the opera.

"You were lovers," she whispered. And now she was trying to picture them together. Trying and failing. Laurent was a staid, quietly masculine sort. Not colorful and energetic, as she would have expected Tagget to prefer. "Or am I mistaken?"

"My... inclinations are no great secret to those who follow the gossip papers," Tagget replied, not looking away from the stage. "If you have any issue with that, I suggest we no longer work together."

"I have no issue with it," she promised.

A small smile tugged at the corner of his mouth, and he glanced at her for an instant. "I'd hoped as much."

"It's a bit difficult to imagine, though," Violet continued, her voice still the barest whisper. "He's so entirely different than myself."

Tagget shrugged. "I admire humankind in all its variety."

Vi sat abruptly back. Variety. Of course. That's what she was. Something different. This month's flavor. And just when she had begun to like him. The opera glasses dropped into her lap and she slumped in her seat—a rare luxury while she was without a corset.

The music sustained her throughout the remainder of the opera, but the final round of socializing was too much. She stopped trying to remember names or even faces. Her greetings were no more than what was necessary for politeness, and she refused to fake a smile. She no longer cared that these people were potential clients with connections to dealers and galleries. They had become enemies obstructing the path to her comfortable bed. What were the chances one of them was her art thief?

When the crowd at last began to thin out, Violet marched for the exit, not waiting to take Tagget's arm. He jogged after her, not catching up until they reached the street where the Peugeot awaited them. He seized her arm, insisting on helping her into the vehicle.

Violet stared off into the distance as they bumped along the road. She couldn't wait to lock her door and burrow under the blankets.

Tagget drove slower than usual, glancing away from the road to look at her every few seconds.

"Tell me what's wrong, darling. Your distress has been growing since the opera ended. Did someone make a nasty remark? Did some man attempt to touch you? Tell me. One word from you and I will destroy his career."

She gritted her teeth. "Enough. I don't want to be your plaything."

He stiffened beside her. "I don't think you a plaything, Miss Dayton. I apologize if you felt I was parading you around like a trophy. It wasn't my intent, but a man does feel a certain pride when he has a spectacular lady on his arm."

"No more compliments, I beg you. I'm not your sweet flower, and when the next interesting thing comes along I won't be such a grand beauty anymore."

"Is this about Laurent? Don't be jealous, my bud. He is but a dying ember beside your blazing inferno."

"Shut up!"

Tagget stared at her for so long he had to brake hard to prevent a collision with the motorcar in front of them. Vi took a great deal of satisfaction from his stupefied expression. She doubted many people had ever rendered Evan Tagget speechless.

He turned his attention to the traffic, while she watched the streets all around, looking anywhere but at him. The uncomfortable silence lingered as they wove their way through the crowd, attempting to forge a path to the hotel.

Everywhere were the conveyances of the wealthy. Thibodeaux's carriage dragons abounded, and she saw at least a dozen motorcars nicer than Tagget's. With nothing else to do, she assessed each vehicle's chances of belonging to their dirigible-owning, machine building nemesis. Just outside their hotel, she grabbed Tagget's arm.

He slowed and looked at her. "What's the matter?"

"Someone is following us."

13

Evan handed the car off to the hotel porter and took Violet's arm, scanning the area for anything unusual. No vehicle or pedestrian on the busy street looked out of the ordinary to his eyes. They entered the hotel, but paused to watch out a window.

"Do you see your suspicious person?" he asked.

"No. That cab continued on when we stopped, but I'm certain it was following us." She kept her face pressed against the glass, shielding most of her body behind the drapery. "Oh, here it comes! They circled around."

Evan looked where she directed, but could find nothing strange about the hired cab. It looked to be from the biggest taxi company in the city, was driven by an ordinary-looking man, and carried a single passenger. From the window he couldn't recognize faces or make a good assessment of the rider's status. The cab drew closer, and Violet nudged him away from the window. A moment later she pulled back as well.

"I think he's coming after us."

"Perhaps he wasn't following us but only seeking a hotel," Evan replied, though his fingers tightened around his cane.

She narrowed her eyes at him. "I doubt it. Quickly. We should hide."

"Hide? In my own hotel? Certainly not. No one would dare attack us here. I will have the man thrown out if you fear him so."

He started for the front desk, but Violet grabbed his arm. "It's not fear. I want to learn what he's up to. Come on."

She dragged him across the lobby and shoved him into one of the three wooden telephone booths, squeezing in after him and yanking the curtain closed.

"This is highly irregular, Miss Dayton." Evan squirmed, trying to get comfortable, succeeding only in rubbing up against her shapely rear. He slipped an arm around her waist, nothing but thin lace and silk separating his hand from her skin. "If you wish to be in my arms we will be a great deal more comfortable in my bed."

She nudged him with her elbow. "Hush. I'm trying to watch. He's approaching the desk. He is unremarkable. Whitish skin, brownish hair, bowler hat, plain black suit—bought off the rack, I'd guess."

"In that case, he may want to seek out lower-priced accommodations."

"He's not getting a room. The conversation is too animated. Your man at the desk looks unhappy. I think they're arguing."

Violet's hair smelled of flowers. Evan kissed the nape of her neck, and she gave a delightful little sigh of pleasure. She tasted divine. It would be awkward and uncivilized, ravishing her in a phone booth, but he was willing to give it a try.

"You're distracting me, Tagget," she griped. Her elbow dug into his ribs again. "Enough. This is hardly the place."

Evan drew back, as best he could manage in the tight space. "You chose the location, my ambrosial nectar," he whispered. "I offered my bed."

"He's leaving now, looking angry. I don't think he got what he was after."

"Good. Have you finished, then? May I ravish you now?"

"No."

"No? But—"

She spun around, squashed him against the telephone, and kissed him. The phone dug into his back, and she was rumpling his suit and mussing his hair, but, God, did she taste glorious. Her tongue warred with his. Her soft breasts crushed against his chest. He was melting under her heat. If this wasn't a prelude to ravishment, he didn't know what was.

The embrace broke as abruptly as it had begun. Evan's skin burned from head to toe, and the snug trousers that looked so good on him were painfully tight. He needed to be upstairs in his bed, immediately, with Violet beneath him.

She yanked open the curtain. "That will have to satisfy you."

"Satisfy me? You will kill me. You have dangled food in front of a starving man and then snatched it away. You're a worse temptress than Carmen."

"And a better pickpocket." She held up his room key and jiggled it about. "Good night." She bolted for the stairs.

Evan swore and hurried to the front desk, hoping no one was looking at him too closely. The concierge wore a frown, but attempted to smile as he approached.

"What can I do for you, sir?"

"That man who was here a moment ago, what did he want?"

The frown returned. "He was asking questions, sir, about you and Miss Dayton. He wanted to know who she was and whether she was staying here with you. That sort of thing. I told him repeatedly we do not give out information about any of our guests, until he cursed at me and stormed off."

"Good man." Evan gave him a hefty tip. "If he troubles you again, have him tossed out and notify the police. In the meantime, could you place a guard outside my suite for the duration of the night? I am concerned for Miss Dayton's safety. Also, if I could have a spare room key, I would appreciate it."

"Absolutely, sir. Glad to be of service. And don't forget your cane, sir. You left it in the telephone booth."

Evan cringed. "Thank you. We will not speak of this incident again."

"I don't remember any incident, sir."

"Exactly."

14

Vi yanked open the door. "Enough with the pounding, already. I'm awake!" She looked Tagget up and down. "How early do you get up to do all your beautifying? I swear, I've never seen anyone as fastidious as you are."

"With my clothes properly cleaned and pressed and in their correct location, it takes me hardly any time at all. It's the shaving that takes the most time, which is why I have invested in clockwork razors. My company began producing them about a year ago. They haven't yet caught on, but I think they are a tool of the future."

She frowned and examined his face. "You missed a spot."

"What?" His hand went to his cheek.

"Kidding."

"Miss Dayton, has anyone ever told you you are exceedingly vexing?"

She grinned. "Only you, darling. Everyone else finds me perfectly agreeable."

"Everyone else didn't go to bed last night painfully aroused and plagued with worries about strange men taking too great an interest in you. I could hardly sleep."

Vi tugged her dressing gown tightly around herself. "That man last night?"

"My concierge said he was asking about you. I've had people snooping into my business plenty of times, but you have no connection to that. This must be related to your investigation. I think we should leave Paris. With the dirigible, we can go anywhere and leave again at a moment's notice. I have already called down to the kitchen to have a breakfast packed up for you. Shall I ring for someone to help you pack, or would you prefer to do it yourself? I wish to leave as soon as possible."

Violet put a hand to her temple, turned, and shut the door behind her. She wouldn't waste her breath scolding him. The man couldn't get it through his head that she wanted to be consulted on such matters. Or else he didn't care what she thought. Both were equally possible.

It would be hard to argue with him in this instance. She didn't like being spied on any better than he liked it, and they needed to get on the move again if they were to prevent another theft.

She stuffed the dressing gown and her nightgown into the large carpet bag she had never unpacked after their trip to Italy. After tossing a few more things in, she pulled on a pair of black hose under a rust-colored corset dress, and slipped into her sturdiest boots. Her hair she left in the braid she'd done up before bed. She could always restyle it on the dirigible.

A quiche awaited her when she stepped into the motorcar, wrapped in a tidy bundle. Tagget had already learned what she liked in it, and the chef had adjusted the recipe accordingly.

"And your tea." He passed her a cylindrical metal flask.

Violet turned it around in her hands, eying it with suspicion. "What is this?"

"A Dewar flask. A two-walled vessel with a vacuum in between to insulate the liquid inside. A brilliant invention."

"Another from your company?"

"Sadly, no. Just one I enjoy using."

The flask did its job. Violet arrived at the airfield with her belly full and her tea piping hot.

Tagget parked his car in a reserved area, where a porter gathered their luggage for transportation to the airship. The familiar discomfort of having another person handle her things crawled across her skin again. Somewhere in that bag was her emerald necklace. She ought to have kept it on her person. That one stone could fund everything she wanted. She did her best not to stare at the porter as they made their way across the field.

Tagget came to an abrupt stop. "Where the hell are my stairs?"

A long rope ladder unfurled from up on the deck, thwacking against the wooden hull. Violet grabbed hold and scampered up, leaving him behind to grumble.

Harrison gave her a hand over the top. "Pleased to see you again, miss. Sorry about the ladder."

"Oh, it was no trouble. Mr. Tagget may have some difficulty, tho—"

He vaulted over the rail, his shiny shoes hitting the deck right beside her, his cane still in his hand. "You were saying, Miss Dayton?"

Harrison clapped him on the back. "I knew you could still scramble with the best of them, Mite."

Tagget smoothed out his suit. "That doesn't make it any less unseemly. What happened to the stairs?"

Harrison rolled up the ladder as he talked. "We had them taken away. More than once yesterday we spotted strange fellows wandering around without boarding any ship. We set a watch and decided ladders only. I won't have any thieves sneaking onto her at night."

"A wise decision. Thank you."

"Maybe spies and not thieves?" Violet conjectured.

"Quite possibly," Tagget agreed. "All the more reason for us to leave promptly."

"We can be off in ten minutes," Harrison said. "Where to?"

"For now you can circle the city. Miss Dayton and I need to decide upon our next destination. I'll let you know."

The pilot nodded. "She's your ship, Mite. Say the word and we'll take you wherever you like."

"Thank you. And have Walton bring our things to our room when they have been hoisted onto the ship. Miss Dayton will want her tea." Tagget offered his arm. "Shall we?"

Violet accompanied him down into the cabin and settled into one of the plush chairs. "Was he calling you a mite?"

"What? Oh, Harrison? Yes, he calls me that more often than not."

"I wouldn't have thought you would approve of nicknames."

"We met when I was five. I'm not certain he knew me by any other name until I encountered him again while looking for a pilot."

She leaned toward him, eager for a glimpse into his past. "You were childhood playmates?"

"No. We didn't play, but there was mutual respect between us."

That had to be the strangest summation of a boyhood friendship Vi had ever heard, but Tagget had already pulled out his notebook to make plans. She wouldn't get any more out of him this morning. Still, she had a new thread to unravel.

"Have you any thoughts on our next destination?" he asked. "I consulted your list of threatened museums this morning. There were more than I realized. We have several possible choices."

Violet unlatched her purse and withdrew her map, smoothing the creases out on the table. "If he follows the pattern, he will move further out than Florence. Rome is possible, though I doubt he would pay two trips to Italy in such rapid succession."

"I agree."

"Vienna could be a target. He has been there once before, stealing a small painting from a gallery." She ran her finger along her penciled circles. "The same goes for Copenhagen. I don't know how we might choose between the two."

Tagget jabbed a finger at the map. "Madrid. He will go there."

"What makes you say that? I think it as likely as the others, but not more so."

"He hasn't yet been there."

"True, though he's hit other cities multiple times."

"Florence was a new location, and by far the biggest of his crimes. Remember, this is a game to him. It's a form of entertainment. He wants new and exciting. Large or famous works of art and new locations. I wouldn't say it's impossible for him to go next to Copenhagen or Vienna, but I think Madrid holds a greater attraction."

Violet considered his words before nodding. If anyone could understand the mind of a bored, wealthy art thief, it would be Evan Tagget. "Madrid it is, then. Your analysis is better than a blind guess."

"Excellent. I will notify the crew. We won't need to waste time circling about the city."

A rap sounded on the door and Walton entered. "Your luggage, boss, and the lady's tea."

He passed Violet the flask and she took a sip. She thought she might continue to drink it slowly just to see how long the device would keep it warm.

"Thank you, Walton," Tagget said. "You may let the others know we will be flying to Madrid."

"Sure thing, boss." He set down the remaining luggage and disappeared out the door.

Violet rose to follow.

"Where are you going?" Tagget asked.

"Up top to watch us lift off. Since our planning is done, I would like to get a better view."

"Ah. As you like. I hope you enjoy yourself."

She turned back to face him. "Why don't you come with me?"

"No, thank you. I prefer to remain in the cabin."

"Why? You said you weren't afraid of heights, and you proved that well enough, scaling that ladder with a cane in your hand."

"It's the air. The ship flies high enough that the air becomes thin. I have weak lungs and can't breathe easily in such an environment. The cabin, however, maintains the same pressure as on the ground."

"Weak lungs?"

"Yes."

"In that case, perhaps you might consider giving up smoking."

He chuckled. "No, the cigarettes won't make it any worse than it already is. The filters see to that."

"Filters?"

Tagget struck a match and lit a cigarette. "A crude word for a complex device. In case you need another reason to reject me, Miss Dayton, I will share my secret with you. I am biomechanical. I have been for near to half my life now. The filters are small machines that replace the top portion of each of my lungs. They both strengthen the lungs and keep out dust and smoke. I'm certain I would be dead without them."

Biomechanical? Violet had to stop herself from gaping in surprise. "I wouldn't dream of rejecting you for such a reason."

"I appreciate that."

"I'm sorry you've had to suffer. Did you contract consumption as a child, or some similar disease?"

"I think that's quite enough talk about myself for the morning. It feels as though we're beginning to rise. If you wish to watch, you may want to head up to the deck. Let me know how you like it." He wasn't actually smoking his cigarette, but just holding it while it burned away. He set it down in an ashtray and opened his notebook. "While I wait I will sketch out my secret project."

"Oh?" She stepped closer.

"*Secret* project, my scented blossom. You will find out when the time is right."

"Then why mention it at all?"

"To inflame your curiosity and keep you by my side, eager to discover what I'm about."

"You're quite the manipulative bastard, aren't you?" Violet retorted, but the words were light, teasing. He'd been frank with her, and right now she quite liked him. She gave him a nod of farewell and headed for the door, taking her tea with her.

Up on deck, she watched in awe as the dirigible ascended toward the clouds and Paris dropped away below her. In minutes the airfield contracted to a square of colored dots. The buildings and streets shrank to map size, then to no more than a cluster of city amidst the browns and greens of the countryside.

Violet had just leaned over the edge for a better look, when the ship lurched, knocking her to the deck. An enormous dirigible with an oblong blue balloon flew past, so close that the wake from its propellers rocked the ship. Vi picked herself up and crossed the deck, climbing the stairs to the bridge. Harrison stood at the helm, steering Dauntless through the rough air. To either side of him were a pair of instrument panels, several feet high and several feet long, covered in dials, switches, and levers. Behind were the large copper boilers that held the water for the steam engines beneath.

Dahlia stood by one of the control panels, bouncing her wailing daughter and watching the gauges.

"Damned freighters," she muttered. "They don't look out for anyone. Hire cheap-as-shit pilots who steer like they're drunk." She stuck a finger in Fern's mouth, and the baby suckled and calmed. "Poor little thing. She likes a smooth ride."

"I'm taking her up and over," Harrison said. "We're faster than any cargo ship, and we'll put her behind us in a half-hour."

Dahlia checked several dials. "Yup. Go ahead. We're looking good. I'll keep an eye on the currents." The baby began to fuss again. "Oh, for heaven's sake. I just fed you, so I know you're not hungry." She lifted her daughter and sniffed at her rear. Violet grimaced. "Ugh. Soiled yourself again? Walton can handle this one. He doesn't have to cook until lunch. You good if I run her below deck?"

Harrison nodded, concentrating on his work. Violet watched his hands as they moved deftly over the controls, turning the wheel and flipping switches to control rudders, propellers, and engines.

"You look like a natural."

"Thank you, Miss Dayton. I'm good with machines. I've been working with one sort or another most of my life. When I first flew, I knew I'd found what God intended me for. The beauty of the earth, the freedom of the skies, and the ingenuity of man allowing us to explore them. It's a gift."

"I'd never flown until our journey to Italy. I'm glad to be here. It's an experience I'll never forget." She paused, then added, "I only wish Mr. Tagget could join us on deck. I feel he's missing out."

"The boss does what he likes."

Violet inched closer. "You've known him a long time, I understand?"

"He was a tiny little thing when we met. No more than five. But you could tell there was something about him. A fierceness. He wasn't going to let others control his life. Smart as a whip, too. And look at him now, controlling just about everyone."

"Yes." He certainly did that.

Violet, on the other hand, felt she had no control over anything. Whenever she was close to Tagget, all rational thought flew from her head. She ought never to have kissed him last night. She'd swiped his key and run ahead solely to prevent herself going any further. Annoying him was merely a pleasant side effect.

"Where did you meet?" she asked. Perhaps once she'd satisfied her curiosity she would find it easier to walk away from him.

Harrison chuckled and shook his head. "That's for him to tell you. He's a private sort of man, and I won't break his confidence."

Violet sighed. It had been worth a try.

Dahlia returned a moment later, without the baby, and set about checking dials and maps. Vi left them to it and returned to the rail until she tired of looking down on endless fields dotted only by the occasional town. She spent a few additional minutes watching Parker and Flynne at their work monitoring the engines and all other mechanical parts of the ship. Parker spoke very little. When she did, she lisped badly. The woman had a sharp mind, but Vi would have wagered many people didn't notice it.

Flynne talked enough for the whole crew, but mostly to the squirrel dragon perched on his shoulder. Now and then he fed it a bit of metal from his pocket.

"Nuts," he explained when he caught her puzzled look. "No screws, bolts, nails, et cetera. Just nuts, like a proper squirrel." His mouth turned in a crooked grin at the joke he must have told dozens of times but still found funny.

"Doesn't it… fill up?"

"Oh, I open the plate in the back and empty her at night. She eats the same nuts every day."

"Sensible."

His smile went from slightly awkward to radiant. "Thank you. She reminds me of home. I lived in the country, once. But there aren't many engineering jobs there 'cept for fixing farm equipment. This one pays well and I can see the world."

"I left my home years ago hoping to see the world, but I'm only now getting to do that."

"Oh, I'm sure Mr. Tagget will take you anywhere you want to go."

"I know. I'm not sure if that's a good thing or a bad thing. Thank you for chatting with me. I'll let you get back to work."

He didn't have a hat on, so he tipped his goggles. "Pleasure, miss."

Down in the cabin, Tagget had finished with his secret project and was sprawled in his chair, reading. He glanced up from the book when Violet entered, but didn't set it down.

"Did you enjoy your time on deck?"

"Yes, it was very pleasant. I like your crew."

"I'm not surprised. I think you are much like them. Smart and competent. Many disregard them merely because they are different, but you notice and admire their wit and skill and loyalty. It's one of the things I like best about you, Miss Dayton."

Her stomach lurched. This was no flattery. There was no teasing or innuendo. He genuinely liked her, and for a fine reason. Dammit, she was in so much trouble. She was going to fall for his clever mind and his quirkiness and then he would leave her bereft when someone new came along to pique his interest. And she was going to let it happen because she was dying to understand what made him tick, to strip him down to his essentials. Her yearning to strip him down in a literal sense helped matters not at all.

"I had a nice chat with Harrison," she said, lowering herself into the other armchair.

"He's a brilliant pilot. And a loyal employee." Tagget gave her a quick smirk to show he had no intention of giving in to her obvious ploy.

She tried a new tactic. "You know, Tagget, if you want me to be your mistress, it might help if you told me a little more about yourself. I like to know what I'm getting into."

"Where's the fun in that, my delectable fruit? Men of mystery are sinfully attractive, you know. Besides, I see no reason to launch into an extensive recitation of my history when you have shared nothing of your own. You are from Australia, where your father is a minister. That's all you've told me."

"Not true. I've mentioned my stepmother's love of frilly tablecloths."

"Which gives me a hint at your family situation without any of the relevant details. You, Miss Dayton, are a tease."

"And you aren't?"

"Who kissed whom last night? And to what did it lead? Nothing. I wasn't the one shutting myself in the spare room. Of course, tonight we will share my bed, as we ought." He waved a hand at the mound of pillows. "In fact, I would be happy to share the bed right now. We will be flying all day, and we must do something to pass the time."

"We have plenty of options."

"None as enjoyable."

Vi grinned as an idea sprang to mind. "Do you play cards, Mr. Tagget?"

"On occasion. I have a deck or two in the cabinet."

"Perfect." She hopped from her seat and flung the doors wide. She fished around until she located a deck of cards, then she poured them each a drink and returned to the table. "You know Écarté, I presume."

"I do. Are we playing for money?"

"Of course."

"Excellent. You may deal first, Miss Dayton."

Violet shuffled the cards with a well-practiced hand while he eyed her with a calculating gaze. His competitive drive and intelligence would make him a formidable opponent, but Vi had always been something of a cardsharp. She'd take his measure today. When they played next, the stakes would be higher than money.

15

EVAN GOT THOROUGHLY TROUNCED and enjoyed every minute of it.

His luck wasn't great, but the chief reason for the drubbing was Violet's expertise. She watched his face, watched his body language, and never forgot a single card that had been played. Her hands were so dextrous with the deck he was certain she could have cheated. He was equally certain she didn't. She wanted to beat him in a fair fight.

When he ran out of French coins, he opened up the hidden safe under the bed and switched to playing for American money. He had lost nearly fifty dollars by the time they stopped for the day. He considered it money well spent.

A day of cards and books with Violet, along with quality meals courtesy of Walton—who continued to expand his chef's repertoire—left Evan in high spirits. He didn't even complain when Miss Dayton took herself off to bed without so much as a goodnight kiss. They'd had fun together, and the situation was looking up.

Now, with the morning rays slanting through the windows, Evan snuggled up beside Violet, feeling her warmth and breathing in her lilac scent. He had no incentive to get up this morning. He'd had one nightmare, early in the night, but the dirigible had long since landed, and he'd slept soundly for several hours straight.

She stirred beside him, her long lashes fluttering as her eyes slowly opened.

"Good morning, my beauteous one." He pressed a kiss to her shoulder, where her nightgown had slipped down during the night.

"Morning," she murmured, her voice dreamy and sleep-fogged. "Why aren't you up?"

"I found no compelling reason to rise and one excellent reason to stay abed." His arm snaked around her waist.

Violet twisted toward him. "Mmm. So you think to seduce me while I'm still groggy?"

"No. I think to seduce you while you're still basking in the warmth and comfort of our shared bed, freshly woken from a night of erotic dreams."

"What makes you think my dreams were anything but ordinary?"

His fingers ran a winding trail down across her hip. "With a woman of your passionate nature, I must assume erotic dreams *are* ordinary." His eyes roved over the thin cotton clinging to her body. "Also, your nipples are hard."

"Perhaps I'm only cold."

"Then I shall warm you." He covered her body with his own, kissing up along her neck and jaw until he reached her mouth.

Her arms circled him. His skin prickled where her soft fingertips glided across his back. She was honey on his tongue and velvet under his hands. She kissed with such fervor as to leave him breathless. God. What sorts of debaucheries went on in her dreams and how did he get into them?

Violet pulled away, breathing hard. "Damn you, Tagget, why are you so delicious?"

"Good fortune in my looks, an exceptional sense of style,

and a sophistication far beyond that of your average man." He nuzzled her neck.

"And the arrogance of a king. Ooh." He had located a sensitive spot. He laved it with his tongue while his hand came up to cup a supple, round breast. "Oh, that's nice."

His thumb stroked her nipple. "Yes. Yes, it is. Exquisite, in fact. You taste like heaven and feel like a goddess. And I'm tired of this nightgown blocking me from the perfection of your skin."

He continued to kiss her neck while his fingers worked the buttons of her nightgown, exposing inch by inch the expanse of her lovely skin. His lips followed his progress, lingering on the hollow of her throat, sliding down between her breasts, and finally over one dark nipple.

"Tagget," she groaned.

He paused. "Evan. I want you to call me Evan."

"I know. You can't..." She sighed when he resumed his explorations. "You can't have everything you want."

"Nonsense."

She was all he wanted. He tugged her nightgown down to her waist, ready to dispose of the thing entirely. Her hand caught his wrist.

"Enough. That's enough."

Her words surprised him to the point of confusion. "Enough of what?"

"I mean stop. Before I can't anymore."

He sat up, staring down at her exposed torso, her tousled hair, the tinge of pink across her cheeks. She would stop now, amidst her flourishing desire?

"Why the devil would you want to stop?"

She squirmed out of the bed, tugging her nightgown up to prevent it falling away completely. "I told you, I won't be your mistress."

"Why not? You are ravenous for me, my sweet. You tremble at my touch. You kiss like a woman possessed. We are living together as if you were my mistress, and the whole world thinks you are."

"But *I* know I'm not. I want to be your lover, Tagget, I really do. But it can only be on my own terms. I won't be bought with jewels and clothes. I won't be put up in a pretty apartment for a month and then cast aside to live on whatever junk you've given me to ease your guilt."

"I've never given anyone anything for such a reason. I like to bestow gifts on my admirers. I don't see the trouble with that. Also, I have no intention of casting you aside."

"Maybe not today, but what about tomorrow? What about next week when you've grown bored of me?"

"Miss Dayton, you may be the least boring person I have encountered in my life. I assure you, I won't be running off due to ennui. You appeal to me precisely because you are not boring."

"You're either deluding yourself or trying to delude me."

He flopped onto his back. "You may be the stubbornest woman I've ever met. Isn't there any way I can win you? Tell me what you want and I will get it for you."

She put her hands on her hips. "You can't buy what I want."

"You can buy anything. Believe me. Sometimes it takes a bit of work, but I'll get you whatever it is."

She started for the closet, shaking her head. "I'm not going to waste my breath trying to get it through your thick skull."

"I beg your pardon!" Evan had been called many things over the years, but stupid had never been one of them.

"Just forget it, Tagget. It's obvious you don't understand." She pulled out several articles of clothing and disappeared behind the privacy screen to change. "And don't do that again."

"Do what?"

"Try to seduce me first thing in the morning."

He frowned at the top of her head, watching it bob in and out of sight as she bent to pull on various pieces of her ensemble.

"Very well, my dear. What time of day would you prefer your seduction? I am at your disposal."

"Never would be good. I would prefer we be friends."

"Now who is deluding herself? You don't want to be friends any more than I do."

"Friends," she insisted. "You do grasp that concept, don't you?"

He didn't. Not really. Intellectually, he could understand the idea of it, but Evan didn't think he could have claimed a true friend before Eden, and that relationship was still new and strange. He owed her a letter. Perhaps she would have some advice regarding Violet. Unusual advice, likely, but Violet was an unusual sort of woman.

He shoved himself out of bed and began his own preparations for the day.

· · · ~~~ · · ·

Friendship, as Miss Dayton thought of it, differed not at all from having a mistress, except for sexual frustration. All day Evan escorted her around Madrid, visiting shops, seeing sights, and sampling the local cuisine. They spent a large chunk of the afternoon sitting by the river while she painted a watercolor and he worked on the secret project he had devised for her. When he suggested they arrange to attend the opera that evening, she readily agreed.

They took their dinner on board Dauntless, discussing plans for catching their thief.

"Being so near to the full moon, he will have a limited amount of time in which to commit his crimes," Evan said.

Violet nodded. "If we patrol the area near the museum between full darkness and moonrise, we should have a good chance of catching him in the act. Our dirigible is discreet enough not to attract notice. The gray balloon and dark wood of the hull should make us nearly invisible in the dark."

Evan quirked an eyebrow. "It's almost as if I took stealth into consideration when making decisions about the ship."

"Did you expect to need to flee in the dead of night?"

"I always like to be prepared."

"Well, it should serve us well. This chicken is excellent, by the way, and pairs perfectly with the wine."

"As it should. Walton has quite taken to French cooking and is turning himself into something of a gourmet. As for the wine, I keep only the best product in the cellar."

She laughed. "Only you would have a wine cellar in your dirigible."

"You'd be surprised. Based on his tastes, I suspect our art thief to have a similar arrangement, though perhaps more flamboyant than my own transport."

"Or he may have built his own dirigible with stealth in mind, or had it altered to be difficult to detect when he embarked on this crime spree."

"An excellent point. If we aren't successful here, when we return to Paris we should pay some attention to any airships that look suitable for that purpose."

Violet arched her eyebrows. "We haven't even begun, and you're planning for us to fail?"

"I told you, I like to be prepared. More wine?"

"No, thank you. I prefer to attend the opera sober, strangely enough."

Evan smiled at her over the top of his glass. "How peculiar."

The opera was lovely, though not as good as *Carmen*, and a delightful way to close the evening. He still couldn't fathom what she thought was the difference between a friend and a mistress. She hung on his arm, wearing the dress and jewels he had bought for her. When he introduced her to his—thankfully few—acquaintances and they gave her that knowing smile and a quick appraisal, she did nothing to disabuse them of their assumptions. The woman was an enigma.

It had clouded over somewhat and was fully dark when

they arrived back at the dirigible. Violet swapped her dress for her nightgown, pulling on a pair of black hose underneath it, and wrapping herself in a warm dressing gown. Evan remained as he was. It would be too chilly on deck to remove his jacket, and he didn't own any casual clothing. He disliked dressing gowns and smoking jackets. Even the clothes he wore in his workshop were simply his old suits.

"You're coming up top, then?" Violet asked, when he followed her up the stairs.

"The ship will be flying low. A mere thousand feet up won't bother me, and we may hover even lower, if the crew deems it practical. We'll want a good view of the museum."

"I must say, they're all remarkably unperturbed by this strange night-time outing of ours."

"They're a loyal crew. They do as I ask, and I pay them well in return."

"That's part of it, perhaps, but I think there's more to it than that. I think your acceptance of their myriad differences makes them respect you when you display your own oddities."

"Oddities? I see nothing odd in what we're doing. How else would one catch a night-time thief?"

"The fact that you're involved in catching a thief at all is odd, Tagget."

"You recruited me to this job, if you recall, my hardy wildflower. I accepted only for the opportunity to take you as a mistress."

"I thought you accepted out of boredom."

"Boredom stemming from the lack of an exceptional paramour."

"You don't ever give up, do you?"

"Not if there's any alternative. I change tactics occasionally, but I rarely give up."

Violet took hold of his arm and guided him toward the rail. "Your tenacity is one of the things I like about you. Sadly, it's also one of the things that makes you annoying. How do you want to conduct our observations?"

He slipped an arm around her waist. "I thought we would stand here cuddling together and distracting ourselves from the task at hand. It would give you a reason to scold me, and I know you love that."

She spun from his arms. "No distractions. The sooner I catch the thief, the sooner I can be away from you."

"Away from me? Darling, you would miss me terribly. Don't do that to yourself."

Violet placed her hands firmly on her hips and opened her mouth to retort, but her words turned into a yelp as the dirigible lurched. Evan caught her as she pitched forward, but couldn't keep his own footing. They landed in a heap on the deck.

"What on earth?" she gasped.

Evan disentangled himself from her clothing and scrambled to his feet, bracing himself for more tremors, motioning to Violet to stay down. The ship swayed beneath him. Wind whipped at his hair. His eyes darted about, seeking danger. Heavy footsteps pounded on the deck.

"You okay, Mite?" Harrison stopped beside them and helped Violet to her feet. "How about you, Miss Dayton?"

"Fine, thank you."

"What caused that turbulence?" Evan demanded.

"The wash from a freighter." The pilot gestured at a large ship heading away from the airfield. "I was given the all-clear for takeoff, but seems it wasn't clear after all."

Dahlia padded over, baby Fern asleep on her chest, despite the excitement. "Hate cargo ships. Think they're so all-fired important. No one should be flying low over an airfield, even this late at night."

Evan stared across the city at the departing ship. "Follow her."

They'd been thinking about this all wrong. A cargo ship

was perfect—unremarkable, common in any large city, plain enough to be easily adapted for stealth, and large enough to transport and hoist heavy burglary machines.

"You got it, boss," Harrison replied. "She came at us from our blind spot, and I'm happy to repay the favor. I'll take us high and then drop down above her. She's so large they'll never know—if I do it right."

"This wind'll make it tricky," Dahlia said. "I'll keep my eye on the currents, and signal Flynne and Parker when to cut the engines."

"Excellent," Violet replied. "We'll keep watch at the rail, and Tagget will stand there pretending he has some idea of how the ship works and bellowing orders for you to ignore."

"I happen to know very well how this ship works, Miss Dayton, and I would thank you not to insult my intellect again. Also, I don't bellow. It's terribly vulgar."

He leaned on the rail and watched the ground fade away beneath him. In the dark it was difficult to judge their altitude, and they were running without lights. Harrison and Dahlia would have to rely only on their gauges, but Evan didn't doubt they could do it. He was proud of this crew he'd cobbled together last December. Hiring on short notice, he'd been forced to pick through candidates others had rejected, but he'd found pure gold among the pyrite.

Evan lost track of the freighter after a few minutes, but remained where he was, drumming his fingers on the rail. As long as the crew showed no signs of panic, he was going to assume everything was under control. Beside him, Violet shifted from foot to foot, unhappy with the idleness. He draped an arm around her once again.

"Would this be a good time for that distraction?"

She turned toward him, dark eyes unreadable in the starlight. The top of her dressing gown was open, exposing her throat and the neckline of her nightgown. Evan thought he might try for that ticklish spot again, and see what new noises he could coax out of her.

"Do you smell that?"

Evan's brow furrowed. He couldn't smell anything but her familiar floral scent. "Smell what?"

She turned back around, put both hands on the rail, and leaned out for a better view. "Smoke. Just a whiff. Wait until the next wind gust."

He pressed up behind her, his arm tight around her middle. He wouldn't risk her toppling over the edge if the ship floundered again. Wisps of her hair fluttered in the breeze. What in hell was he doing chasing a woman who preferred stalking thieves in the dead of night to snuggling in his cozy bed?

A trace of smoke hit his nostrils.

He was staving off boredom, that's what he was doing.

Evan took a good sniff. Something in this city was on fire. His eyes tracked across the horizon, looking for a flicker of orange.

Flynne saw it first. "Fire! Dead ahead! On the ground, so if we keep high it won't affect us."

"Ignore it," Violet ordered. "It's a distraction. Head for the museum and find that freighter."

"We're on it, ma'am."

Dropping down above the cargo ship required finesse, and Evan paced the deck while his crew executed the tricky maneuver. He tried to smoke, but the unyielding winds forced him to wander about with the unlit cigarette dangling from his fingers. Behind him, the city glowed from the growing inferno. The fire was several blocks away, he guessed, though he avoided looking directly at it to preserve his night vision. Close enough to pull attention away from the museum, but far enough that the building itself wasn't in imminent danger.

The freighter hovered near the museum, so low Evan wondered if it was landing. From directly above, it was impossible to tell. He strained to hear any sounds of machinery below, but the clangs of alarms from the fire masked whatever their thief was doing.

Violet grabbed Evan's arm. "We have to do something. This is taking too long. He'll have people inside the museum by now. I'm certain they'll know the layout and make quick work of the burglary."

"I would hope so. Otherwise he's no great mastermind, and I can't imagine why we would even bother."

"I bother because I have to! Need I remind you that this is the price of my freedom?"

"I can buy your freedom."

"I don't want you to!"

Harrison came padding over. "We're in position. What next? Hover until they move?"

"I want to see what's going on down there without exposing our presence," Evan replied. "Any ideas?"

"We could drop you down using the cargo hoist. The chain is long enough that you could get out to the edge of their balloon and look down at the freighter's deck and the ground below."

"That's insane," Evan said.

"I'll do it." Violet shrugged out of her dressing gown and began to tie up her nightgown above the knees.

"What? No! Are you mad?"

"I'm going to catch that man in the act if it's the last thing I do," she vowed.

"This *will* be the last thing you do! One slip and you'll plummet to your death!"

"I trust the crew to strap me in securely."

Harrison's arm landed on Evan's shoulder. "We would never put her life at risk, Mite. Parker will tie up the safety lines. She's a whiz at knots."

"Fine. Then I'm going too."

Evan stood tapping his foot irritably while Parker lashed

a rope snugly around his waist, tying the opposite end to the steel hook at the bottom of the cargo hoist. A second, longer rope secured him to the ship. She repeated the procedure for Violet. Flynne moved to man the controls.

"If these ropes damage my suit, I'm going to be extremely unhappy," Evan muttered. The hoist jerked them upward. They hung several feet below the end of the chain. "And if this breaks my back, I will rescind my commission for the de Heem and make you paint naked baby angels instead."

Violet pulled a face. Her arms wrapped around him as Flynne swung them over the rail. "You'd never be caught dead with such a painting."

Evan clutched her against his chest, half because he feared for her safety, and half because he didn't want her dangling free and smashing into him. "I'll donate it to a museum. Put it in a very prominent location."

"Are you sure you're not afraid of heights? You're clinging to me like a leech."

"We are hanging hundreds of feet in the air. I intend for you to break my fall if necessary."

"How chivalrous."

The hoist dropped fast and smooth, and Evan found his feet hitting the balloon of the freighter sooner than expected. He relaxed his grip on Violet, and they sidestepped along a bit of the framework toward the edge. Above them, Flynne kept the hoist in check, allowing them enough slack to move. When the footing became too treacherous, Evan and Vi sat together and slid down the side of the balloon. The ropes bit into Evan's side as they once again took on his weight. His gaze drifted down to the ground, approximately one hundred feet below. This was madness.

Violet yanked on his sleeve. "Tagget, there," she hissed. "Look."

Evan turned his attention to the freighter. It hadn't landed, but it hovered so low the hull dipped below the level of the museum's roof. A slapdash metal box sat on the deck, a pair of spindly arms jutting out of it over the starboard rail to wave in the wind. The contraption looked to be at least ten feet in both height and width, though only a yard or so deep. A man standing beside the box spun a wheel, and the arms extended further, spreading wide.

Violet leaned down for a better look. "I think it's hollow. He's going to grab a painting and pull it inside."

She twisted upright and gave a single tug on her rope leading up to the ship. The hoist lifted them up until they were once again standing atop the freighter's balloon. Violet began unknotting one of her ropes.

Evan grabbed her wrist. "What in God's name are you doing?" he hissed. "We are thirty-four yards above the ground, give or take a foot, and you want to untie yourself?"

"If we free ourselves from the hoist, we can lower it down and hook it onto that machine. We'll disrupt the theft."

"I'm not certain it goes much lower."

"Then we'll have to get Harrison to descend further. Let him drop the ship all but on top of this thing. It doesn't matter if we expose ourselves now. L'Exploiteur will know we're here the moment the hook hits his device."

"You might very well be a madwoman."

"See? Aren't you glad I'm not your mistress now?"

"Not at all." Evan released her and began to untie his own rope. He stepped up onto the cargo hook, then stuck a toe into a link of the hoist chain to test the footing. A bit slippery in his slick-bottomed opera shoes, but it would have to do. His coattails flapped in the breeze. "If I had known I would be climbing, I would have changed. I'll be right back."

"What? Tagget…"

He hurried up the chain to inform the crew of the new plan. His palms smarted and his arms ached by the time he reached the top, and his breathing was slightly wheezy, but he wasn't about to admit that to anyone. He briefed the others, who scrambled to make adjustments, then made his way back down to Violet.

"Walton and Flynne are manning the ropes tying us to the ship," Evan informed her. "They'll lower and raise us while Parker works the hoist." He gripped a narrower rope that hung down from the ship and circled loosely around his waist. "Parker gave me this for a signal rope. When I give it a single tug, the ship and the cargo hoist will drop. Two tugs and they pull us back to safety."

Violet nodded, then sat and scooted once again down the side of the balloon. Evan moved to follow, but his slippery shoes lost traction and he fell. For a second, he couldn't breathe, as his body went sliding over the curved edge, hurtling inexorably toward the earth.

An instant later, his safety rope caught. He gasped and steadied himself against the balloon, willing his racing heart to slow.

Beside him, Violet drew in a sharp breath. "We have to go now. Look!"

Evan followed her pointing finger. Four men rushed from the wide museum doors, a massive painting in their hands. The claws of the box-like machine extended nearly to the ground now, ready to clamp down on the artwork.

He'd be damned if he'd dangle perilously from an airship, scare himself half to death, and ruin perfectly good eveningwear for nothing. He gave the signal rope one sharp yank and Dauntless' engines roared to life. The ship dropped, and Evan, Violet, and the cargo hoist dropped along with it.

They swung over the freighter's rail and Evan grabbed hold of the swaying cargo hook, wedging it into a joint on one of the machine's arms. His fingers had just curled around the signal rope again when Violet cried out.

"Wait, stop! It has the painting!"

"Seize them!" the man at the controls screamed in guttural

French. L'Exploiteur, no doubt. His scarf, aviator's cap, and goggles entirely obscured his face. Damn.

"Get it off, get it off!" Violet tried to free the hook from the arm, but it stuck fast.

Evan tugged with her, to no avail. The point of the hook had caught on some internal mechanism and it wouldn't budge. A trio of men came racing toward them, knives drawn. With a curse, Evan abandoned the attempt. He grabbed Violet by the shoulders and pulled her away from the hook.

"Time to go."

She squirmed in his grasp. "No! The art! It'll be destroyed!"

"Hang the art, we're getting the hell out of here!" He gave two firm tugs on the signal rope and wrapped his arms tightly around her.

They flew upward as Dauntless pulled away from the freighter. One of l'Exploiteur's men grabbed at their legs, and Violet took him out with a swift kick to the nose. Metal creaked and groaned as the hoist pulled at the art-stealing machine.

Evan and Violet clung to one another, dangling above the freighter's deck. Below them, the painting continued its upward journey. A piece of the machine broke off with a loud *snap*, but the cargo hook remained stuck.

"Stop them!" the man in charge screamed again, yanking on the wheel in an attempt to get the painting onto the ship before the machine was torn apart. Two more crewmen raced across the deck, rifles in hand.

"Faster!" Evan shouted up to his crew. He grabbed the signal rope and pulled it repeatedly. "They've got guns!" A shot rang out and he let out a yelp of alarm. "Get us the fuck out of here!"

The mechanical arm gave a final squeal of protest, then broke free from the machine, sending one crewman flying. The claw lost its grip on the painting just as the towering canvas cleared the rail. No longer encumbered by the weight of the large device, Dauntless rocketed upward.

In moments they were out of range of the guns and sailing swiftly away from the freighter.

Walton and Flynne hauled Evan and Violet up onto the deck. Parker reeled in the broken mechanical arm, setting it down beside them with a gentle thunk.

"We failed," Violet sighed. "We didn't stop the theft or learn the thief's identity. Thankfully the art wasn't destroyed. We still have a chance to recover it."

"I wouldn't call it a failure," Evan replied. "We have learned many things we didn't know before. And this…" He patted the twisted metal claw. "Will tell us even more."

16

It was awful. Unfixably awful. The colors were wrong, the shading was wrong, the composition was wrong.

Violet turned away from the painting, gathering her brushes and tools to clean them. She knew she would never make progress until she stepped back and gave the self-doubt time to dissipate. Another day, with a clear head and better lighting, she would be able to tackle the problems and make the work into something she could take pride in. She could only assume the real de Heem had struggled with his own lack of perfection. It was the artist's lot in life.

Outside the studio's large windows, the rain continued, dreary and unrelenting. The bleak weather offered no respite from her dour mood. She had found little solace in her work, and she had nowhere else to go to find relief.

And it was all her own fault. Despite plenty of warning signs and her own good advice, she'd continued to harbor some ridiculous hope that Tagget liked her for her own true self—that she was more than just an interesting new thing or a difficult challenge.

The reality of it was that she was less interesting to him than a bit of broken machinery. Since obtaining the claw arm, he'd been studying it incessantly, taking measurements and notes. The only time she'd seen him do anything else was when he'd written a lengthy letter to a Mrs. Eden Caldwell in America. Vi had no idea what all he'd written, but she'd caught a glimpse of the salutation, where he addressed her as "my ever verdant garden." His flatteries were nothing special. Violet hated that even a small part of her had been swayed by them.

She finished cleaning her tools and washed herself up, changing from the old painting frock into a cute flouncy skirt and a matching top. If nothing else, she could take herself out for dinner. She felt rich as Croesus with the money she'd won playing cards. It was time to splurge on an excellent meal and a top-notch bottle of wine.

She opened the door to Tagget's half of the warehouse, making no attempt to keep the door or her footsteps quiet. Better to make her presence known than to walk right up and startle him again. She had no desire to find herself burned with a welder or skewered with a screwdriver.

To her surprise, he wasn't working on the arm. He had dismantled the thing entirely, and its parts were spread neatly across the workshop floor. Tagget sat at his workbench, intent on some small project. Perhaps he had found an interesting mechanical bit inside the arm.

He glanced over his shoulder as she neared. "Ah, Miss Dayton."

Violet's spirits dropped lower. She didn't even rate a "flower" or "blossom" today?

"I'm very near to completion of this secret project. If you could give me five more minutes, I will be right with you."

For lack of any better occupation, Violet made her own examination of the confiscated arm. If she'd hadn't known what it was, she would never have been able to guess from the pieces. The plates, rods, and bolts meant nothing to her. She looked at them anyway, because it prevented her looking at Tagget. She didn't need to see him with his hair tousled and his sleeves pushed up, an array of small tools strapped to his left arm and screwdriver in hand, his green eyes dark with intensity.

Dammit, Vi, you are such a ninny!

She couldn't see his eyes under the goggles, even if she wanted to. As usual, her imagination was a curse. She should have just slept with him. Gotten it over with. If she'd given in to her attraction, she would have discovered by now that he wasn't anything special and she would be happily indifferent.

At least this wasn't as bad as when she was eighteen and fell in love with a dance instructor. She'd blown all her money on lessons and gotten nothing out of it except some mediocre sex and several days of brokenhearted crying. She could, however, dance an excellent polka.

"Finished," Tagget announced. He set down his handheld welder and slipped whatever he'd been working on into a pocket before Vi could get a good look at it. "Thank you for your patience. I assume you wish to know what I learned from all that?" He waved a hand at the dismantled device.

"Yes, please. I contacted your man, Durand, and requested a list of businesses that own or rent cargo dirigibles, but I haven't heard back and I feel as if I have accomplished nothing today."

"He'll get you your list, never fear." Tagget pushed up his goggles and joined her beside one of the largest pieces. "This is a good place to start. See that brand marking?"

"Fabrique de Saint-Juste?"

"Yes. They make boilers, furnaces, and the like. There's another partial brand mark over here, from a company that makes steel furnishings—the stool at my workbench is of their manufacture." He prodded another piece with his toe. "This bit has a scratched-off serial number. These parts are all scrap, gathered from multiple places and assembled into a machine."

"Our thief isn't a factory owner, then," Violet surmised. "He doesn't have raw materials at his disposal. Anything else?"

"Yes. In spite of its haphazard origins, this contraption was well-made. Bolts were tight, and moving parts lubricated, but not dripping with oil. The welding is excellent. He has talented engineers working for him, and not only Thibodeaux's cousin. These welds here were done by a different hand than those I grouped together on the opposite side of the room. Both very professional, though. We might want to ask what other businesses have lost top workers recently."

"He must pay well to drag quality workers away from good jobs."

"Perhaps. Or else he seeks out manufacturers who underpay their people. Thibodeaux's wages aren't stellar, by any means. A promise of good money for a temporary position followed by a glowing recommendation could draw many a disgruntled employee, and even inspire loyalty enough to keep secrets."

Vi rubbed a finger across her bottom lip as she thought. "He won't be confiding what the machines are for, or giving a true name to any of these workers."

"No. He will have a pseudonym, and a better one than 'Exploiter.'"

"Perhaps we should pay a visit to Thibodeaux's cousin. Though I'm a bit afraid I might have to agree to accompany him to the theater in order to get the address."

"I already have it. As I said, Durand is quite capable. Apparently, Thibodeaux telephones his sister often. Learn a few names, ask a few questions… Voilà."

"It seems I hired the right man for this job after all."

Tagget grinned. "You have hired me? Excellent. What is my pay? I accept outings to the opera and well-aged cognac."

"I'll remove one reference to your many faults from your fake de Heem."

His brows rose. "You're insulting me with my own painting?"

"It's a vanitas. It's meant to remind you of your miserable mortal state. Each item in the still-life is symbolic. Which would you prefer I remove, lechery or narcissism?"

"Keep whichever looks nicer."

Violet laughed. "Lechery it is, then. I couldn't possibly remove narcissism and still consider it your painting."

He stepped close enough to make her skin prickle. "You must include some reference to lust. I'm overcome by it whenever you're near, and I don't think you could do without it."

An urge to sway into him coursed through her, but she caught herself at the last second.

Control yourself.

She wasn't going to fall for that sensual voice and come-hither smile. She sidestepped him, putting one of the larger chunks of the mechanical arm between them.

"Don't worry, I'll work all your deadly sins in there. But now, you need to change. Thibodeaux's words about his cousin suggested that the boy lives with his parents. If we are prompt, we can catch him coming home for dinner."

"Excellent idea. I will rid myself of these grimy clothes. I'm afraid you won't be able to assist me, as we don't have time for such a distraction. I know you're disappointed."

"Terribly."

He twitched an eyebrow at her as he disappeared into the small office in the corner. Violet could only shake her head.

· · · ~ · · ·

The Thibodeaux cousins lived in a middle-class neighborhood near the airfield. The moment Vi saw the house she knew this was a family yearning for a higher social station. The fence around their small garden mimicked the ironwork she'd seen at fancy townhouses, but the construction was subpar. A steam car several years old was parked outside. The leather seats were worn, and the trim had a number of dents. Either they had bought it used or were wringing every last mile out of it.

She walked toward the door, but paused when she spied a young man approaching from the direction of the airfield. He was of a similar body type to Thibodeaux, tall and burly. He wore loose gray trousers, a plain waistcoat with no jacket, and a pair of goggles perched on his head—the unofficial uniform of an engineer.

"Good evening," she greeted him in French. "You are Monsieur Florian Thibodeaux?"

The boy looked her up and down, his features twisting into a scowl of disapproval as he assessed her appearance. Violet wore skin-tight black trousers today, beneath a lavender skirt that didn't even reach mid-thigh. Her blouse, also lavender, was semi-transparent, and topped by a lace-trimmed ivory corset that could easily have been worn as an undergarment instead. Perfectly ordinary for her personal style, but by no means conservative. She ought to have considered that Florian might disagree with his uncle over more things than a job.

"Whatever you're selling, I don't want it," the boy snarled.

Violet kept her tone civil. "Monsieur Thibodeaux, we represent the Société des Arts in an important investigation that relates to your current employment. If you could answer a simple question or two, we will be on our way."

Thibodeaux loomed over her, curling his fingers into fists. "You'll be on your way right now, bitch."

Violet flinched at the naked hatred in his glare. At six feet tall and bulging with muscles, this man could do her serious harm. Leaving was the only sensible choice.

She began to turn away, but Tagget was having none of it. "I suggest you apologize to the lady," he said, his voice as cold and sharp as ice.

"Go sell your whore somewhere else," Thibodeaux shot back. "I don't fuck foreign strumpets."

Rage blazed in Tagget's eyes. His cane flew upwards. Vi reached for his arm to stop him. "Tagget, forget it. Let's go."

He dodged her hand and caught the bottom of the cane. When his fingers curled around the copper cladding, the walking stick emitted a series of mechanical clicks. He yanked on the top of the cane, and a slim blade slid free of its sheath. The tip of the sword swung toward Florian Thibodeaux.

"Apologize to the lady," Tagget repeated.

"Or what? You scratch me? Fuck off, little man."

"Evan," Violet said, more sternly.

Tagget flicked his wrist and a button flew from Thibodeaux's waistcoat, dangerously near to his heart. The boy staggered backward. Tagget slashed, slicing the waistcoat open.

"Perhaps you wish to reconsider? I will offer you one more chance to apologize. I prefer not to stain my new sword with your filthy blood."

Thibodeaux opened his mouth as if to speak, then darted for his house, slamming the front door behind him.

Tagget thrust the sword back into its sheath. "I should have skewered the bastard."

Violet rounded on him. "That was stupid," she chided. "Stupid and dangerous."

He shook his head. "That man was a bully, not a fighter. The worst that would have happened is he would have landed a few trifling blows and then gloated when I feigned agony."

"You couldn't know that." She stormed off, back the way they'd come. Tagget could do what he liked, but she was done here. She'd regroup and try a different tactic.

Tagget hurried to catch up, falling into step beside her. "I have some experience with both sorts of men," he explained. "Young Thibodeaux didn't hold himself like a fighter. He balked the moment I showed skill. His sort would rather prey on weaker foes than chance a fair fight."

Vi huffed. "I don't care. I told you to forget it."

"Yes, but I've been practicing." He waved the sword cane. "You had no way of knowing, of course."

She shook her head and picked up the pace. "You don't understand." Of course he didn't understand. He could never truly understand.

"Understand what?"

"You're a man. Fighting a bully might make sense to you. For me, it would only make things worse. The physical danger is only part of it. Who do you think society is going to support in a confrontation? The 'trouble-making woman' or the 'respectable working man'? Because I guarantee that's how we'd be portrayed. You don't ever need to consider such things. You'll never fully grasp why I would just walk away when a man like that deserves to be taken to task. But maybe you could listen when I say something instead of assuming you're always right." She sniffed. "Though I don't know why I'd expect that of you."

They continued on in silence. Tagget was strangely still as he walked beside her.

"I'm sorry," he said at last. "You're right. I didn't listen. The urge to defend you was… unexpectedly strong, but I ought to have given more consideration to your wishes. I will try to listen better in the future."

Violet almost stopped walking, her mouth dropping open in astonishment. "You— Did you just genuinely apologize?"

His usual smirk returned. "I *do* make mistakes, my lovely blossom. Humans are foolish, weak things. Myself included. If I didn't learn from what I did wrong, I'd hardly be where I am today. So, thank you for the scolding and the explanation. I appreciate learning something new."

"You are something else, Evan Tagget," Vi marveled. "You repeatedly defy expectations for a man of your class."

"My class?" he scoffed. "There are no more than a dozen men in the world who could be said to belong to my class."

She rolled her eyes. "Thank you for that bit of snobbery. I was in danger of liking you for a moment, there."

"Another mistake." He sighed theatrically. "But perhaps it is time to move on. Our plans will need reworking now that we know we cannot find the machine shop directly through Thibodeaux. Shall we head for home?"

"Not quite yet."

A used furnishings shop across the street had caught Violet's eye. Its large windows were crammed with items on display, and additional wares overflowed into the street. She hadn't gotten her dinner and wine, but maybe she'd pick up something nice for her studio instead. A pretty plant stand, or an elegant vase. Perhaps even a cozy chair for when she needed a break. She started for the shop.

Tagget hurried after her. "Where are you going?"

"Shopping."

"Shopping?" He scanned the furnishings with a grimace of distaste. "In a junk pile?"

"One woman's junk is another woman's treasure. All my clothes except those you've bought me came from second-hand shops."

Tagget edged past a rickety table as if the least touch might contaminate him. "Then I shall have to buy you more. You deserve better than old cast-offs."

"No. I love my clothes. I love the hunt. I scour piles of beauty that foolish women have thrown aside for no good reason and I reassemble the pieces into something all my own."

"I see."

He didn't, but the foolish part of her that fancied him yearned to make him understand. She wandered into the maze of furnishings, perusing chairs and tables that had once graced fancy dining rooms or elegant parlors. Surely something here could prove her point to him. She sidestepped a carved headboard that blocked her view and pulled up short.

"Oh."

The graceful line of an old fainting couch lured her across the room. Finely carved from a dark cherry wood, it held marks and dings of age, but had lost none of its splendor. The top edge gleamed from years of hands running across its surface. Its worn fabric had once been a masterpiece of upholstering. The rolled arms and flattened S of the back were splendid in their simplicity. Violet stretched out on it, imagining herself courtesan to a king or a duchess in a castle, her lands running for miles in any direction.

"This. This is what I came here for."

Tagget peered down at her. "You like this style of couch? I will have one made for you."

"No. I want this one."

"You must be joking. It's full of holes, and there are great gouges in the woodwork. I can have someone copy it exactly, if you fancy it so."

"It needs new upholstery, yes, but the body is solid, and the legs are strong. Its imperfections give it character. It has history. Generations have lived and loved on this couch."

"Generations have dirtied it and worn it down. How can you not prefer a new piece?"

"How can you fail to see the beauty in it? Have you no soul?"

Tagget looked thoughtful. "I expect not. I doubt the soul is anything more than a fairytale people use to ease their fear of the oblivion of death."

Vi threw up her hands. She swung her legs to the floor and stood to look him in the eye. "I'm buying this, whether you like it or not."

"Very well. I will instruct the shopkeeper to have it shipped to a quality upholsterer for repairs."

"That is acceptable."

She expected he would pay for the couch as well, and she wouldn't stop him. She could save her money for future dinners and that bottle of wine, or maybe a writing desk to claim the last empty corner in her studio. The studio that a sensible woman would vacate immediately to escape being alongside, and indebted to, soulless Evan Tagget.

Of course, Vi had lost all claim to the moniker "sensible" when she left home eleven years ago. Her silly, teenaged self had actually thought she could simply wander into Paris and make a living with her brush. Legally. She got by, though. She'd slowly built her savings, and she loved her freedom.

Freedom that was in jeopardy. Crevier could rescind his agreement at any time if she didn't stop the thefts.

"We're going to get up extra early tomorrow and follow the Thibodeaux boy to his workplace," she declared.

Tagget nodded in agreement. "Excellent. That will give me an opportunity to test out one of the new alarm dragons. The plan is to have them in shops by month's end. Which style would you prefer, an owl or a cock?"

"An owl, please." Violet honestly didn't care, but she wouldn't allow him the chance for a salacious pun.

"A fine choice. I, too, prefer creatures of the night."

Damn him, he didn't need any puns. All he needed was to widen his eyes and arch those dark eyebrows, and any words at all turned into innuendo.

"Let's just buy the couch and go to dinner. I'm starving."

"As you wish, my radiant flower."

Several hours later, Vi hauled herself up the rope ladder onto the dirigible, ready to crawl beneath the covers until the screeching mechanical owl woke her before dawn the next morning. She slipped into her private corner to change, pulling off boots and stockings and unbuttoning her blouse. She could hear Tagget undressing on the opposite side of the screen.

"Before you turn in," he said, "I have something for you. That secret project I was working on."

"Oh." Feeling covered enough in her corset and skirt, she walked out to see what he wanted.

He stood near the closet, stripped down to trousers and an untucked shirt, and he held something small and metal in his hand.

"I made this out of my scraps, since you seemed to like them so much. May I see your arm?"

Violet held out a hand, and he slipped a bracelet over her wrist. The design was simple and elegant—pieces of copper rod flattened and bent into s-shaped curves, then welded into a single unit.

Her heart skipped a beat. This wasn't the work of a man with no soul. It was a thing of beauty, crafted from nothing. It was his skill, his imagination, molded into art for no reason but to please her. Special. For her alone.

His fingers against her wrist burned like fire. She couldn't tear her gaze away from the bracelet, or wrench her mind away from his touch. She had found a crack in his imperious shell, and she wanted to pry it open and expose him to the world.

"It's worthless, of course," he apologized, "but I thought as an artist you would appreciate the craftsmansh—"

She flattened him against the closet door and stopped his mouth with a crushing kiss.

17

EVAN HAD BEEN KISSED countless times. Many of those kisses had left him yearning. None had ever before left him gutted. He floundered, swept away in her deluge. Everything that was Violet Dayton poured into him. Her beauty, artistry, wit, and passion scorched him with every sweep of her lips, every flick of her tongue. She was a tart bite slicing through sweet essence. Fruit and flowers, heat and spice. When her mouth slipped away, it took some deep part of him with it, leaving a void that none but she could fill.

The floor swayed beneath him. He would have sworn the dirigible was bouncing through rough air and not solidly on the ground. Somehow during the kissing, Violet had gotten his shirt unbuttoned, and she pried it open now, gazing at him under the warm glow of the lights. She traced a finger over the crescent-shaped scar above his right lung.

"Was it painful?"

His own voice answered her, from some faraway place. "I was unconscious at the time. For a few hours after I woke, every breath was agony, but the worst of it was the frustration of lying in bed for a fortnight, too weak to even walk across the room. If I hadn't had dozens of books at my disposal, I would have gone mad."

Mad.

He hovered near madness now, while her fingers rubbed gentle strokes across his nipples, and her velvet lips grazed his neck. So warm. So soft. Everything he craved. Kisses covered his hammering pulse. She flattened her hands against his chest, sliding them up to push the shirt off his shoulders. Her fingers trickled down his arms, never leaving his skin. One hand tightened on his biceps.

"Not scrawny at all."

"No." Though Evan preferred small, precise tools, he could wield a blacksmith's hammer with ease. He was by no means a bruiser, but people misjudged him based on his size, and he took advantage of it.

Violet kissed his shoulder. "Maybe you could have fought little Thibodeaux."

"Not a chance."

She laughed. The sound ringing through the cabin thrilled him almost as much as her touch.

"What's this scar? More biomechanics?" She paused in her kissing to examine the ugly white slash across his upper arm. "And this other… Lord, how did you do this?" She seized his opposite arm to search further.

"Later." Now he wanted to make love. Needed to make love. He nudged her toward the bed, his limbs finally waking from the paralysis her ministrations had inflicted on him. It was time to take charge and lavish her with all he had to offer.

"Three on this side," she continued, ignoring him. "And the one across the back of your right hand. Gad, that's half a dozen serious scars, not counting the surgical ones. Where did they all come from?"

She hadn't even seen his back yet. This was why Evan preferred dim lighting for his romantic encounters. Few people ever saw him naked in good light, and then only the incurious ones.

Violet, though. Violet made him want to explain, damn

her. But not now. Not today. Not while he stood undressed in her arms with an aching cock and a fire in his chest that screamed for her to extinguish it. It had to be now, and it had to be her.

"Later. I promise."

He kissed her, teasing her lips apart with his tongue, eager to lose himself once again in the taste of her.

She turned her head. "I don't believe you."

Evan found the loops at the back of her corset and began to untie it. His lips caressed her cheek, but she wouldn't turn back to him.

"You will give me some half-answer that reveals none of the truth," she said. "You will gloss over any important parts."

"You are speaking of your own tendencies, fruit. You dangle yourself in front of me and never let me get hold of you. But I'm done with games."

He unhooked her corset busks, but as he pulled the garment open, something fell from between her breasts. He bent to retrieve it, and they smashed heads as Violet dove to do the same. Evan's hand closed over the mysterious object, and he straightened, rubbing his temple and wincing.

"So sorry, Miss Dayton, but I'm not one of those men who like to mix pain with their pleasure. I hope your head fared better than mine?"

She reached for his hand, and he opened his fingers to reveal a pair of small, conical shells strung on a bit of black ribbon. They sparkled an iridescent blue-green in the light. One shell was missing the very tip. He had no time for further examination, as she snatched the bauble from his grasp and spun away to hide it among her things, leaving her corset abandoned on the floor.

"See, you have secrets, too, darling. Perhaps tomorrow we can trade one for another." He followed her around the back of the privacy screen. "Tonight, however, it's time for us to enjoy what we have both been wanting." He held out a hand to her. "Come to bed, my sweet. I swear I will make it worth your while."

Her hesitation was palpable. Evan's palms began to sweat.

He quashed the panic with determination. He would not be denied. He had to have her. Anything else was unthinkable. The usual tactics had failed. Violet required something special. He swallowed his pride and uttered a word he had rarely ever spoken.

"Please?"

· · · ⸺ · · ·

You shouldn't be doing this. You shouldn't be doing this.

Violet wished there was a way to get that nagging voice in her head to go away. Maybe it was right, but she'd made her decision, and, oh, did her body approve.

Tagget's lips were like silk on her skin. He lavished attention on her breasts, drawing little noises of encouragement from her throat when his tongue touched her sensitive nipples.

Tonight she was ready for more. She would satisfy her cravings, and tomorrow she would face the world with a clearer head. Evan Tagget would cease to be a distraction.

Evan Tagget will break your heart.

No. She was no longer a silly girl. She knew better than that. This would be a fling and nothing more.

He placed a kiss squarely between her breasts. "You are the picture of perfection, my flower. A veritable goddess."

Don't believe him.

There was nothing goddess-like about her. Her limbs were lanky, her knees and elbows pointy. Despite the long legs, her torso was short, with a waist that wasn't fashionably thin. He couldn't possibly be sincere.

"Honestly, Tagget, your flatteries are ridiculous. For heaven's sake, my breasts aren't even the same size."

He sat up and cupped one in each hand. "Ah, but they are

lush and round, and they taste of honey and lavender. Each exquisite."

No matter how silly the words, the deep caress of his voice never failed to bring a tingle to her skin. Absurd, beautiful, tantalizing man.

He moved lower, scattering kisses across her belly. His fingers snaked up the inside of her thigh. "Sweet and smooth. So soft against my lips. You are every man's dream."

"Hardly." The word came out on a ragged breath.

"You are *my* dream." He eased her legs apart, settling himself between them and replacing his fingers with his mouth. "Every night since we met. You haunt my nights."

Violet gasped as his tongue touched wet, eager flesh.

"You haunt my days."

Another flick of the tongue. Her back arched, her body pleading silently for more.

"You have driven me to the edge of madness."

Her fingers clenched in the sheet.

"Now I shall return the favor."

Here, at least, he was telling the truth. His mouth did beautifully unspeakable things to her most private parts.

"Yes, Tagget. Please."

Lord, he was good. He teased her clit with gentle lashes of his tongue, sending shudders of pleasure pulsing through her body. Each stroke drove her nearer to climax, but before she broke, he pulled back, pausing only momentarily before redoubling his efforts. Closer. Higher. On and on, edging her so high she was certain she would crack in two. She writhed, groaned, clung to the bed in a vain attempt to stay grounded.

"Evan. Oh, God, Evan."

Bliss shuddered through her. She was flying, soaring, falling, then drifting down to reality, the back of her arm flung across her brow, feeling the perspiration there, sensing again her deep breaths and her pounding heart.

Evan crawled atop her, his lips stroking hers in the barest whisper of a kiss. Gentle. Sweet. He would be a good cuddler.

Nonsense.

Men like Tagget didn't cuddle. They took what they wanted and then they paid you for it—whether with money, jewels, favors, pleasure. Tonight he had paid in advance.

His kisses grew bolder. He ground his heavy erection against her thigh, making her excited all over again. Violet ran her hands over his chest, enjoying the soft hairs covering his hard, lean frame.

Thud.

They both jumped at the heavy knock on the cabin door. Evan swore, then went right back to kissing her. A moment later, the knock sounded again.

"Go away," Tagget shouted.

"This is the police," a scornful voice replied. "Open this door or I shall use my authority to break it down."

Tagget shoved himself up and off the bed, his eyes blazing with fury. "Damn stinkin' pigs," he snarled, his New York accent coming out thick and unrefined.

He yanked the ties off the curtains and drew them closed to give Violet privacy, but she preferred to see what was going on. She hopped from the bed and grabbed up her dressing gown, throwing it over her naked body and tying it up in a haphazard knot. She peeked out from behind the curtain in time to see Tagget fumbling to get his trousers buttoned before jerking the door open.

Crevier met him with a nasty grin. "Good evening, Monsieur Tagget. I hope I'm not interrupting anything of importance."

"Get the hell off my dirigible."

"I'm afraid I cannot do that. I have come for Mademoiselle d'Aubergine. She has failed to uphold her end of our bargain. No thefts have been thwarted, and they have only grown bigger."

Violet stalked across the room. "What, did you think I could just put an ad in the newspaper, inviting him to turn himself in? I have made more progress than you made in months."

"I suppose bedding a millionaire must seem like progress after the scum you no doubt had before. I'm afraid, however, that your little affair is over unless you can provide me with some useful information in regards to this case."

Violet didn't want to tell the bastard anything, but she wasn't about to give up Tagget's cozy bed for a rusty cot in a jail cell. She sought about for a juicy bit of information to share.

Tagget spun toward her. "May I defend you from this cretin, Miss Dayton?"

Vi goggled at him. He'd asked her permission. He'd actually asked. Apparently he did learn.

"Yes, you may."

His smile was lethal. He rounded on Crevier. "You will not touch her," Tagget threatened. "Get off my ship and stay far away from her or you will rue the day I laid eyes on you."

Crevier was either too stupid or too arrogant to grasp the dangerous truth of the words. He only laughed. "You defend her after she implicated you as a criminal?"

"That was a test for me and a punishment for you. She is no fool, Crevier. I had to prove myself a worthy partner."

"Worthy?" he scoffed. "Of a slatternly criminal gutter-bird?"

Evan punched him.

Vi almost smiled at the stunned expression on Crevier's face when he hit the floor. Blood trickled from his nose. A fat red welt was rising on his cheek. Behind him, the crew of Dauntless looked on, nodding in approval.

"Engineers can be tougher than you expect," Flynne opined. "Isn't that right, Mrs. Chatsworth?" He fed a nut to the squirrel, who responded with a mechanical squeak.

Crevier's expression turned to thunder. He sprang up and

snapped a cuff around Tagget's wrist. "You are under arrest for the previous escape from your prison cell and for assaulting an officer of the law."

Tagget turned an impassive expression on the police inspector, but anger burned in his eyes. He looked at his crew as Crevier dragged him toward the stairs.

"Parker, my brilliant flame, come give me a kiss before I depart."

The petite engineer rushed over and flung her arms around him. He gave her a wink and a peck on the cheek. For a moment, Violet wondered why he would choose now of all times to flaunt his rakish reputation, but as he and Parker drew apart, Tagget discreetly slipped a tool under the waistband of his trousers. He wouldn't remain long in Crevier's clutches.

"I will return for you tomorrow, Madame Vérité," Crevier snarled. "You will give me every scrap of information you have, or you will become a permanent resident of one of our lovely rehabilitation facilities."

Violet cared nothing for the inspector's bluster. Her eyes locked with Tagget's. The moment before he disappeared up the stairs, he pressed his fingers to his lips, then held them out to her in a goodbye kiss. She turned back to her cabin. There was work to be done in the morning, even if she had to face it alone.

18

"What self-respecting engineer works in a barn?" Tagget sneered, cupping his hands around his eyes while he peered through a crack in the wall.

"Hush."

They'd managed to get all the way here without being caught, and Violet wasn't about to let him ruin it with his chattering. He'd been surly all morning, though she couldn't blame him for that. He'd been stolen from the promise of a pleasurable bed and dragged away in cuffs, and hadn't returned until hours after midnight. Far too late to get enough sleep.

He'd thrown the alarm dragon across the room when it woke them. The poor thing had flapped about the cabin, hooting madly, until Violet caught it with a pillowcase and reset its clock. It would be staying on her side of the bed from now on.

Tagget wrinkled his nose. "This place smells like animal. Isn't the entire point of machinery to free us from the reliance on stinking, shitting animals?"

"As if humans are any better."

He looked at her, and his mouth quirked upward. "You have a point." The smile vanished before it could fully form.

"Let's go. We can't learn any more without going inside, and then we would certainly be caught."

"No. I have an idea."

She gestured for him to follow, and crept around to the end of the barn. "If you boost me up, I can get in through that upper door to the hayloft. From there I should be able to look down on what they're doing inside."

"And if they're using the hayloft?"

"Then I don't go in. And if they see me, we run."

"I can't run." Evan tapped his chest. "Filters, remember?"

"If they see me, I run and leave you to your fate. You seem to have a talent for escaping captivity."

He scowled at her, but cupped his hands to make a stirrup for her foot. She stepped up, and with a single, smooth motion he hoisted her into the air. Strong for a small man. Her hands grasped the edge of the opening, and he lifted her clear over his head to push her through.

"I like your lacy underthings," he remarked. "Hurry up so we can go home where I can take them off you."

Men. Only one thing on their minds. One delicious, thrilling thing she absolutely had not been thinking about all morning.

Vi didn't waste time in the barn. She found what she wanted and then dropped back down beside Tagget, ready to head home and celebrate her triumph.

"I've seen enough," she said.

Tagget nodded. "Good. Give Crevier this address. He can waste his time interviewing engineers who probably don't know who their employer is. When he's arrested them all, we can come back and search the place while it's empty."

"Not necessary. I know who l'Exploiteur is."

His eyes went wide. "Do you? What did you see in there?"

She grinned. "If you want my secrets, you'll have to win them from me."

The weather had grown stormy, but l'Exploiteur's secret manufactory was close enough to the airfield that Violet and Tagget had made it onboard Dauntless before the downpour began. Now, as rain sluiced down the windows, they faced each other across the small table in the cozy cabin, cards in hand and drinks at the ready.

"What did you see in that barn?" Tagget asked, after winning the first hand with ease.

Vi shook her head. "Uh-uh. That wasn't the deal. You get your point, but you need four more. Win one game, ask one question." She shuffled and dealt out the cards in threes and twos, flipping up the eleventh card. "Hearts are trumps."

"This is absurd. You will be badgering me with queries that are none of your concern, when all I want is to know the one thing relevant to our business. I'd like three cards."

"Nope." Vi had a good hand and no need to swap out any cards. "I refuse. Play what you've got."

Tagget scowled at his cards and dropped one onto the table in irritation.

Violet tossed a heart atop it. "If you don't like it, why did you agree to my terms?" she inquired.

"I enjoy playing cards with you. And, since I just answered your question, you will not get another upon your first win."

"Rubbish. You answered of your own volition. It doesn't count."

He sniffed. "I don't like games where you make up the rules as you go."

"Really? I thought that was the sort of game you played most." She took a third trick. "One hand to me."

Three more quick hands and a king of trumps, and Vi looked across the table at him with a grin and arching eyebrows.

"First question to me. Remember the rules: no one-word answers. You must tell the truth and answer fully."

He nodded, scowling at her and shuffling the cards without looking down.

"Who is Mrs. Caldwell?"

Tagget looked startled. "Who? Oh, you mean Eden? She's a friend."

"Who addresses a friend as 'my ever verdant garden'?" Vi scoffed.

"Is that your question for the next time you win?"

"Is that yours?"

He smirked. "This could go on for some time."

"It wasn't another question. It was me not believing you. People don't talk that way to their friends."

"I wouldn't know how 'people' do things. She is my friend, and I address her as I wish. She isn't my lover, if that's what you're getting at. She abandoned me for another man, and seems satisfied with the choice. The longer we are apart, the clearer I see how we were not suitable, in any event. She likes saloons, beer, and sports, and I find such things…"

"Vulgar?"

He shrugged, which was admission enough.

"Thank you. That was a satisfactory answer to my question."

"Satisfactory in that it has assuaged your jealousy?" he teased.

"No questions until you win. Deal."

He slid three cards toward her. She watched his hands, eyeing the white line that slashed across his knuckles and considering her next question.

Violet took the second game in five straight points. Today's session was already shaping up to be as thorough a beating as their previous one.

"How did your lungs get damaged enough to need the filters?"

"I spent too much of my childhood breathing unclean air. I had terrible coughing fits, and frequent wheezing. It only grew worse during my teenage years. I could hardly walk up a flight of stairs without feeling out of breath. I sought out a biomechanologist the moment I had enough money."

"There can't have been many biomechanologists that long ago."

"There weren't. The man who did mine was the pioneer of his field, and to this day he is the best at the craft." Tagget smiled at her. "I trust you will be answering my questions as fully as I have answered yours."

"Naturally."

Violet collected the cards and began to shuffle. The way he played, she wouldn't be answering much of anything. The next game went almost as smoothly as the previous two.

"Where did you grow up?"

"New York City."

"Well, I knew that much," she huffed.

"Then why did you ask?"

"I wanted more details."

Tagget responded with that flirtatious smirk she both loved and hated. "My answer was more than one word."

"Jackass."

He held her gaze, sliding the cards over the polished wood of the table in a slow, smooth stroke that made her yearn for his hands to be elsewhere. "I've been called worse."

Vi pretended not to notice when his fingers brushed hers. She wouldn't be seduced out of a victory.

Tagget's luck improved, however, and he won a narrow five-four victory in the next game. Violet didn't mind. She had always intended to tell him her news, whatever the outcome.

"I know you've been waiting for this," she said. "Go ahead and ask."

"What is the significance of those bits of shell you hide on your person?"

Her mouth dropped open. What about their work? She snapped her jaw closed. She kept forgetting he didn't care. It was only a reason to remain close to her. He knew she would have to tell him eventually. Why waste a question?

He folded his hands atop the table, waiting, not smiling, but looking smug nonetheless. Bastard. She sighed.

"They are all I have of my mother."

Violet shuffled and dealt, wondering whether the things she learned were worth the things she might have to confess. When he won three straight points, she began to think not. Her luck had turned, and the questions came hard and fast.

"Is your mother dead?"

"Not as far as I know."

Another round.

"Who all is in your family?"

"My father and stepmother, their two sons and daughter, and another little sister who has a different mother. We also have an older brother who's always lived elsewhere with his mother, but we've never really known him."

Evan laid down his cards. "Your father seems a champion of infidelity."

"Yes."

Vi motioned for him to resume playing, and managed to win another question. "Who's in *your* family?"

"No one."

Damn. And technically it wasn't a one-word answer. Speaking of her own family, however briefly, had caused an upwelling of homesickness greater than any she'd experienced in years. She missed them. How awful must it be to have no family at all?

Tagget took advantage of her distracted state to win yet another round.

"Why weren't you raised with your birth mother?" he asked.

Violet squeezed her eyes closed. The question stung, for reasons he knew nothing about, but she'd given her word. She would play by the rules of her foolish game. Her eyes opened and lifted to meet Tagget's.

"Because my father thinks everyone needs to live by his religion and his rules. Because he won't allow any child of his to consort with someone outside his restrictive social sphere."

"And yet he doesn't stop himself forming attachments with women outside that sphere," Tagget scoffed.

Vi shrugged.

"Was your childhood an unhappy one?" Evan asked, not even making a pretense of continuing play.

She shook her head.

He shoved the cards aside. "Tell me everything."

Vi knew she shouldn't comply with his imperious command. She didn't talk about these things with anyone. Even her artist friends knew only vaguely where she had come from and why. Tagget was a terrible choice for a confidant. But now that she'd begun to unburden herself, she found she couldn't stop. She tugged the shells out from beneath her shirt, watching the play of light across their iridescent surface.

"My childhood was comfortable and happy. I loved my siblings and we got along as well as any siblings can. We fought, of course, but also played together happily. We still write one another regularly. My father, unsurprisingly, was often absent, off evangelizing while he hunted for new lovers. But my stepmother was kind and she loves all children, even those not her own. She was my first art instructor and always encouraged my passion.

"My parentage was no secret, though. My brother and I are only two months apart in age, and anyone can do that math. I begged my father to tell me of my birth mother, but he would say nothing but that she was a 'great beauty.' He always had a dreamy look in his eyes when he spoke of her. The one good thing in his philandering is that he shows genuine affection, perhaps even love, for all his mistresses. Eventually he admitted my mother had left me some things."

Vi closed her eyes for a moment against the suddenly vivid memory. She rolled the shells between her fingers, the familiar texture comforting.

"When we dug the box out of the cellar, it was crushed and waterlogged," she continued. "All the papers were destroyed. I could read only a small portion of a newspaper clipping about a group working to protect the native flora and fauna of Tasmania. I like to believe that is her passion. These shells are from the island. They were the only salvageable bits from the necklace she'd left for me. I carry them always. Even if I never know her, I have a piece of her with me. It's more precious than I can express."

Violet blinked away a tear. Until she'd started to talk, she hadn't realized just how much she missed her homeland. She missed the mother she didn't know, of course, but also her father, who did love her, despite his backwards ideas about the world. She missed her stepmother and those ugly lace tablecloths she tatted. And it had been far too long since Violet had written any of her siblings.

Australia itself called to her as well: the sprawling city of Melbourne with its trains and trolleys, the wide open land around her family's home, the sparkling, seemingly unending ocean.

"I didn't become unhappy until I was a teenager," Violet went on. Why was she telling Tagget all this? He didn't need to know her history. Perhaps it was only that the talking eased her homesickness. "That was when my father decided I ought to be trained to be a governess. A governess! Me! Can you imagine?"

"It would have been an appalling waste of your talents and independent spirit," Tagget agreed.

"It was awful. The training was awful, the idea of it was awful. I wanted to be an artist and to control my own life, not work for some rich bastard."

Evan chuckled. "Ah. So that's why you wished to have a

rich bastard working for you instead. Well, I am at your service, my intrepid artiste."

Vi smiled back at him. A sense of relief began to settle inside her. She'd needed to share, and she'd been holding back too long, it seemed.

"So, that's my story. I trekked off to Europe to become a master artist. I was young and foolish. I didn't realize how difficult a task I had undertaken."

Evan reached across the table and covered her hand with his own. The expression in his fierce, green eyes wasn't one of pity or sympathy, but something far more dangerous. Admiration.

"Few would have had such courage, my bold, tenacious wildflower. You didn't quit and run home. You forged a new life for yourself. Ow!" He rubbed his hand where she'd pinched him.

"You got off easy. That pun deserved a slap."

"It was brilliant wordplay! Have you no appreciation for the linguistic arts?"

"You're no Lord Byron," she scoffed.

"No. I'm smarter and better looking. And thankfully, not dead."

Violet rose from her seat, shaking her head, fighting the grin that tugged at her mouth. She had some letters to write, and a painting to touch up. "I'm going to the studio. But I'll leave you with this, to give you something to do this afternoon: in the barn, they fueled their furnace with old shipping crates. Several pieces were branded with the mark of Continental Freight. Find the owner, and I wager we will find our thief."

"I can have his name within the hour."

"No rush. You can update me at dinner. Here on the ship or at your hotel?"

"Here. I prefer this bed."

"Because it's smaller and there isn't another one I can use?"

"That does make it attractive, yes. Perhaps tonight we

can turn in early. I will make certain no stairs or ladders are let down and the crew is given strict instructions to fly off if anyone should attempt to board."

Vi grinned at him. "I see no need for such precautions. I was plenty satisfied last night." She winked and scampered out the door before he could reply.

19

"ALBRECHT WECHSLER," Evan reported. "A Belgian. Son of a German father and Flemish mother, he grew up in a small town near the German border. Lives in a castle now, in the same area."

He took a sip of his port and eyed the chocolate confection Walton had created. The chef had thrown himself into his French cooking with great gusto, particularly for a half-Italian, half-English New Yorker. Evan reached for the knife.

"You cut. I choose," Violet said.

"What?"

"To make it fair. You slice the pastry in half, and I choose which piece to eat. The cutter has an incentive to make it as fair as possible."

Evan regarded her with raised eyebrows. "I won't begrudge you the larger piece, if you desire."

She shook her head. "I can tell you don't have siblings."

"None that I know of."

"How would you not know? Unless your father also sowed his oats in too many fields?"

"My parents died when I was four. I was sent to an orphanage." He owed her that much of an explanation, after she had given him so much of her own story.

Her mouth opened in surprise. "I'm so sorry. I had no idea."

"It's not something I advertise." He sliced the cake and turned the larger piece onto her plate.

"Thank you. So, this Mr. Wechsler owns Continental Freight?"

"He does. The company began by shipping Belgian goods to Germany and France by train. Their expansion to cover all of Europe coincided with the surge in dirigible transport. He loved the airships and moved the center of business to Paris."

Violet waved her fork. "They have dozens of dirigibles, correct?"

"Correct. And dozens of routes."

"It's perfect. He can take his hand-picked crew and hop aboard any freighter he chooses. No one suspects anything because these ships are flying their ordinary routes." She took a bite of her chocolate and closed her eyes, sighing in pleasure. "This is spectacular."

"Mmm," Evan replied, tasting his own and imagining her making that same expression in his bed, hair tumbling over her naked shoulders to brush the curves of her breasts.

"Walton is a skilled chef. How did you find him?"

"I didn't. He came with Dahlia."

Violet's dark eyebrows arched. "Oh?"

"When I gathered this crew, she wouldn't hire on without him, and I needed a man-of-all-work. He took up the chef's duties because he liked to cook. He has proven more than satisfactory."

"He's the baby's father?"

"Yes. They have a puzzling on-off relationship. It doesn't negatively affect the running of the ship, so I leave them to it."

"At one time I thought she might be yours."

"The baby?" Evan laughed at the idea. "Certainly not. You

weren't here to witness the one time when Dahlia handed her to me. The child screamed bloody murder."

"Babies have good instincts. They can recognize a villain."

"I've held other children, and they haven't reacted so."

"Other people's children, or your own? You're a notorious playboy. How many unfortunate offspring have you sired?"

"Fourteen, fifteen, maybe. I can't remember."

Violet's bright eyes grew round with shock. Evan wasn't certain whether to be proud of his reputation or horrified that she wouldn't even question so ludicrous an answer.

"I... that..."

Horrified. Perhaps even as horrified as she now looked. He knew too well the lot of an abandoned child. A queasiness clenched his stomach. His chest ached, knowing she believed he would show such casual disdain for one of his own blood.

"Violet." He held up a hand to stop her. "I have no children. No family, remember? The closest I've ever come is that I offered Eden the opportunity to join me here in Paris and bear me an heir. And I did that knowing she would refuse."

"Oh." Violet looked down at the remains of her pastry.

"I'm not as horrible as people make me out to be." He spoke truthfully. He'd nowhere near the number of wild affairs the papers claimed, and never more than one at a time. The affairs he did have ended calmly, amiably. He didn't break hearts. His lovers had always known what they were getting into. So why did the words feel like a lie?

"I don't think you're horrible." Violet lifted her head, and a mischievous smile touched her lips. "At least not all of the time. You provide good food, at the least." Her eyebrows twitched as she took another bite.

Heat coursed through Evan's body. God, to be that fork, sliding between her lips. He gobbled down the rest of his dessert, anxious to move on to the more important business of the night. Violet taunted him, in her coquettish way, finishing her own food with agonizing leisure. Evan watched every bite touch her mouth as he gathered up the dishes.

"For a rich man, you clean up after yourself strangely often," she observed.

"You're confusing me with your British nobility. In America, we work for our money and take pride in it. I didn't get rich by standing around waiting for someone else to do things for me."

"No, I don't suppose you did."

She set her plate and fork atop the pile, and he carried it out the door, setting it down in the hall. No one would have any reason to disturb him further this evening. He locked the door and turned to face Violet.

She had wandered over to the desk to play with his dragon. The metal creature belched flame, too close to the flocked wallpaper for Evan's liking. It looked like an animal, but hadn't the sense of a living creature to not set things on fire. An idea for adding proximity sensors flashed in his mind, warring for an instant with the screams of his body to hustle Violet into his bed.

"What's its name?"

He frowned at her. "It doesn't have a name. It's only a machine."

"It's cute. You should name it. I suggest Ignatius."

Evan winced. "Please don't."

"I named the owl already. I call her Selene."

"Darling..." He wrapped his arms around her waist and nuzzled her neck. "I'm concerned, my bouquet of beauty, that you are not fully in your right mind tonight. I must assume it is the result of your desperate longing for me."

"Longing?" Her head fell back against his shoulder. "I don't know what you're talking about."

"Mmm-hmm." He caught her earlobe between his teeth.

"I'm entirely indifferent to you." She tilted her neck to give him better access. "I rarely think of you, and I certainly haven't… ooh… haven't spent the day hoping for a repeat of last night."

Evan teased the ticklish spot just under her ear and was rewarded with an appreciative sigh. His tongue and lips gorged themselves on the taste of her skin. She put the world's finest cognac to shame.

"Most of all, I don't want you to undress and let me run my hands all over your body."

He eased the sleeve of her loose top off her shoulder, kissing the exposed skin. His hands dropped to untie the gorgeous silver brocade corset covering it.

"That's unfortunate, as it was precisely what I had planned. I shall have to restrain myself. After all, my aim is to please you." She shivered in his arms. "To unrelentingly please you."

"Perhaps I could allow you some small concession," Violet murmured. "It *is* getting warm in here."

"Very."

Evan pulled away from her. He had tangled the laces of her damned corset, and he couldn't get it undone while he kissed her. He growled at the knot until it loosened beneath his fingers. Violet's hand found his before he could make further progress on the garment.

"Why don't you remove your own clothes? I hate to think of you sweltering in that suit."

He pressed one more kiss to her neck. "Ah, so you do think of me."

She pushed him aside to work on her corset strings with practiced fingers. "Go on, Tagget. Don't leave me waiting. I'm tingly all over."

He started for the closet, removing his jacket as he went. He felt rather tingly himself, and he had doubts about the practicality of his tight trousers when he was so frequently in Violet's company. Some subtle alterations might be in order. That would be an awkward conversation with his tailor.

Evan had just hung his shirt when a frantic rapping came at the door.

"This ship had better be on fire," he threatened, yanking it open, contemplating the immediate dismissal of whomever had disturbed him.

Flynne stood in the hall, with what looked to be a playbill clutched in his hand. The boy's eyes were wide with fear, but his posture was one of determination. Whatever his concern, he thought it worth the risk. Admirable.

"So sorry, Mr. Tagget, but I took Mrs. Chatsworth to the park to play with the real squirrels, and I saw this. I thought you should know at once. They're all over. I spied two more on the way back." He thrust the paper at Evan and backed away. "Sorry. We won't bother you again."

Evan glanced down at the poster. "Hell. Thank you, Flynne. We'll talk in the morning." The engineer scurried away, and Evan shut and locked the door behind him. "Our thief has started advertising."

A soft finger ran down his back. "Do we need to act upon it tonight?"

"Do you think I care?"

"No."

He made a noise that was halfway to a laugh. "You'd be wrong. If it concerns you, then I care. I won't have that police inspector throwing you into some filthy dungeon."

The one finger turned into a full hand. "Show me the paper."

Evan held it up. Styling his announcement like a theater pamphlet, l'Exploiteur had splashed his moniker across the page in swooping red letters, claiming, "The greatest heist in history!" and, "Theft on a scale heretofore unknown!"

"Coming soon," Violet muttered. "If he has to be such a grandstander, the least he could have done was put in a time and a date."

"He's too cowardly."

"Or perhaps just not that stupid."

Her fingers moved over Evan's back in criss-crossing motions, tracing the scars. Faded by time, none were as bad as those on his arms, but they were plentiful.

"We have time before he acts," she said. "He will want to build tension. I won't ask you to go out hunting him tonight."

"I would go, if necessary. I mean to see this through and help you secure your liberty."

"Thank you." Her hands stilled, and she pressed a kiss to the back of his neck, sending a tremor of arousal down his spine. "Did they beat you at the orphanage?"

Evan had no memory of his time in any orphanage, only the lingering knowledge that he'd been sent several places in rapid succession. He knew the exterior of the last orphanage, across from the factory, and could never forget the haunted faces of the boys who lived there, but any more was lost.

He shook his head. "Not now. Another time."

Violet's arms wrapped around him, her soft breasts pressing into his back. Her corset was gone, but the silky fabric of her shirt kept him from her magnificent skin.

"In the morning?"

He turned to face her, grinning. "You'll have to beat me at cards."

She backed him into the door. "Not even a challenge. You'll never get as lucky as last time. I prefer to beat you at your own game."

Her mouth crushed his, driving the breath from his lungs. She kissed like no one he had ever kissed, taking what she wanted with such sweet fierceness it was all he could do to hang on and let her carry him away. It was terrifying. It was heaven.

"Violet," he gasped, fumbling to get his hands beneath her clothing.

She unfastened his trousers and tugged them down over his hips. "You never finished undressing."

Her fingers curled around his cock, squeezing and stroking

as she kissed him again. Evan moaned against her lips. Never had he needed release so desperately. He groped through the layers of her short skirt. He would take her here, up against the door. Never mind that it was uncivilized. The bed was miles away.

Violet released him and nodded toward the bed.

Evan reached for her. "Too far."

She ignored him, as usual, and walked across the room, shedding clothing as she went.

Groaning in frustration, he followed, kicking off his trousers and trying not to think about the mess they were leaving. He caught her at the foot of the bed, and they half-climbed, half-fell onto the sheets as they grappled with one another.

Evan rolled atop her, kissing everywhere his mouth could reach, his fingers sliding between her legs to find her hot, wet core, ready and eager for him. He stroked her silken folds, needing her to want this as much as he did. The waiting was agony.

"Evan."

The sound of his name washed over him in an erotic caress. He was drugged on the taste and scent of her.

His lips trailed along the slope of her breast as he slipped a finger inside her, and she answered with another delicious sigh.

Good God, she was magnificent. Every touch of his hands and mouth brought a new response. Evan reveled in each tiny twist of her body, each noise that passed her lips. He ached to be inside her, to feel like a part of her, but he had to see her find her release first. Had to know he'd brought her pleasure.

Her movements became wilder, more desperate, until at last she climaxed, her lips parting in a gasp of glorious bliss. No one had ever looked more beautiful.

"Violet," he groaned. *I want you. I need you.*

"Evan." Her hands caressed him, gliding down his back, tugging him closer as she canted her hips upward. In a throaty, lust-thickened voice, she echoed his inner thoughts. "I want you."

The most glorious of words. Evan withdrew his hand, shifting to slide inside of her. Tight. Slick. Perfection. He began slowly, finding a rhythm she liked, moving with her until they were straining as one for that elusive release. Their lips crashed together, tongues sparring, their kisses growing wilder as his thrusts became harder, faster.

She was bliss. What insane lovers in her past had let her go? Evan couldn't conceive of it. He was consumed by her, body and mind. Violet was pure passion, unafraid to unleash the full force of her desire. At the same time, her hands moved over him with the softest, gentlest touch, as though he were something precious.

She began to writhe against him, arching her back to take more of him, and he gave himself over to his desire, thrusting faster, deeper still, until he could no longer stave off his impending orgasm. Violet broke beneath him, crying out her delight. The sensation of her body clenching around him sent Even reeling. He clung to her, the tremors of his own climax wringing every drop of stamina from his body.

He collapsed and rolled over, breathing hard, his half-mechanical lungs vibrating in his chest. Violet curled up beside him, pillowing her head on his chest and wrapping an arm tightly around him.

Evan stroked her hair and the soft skin of her back, spent, sated, but not satisfied. Her perfume still infiltrated his nostrils. Her warm flesh still heated his own. Even the sound of her slow, steady breathing sliced into him, burrowing its way inside until it was too deep to escape. He couldn't say why, but he knew he would need her again tomorrow, and the next day.

When she fell asleep he continued to hold her, afraid to let go and break the spell she had cast over him. He fought sleep, knowing no dream could compare to the reality of her.

He'd known when they met that she was special, but he'd

never imagined how utterly she would destroy him. She had forever ruined him for anyone else.

So be it. All that mattered was that he had her. And he would never let her go.

20

"Hoo-oot! Hoo-oot! Hoo-oot!"

Violet made an incoherent grumbling noise as she fumbled for the dragon at her bedside.

"Hoo-oot!"

"Be quiet!" She opened her eyes, squinting at the morning light slanting through the windows.

"Hoo-oot!"

"Shut up!" Her fingers touched a metal wing, and she dragged the small creature closer, spinning the dials to silence it.

Evan snuggled up against her back. "Would you like voice controls? Eden's father has a fabulous design. I will license it if you wish."

"I want you not to keep me up so late."

His fingers trickled down her side to her hip. "Is that so?" he murmured against her ear. "I thought you seemed pleased with our nighttime activities."

"Very." She turned toward him, content to relieve her crankiness with yet another bout of amorous sport. "I simply don't like mornings."

"This particular morning may be better than you think."

Violet leaned in to kiss him and ran the tip of her tongue across his upper lip. "Prove it," she breathed.

He flipped her onto her back, hands and mouth taking up her challenge. She sighed in his arms and gave herself over to the pleasure.

When at last they were satiated, they curled up together in the middle of the bed. She left Evan the one pillow they had yet to knock to the floor, content to rest her head on his chest, listening to the faint whirr of the filters as he breathed in and out.

He was as excellent a cuddler as she had hoped, one arm curved protectively around her while his opposite hand stroked her hair and slid gentle caresses across her skin. She'd fallen asleep twice this way last night, and she didn't mind doing so again. Both times she had awakened with him close beside her.

The more time they spent together, the more she believed his haughty persona to be a sham. Where he should have been cold and detached, he was warm and gentle. The real Evan Tagget loved a good snuggle. Bit by bit she was unraveling him.

Violet did fall asleep again, and woke a short time later feeling refreshed. Tagget was no longer in bed with her, but seated at the table, fully clothed, writing a letter.

"Good morning. Breakfast will be here any moment."

"Excellent."

Vi tossed back the sheets and ducked behind the privacy screen to paw through her bag for something to wear. Her little corner of the cabin was a mess. It felt very much her own, however, leaving her reluctant to use the closet instead.

Her fingers closed around her fluffiest, brightest purple dress. Perfect. She'd match her clothing to her glorious mood. Happy, energetic, and free. Free from all the wondering and wanting. She'd spent a long, uninhibited night satisfying her desires and her curiosity. Evan Tagget would no longer be a distraction.

The door opened, accompanied by the smell of freshly

baked quiche. This morning grew better all the time. She wrapped an emerald green underbust corset around her torso, tugging the laces tight before tying it. She'd be gleaming like a jewel today.

"You know, Tagget," she called, "I'm quite fond of this room, but it's not set up properly for ladies. I'm adaptable to the conditions, but others may not be."

"It's fortunate, then, that I have no intention of sharing this room with other ladies. Or men, for that matter."

Violet's stomach flip-flopped. Her heart began to beat wildly. The conviction in his words was more seductive even than his sultry voice. It promised long-lasting affection, told her she was special. If the privacy screen hadn't been in her way, she might have run at him and smothered him with kisses. This was *not* how "over him" was supposed to feel.

"Perhaps we could do away with this privacy screen and replace it with a dressing table?" she requested, forcing herself to remain casual. "I could use a place to sit and do my hair."

"Hmm." She could imagine him stroking his beard, a thoughtful expression on his face. "Do you know the dimensions of a standard dressing table?"

"Dimensions?"

"Yes. If the screen is removed, you have five feet, seven inches along the outer wall, and four feet, four and a half inches beside the bed. I can't be more precise without taking measurements."

And there he went again, piquing her interest with his oddly specific mathematical observations. She wasn't over him at all. If anything, he was even more of a distraction than before. She'd had a thorough taste, and she wanted more.

I told you, she scolded herself. *I told you to hold back. I told you not to get involved.*

Violet brushed out her hair in silence, pulling it back with a single ribbon before stepping out into the room. She wasn't "involved," she was merely interested. Maybe she needed a few more nights to completely satisfy her.

Tagget rose to greet her. "You look gorgeous, my sweetest blossom, even without a place to do your hair. I will, of course, buy you any dressing table you desire. We can order a custom size if it doesn't fit. Please, sit. Walton has made your favorite."

He was smiling at her, not with his usual smirk, but with an expression of boyish good cheer. Her sweet cuddler.

Goddammit, Violet, he is not yours. This is only a fling. No attachments.

Her gaze fell to the table. For the first time she had ever seen, Tagget's plate was empty, the only evidence of his morning croissant a few stray crumbs. He had also finished an entire cigarette, crumpling only a small butt into the ashtray. A bottle of champagne sat open on the table. His glass had been filled.

Champagne? For me? The urge to kiss him took hold again, warring with the urge to flee before she let herself get too close.

Tagget pulled out a chair for her, then picked up the bottle and began to fill her glass. "Champagne, darling? What better way to celebrate our exceptional morning?"

Celebrate. The word echoed in Violet's mind. All the joy rushed out of her at once, replaced with a mix of fury and shame. Of course he was celebrating. He thought he'd won. Hadn't he told her from the very beginning that he meant to win her?

All along she'd warned herself. This was what came of ignoring her own good advice. She'd succumbed to temptation and allowed herself to foolishly imagine she was something special to him. In truth, she was nothing more than the new plaything he'd acquired. The new prize he'd claimed.

Violet's jaw clenched. Well, he didn't get to win her. She wasn't going to be his trophy. And no one was going to celebrate a damned thing.

She grabbed both glasses of champagne and upended them

onto the table, then stormed out the door, barely remembering to grab her plate of quiche. She stomped up the stairs to the deck, directly to the bridge, where Harrison and Dahlia were at work checking gauges and making notes.

"Take us to Liège," Vi commanded. "I have some shopping to do."

They both looked past her at Tagget, who had followed behind, dabbing at the champagne that had splattered his suit.

"What in hell was that for?" he demanded.

Harrison turned to the controls. "Liège it is. At your service, ma'am."

21

Dahlia linked her arm through Violet's, a huge smile splitting her face. The warm summer sun beat down on the small group as they made their way down the long gravel drive that led to Wechsler's enormous home on the Belgian-German border.

"I'm so excited, I'm about to burst!" the navigator exclaimed. "I've never been in a real castle before. Thank you so much for inviting us."

Vi couldn't help but return the smile. "You're welcome. It's fun to have friends along."

Not that fun had been her primary reason for asking Dahlia and Walton to join them. The lively American couple would keep attention off of herself and Tagget, allowing them to better scrutinize Wechsler's home. Seeing Dahlia's delight was an extra bonus. Vi would be certain to invite her on future outings that would be purely pleasure.

A cold feeling settled in her stomach. She might never see the crew again once her work was completed. There would be nothing holding her there. She wasn't going to let Tagget parade her around like a trophy. She loved living on the dirigible, and couldn't get enough of the thrills of his bed, but her imagination promised her impossible things, and repeated disappointment would be unbearable. This needed to be a fling and no more.

Breaking off the affair wouldn't be difficult. She only had to look at him to feel a hot flash of anger. That and amusement. Her latest idea was delicious revenge. Since Tagget couldn't fake an accent to save his life, Vi had decided to have him and Dahlia pose as siblings from New York, bringing their spouses on a once-in-a-lifetime European holiday. Violet had chosen clothes to make them look prosperous enough to get here, but not for fancy hotels or expensive restaurants. They looked like the people who had the bad seats at the opera.

She'd dressed Tagget in an ill-fitting tweed suit and a straw hat. He had uttered some choice words upon seeing the outfit, but had accepted the plan as sensible. He couldn't stop fidgeting, tugging at the cloth and kicking at the ground with his less-than-shiny boots. Without his perfect clothes, he went from staggeringly handsome to unremarkable. The ugly hat obscuring his pretty face completed the effect.

Violet had to admit she didn't like her own outfit any better. She had found herself a high-necked white blouse and a slim navy blue skirt that fell to her ankles. The clothes were as restrictive as they were boring. To accessorize, she had donned gloves and a big hat with a ridiculous number of fake flowers. Its sole benefit was that it allowed her to conceal a finely-honed, six-inch hatpin.

Dahlia's eager bouncing made Fern giggle, and Violet couldn't stop a smile from forming whenever she heard the baby's laughter. Walton, too, was pleased by the outing. He grinned and walked close to Dahlia, looking every bit a proper, devoted father and husband.

"We have a lucky daughter, to be able to experience such things already at her age," he said.

Dahlia looked up at him. "Yes. Growing up on an airship, she will travel the world and see incredible things. I want this to be only the first of many for her."

"This could become a normal thing, taking her on outings."

"It should. This is lovely. I will try to take her off the ship more often."

"I'd like to do it together. As a family. Perhaps you and I could get married." There was a hopeful note in his tone that made Violet think this wasn't the first time he had made the suggestion.

"Oh, I'm not ready for that. I have more things like him to explore first." Dahlia waved a hand at Tagget.

"I thought you said he was inadequate," Walton replied.

Tagget spun around. "Excuse me?"

Violet smothered a hysterical gasp of laughter. She didn't find him inadequate in the slightest, but perhaps next to a giant of a man like Walton he might seem so.

"No, no, not like that," Dahlia sighed. "It was all terribly exciting at first, but then… just ordinary. Dispassionate."

"Dispassionate?" Violet echoed in disbelief. It was the last word she would ever have used to describe Evan, except perhaps for "humble."

Dahlia shrugged. "Sorry." She turned back to Walton. "Yeah. Still need a few more excitements. But maybe later on, when I'm ready to have another baby."

Walton put an arm around her waist. "Fair enough."

Vi turned her attention back to Tagget. He wore a twisted expression, as if he couldn't decide between fury and bafflement. He banged his cane as he walked, looking more uncomfortable than ever. Her plan was going well. No one would know him for anything but a grumpy American tourist.

The plan went awry the moment they arrived at the visitor's entrance. Tagget's shoulders straightened, his face grew calm, and his eyes hard. Before Violet even realized what was happening, he had introduced their party, given a glowing thanks to their English-speaking guide, and charmed her to the point of giggles. She hung close to his side, talking as if to him alone and fluttering her eyelashes.

"You are from New York, Mr. Jones?"

"Yes, as are my sister and her husband. My wife is Australian."

"How lovely that you are all able to travel so far! Right this way, please." The guide ushered the group into a large parlor.

Violet wandered over to gaze out the window at the pond that acted as a moat across the front of the castle. She lifted the camera Tagget had supplied and pretended to take a photo.

"The castle had fallen into disrepair before Mr. Wechsler purchased it," the guide gushed. "He has restored it to its former glory, and opened it to the public for all to see. The proceeds from the tours go directly to the castle staffing and maintenance, and anything left over is donated to the village as a show of thanks for those who supported him in his dream."

Violet had to work not to snort. Their guide might be dazzled by Tagget's charisma, but next to their local hero Wechsler he was nothing.

"He sounds like quite a man," Tagget said, keeping most of the irony out of his voice. He began to pepper their guide with questions about Wechsler's past, his business, and the castle, speaking in French to further enchant her.

Violet used the distraction to poke around for any place where the stolen art might be hidden. She slid her hands behind tapestries, eyed every canvas for a potential paint-over, and scratched her nails on statues in case cheap plaster hid something beneath. An hour of wandering the massive home turned up nothing.

"That was amazing," Dahlia exclaimed on their way to the exit. "Are we able to tour the gardens, too?"

"Of course," the guide offered. "There is no formal tour, but you may walk around for as long as you wish. The gardener is at work and can answer questions."

Violet waited through another absurdly long thanks before Tagget at last took her arm and escorted her out the door.

"I saw no place to hide art of the size he has stolen," she

whispered. "He can't have crammed it into his personal rooms unless his entire staff is complicit. That seems far-fetched. In a cellar makes no sense, either. The man is a huge art lover, and he wouldn't hide important works in a dark, dank space. He would want to see them. The stolen works must not be here."

"I agree with all but that last statement."

"Why? What did you see?"

"There was a space missing."

"What?"

"The castle we saw plus the personal rooms we skipped couldn't account for the full square footage of the building," Evan explained. "There was a chunk missing on both the first and second floors that had no apparent entrance. I need to walk around the outside and into the courtyard to get a clearer picture. I will draw a floor plan when we return to Dauntless."

"You and your strange, mathematical mind."

"Useful, isn't it?"

"It's why I hired you."

"Of course. About my payment? We never did work out the details."

"Get me into that 'missing' space, and then we'll talk."

He bowed. "You have yourself a deal, my sweet."

22

EVAN DID NOT HABITUALLY keep his dirigible stocked with appropriate tools for breaking and entering. He dragged his toolbox out of the closet and into the center of the cabin. Full darkness was already upon them, but the ship's electric lights kept the room bright. Kneeling beside the box, he began pulling out potentially useful objects and setting them on the table. A flashlight. A wrench. A pair of long-nose pliers.

"We need a lantern," Violet informed him. "Adjustable brightness and beam if you have one."

Evan glanced up. "This is an airship. It has multiple lanterns for signaling, and they all fit that description. You don't find my flashlight suitable?"

Violet hefted his camera. "We need to take photos of the stolen art for evidence, and it will be impossible without better lighting. Even a good lantern will be less than ideal. This camera is terrible."

"That camera is astoundingly popular. Its sales alone earned me enough to pay for this dirigible and everything on it."

"It may be popular, but it's awful. It doesn't focus well, its lens gives neither good distance nor a wide enough angle, and it can't be adjusted for changes in lighting conditions."

"It's a good value and sufficient for most casual photographers."

She scowled at him. She really did have a lovely scowl. "I've been taking photographs since I was seven. I could recommend three different cameras for only a fraction more money that are all at least twice as good."

"Yet people are buying my Ready-Cam."

"Evan," she sighed.

His heart skipped a beat. Every time she used his first name he felt a rush of excitement.

Her clear, brown eyes locked with his. "It's a shit camera."

Evan shook his head in resignation. She was probably right. "Shall I fire the engineer who designed it?"

"No! Heavens, why would you consider such a thing?"

"I don't like having my name associated with junk."

"Then you shouldn't have approved it in the first place."

He chuckled. "I approve very few products these days. There are still bits of my handiwork in our teletics infrastructure, and I have a small involvement in our experimental technologies—wireless teletics, telepictures, and the like. Everything else is done by others. There was a time when everything in our small machines division had been built, designed, or altered by myself, but those days are long gone. I created a self-sustaining operation, and it no longer needs me."

Violet's lovely lips pinched into a frown. "I find that rather sad."

Evan shrugged. "It's not so bad. It makes me plenty of money, and I have absolute authority over any product or service we offer. As long as things are running smoothly, however, it's not worth my time to meddle."

"What do you make in your workshop, then?"

"Whatever I want. Sometimes I do custom dragons. You wouldn't believe what people pay for one that I have personally built."

"I am an artist. We earn our livings by making people

pay as much as possible for our own creations. I would believe anything. Hand me that set of tiny screwdrivers."

He passed it up to her. "May I express my skepticism regarding your plan?"

She put her hands on her hips and stared him down with an exasperated look that didn't reach her eyes. Most of the morning's anger had faded. He still didn't know what had upset her. They'd had such a happy night together, and she'd appeared to wake in a good mood.

Then something he'd said or done had caused her to lash out in anger. He couldn't fathom what that might have been.

"Express whatever you want," she declared. "It won't change anything. I'm going up top to watch our approach. Are you coming, or do you prefer to hide here?"

"I need to fortify myself with a stiff drink before we proceed. I will join you shortly."

Evan watched her swirl away in a flourish of purple skirts. She confounded him, yet still delighted him. Even now, when she was annoyed with him, he wanted to hold her close. Wanted to understand.

Again, he replayed the morning in his mind. Nothing he'd said ought to have made her angry. Unless he'd touched on something he didn't know about. Some inner pain.

Fear. Not anger. She was protecting herself.

Evan admired that self-reliance. Violet was a woman of strength and pluck, who strode from every room with her head held high. Who dared to challenge him like no one else. The glimpses of vulnerability beneath her armor made him long to defend her and promise her the world. She had nothing to fear from him. But how to tell her? How to convince her?

He'd learned so much about her, yet the distance between them stretched like an uncrossable chasm. The more she opened up to him, the more he craved her, and the more he yearned to know. It could take years to uncover all that she clutched close to her heart. Hell, it might take his entire lifetime. He was prepared to wait. He was also prepared to offer her his own secrets. Everything had its price.

Evan skipped the drink and followed Violet to the deck. Dauntless hovered, engines low, lights off, another formless shape among the clouds. Harrison's expert hand brought her down in a smooth motion, freezing twenty feet above the turrets.

Walton unfurled the long ladder, and Evan swung himself over the rail. Moments later his feet were planted solidly on the roof of Wechsler's imposing home. Violet followed, hopping the last several rungs. The ladder zipped upward, and the dirigible floated away, rising to rejoin the denizens of the night sky.

They slid down to a rooftop terrace, where Violet plucked the set of tiny screwdrivers from her purse and went to work on the door lock.

Evan leaned in close, letting his hand wander down over her backside. "You are certain you know how to do this?"

"I've been a forger for a decade. When one is in regular contact with criminals, one can't help but pick up a trick or two. I'm surprised you can't pick locks yourself, given your general amorality."

"I did all my thieving through stealth and deception. Please don't damage my tools. Those screwdrivers are made to exacting specifications."

"Buy yourself a new set."

She nudged him away, and he left her to it. She could take as long as she needed. Wechsler's security was amateurish—intended to look as though he had nothing to hide. After pacing the terrace for several minutes, Evan paused to light a cigarette. Violet's head swung around the moment the match flared.

"What are you doing?"

Evan shook out the match and took a long draw on the cigarette. "Having a smoke. I need something to do while I wait."

She turned back to the lock, shaking her head. "You're anxious."

"Pardon?"

"You smoke when you're anxious. Or excited. It's a nervous habit."

"Is it?" He blew out a long, thin stream of smoke, pondering the habit in a new way. No one else had ever commented on it before, even people he'd known for years. His chest constricted. Violet had noticed. And for reasons he didn't entirely understand, that mattered.

When at last the lock opened, he flicked the cigarette away and followed her into the castle, using only what little moonlight seeped through the windows. In the darkness, her body was no more than a shadowy form, but he could feel her warmth, hear the rustle of her skirts, and smell a trace of lilac. The memory of the taste of her danced on his tongue. Had he always been so aware of her? He swore he could pick her out of a mob using any one of his senses alone.

She led him in silence down to the second floor, finding her way without error to the mysterious space, though she had spared his diagram no more than a few seconds' glance. He loved the ease with which her artist's mind jumped between two-dimensional representations and the real world. She was like an engineer, but more vibrant and fanciful, a perfect, sparkling companion to his crisp, calculated black.

God, did he want her, and not just for the delights of her body. He wanted to hold her and sleep curled up beside her. He wanted to watch her eat breakfast while she frowned at his meager morning meal. He wanted to walk hand-in-hand with her and sneak kisses in front of prim, scowling governesses. Talk with her. Laugh with her. Work in their side-by-side studios, where he could peek in at any time just to see her.

Damn. She was driving him out of his mind. Maddest of all, he liked it.

Violet's elbow dug into his side. "Why aren't you looking?" she whispered.

"Huh?"

"For the entrance?"

His mind jerked back to reality. This wasn't a lark. They were engaged in an unlawful search in the home of a dangerous man. And nearly two decades had passed since Evan had last broken into a house. His sneaking skills had moved past rusty and into decomposing.

Moving as silently as possible, Evan ran his hands along the wall, feeling for anything strange. God, to be back on the ship, running his hands over Violet instead. Where his ears were pricked to catch her little sighs and moans rather than the footsteps of a security guard.

The sooner we find the secret room, the sooner we can leave.

The thought kept him going, distracted as he was.

Violet, though, was determined. Where his efforts were meager, she was thorough, squeezing between furniture, reaching behind paintings, checking high and low. Evan tried to keep pace with her, wincing at every creak of the old castle floorboards. Had he actually believed in a god, he might have prayed for the interminable search to end.

He paused by a window, trying to check his watch by the light of the moon. They were taking too long. If they didn't move on soon, they risked being caught by a patrolling guard.

He turned to Violet in time to see her jerk her hand away from the wall. Carefully, she reached out again, then beckoned Evan to join her.

"Here." She took his hand and drew it beneath the edge of a tapestry. Evan's fingertips traced the slight gap between wall panels.

"I think you're right. Now, how to open it?" His hand moved over the wall, feeling for any latch or recess that might open the hidden door. The wood was smooth and unchanging beneath his fingers.

"No locks that I can find," Violet sighed. "What about down below? Something you could kick with your foot?"

"Good idea." Evan knelt. "Out of the way, to avoid accidental openings."

He reached behind a pedestal that held a marble bust. He remembered it from the tour. It looked to be Roman, but he guessed it was a fake. Behind the statue, in a spot just wide enough to poke with the toe of one's shoe, he felt a section of wood different from the others. Not a button, but a sensor, set to trigger the mechanism when it was hit with enough force. He rose to his feet and kicked the spot.

The clank of pulleys and turning gears made him jump. He tensed, certain someone would come charging in at any moment. A section of the wall swung open, large enough to admit a person, but too small for the ten-foot-tall *Las Meninas* stolen from the Prado.

"Quickly," Violet murmured, darting through the gap. She pulled a lever to close the door so quickly Evan almost didn't make it inside. For a long moment, they waited in the darkness, listening for evidence they'd been heard. Nothing.

Violet lit the lantern. They stood at the top of a steep wooden staircase that led down to the floor of a multi-story gallery. She rushed down the steps, opening the lantern wider and swinging it in an arc as she surveyed the room.

Evan followed the beam of light across the wall. Art, both familiar and unfamiliar, crowded the space. The enormous Velasquez painting took pride of place on the opposite wall, surrounded by smaller paintings and shelves holding statuettes. Violet pointed the light up to the ceiling. A seam ran down the center roofline, the metal support beams on either side attached to hinges at the wall.

"Ah." Evan nodded. "He opens the roof and lowers the artwork down directly from the dirigible. Sensible."

Violet handed Evan the light and lifted the camera. "These

pictures won't be good, but I hope they will be enough to prove him the art thief."

Evan nodded, angling the beam to give her as much light as possible. He grinned at the reclining Venus. "That emotional Italian fellow was right. She really is something. I might like to take her for myself. We can say we didn't find that particular painting."

"Honestly, Tagget, do you want to be the next person they send me after? It goes back to the museum."

"You're no fun at all."

"I'm glad you think so. Turn the light this way, I want to see what's in the back corner."

Evan swiveled around, widening the lantern beam for a good view. The light fell across what appeared to be a large stone ship's prow. Violet gasped. He stiffened. He knew that pedestal. He had stood on the Daru Staircase in the Louvre, admiring the power and beauty of the marble figure above.

Violet's hand clenched on his wrist.

"He's going to steal the *Winged Victory*!"

23

"THE STATUE FROM THE LOUVRE?" Dahlia asked. "The headless one with the wings that's above the big staircase?"

Dauntless lay still, her crew waiting for the early-morning fog to dissipate before they began their ascent. Violet leaned on the rail, eyeing the rays of sunlight that cut through the mist. Eerie, but hopeful. The scene would make a wonderful backdrop to a painting. Maybe her next series could all be of airships and airfields. Assuming she ever caught her thief.

"Exactly," Violet replied. "Do you remember how it sits on a large stone pedestal made to look like the prow of a ship?"

"Yes."

"He's replicated the pedestal exactly. Cracks and all. It's sitting there in his room of stolen works, waiting for the statue."

"Wow. It would be something to steal that statue. I've seen it, and it's huge! I wonder if Walton has ever gone to the Louvre. We should take Fern there for our next outing. But maybe not until after this thief of yours has been caught. What are you going to do?"

"I don't know. Report him to the police, first of all."

Dahlia snorted. "The police who haven't done anything to help you?"

"Hence the 'first of all.' I can't leave it there, but I have no good ideas at the moment. As you can imagine, I didn't get much sleep last night."

Dahlia laughed and patted her daughter. "What's sleep?"

"Sorry. You must have it worse."

"No, truthfully, this job has been perfect. The strange hours and long periods of rest in between have worked so well for us. I'm forever indebted to Mr. Tagget for hiring me on."

"Top-notch navigators are hard to find, I understand."

Dahlia beamed. "Thanks. I should get to work. Back to Paris, I assume?"

"Yes, but no hurry. Wechsler can't make a move during daylight hours. We'll want to be back at the hotel by evening. Hopefully all of you can grab a few days off while we wait and watch."

"We're up for anything. This is exciting, helping you chase a famous criminal."

Vi shook her head. "I hate to spoil your fun, but I hope the excitement ends soon."

"Oh, that's okay." Dahlia waved a hand. "When you've finished, Tagget will fly you around the world and that will be plenty fun."

Violet nodded and faked a smile, not wanting to admit that she intended to leave the moment Wechsler was behind bars. She would miss Dahlia. She would miss all the crew, for that matter. Dauntless was as close to home as any place she'd lived in years.

Oh, hell, she would even miss Tagget, just for those times when he seemed to escape being an ass. Or maybe for those hidden depths that lurked behind his dappled green eyes.

"I should be heading below deck, myself," she said. "Tagget promised me a round of cards, and I can't pass up the chance to give him another drubbing." She'd uncover some of those depths today. Learning a secret or two from his unsavory past would ease her departure.

Dahlia chuckled. "Have fun!" She bounded off to take care of her business.

Violet headed below. The door to the cabin stood wide open, a rarity that suggested Tagget had expected her some time ago. He sat with his back to her, sliding cards around the table. Vi paused in the doorway to watch. The cards were all facedown, but he moved them with deliberate motions, sorting them into piles, and arranging each pile in order. She may have questioned his sanity, if not for the obvious solution—the cards were marked.

Damn him. He'd been cheating this entire time. All those questions she'd answered, the things she had confided—cheated out of her. Had he been stacking the deck, as well? She'd thought herself adept at catching such tricks, but she couldn't put it past him, and a marked deck couldn't account for all of her losses that day. Her cards had been terrible.

"You look bored."

He jumped. His tendency to forget the outside world amused her. She could lose herself in her art, but never to that extent. Being startled could cause her to ruin a brush or a canvas.

"A bit," he replied.

Violet hurried to the table, knocking a handful of cards to the floor before he could gather them up.

"Sorry! I got caught up telling Dahlia all about last night's adventure." She bent and scooped up the scattered cards, getting a good look at both sides.

"You like her."

"Very much."

"I'm glad. She's a sweet girl, and as good a navigator as I could ever want."

Violet set the cards facedown, giving herself another chance to scrutinize the pattern. The marking was subtle, but easy to pick up once she knew where to look. She placed her cards atop his pile.

"Do you want to deal first?" Vi had handled cheaters before. Tagget would be sorry he'd ever agreed to play her. She would make this hurt more than their first game, when he'd let her win all that money. She should have known then he was toying with her.

He pushed the cards toward her, his delectable mouth curling into a come-hither smirk. "After you, my blooming beauty. I wouldn't presume to give myself precedence over a lady."

Vi stared him down while her hands shuffled the deck. "I'm immune to your charms, Tagget."

His eyes glinted. "No, you're not."

"Perhaps I should say instead that I choose when to react to them."

"Would that I could say the same," he sighed. "Alas, I react to everything you do, whether I will it or no."

Melodramatic nonsense. Did the man possess a single sincere bone in his body? She tossed him his cards. It was past time for someone to wring a bit of truth from him.

Violet watched his eyes as he frowned at his hand, using the markings to plot her strategy. He held two trumps and an off-suit queen, a better hand than hers at the moment.

"Three cards," he requested.

Three? With only two poor cards? Curious. "I accept."

He discarded the higher trump and the queen, leaving himself only a single trump and whatever new cards he scooped up. Violet exchanged three cards of her own, struggling for an impassive expression. He was playing to lose. Why? To lull her into complacency? She had begun well in their previous outing, also.

When she won the first game, she started easy, with a topic already broached. "About those scars: did they beat you at the orphanage?"

"Not to my knowledge, but my memories of the time are

scant. What I recall is that I was a strange child, and they didn't know what to do with me."

"Of course you were a strange child. You're a strange man."

"I was bounced from one orphanage to another, then sent to a home for 'troubled boys.' That place terrified me, and I fled within days."

They began another game, where Vi again watched him toss out all his best cards. "Were you on the streets, then, after you fled?"

He flinched at the question. "God, no. The street boys carried knives and ran with rabid dogs. They were as terrifying as the tortured faces of the boys in the home. I hid in the factory."

A flood of new questions filled Violet's mind, but Tagget played the next several hands without cheating and eked out a victory. He leaned across the table, letting his fingers graze hers. Her eyes flicked to the bed before she could stop herself.

"Why do you still hold yourself back from me?" he asked.

The unexpected question caught her off guard, and it took Violet a moment to collect herself, bringing her focus back to his cheating. She set her jaw. "Because you're a selfish bastard."

A look of pain flashed across his features. "I try to be good to you."

"For your own selfish reasons."

"I like you!"

"Yes. So you think you can claim me as yours. You can't. I'm mine."

"I don't—"

"Enough. Back to the cards."

Evan leaned back in his chair. "Whatever you wish."

Violet blocked out everything but the game before her. He would expect to win, now, and it would take effort to counter his moves. With both of them cheating, tactics would be key.

Tagget surprised her by continuing to discard his good

cards. She won easily, then struggled to come up with a question while her mind puzzled over his strategy and motives.

"What was that factory you mentioned hiding in?"

"A machine manufactory. It built small machines for industrial and personal use."

Dammit, that told her nothing. She was ready to be done with this whole farce. One more game, and then she'd call him out for the cheat he was.

He discarded a king in the next hand. She tried misplaying, but he followed up with the same trick, giving her the point. Violet discarded her own good cards in the following hand, causing him noticeable frustration when he couldn't avoid taking three tricks. She pushed him all the way to four points before relenting and letting herself come back to win. His pinched lips and gritted teeth gave her much satisfaction. It was time for her question.

"Why are you cheating?"

"Why are *you*?" he snapped. "You should've had that game in five straight points."

"Answer the question."

"The whole point was to answer your questions."

Violet blinked, confused. "To what?"

"You want to know about me. I want to tell you. I can't do that if I'm winning."

"Wait." She rubbed her temple to fend off the headache that had been threatening since the game began. "You want to tell me about yourself?"

He spread his arms, palms turned upward, and leaned back in his chair. "Whatever you would like to know. Ask away."

"Then what are we doing with these cards?"

"You wanted to win the truth from me."

Her eyes squeezed briefly closed. "Goddammit, Tagget."

"You see? I'm trying to give you what you want."

"Fine." She leaned back, crossing her arms over her chest.

"Tell me everything. The factory, the scars, the filters. I want it all."

He grimaced. "I will summarize to start. The home for troubled boys sent its orphans to work for next to nothing in the factory across the street. Twelve hours a day got you two meals and a bed at night. Any given day, about half the boys were in the factory, the others were at the home for 'schooling.' It must have been awful, from the way they looked. They all preferred the factory, though every foreman we had cursed us and smacked us around. I found a hiding place under one of the biggest machines and lived there."

"You lived in the factory? For how long?"

"Five years."

"Five *years*?" she blurted. "How did you survive?"

His eyes locked on some distant point out past her. "When they realized I wasn't coming back to the orphanage, they stopped sending food for me. I had to sneak whatever I could get, or take the rotten bits the others didn't want. I stole old rags to use as blankets and took any clothes the bigger boys discarded. The meager pennies they paid us I hoarded."

Violet had imagined a home with proper food and shelter, marred by an angry schoolmaster who took a switch to sassy pupils. This went beyond anything she would have guessed, and she found herself grieving for the frightened, starving boy with the mottled green eyes.

"They beat you at the factory," she guessed.

Evan lifted one shoulder, then let it drop. "A slap or a smack here and there. I avoided it most of the time. It was easy to learn what set them off."

"Then how did you get the scars?"

One corner of his mouth quirked up. "I was a rat catcher."

Vi shuddered. "I hate those filthy, biting things."

"Not real rats. Cleaning rats."

Tagget rose from his chair and went to the closet, rummaging around for a few seconds before returning and placing a battered bit of machinery on the table. Six inches long, it resembled a blocky beetle, with legs jutting from the sides, and a wind-up key on the back. This one looked to be missing a leg, and the key was bent so far it could no longer be turned.

"This had little cloth pads on its nose and feet, originally," he explained. Again, his gaze drifted away, as if lost in the memories. "They were made to scurry under the machines and wipe up dirt, oil, and so forth. The design was poor, and the splayed legs and angled bodies meant they were stuck often. The small boys were rat catchers. We would crawl under the machines and pull them out. That's where the scars came from. Moving parts you couldn't see, or sharp edges poking down. Hands and arms took the brunt of it. A few boys lost fingers. Backs were protected somewhat by clothing, but not entirely."

"And that was your life? As a little child?"

"Yes."

"And you didn't flee?"

"To what? I told you, the street was worse. Half the boys that ran off turned up dead. The rest just vanished. I assume some survived to become pickpockets or the like."

Violet picked up the old cleaning rat, turning it over in her hands. "I'm so sorry. I can't even imagine how terrible it must have been."

"As you can see, I have survived and improved my lot in life."

Survived, perhaps, but not escaped. There was a hollowness to his voice, and a flicker of panic in his eyes that hadn't been there when the conversation had begun. She didn't need to ask about the nightmares.

"Do you keep this as a reminder?"

He shifted in his seat, and for a moment didn't answer. Violet had just opened her mouth to tell him he didn't need to tell her more, when he spoke.

"I keep it because it's mine. I freed it from under a machine where it must have been stuck for months. I was the only boy small enough to reach it. When I pulled it out, the foreman told me it was junk and to toss it in the scrap pile. I asked to keep it, and he shrugged. It was permission enough. I made a toy of it."

Vi ran a finger over the pitted metal shell. "Such a sad, broken little thing."

"I loved it." His voice was so harsh Violet set the cleaning rat down for fear of damaging it further. "It was my very own at a time when I had nothing."

Evan's green eyes were bright with pain. He quickly looked away. A moment later, he stretched out a single finger and gently tapped the bent key on the rat's back. To Violet's astonishment, the fragile little legs began to move, and the rat limped its way across the table.

"And as you can see, I fixed it," Tagget said, his voice still tighter than normal. His expression turned hard. "Then I designed a better one, which has since been imitated countless times and started me on the path to where I am today."

Vi felt tears prick at her eyes. The rat was not the most damaged thing in the room. Somehow, though, Evan had persevered, survived, pieced himself back together the way he did with his machines. He was scarred, but that only made him more remarkable, more beautiful.

He shoved himself away from the table and stood, taking the rat with him. "We are done here. What do you want for lunch? I'll tell Walton to make it."

"Anything is fine. Pick what you want."

"A cigarette and a bottle of cognac."

She sighed. "I'll have a sandwich."

"A wiser choice."

He stashed the rat in the closet and disappeared out the door.

"Walton!" he bellowed, "Miss Dayton requires a sandwich. Make it a good one. And why the hell hasn't this ship taken off yet? We had better be in Paris by dinner or I'll find myself a new dirigible crew!"

Violet put her head in her hands. That haughty, demanding temperament was his armor, and it had cost him something dear to remove it for her. She still thought his behavior selfishly motivated—he gave her what she wanted in order to keep her around—but the lengths he would go to staggered her. Maybe she'd been wrong. Maybe he wouldn't leave her for the next new thing. Because this wasn't a game anymore. He had allowed her to rip him apart and expose all his layers.

And what a picture it made. The armor on top, cold, hard, and arrogant. Then the charming layer: still arrogant, but deservedly proud of his intellect and accomplishments. This was the layer of many paramours, that loved opera and a good drink, and it twisted and tangled with the passionate layer beneath.

The true passions were rarely exposed, and Violet considered those the first layer of Evan the orphan boy, who lost himself in his work and craved a good cuddle. Under that came pain, fear, loneliness—a terrible mess that threatened to crack through at any moment.

Vi had battled enough of her own demons to know what a struggle it must be. He wouldn't let it defeat him, though. She had seen down to his fiery core, which was ablaze with strength and determination. He would do what had to be done. He would strip his soul bare just to win the woman he wanted.

And, damn him, it had worked. Her heart sang for his triumphs and wept for his sorrows. He was obnoxious and overbearing, gentle and generous, powerful, beautiful, and wounded. And she loved him for it.

A knock sounded on the door. "Your lunch, Miss Dayton?"

She went to retrieve her sandwich. "Thank you, Walton. I'm sorry about Tagget's shouting. I pushed him too hard, I think. I'm certain he doesn't mean to get rid of you all."

The chef chuckled. "I'm not worried. That man's too smart to let go of a good thing."

"Could you make him some lunch? He shouldn't go all day without eating."

"I'll make his favorite and tell him you were concerned for him. That should do the trick."

"Thank you."

"It's my pleasure, miss."

Violet returned to the table and nibbled at her food, willing the ship to rise faster, in the hopes the altitude would drive Evan back to the cabin. In a fit of optimism, she set out a glass and the bottle of cognac. By the time her plate held only crumbs, she was itching to go find him. She didn't need words, or even his touch. She simply wanted to be near him.

She poured herself a glass of the brandy and lifted it in a toast.

"To you, Evan Tagget, and to this fool heart in love with you."

She tipped her head back and drained the drink.

24

Evan lit another cigarette. Violet was right. He smoked when he was anxious. It never seemed to help, either. It was merely something to do.

He surveyed the assortment of wine bottles in front of him. He'd pulled them down from the racks and sorted them alphabetically by vineyard. Not the best idea, to set the wine sloshing about, and he'd have to wait several days for the sediment to resettle before drinking any, but it was better than smashing something.

Now he was resorting the bottles mathematically, adding up the digits in the vintage and subtracting the number of letters in the variety of grapes. Blends with unspecified ratios were giving him trouble.

"Ah, excellent. A 1900 Cabernet Sauvignon. Negative seven."

He placed the bottle in the top left corner of the rack. This was absurd, but it kept his mind occupied, and he needed some way to suppress the torment he had unleashed. He hadn't expected revisiting his past to cause so acute a reaction. After all, it was more than twenty years since he'd set foot in that godforsaken manufactory. Never speaking of it to anyone now felt like one of the most sensible decisions of his life.

The door opened behind him, and he spun to find Walton holding a sandwich.

"What's this?"

"Roast beef on rye with grilled onions and extra cheese. And a nice, fresh apple."

The sight of the oozing cheese made Evan's stomach rumble. Walton had grilled the sandwich to perfection and the apple had been scrubbed to a shine.

"Miss Dayton requested it for you," Walton explained. "She was greatly concerned you might miss lunch."

Of course she was concerned. She had a kind heart. He'd nearly cracked when she'd gazed so mournfully at Ratty. As if she wanted to hug the toy. As if she wanted to hug the boy Evan had once been.

"*Greatly* concerned, you say?" Evan asked. Maybe it was more than pity for a long-ago child. Maybe Violet cared about *him*, as he was now.

"Extremely. She had a little worried crinkle between her brows, and her eyes were big and round."

Evan could picture it. He frowned as he accepted the lunch. "Is she unhappy, do you think?"

"Oh, she'll be all right as soon as I tell her you're eating something. No need to rush off to check on her."

"Odd. It feels rather as if I'm being manipulated."

"Would I do that to you, boss?"

"At Violet's prompting? Of course. This entire crew would bend over backwards for her."

"We adore her, sir. My Dahlia hasn't had so great a friend in years."

"How long have you and Dahlia been acquainted?" Evan wondered. It was strange, how little he knew of the lives of his crew. He needed to talk with them more often.

"Oh, since we were kids. 'Bout five years, I guess it is now. I got a job on her uncle's airship where she was working. I hadn't known her more than two days before I wound up stealing her virtue."

"Knowing Dahlia, I question your definition of 'stealing.'"

Walton's cheeks reddened. "She's a generous girl. She told me I was 'the right man.' I hope she'll marry me someday, because I love her like crazy."

"This is her dream job, and she was prepared to turn it down—and risk never getting another offer—if you couldn't come along. I would say it's only a matter of time."

A boyish grin split Walton's face. "Thanks, Mr. Tagget. You want me to clean up these bottles, or do you prefer to do it?"

"I'm going to do it, and then we'll see which one of you can figure out my sorting system."

"Parker. Her brain works like yours."

Evan grimaced. "Poor girl."

Walton laughed. "I'll leave you to it, boss, and let your lady know you're eating lunch."

"Thank you."

Evan took a bite of the apple, chewing slowly, letting the sweet taste linger on his tongue, his spirits much improved. Violet was thinking about him. Violet cared about him. Stranger yet was that Walton, too, seemed to like him.

Bizarre. His lovers liked him for the pleasure and gifts. Those he flirted with liked him for the same momentary gratification he received from them—quick fun, soon forgotten. People didn't like him for other reasons. They respected him, hated him, envied him, and occasionally were in awe of him.

Why would Walton like him? For that matter, why did Violet like him? She never hesitated to express her annoyance with various aspects of his personality. The words "selfish bastard" still rang in his ears. He'd heard the phrase plenty of times. It had never stung before. It was a weight off his chest, knowing she liked him regardless.

Perhaps it was a combination of everything. She liked his

body, his dirigible, the good food, the new studio. She liked that he would exchange his secrets for hers. Her price was high, but he would keep paying it. He had begun to think he would go to any length to keep her around.

When he had finished both the lunch and the sorting, Evan climbed up out of the wine cellar and headed back to his cabin. Hearing voices, he paused at the door.

"You don't actually need as much luxene to power a car as people think," Parker was saying. "It's only a matter of reconfiguring the internals to distribute the power as needed. That and keeping the fuel free from any contamination. Luxene doesn't do well when it has gunk in it. I think Pure-Lux has it right; we should apply special filters to it to clear out all the impurities we can."

Evan didn't think he'd ever heard the engineer put half that many words together at one time. Violet's rapport with his crew was remarkable.

"That explains my difficulties with the ink," Violet replied.

"Ink?"

"Before I became a forger, while I was struggling to sell anything, I painted on the streets for coins, mixing colors from whatever materials I could find. A man saw me making a new pigment one day and said he had a job for me. A certain underworld figure whose name I won't disclose wanted a special ink made with luxene. I spent days mixing paints and inks until I found what worked. India ink, made fresh with lampblack and water, and no binders. The luxene must be mixed in while making the ink, not after. And I discovered a couple other little fun secrets during my experiments, too."

"Nifty!"

Evan agreed with Parker's assessment. It sounded fascinating. He wondered what ratio of ink to luxene was necessary, and what other tricks Violet had learned. He reached for the doorknob, ready to join in, then froze. She wouldn't want her conversation interrupted. He knocked.

"Come in," Violet called.

Evan entered. The stunned expression on her face was worth the absurdity of knocking on his own door.

"Evan! Are you well? Walton said you were eating?"

He greeted her with a grin. Her use of his first name betrayed the true depth of her concern.

"Yes, the food was excellent. Thank you for sending it down. I'm touched by your regard for me."

A hint of a blush colored her cheeks. "I'm sorry if I caused you pain earlier. It wasn't my intent."

Evan's muscles clenched. Sending him lunch was one thing, but he didn't need pity or coddling. He forced a chill into his voice. "I am entirely well, Miss Dayton. You can hardly think I could be brought low by a single conversation?"

"Certainly not." She didn't believe him. Her eyes were wide and sad, and her hands twitched toward him, as if she wanted to hug him. If she offered, Evan wasn't sure he'd be able to resist. He looked away.

Parker's face was alight with interest. Evan hadn't asked Violet to keep anything confidential. It would be interesting to see how much she shared with the crew. He expected she would seek out Harrison at the least, to get his perspective. If the whole crew began to give him those pitying looks... Evan shuddered.

"You ladies must excuse me," he said crisply. "I have a letter to write. Feel free to remain at the table and continue your conversation, unless you have need of privacy?"

"Actually, Parker intended to give me an overview of the workings of the ship. We got distracted with talk of dragons and luxene when Selene began to hoot. I think her controls need to be more intuitive."

"I will pass that along to the designers." He nodded to the ladies as they departed, then sat himself at the desk and took up a sheet of paper.

My dearest Eden,

I must apologize, my pristine paradise, for inundating you with so many lengthy missives. In truth, these past weeks have been among the most eventful of my life, and I cannot cover all the significant details in brief notes. Suffice it to say that my telegraph operators surely hate me more than you do.

Today, however, I do not intend to bore you with recountings of events, but rather to ask your advice. The question is a simple one: How does one go about making friends?

Don't laugh at my ignorance on the matter, I beg you. I expect it is something that most learn in the course of an ordinary childhood, a luxury I did not experience.

I consider you a friend, but our relationship came at your instigation—a grand gesture of forgiveness from your sweet heart and one I am still entirely unworthy of. I think Violet may be a friend as well, but our romantic liaison muddles the connection and makes it impossible to use as a basis for comparison. Also, I am entirely unsure how it came about.

Violet has befriended all my crew, and I believe they are excellent candidates for friendship, as I admire their intelligence, competence, and dedication. Should I be considering other qualities? How do I broach the topic with them? Any thoughts would be most appreciated.

Yours in bafflement,
Evan Tagget

・・・⚙・・・

Evan had recovered himself by the time Violet returned from her visit with Parker. Violet was glowing with happiness and flush with new knowledge.

"It will be invaluable when painting realistic renderings of machines," she gushed, those dark-amber eyes gleaming with happiness. "I'm plotting out a series of dirigible and airfield scenes that show the beauty not of the bright colors and decorations, but of the engineering itself. Part of a larger Paris collection, eventually."

"I look forward to seeing that." Elated by her enthusiasm for his own vocation, Evan retrieved an old notebook from the bottom shelf of his bookcase. "Here are some of my notes and designs, for your reference and reading pleasure. Any useful designs have been long since drawn up in proper schematics or given over to my employees for manufacture, so you may do with it as you please."

It happened that what she pleased was to take up her own pencil and sketch beautiful skins atop his diagrams. Evan watched, mesmerized, as simple machines became works of art in her hands. If Tagget Industries were to suffer some catastrophic collapse, he and Violet could make a fortune designing and selling magnificent, functional creations. Thibodeaux's carriage dragons would look drab by comparison.

"I could stare at you all day, my artistic genius," he murmured.

She set down the pencil and looked up, her cognac-colored eyes sparkling. "Oh, but I would be disappointed if all you did was stare."

Evan was in her arms in an instant. "I would never wish to disappoint you, my fruit." He pressed a kiss to the soft skin where neck met shoulder.

She made a murmur of appreciation. "Why 'fruit'? That's not a flower allusion."

"Do you think I would forget your name? You are my tender aubergine." He unbuttoned her dress, his lips following his fingers over each bit he exposed. "Though your taste is sweet honey, with a crisp edge and not the merest hint of bitter."

"Mmm. You taste like high-quality tobacco and well-aged liquor: smooth and strong, with a bite. To be savored, not gulped."

He pulled her toward the bed. "Come along, then, and savor me, my sweet. We have hours yet to Paris."

Hours that flew by, filled with passion, warmth, and laughter. They made love and cuddled among mounds of pillows. Violet spoke of her art, Evan of his machines, and they tossed about ideas for collaboration—most of them ridiculous, but neither cared in the least.

Too soon, a sinking sensation told Evan the dirigible had begun its descent into Paris. He cursed under his breath, wishing he had told the crew to take a long, circuitous route. The afternoon had been perfection and he didn't want it to end.

Seated at his desk, he idly jotted notes for several of the less silly ideas they'd come up with while he watched Violet draw. She had never looked more beautiful.

She lay on her belly on the bed, the tangled sheet having slid down her back to just cover her rump. Tendrils of dark hair had come loose from her coiffure, brushing her smooth cheeks and dangling across her shoulders. One long, lean arm propped her up, blocking much of her torso from view. He could see only a small curve of one shapely breast, but even that glimpse gave him an erotic thrill.

"Is the camera with your things?"

Her eyes flicked up at him, then back to her work. "It should be. Why?"

"I want a photograph of you. Exactly as you are now."

Her head came up, her brows arching. "For your own personal use, I hope? I wouldn't like to be sold to the highest bidder."

"If you think I would share you with anyone else, you don't know me very well."

A laugh danced in her eyes. "I think that if anyone tried to pass around copies of the photograph, you would hunt down and buy every one. You don't do things halfway. Go ahead, take your picture. But I expect the favor to be returned."

"You want to photograph me? Lounging naked on the bed? I shall look ridiculous."

"I agree. You only lounge in a large chair, with an expensive drink in your hand. Just sit there at your desk without your shirt. I'll catch you when you least expect it." She gave him a grin and returned to her drawing.

Evan took his time setting up the correct angle to capture her in the best possible lighting, still bristling from her criticism of the camera. When he was satisfied, he left it on the bed and picked up his pen, much of his distraction gone.

Violet teased him for a time, circling with the camera, threatening to snap a picture. Evan concentrated on the page, pushing away everything but her. She could still distract him with a word or a touch, but he found her silent closeness soothing, and soon her presence faded to a distant sense of rightness.

He didn't look up again until a knock sounded at the door.

"Hey, boss?" Walton called. "Do you want us to arrange transport to your hotel?"

Evan flipped open his watch. "Damn. It's near dinner already, and I suppose you're hungry?"

Violet grinned at him. She had dressed herself while he wasn't paying attention. "A bit, but I will be more hungry soon enough."

"I apologize for not giving you a good shot for your photograph. I got caught up in the work."

"As you do. Your apology is misplaced, however. I got an excellent picture. I can't wait to see it developed."

His brow furrowed. "I see."

She laughed and bent to kiss his cheek. "You're cute. Get dressed. It's time for dinner."

Cute? Good Lord. That was not a word anyone had ever applied to him. It made him giddy, and he couldn't decide whether that was a bad thing or a good thing. He hadn't even dropped off the letter to Eden yet, and he found himself wanting to write another one.

"Hell," he muttered.

"Stop cursing, Evan. We're going to a nice restaurant, not a tavern."

"Are you attempting to jump from mistress to nagging wife?"

"I'm not your mistress. I don't need you to put me up or buy me off."

"If that's how you care to define the term, I suppose."

"Call it what you will, but I am my own person, and I'm free to come and go whenever I please."

He nodded and let the conversation drop, but the ideas continued to swirl around his brain. A lover or mistress was always free to leave. If he wanted her forever, he would have to marry her.

Oddly, it didn't seem a bad idea.

25

Crevier grinned down at the stack of photographs. God, did Violet hate that smile. He looked like a dingo about to devour a wombat. Except that instead of simply eating the wombat, like most predators would, he was nipping and batting at it. Taunting it. He wanted his prey to be cowed and terrified before he pounced.

Vi met his mocking gaze with her best card-playing face. She was ready to be done with this. He had the information he needed to bring Wechsler down, but she would give him no further satisfaction.

"I will analyze these photographs, of course," the inspector said, the nasty smile unwavering. "But you must understand, Mademoiselle d'Aubergine, that such... dubious evidence as this may not be sufficient to apprehend so notorious a criminal. Naturally, I would not expect you to understand the complexities of the law enforcement profession."

Violet gave him a smile, imagining he *was* a dingo and preying on the family chickens. She'd shoot him.

"They must be complex, indeed, if such intellectual prowess as yours is necessary to understand them."

His eyes narrowed. She had to credit him with enough sense to feel her insult.

"Be warned, mademoiselle, that I also question how these photos came to be in your possession. It would be a shame if you were to be caught in further illegal activities."

The threat did nothing more than cement Violet's suspicion that he had no intent to let her walk free. The signed paper she had with her things would serve her about as well as a laundry receipt. So be it. She would stop Wechsler herself and use the notoriety as a weapon. No one would dare to imprison the woman who captured l'Exploiteur.

Unless Tagget received all the notoriety. She grimaced. It was a distinct possibility. He wouldn't do anything so callous as to push her aside and ignore her role in their work. He respected her abilities and he wanted to please her. But he was a known name, and a man. He would get all the credit. To the rest of the world, she would be his mistress and nothing more.

"Dammit," she cursed under her breath.

Crevier chuckled, thinking he'd won. "Thank you for the information, mademoiselle. You are free to go. For now."

Violet rose and departed without another word. Better to leave him feeling overconfident. She would finish the job and outmaneuver him, and it didn't matter that she had no concrete plan for doing either. She was an artist. She created. She would come up with something.

By the time she arrived at Tagget's hotel, that "something" had begun to take shape. She couldn't capture Wechsler without Tagget's money and resources, nor did she want to downplay his part. Being his mistress, his lover, or simply his business partner afforded her no protection. He would get the acclaim, and she would be irrelevant. Expendable. Replaceable. What she needed was to be the opposite. All at once, her method for eluding the police gelled in her mind.

"Good morning, Miss Dayton," the young man at the front desk greeted her. "Is there something I can do for you?"

"Yes, please. Do you have a pen and paper? I need to jot a letter."

"Of course." He retrieved the necessary supplies from behind the desk and handed them over with a shy smile. "I shall post it for you as soon as you are finished."

"Thank you. I'll be only a moment."

Violet found herself a secluded chair and penned a note to the queen of the unruly pet dragons, Mrs. Virginia Gaillard.

I wish to give you my sincerest thanks for your assistance as my fiancé and I work to track down this criminal. With your help, we have identified the culprit and have turned our attention to the task of arresting him and bringing him to justice. I am happy to tell you that I have seen your Daphne statuette with my own eyes. She is unharmed and I am certain she will be returned in pristine condition.

I would also like you to be the first to know that Evan and I will be hosting a gallery exhibition in the weeks ahead to showcase some of the beautiful works in his collection and to auction off a variety of art, both old and new. The highlight of the auction will be a recently rediscovered de Heem masterpiece we have located through our work with the Société. Be on the lookout for a formal invitation soon! Pets and dragons welcome on a leash.

(Also, please bid on the de Heem to drive the price up. Evan wants to gift it to me for our wedding, and he will feel especially generous if he must pay a grand price. The Société will thank you!)

Thank you again, and I look forward to seeing you soon.

Sincerely,
Violet Dayton

Violet reread the letter, folded and sealed it, and dropped it at the front desk. A nervous shiver ran down her spine as the dimpled boy at the desk took it from her. There would be no undoing her plans now. She had given no indication that her words were confidential, and she didn't think Mrs. Gaillard the sort to keep breaking news to herself.

This wasn't precisely how she'd imagined her dream unfolding. Everything would be done in a rush, and she would have to borrow money from Tagget—she would never let him or anyone else pay for this outright—because he hadn't yet purchased the de Heem. The short notice might make it difficult to include all the artists she'd meant to invite.

She would make it spectacular, though, whatever it took. This art show needed to be the talk of the town. No longer would they see her as a mistress or hanger-on. She would be notable in her own right. A worthy partner. Someone a man like Tagget might actually unite himself with.

Putting on a show of that magnitude would take constant work, and every connection Violet had in the art world. It would also require admitting to Tagget that she'd given up his Vérité to the auction and—worse—that she'd flaunted the false relationship they'd used as a cover story. Chances were he'd forgotten all about it. Cold fear gripped her heart. He might never forgive her.

No. He was a rational man, as much as any human could be. He would see the sense in her ruse. She would promise to break the engagement once she was safely free from the Paris authorities and had established herself elsewhere. London still seemed promising. Tagget could then claim a broken heart and garner the sympathies of the entire city. He wouldn't be lonely for long.

Violet gritted her teeth. There was the flaw in her otherwise excellent plan. What good was a promise she couldn't keep? The thought of him with anyone else lit a possessive fire inside her. She cherished him, flaws and pain and all. No casual liaison could match that.

The fire twisted into pain. She doubted he could return her feelings, now or ever.

"Not helpful, Vi," she admonished, but the best she

could manage was to tamp her worries down to a simmering irritation. The truth was, she would rather suffer his anger than lose his interest.

The future could sort itself out later. No promises would be needed if she failed step one of the plan. It was time she headed upstairs and tried out the dresses that had been delivered from Madame Rochette. Today had one purpose: make the world believe Evan Tagget was head-over-heels in love with her.

. . . ~~~ . . .

"You look ravishing, flower of my heart." Evan gently extricated the emerald necklace from Violet's fingers and fastened it around her neck. Already she wore the matching earrings he'd purchased to accompany her new clothing. "What's the occasion?"

"You are."

Evan froze, his fingers hovering above her skin. What had gotten into her lately? Ever since he'd told her about his past, she'd been sweet as honey. She hadn't lost her biting wit, but it was always playful, never harsh. It was almost as if she loved…

No. He wouldn't even think it. That way lay madness.

She wanted to soothe him, that was all. Her interrogations had hurt him, however unintentionally, and she was making it up to him. Underneath her stalwart exterior beat a gentle heart.

He let his hand fall to her shoulder, stroking the lush velvet of her dress. "Me?" he asked.

"Not you, yourself, though you are the cause. You have bought me these incredible dresses, and I want to make use of them. Therefore, we are going out. We will spend the afternoon about town, and this evening we will go to a show. Is there another opera playing, do you think?"

"There will be a performance of some variety, I'm sure. My box is always available. If you would like to go, we shall do so, even if the entertainment is subpar."

"Subpar? Evan, you are a snob. Most people would jump

at the chance to attend any event at all at the opera house." The corners of her mouth turned down, and a faraway look filled her eyes. "Your box can hold up to eight, yes? Could we invite your crew? They deserve a night on the town. Oh." The faraway look faded into disappointment. "I suppose it isn't proper decorum to mingle with employees."

"Darling, if you wish to bring along your friends, we shall do so. It makes no difference to me if people will talk."

A wide smile made her whole face glow. "I suppose you aren't the sort to care, are you?"

"The opinion of others is irrelevant. I'm concerned about your happiness and mine. Invite the crew. Invite them to dinner, even. I will pay to have Dauntless guarded while they are out."

"They will need appropriate clothing, I would think."

"I'll pay for that, too. They've earned a hefty bonus for all our strange travels of late." He stepped away from her. "Now, speaking of clothing, show me this incredible dress you have donned."

Violet turned a full circle to allow him to take her in. She shone like a jewel. A skirt of luminous blue silk fell just past her knees. It was gathered in the back in an elegant nod to the bustle fashions of his youth. Her tall boots left two scandalous inches of bare leg showing beneath her skirt. The velvet bodice was done in a darker blue—a crisp, military cut jacket with ornate buttons and a sharp v-neck that ended just between her breasts. It drew attention there but revealed nothing. The outfit was pure Violet: sexy, smart, unique, and bold. Some would gasp. Some would sneer. She would stand tall and proud.

God, did he love her.

Damn it all, there was that word again. The one he'd sworn not to think about since making a mess of things with Eden. He was out of his head over a woman again, and this time it was worse. Unless, perhaps, it could turn out better?

"Evan?"

He blinked.

"You have an odd look on your face. I can't tell if you love it or hate it."

Love. Again. He needed to get far, far away from that word. He gave Violet his best flirtatious smile.

"Its perfection can only be outdone by the wearer."

She rolled her eyes, but they glittered with merriment. "You haven't even seen the best part. It transforms for the evening."

"Show me."

"Oh, no. It's not evening yet. We have an entire afternoon for a peaceful, romantic stroll about town. Only then do you get to see."

"You are a very commanding sort of woman. I don't know why I put up with you," he teased.

Violet's smile was radiant. "What you mean is, I have excellent leadership skills and you have the utmost respect for my decision-making."

Evan considered her words a moment, nodding at the truth in them. "There is no one I respect more." He offered his arm. "Come. We must send out messages if we intend to bring the others to the theater tonight."

"You are a very commanding sort of man." Her eyes sparkled with mischief.

"Yet you put up with me."

"For now."

She was laughing, but the words made his blood run cold. He couldn't lose this woman. It would wreck him.

He would do anything to keep her. He would give her the world. The trouble was, she didn't want him to give her the world, and he had yet to grasp what she did want.

"Are you coming?" she asked. "I swear, you're so distracted today. Do you have a new invention bouncing around in your head? Bring your notebook. We can sit by the river and you can write it down while I sketch."

He had no invention, but it made a convenient excuse. "You will have to beautify it."

"Naturally."

Evan snagged the camera and his smallest toolbox on the way out the door. They made their calls, sent their telegrams, and spent a lazy afternoon picnicking, walking, and creating.

Violet was creating, at least. Evan did no more than disassemble the camera and draw all the parts. The truth was, he wasn't much of an inventor. He was a re-inventor. He rarely had a brand new idea, but he excelled at looking at things and deciding how to improve them.

She was right about the camera, of course. Corners had been cut to make it small and simple, but adjustments could be made. Affordable didn't have to mean shoddy. They would advertise the improved quality of version two. Violet could help with the exterior. Maybe they could have multiple colors and shapes. The camera could become a fashion accessory.

"Do you want to join the business?"

She looked up from the window of the sweets shop she had plastered her face to. "Pardon?"

"Are you hungry, or do you just want me to buy you an expensive treat?"

"Yes, and yes," she laughed. "What were you asking? About business?"

"Do you want to join my company?" Evan asked. "I will pay you to add your touch to the designs."

She shook her head. "I don't want to be your employee. I'm certain you can find another artist to fancify your machines."

"If you prefer, you can become a partner and take a share of the profits."

Her head shook once more. Evan was baffled. She didn't want a steady job with good pay? Or, God forbid, did she merely desire to be away from him?

"What *do* you want?"

"Freedom," she answered immediately. "To be myself. To create my art. To not have to answer to anyone else."

"I can hardly imagine you answering to someone else."

Her eyes grew hard. "When you need to pay rent and buy food, sometimes you settle for doing as you're told."

Evan took her hand, letting his fingers entwine with hers. This, he understood. "And sometimes you plot day and night how you will escape that trap so no one will ever again tell you what to do. What sort of a sweet do you want? I'm not certain I have ever seen such a variety."

"Chocolates. A big box. Dinner is soon, and I want to share with everyone after we eat."

Evan bought a dozen chocolates, making two for everyone but himself. Violet would certainly scold him for not eating any, but since he liked her fussing more than sweets, he considered it an excellent deal.

His entire crew awaited them outside the hotel, decked out as he had never seen them. Harrison looked utterly devastating in a suit. Walton, too, looked fine, but as a fidgety man he couldn't match the pilot's calm style. He pleased Dahlia, though, which was all he wanted.

"Doesn't Walton look smashing tonight?" she enthused. "I picked out his suit. The pocket square matches my dress. Do you like it?"

The baby giggled and clapped as Dahlia twirled. She was pink, frilly, and adorable. Evan couldn't help but smile at her. "A lovelier navigator I have never seen. But then, you need only be a tenth as pretty as you are competent, to be considered a raving beauty."

She blushed. Walton scowled.

"Why can't I ever say stuff like that?" he mumbled.

Harrison gave him a reassuring pat.

Dahlia soothed her man with a kiss and Evan turned to his engineers. They looked about as un-engineer-like as he could have imagined. Parker's flowing green dress hugged curves he'd never noticed beneath her work clothes, and Flynne was a dandy in black and white with a tall top hat. He would have a lady or two by night's end, Evan was certain, hanging on his arms and telling him how cute his dragon was. Good. The boy needed a good tumble.

"You all look fabulous," Violet said, her broad grin bringing a glow to her perfect cheekbones. "I'm so happy you could join us tonight. I need to change into my evening gown now, to match."

She unhooked something at the back of her skirt, and it unbunched and flowed downward to create an elegant swoop that just brushed the ground at her heels. A quick unbuttoning and she tossed the velvet coat at Evan, leaving him staring at a bodice that clung like a second skin. Madame Rochette was a magician with a needle. He wanted to run his hands over that luscious, blue silk. He longed to kiss it, teasing the flesh beneath before he peeled the dress away with agonizing slowness. He wanted Violet aching for him the way his unruly cock was aching now. Dammit, he needed looser trousers.

"Wow," Parker blurted. "I want a gown like that, one day. It looks like you were poured into it."

Violet chuckled. "It is a little tight, isn't it?"

"No. It's perfect."

"We'll plan another outing someday with enough time to order everyone clothes made to their own measurements," Evan declared.

Flynne whistled. "My family isn't going to believe Mr. Tagget buys us fancy clothes and takes us to the theater as a bonus."

"Mite does as he pleases," Harrison said with a grin. "And I think there is some of Miss Dayton's influence in this plan."

"Violet gets all the credit," Evan replied. "I merely supplied the funds. Shall we go in to dinner? You've all earned a grand meal, as far as I'm concerned."

Violet took his arm and leaned into him. "You like the dress, I see."

"Is it that obvious?"

"Yes."

He cringed.

"Don't worry. No one else is looking."

"No. They're all looking at you."

She dropped a quick kiss on his cheek. "I promise I'll help you with your 'difficulty' later this evening."

"I might not make it to later. You're killing me."

Her laughter was music. "You have something of a dramatist in you, Evan Tagget. You could have made a living treading the boards."

"I would have gotten distracted by the trap doors and the machines that change scenery and do other stage tricks."

"Perhaps. But I like to imagine us as moving in the same circles."

His brow furrowed. "We move in the same circles now. I don't follow your reasoning."

Violet's smile turned sad. "I don't fit in this world of yours."

If he needed a demonstration of her words, he got it over dinner. Their motley crew looked the part, but they couldn't hide their wonder at the high-class surroundings. They looked around with wide eyes and exclamations of awe. They puzzled over the complex table settings and held eager discussions over various points of manners. Most of them spoke little French. Walton knew all the food words, but couldn't read more than half of them. Parker, with her ultra-quick mind, was left to do most of the translating.

Evan could have stepped in and done all the talking for them, but he found it rather enjoyable to see how they worked together to read their menus and order dinner. It wasn't until he heard a neighboring table mocking Parker's lisp that he realized his earlier words to Violet were a lie. He did care if people talked. He just didn't care if people talked about him.

He hopped up from his seat and addressed the man who looked to be the instigator of the taunting. "If you utter one more insult directed at my companions, I will have you thrown out of my hotel and have your name published in the papers as an unwelcome guest."

The man blanched. Evan felt a great satisfaction watching the group hurry to finish their meal and leave, but his own table had lost much of its joy, and the remainder of the dinner was conducted in a subdued fashion. He wouldn't go back on his word to Violet, but he braced himself for disaster at the opera house.

26

Evan was her shining star. He always carried himself well in public, but Violet had never seen him so smooth, so far above each raised eyebrow and pointed cough. He introduced his crew to his upper-class acquaintances with as much dignity as he might have afforded the queen. More, probably, with him being an American. Veiled insults rolled over him like oil on water. Nothing could touch him.

"What's this, Tagget?" laughed a man whom Violet recalled meeting during her previous visit. "Have you brought your domestic staff to the opera?" He eyed Violet's dress. "I'd be happy to employ *her* services when she's finished with you."

"Do you not remember me, Monsieur Lafosse?" Violet asked, mimicking Tagget's unflappable armor. "We met recently at a showing of *Carmen*. I believe Evan introduced me and explained how we are collaborating on behalf of the Société des Arts."

Lafosse looked startled for a moment, then gave her a feral smile. "Ah, yes. His *associate*." He turned to Tagget. "I will, naturally, give you a discount on your next order as payment for borrowing your whore."

A large presence appeared on either side of Violet—Harrison and Walton. The rest of the crew flanked Evan, ready to fight beside him, or possibly hold him back if he went for Lafosse's throat. Violet thanked God he hadn't brought the sword cane. His eyes, ablaze with fury, swept the crowded corridor, and a deadly smile played across his face.

"Evan," she murmured softly.

"Merely business this time, darling." He raised his voice loud enough for dozens to hear as he addressed Lafosse. "There will be no next order. As of this moment, our arrangement is severed." Tagget turned away. "Monsieur Berthier," he called, "where does your company purchase its springs? I'm in the market for a new supplier. And I don't believe you have met my guests. Please, allow me to introduce them."

Whispers ran through the crowd, carrying the gossip to all corners of the opera house. Evan Tagget would consort with whomever he pleased. Anyone objecting would lose his business.

"Have you worked with Lafosse for long?" Vi whispered.

Evan's voice carried across the hall. "Fifteen years. I bought supplies from his New York factory back when I was still on my own. He was my first connection here in Paris."

A fifteen-year-old association, dissolved in an instant on her behalf. Violet's plan for the day had taken a strange turn when she had impulsively invited the crew, yet she had achieved her desired outcome and more. No one would think her expendable or doubt the rumor of their engagement.

A wave of guilt made her stomach flip flop. Maybe she could appear indispensable without a false relationship. Maybe the letter to Mrs. Gaillard hadn't been necessary. She'd done it, though, and she ought to have told him of her plan. Today had been busy with preparations for the evening, and she'd never quite found the moment she needed to bring up the matter. Or maybe she simply feared his wrath. People weren't likely to believe him madly in love if he was furiously angry with her. Tomorrow she would explain everything.

Her worries were forgotten once they stepped into the

box. The show was delightful, and the happiness of her friends even more so. She sat hand-in-hand with Evan, unconcerned with the opera glasses that would be trained on them. She didn't even scan the crowd herself, leaving the opera glasses to Flynne. He spent most of the performance flirting with a girl in the balcony who had a mechanical bird perched on her shoulder, casting bashful smiles across the theater as they showed one another their dragons.

They would do this again, Violet decided, as the party gave the performers an enthusiastic applause. It didn't have to be the opera, either. They could attend any theatrical performance, stroll through a park, or go out dancing. Drinks at a bar would be fun, and she would love to see Tagget squirm at the idea of such lowbrow entertainment. She grinned at him when she took his arm to wend their way to the exit.

"You have a devilish smile, my vibrant petal. What are you plotting?"

"Something you will hate."

His eyes sparkled. "Perhaps. You should know by now, though, that I'm more resilient than I appear."

"Miss Dayton!" The feminine cry sliced through the crowd. "Miss Dayton, I'm so pleased to see you!"

Virginia Gaillard rushed to Violet's side, dragging a sausage-shaped, dog-like dragon behind her. Her husband hovered nearby, looking far more interested in his glass of wine than in socializing.

"Mrs. Gaillard." Violet gave her a polite nod. "A pleasure."

"This is Percy, one of our guard dragons." She tugged on the leash to prevent the creature from wandering aimlessly. Vi could see why the guard dragons hadn't deterred l'Exploiteur.

"Anyway, I received your letter," Mrs. Gaillard continued. "I'm terribly excited about this art show of yours. I do love events, and the unveiling of a masterpiece will bring so many people. I trust it will be a tremendous success."

"I certainly hope so." Vi didn't glance at Tagget, but she was certain his dark eyebrows were raised.

"And, of course, we are eagerly awaiting the capture of your thief. How dreadfully dangerous!" Mrs. Gaillard sounded thrilled. "Are things well with you? You must be so busy. How goes the planning?"

"Oh, well, we know where he plans to strike next," Violet said. "We will do what we can to catch him in the act, but—"

"No, silly, the planning for your wedding!"

At least a dozen heads turned in their direction. Parker gasped aloud, and Walton muttered a barely audible, "Damn."

"Really?" Dahlia squealed. "When did that happen?"

Evan had gone stiff as a board. Violet tried not to wince. She hadn't expected the "news" to go public quite so rapidly.

"Will it be a huge gathering, or private to the family?" Virginia Gaillard asked. "Armand and I had only three hundred guests, but we don't have as much money as your Mr. Tagget. Have you chosen a dress? I don't know what the fashion is in trains anymore. Mine was exactly seven feet, but things change so much in eighteen months, don't you think?"

Vi forced a smile. "Er, yes, I'm sure they do."

"Well, I must be getting home. Armand has a terribly busy schedule and must rise early in the morning. I will leave you to your friends and your fiancé, but I will certainly write to you, and you must continue to write me as well. I am dying to hear about your art exhibition and Mr. Tagget's extravagant wedding gifts and everything! Ta!" She seized her husband's arm and dragged him off, yanking the dragon along.

"Darling." Tagget's hand settled on Violet's waist, drawing her close. His hot breath caressed her ear. "I think you and I need to talk."

27

The new door to Tagget's hotel suite slid closed with a gentle hiss. Violet braced herself for harsh words, but none came. Evan wandered into the bedroom with the same casual ease he'd exhibited all night, unknotting his necktie as he walked.

"Well. I would term the evening a success, despite a few small difficulties, wouldn't you?" He pulled open the closet and hung the tie on a rack with a dozen similar neckcloths.

Violet sat at the dressing table and reached to unfasten her necklace, her fingers struggling to remove it while her attention was focused on watching him in the mirror. When was he going to snap? He had to be fuming beneath his chilly exterior. When would he drop the act and shout at her?

"I think your crew enjoyed their night out," she replied, shivering a bit at her own unnatural calm.

"Or are still enjoying it, perhaps." His waistcoat went into the closet, and the shirt into a basket of things that needed laundering.

Violet nodded, turning her eyes away from the distraction of his bare chest. Their party had split up outside the opera house, with Harrison escorting Parker back to the ship, Walton and Dahlia taking their baby for a stroll, and Flynne chasing after the girl with the bird-dragon.

Tagget had hardly spoken except to bid them all good night. He'd been a perfect gentleman, and as unflappable as he'd been all evening. It couldn't last. Not now that they were alone. He would demand answers. His inquisitive mind had to be pondering, analyzing, longing to learn what she had done and why. Yet he said nothing.

The necklace clasp at last came undone, and Violet dropped the emerald into her jewelry box, along with the new matching earrings. Out of habit, she hid them under a few pieces of junk. They were her emergency fund. She needed to hold that exhibition, and catch Wechsler once and for all. If Evan became so furious he severed their connection, she would need the gems to cover costs.

Her stomach lurched at the thought. No. It wouldn't come to that. It couldn't.

Dammit, why didn't he just shout at her? Get it over with? They could scream and throw his dozens of pillows at one another and have it out.

And then get on with their mission.

Vi pulled the hair sticks from her bun, shook her hair loose, and began to brush it out.

"Did you enjoy our evening?" she inquired, continuing the absurdly mundane conversation.

"For the most part."

Tagget crossed the room toward her. This was it. He would qualify that statement with a "but" and proceed to tell her exactly what he thought of her manipulations.

He didn't. He paused directly behind her, fingers skimming along her back. She could sense no tension in his body, no indication of anger at her deception.

"Would you like some assistance with your buttons?"

His words weren't seductive, but matter-of-fact. Violet's lips parted, but no reply would form. She was mystified, unnerved by his unnatural calm. A shiver raced down her spine.

"Are you chilled, my sweet flower? Shall I fetch your dressing gown, or do you prefer to retire to bed and let me warm you?" Again, the lack of passion in his voice sent an icy tremble through her. What had she done?

"I'm not cold."

"Excited, then?"

His fingers moved down her dress with speed and precision, and none of his usual leisure. Vi missed the tiny strokes of his fingertips over her skin and the kisses that usually followed. A bitter realization settled in her gut. This was how it felt to truly be Evan Tagget's mistress. Tonight their relationship lacked the fire she had thought unquenchable. He had become businesslike. Passionless. This was why Dahlia found him boring, and why others termed him cold.

"No," Violet blurted. She sprang from her seat and moved away from him, clutching her unfastened gown to her chest like a shy miss.

Tagget didn't come after her or say anything. He just stood there, waiting. He had been waiting all evening, she realized. For an apology, an explanation, anything from her. She'd been so braced to defend herself against his accusations she had never even thought to speak first.

Those deep, green eyes locked with hers, traitorously confessing everything his body language concealed. His passion was as intense as ever. She could see it simmering in his sorrowful gaze.

Sorrowful. Not angry. Her stomach, already churning, twisted into yet another knot.

"Evan…"

What could she say? "I'm sorry" seemed so trite, true though it was. She had expected him to be annoyed by her plan, even angry, but not hurt. If she had known, she would have found another way. Now it was too late.

His shield cracked, the sadness spreading from his eyes to the rest of his face.

"Why?" he asked. "What was your purpose in devising such a deception? To entrap me into marriage and make off with my money? To set up some sort of public humiliation?" He raked all ten fingers through his hair. Standing there, shirtless and tousled, he ought to have been alluring. Instead, he only looked vulnerable. "No. That's not you. I can't believe it of you."

His pleading expression pierced her heart, and she felt a hot rush of shame for scheming behind his back. "It was unintentional," Vi explained, channeling her emotions into a new determination to set things right. "I made a plan without consulting you. I'm sorry. I did mean to explain it all when I had the time, and I hadn't expected any of it would go public so quickly. I would never force you into anything, or want to humiliate you in any way." She clutched her dress tighter, afraid if it slipped in the slightest he might take it as an attempt to distract him.

"Why, then? What purpose could such a ruse possibly serve other than to cause me trouble?" He huffed a mirthless laugh. "Though I suppose I likely deserve whatever trouble you choose to heap upon me."

"No. You don't. The plan was meant for me, not you. Crevier isn't going to let me go. I need an escape, and being your lover isn't good enough. But an engagement—a false engagement—will protect me. Who would dare throw Evan Tagget's bride in jail?"

His jaw dropped. "You think I wouldn't protect you? You think I would allow that maggot to get his filthy hands on you for even an instant? Did I not just dissolve a multi-million dollar contract over an insult to your person?"

Vi turned away. "I protect myself. It's what I've always done. You should understand. You do the same."

Except he hadn't been doing that. He'd been opening up more and more, while she'd been holding back as much as ever. But she had to guard her heart. Wanting her wasn't the same as loving her. The ultimate fate of any mistress was to be discarded and forgotten, the way her father had done to her mother. She couldn't—wouldn't—let the same happen to her.

Tagget's arms encircled her waist. Soft lips pressed against her bare shoulder. "You no longer need to protect yourself. You will never lack for anything. I will let no harm come to you. I swear it."

The ice had left his voice. It was warm now. Seductive. She twisted around in his arms. She hadn't lost him. All he'd needed was to understand what she'd done and why.

Violet placed one hand on his chest. "Evan, I don't need you to protect me. That's not what I want."

His grip tightened. "Then what *do* you want? Tell me. Whatever it is, I'll get it for you. Anything." His voice trembled with emotion.

She relaxed into his arms, her fingers unclenching. Her dress slithered to the floor.

"I want this," she murmured, winding her arms around his neck. "The real you. The man full of passion. The boy who likes to cuddle. That's all I want."

Calloused hands slithered up and down her spine. "There must be something. Tell me. What can I give you?"

"Nothing. I need nothing."

His mouth found that spot on her neck that never failed to make her tremble. "Very well. Since you will not tell me, I will settle for giving you a night filled with sensual pleasure." He drew back to look into her eyes. "I will tease you and torment you until I hear you moan my name and feel you convulse around me, carried away in a flood of bliss."

The flecks in his eyes grew darker as his searing gaze traversed her body. Violet's own body warmed in response. As delicious as that sounded, she had a better idea. Tonight *she* would torment *him*. She would feast on him with hands and lips until he was the one moaning and pleading for release.

When he leaned in to kiss her, she allowed him no more than a nibble. She wouldn't rush this.

"Slowly," she murmured. "I'm savoring." She stroked his face with the back of her hand, from earlobe to jaw, then back again. "You have a few gray hairs, right here at your left temple."

"I know."

"My fault? Am I causing you to age prematurely?"

Evan laughed. Vi loved the sound of his genuine laughs. They were all too rare, she feared. "No. They've been there for years. I don't pluck them because I need to look old enough to be respectable."

She began to kiss the same path her hand had traveled, creeping toward his mouth. "You will never be respectable."

He turned just enough to bring their lips together. "And you like me that way."

I love you that way.

She kissed him hard and pushed him toward the bed, her hands running down his back to cup his buttocks.

"You have a nice arse, Evan Tagget."

"So I've been told." Nimble fingers found the ties of her frilly, pale blue drawers. "I'm a fan of yours, as well, but I prefer it bare."

Violet nudged his hands away. "You first."

He stepped back, regarding her with raised eyebrows. "You want an eyeful today, my blossom? I'll be certain to leave the lights on."

He stripped off his trousers, peeling each leg away with a languor that defied his obvious desire, his eyes never leaving hers. His tongue snaked out to wet his lips as he worked the knot on his drawers.

Violet's skin burned. Her face flushed. Could a string possibly unwind any slower? Wet heat dampened her underthings. The man was driving her wild. But this was about him, not her, and Vi was determined he would get as good as he gave.

She backed toward the bed, discarding her own

undergarments the moment his hit the floor. Two quick strides and he was at her side, arms around her, mouth seeking hers.

She kissed him just how he liked, holding nothing back—a slow exploration to begin, then hungrier, urging him deeper, opening herself as she took all she wanted of him. His low groan of pleasure sent a quiver straight to her belly.

Without a word they separated and clambered onto the bed, coming together again an instant later, arms and legs entwining. Tagget climbed atop her, pressing a kiss between her breasts, his hands roaming eagerly. Violet wrapped her arms around him and rolled them both over.

He frowned up at her, brows knitting together in a puzzled expression. She straddled him and kissed his chest, just as he had done to her.

"Violet?"

"Relax. Let me please you."

"Pleasing you pleases me." His hands squeezed her rear. "Yours is better than nice. Resplendent." One hand slipped between her legs. Even beneath her, he couldn't relinquish control.

"Evan."

He paused at her sharp tone.

"You don't always have to be in charge," she said softly.

"Yes, I do."

With gentle fingers, Vi grasped his wrists and eased his arms away from her. "You don't. Give in to it. Let go."

He stared up at her, eyes wide, and shook his head. "Impossible."

She kissed him, softly, lovingly.

"You asked what you could give me. Give me this. Trust me."

28

TRUST ME.

The words hung in the air, as seductive an offer as Evan had ever heard. Lord, did he want to. He wanted to believe her every word, to lose himself in her eyes and let her sweep him away with her touch.

A lifetime of experience screamed that he couldn't. He trusted no one but himself. People were undependable. They could always be bought for the right price. They were irrational, self-serving, horrible. *He* was horrible.

Violet, though. Violet was kind and optimistic. She smiled and laughed and had friends she cared for and defended. She was as good a person as he'd ever met, but even she knew better than to rely on others. The walls she'd built to protect herself were proof enough of that.

Her mouth moved over his, coaxing, but not teasing, the sweetest thing he had ever tasted. Her warm hands moved in slow, comforting strokes.

"Trust me, Evan," she whispered.

"How can I, when you don't trust me?"

Her head came up, but her fingers continued their dreamy caresses.

"You didn't trust me with your plans," he pointed out. "You won't come to me for help."

Her mouth scrunched into a worried frown, and her body tensed. "You're right. It's hard. I'm accustomed to being always on my own."

"I know."

Her clear, brown eyes grew hard, shining with inner strength. His unbreakable flower. Winter might crush her beneath ice and snow, but she would bloom every spring without fail.

She took a deep breath. "What can I do for you, to show my faith in you?"

A bargain? Evan could handle that. Give a little to get a little. "Let me protect you. Let me go after Crevier."

Violet shook her head, then sighed. "Fine. Do it. Get rid of him." She kissed him once more. "And now you must believe me when I say nothing I do is meant to hurt you. The opposite is true. I want to make you happy. Let me."

Evan answered with a single nod. He squeezed his eyes closed and tried to think of nothing but her touch. He never let lovers do this. He told them what to do, or directed their attentions without words. They touched him where and when he wanted.

Not knowing what Violet intended was terrifying, and Evan wasn't the sort to be aroused by danger. She could hurt him without meaning to. He adored her vigorous kisses, but some men liked it rougher still.

His eyes flew open. "Don't strike me," he gasped.

She brushed his wayward forelock back into place. "Never. I promise. Nothing unusual unless you ask for it." Her lips grazed his brow, then his mouth, before moving lower.

Violet chuckled against his chest. "Not that you would ever ask. For a notorious rake, you are adorably conventional. We've never even done it anywhere but the bed!"

"The bed is comfortable. Where else would you want do it?"

She twined her fingers through the hairs on his chest, grinning up at him. "We'll get there. One step at a time." Her tongue flicked at a small, flat nipple.

"Mmm."

"Like that, do you?"

"Yes. You might try—"

"Hush." One hand drifted down between his legs. "Only pleasurable noises allowed. 'Yes,' 'please,' 'more,' and various obscenities also encouraged. Or 'stop,' if I do anything you don't like."

Her long fingers curled around his cock, squeezing and stroking while her mouth inched ever lower. God, did he hope she would suck him off. It took all Evan's willpower not to tell her to do just that.

She took her time about it, her wicked, teasing tongue licking the salt from his skin and tickling his inner thigh until he clutched at the sheets and begged.

"God, Violet, please."

Her hot, wet mouth closed around him. She was perfection. Eager, hungry, and mischievous. Teasing and tormenting. Evan arched into her. He longed to tell her exactly what to do. He yearned to bury his hands in her hair and position her just right. Instead he held still and let her explore. Her technique may have been imperfect, but her enthusiasm and desire to please were unparalleled. It was heavenly.

"Fuck, that's good," he moaned, testing her obscenity tolerance.

She paused long enough to smile up at him with flushed cheeks, then redoubled her efforts, carrying him to the brink. Somewhere along the way he forgot about his lack of control and succumbed to the exquisite feel of her. When she stopped, he was too enthralled to do anything but gasp her name.

A moment later she was astride him, sliding down atop him until he was buried to the hilt.

Yes. More. All of you.

She began to slide up and down atop him. Evan thrust in time to her movements, reveling in the expression of pleasure she wore.

Take me. Make me yours.

"Touch me," she sighed. She guided his hand to her breast. "Here." His opposite hand she pulled between her legs. "And here."

His greedy hands stroked her everywhere she desired, even as his head swam from the ecstasy of their joined bodies. Lost in her, he tumbled among the waves of passion until they hit the crest and crashed together. Violet crumpled against him, breathing hard. Evan could feel the filters vibrate in his chest with each heaving breath of his own.

He pressed his lips to her cheek. "You are transcendent, my Violet."

In response, she nuzzled his neck and squirmed against his side until they were nestled together like a pair of spoons. Her breath tickled the back of his neck and her arms curved protectively around him. She stroked a finger across one of his scars, her touch gentle and soothing, as if trying to replace his old pain with new pleasure.

Evan closed his eyes, breathing her in, as content as he could ever recall being. Warm. Safe. Cherished.

He hovered on the edge of sleep when she mumbled something.

"What's that, love?"

"Don't kill him," she murmured.

"What?"

"Crevier. Don't kill him. Don't want you… murdering…"

"I never intended…" Evan began, but she was already asleep.

He let out an exasperated sigh. All that, and she still didn't truly trust him. He covered her hand with his own. Clearly he'd have to keep trying until she did.

29

MORNING SEX was the best.

Violet lay amid rumpled sheets and scattered pillows, her hair in a wild tangle, yet she felt the most beautiful creature in the world. Evan was leading things again, but in an easy, playful manner. She had woken in his arms and immediately been smothered with kisses and flatteries. He had even tickled her, and not protested at all when she tickled back.

Last night had done him a world of good. And the sex had been rather spectacular, too, once he had relaxed. Perhaps she would amend her statement. Sex with Evan Tagget was the best, regardless of time of day.

He settled down between her legs, glancing up at her with a lascivious grin.

"Ah, my luscious flower, the sweet kiss of your skin lingers on my tongue and I die in the pleasure of your liquid embrace."

Vi laughed and ruffled his hair. "You're ridiculous."

"You like me that way."

She didn't answer, just closed her eyes and surrendered to the ecstasy.

"Dearest," he said, some time later, "could you reach behind you and grab one of those pillows for me? You seem to have sent them all flying."

She snared one that was teetering on the edge of the bed and tossed it at him. "You're equally responsible, Tagget. Don't deny it."

He tucked the pillow under his head and held out his arms to her. She wasted no time crawling into his cozy embrace.

"Why do you have so many pillows, anyway? We kick them to the floor every night and then have to pick them up again."

"As a child I used to pile up my rags and pretend I was a king in a fine bed," he explained. "I always imagined such royal beds were heaped with fluffy pillows. When I had the money, I bought myself the finest of beds."

"I would expect kings to have fewer pillows and more eager women."

He planted a kiss in her hair. "I have both."

"And when you have too many eager women, you can just spread all the pillows on the floor and they can sleep there."

"You provide as much eagerness as any one man needs. But if you like the idea of pillows on the floor, perhaps we can try that next time you are in charge."

It was the most wonderful thing she had ever heard him say. "On Dauntless, where you have that nice, soft rug."

"Another time, then. Now, let's ring for breakfast. I'm famished."

Famished? He was full of wonderful things this morning. "Yes, please. I'd like a quiche with ham, cheese, and spinach, and a pot of tea—Ceylon if you have it. What are you having?"

"A croissant and a cigarette."

Violet sighed. "You are consistent, at least."

They remained in bed until the meal arrived, then repaired to the sitting room for a lazy breakfast. Evan glanced over the stack of mail that had arrived with their food.

"Oh, excellent. A letter from Eden. I've been hoping for a reply to the question I posed the other day." He tore open the missive.

Violet frowned at the paper. It looked to be typed out, like a telegram. "Won't that be a reply to an earlier letter? Even by airship it takes days to cross the Atlantic."

His mouth twitched in a tiny smirk. "There are advantages to having a global teletics network. I drop my letters off at the nearest telegraph office, and they send it off over the wire. The original follows by ordinary post. Eden takes her letters to the office in Ann Arbor, where they do the same. It's vastly more efficient."

"And madly expensive."

"I don't have to pay." His attention dropped back to his letter. "There looked to be something for you in that pile, also."

Violet thumbed through the papers until she found it. The square envelope was of high-quality paper and bore her name and the address of the hotel in typewritten letters. She opened it carefully and withdrew an elegant invitation.

> *The Esteemed M. l'Exploiteur*
> *requests the presence of*
> *Mlle. Violet Dayton*
> *at*
> *The Greatest Heist in History*
> *location known to you*
> *time and date to be revealed*

"Tagget."

His head snapped up. "What's wrong?"

"Look." She laid the invitation in front of him. "I think you've received one also."

He read the note, found his own, and set them side-by-side, glaring down at them. "Damnation. He not only knows we're onto him, but he knows exactly who we are."

"If he knows me by my real name, I suspect he knows my aliases as well. Remember that man who followed us to the hotel? He was probably only one of many."

"I'm hiring bodyguards. I don't like this."

"Bodyguards?" More protection she hadn't asked for and didn't want. "I agree we should take care, but isn't that a bit of an overreaction?"

"I don't want you coming to harm."

"And I don't want to be tailed by a cadre of oafish men. I know my way around town. I know how to hide. I carry a knife."

Evan's expression was uncompromising. "I'm upping the security on this hotel, whether you like it or not. As for guarding your person, that can be determined if and when you decide to go out on your own."

Violet regarded him across the table. "You will set a spy to follow me."

"I'm glad we understand one another."

She turned her attention from the invitation to her food. There was no sense arguing. She couldn't stop him from sending people after her any more than he could stop her from going out wherever and whenever she wished. And she truly appreciated his concern for her. She simply preferred to take care of herself. Maybe she needed to turn the tables and hire someone to protect *him*.

Evan flicked ash from the end of the cigarette he wasn't really smoking. "The obvious solution to this problem is to bring our criminal to justice as swiftly as possible."

"Yes." Vi pursed her lips in thought. "He will have crafted another machine. One meant to smash his way in, snare the statue, and fly off. He will have to come down through the roof."

Evan nodded his agreement. "It will require one of his larger ships. Were I attempting such a crime, I would modify the cargo lift, and use a two-step approach. First, break in, with a battering-ram-style device. Smash a window in the dome and only as much of the roof as necessary to make the correct sized hole. Minimize risk to the art. Second, lower the modified lift, clamp it around or under the sculpture, and haul it away. It would require a team of helpers, but we already know he has that."

Violet poured herself another cup of tea and leaned back in her seat, pondering. "We know the where and the what, and we can make educated guesses at the how. When is more difficult, but we know it will be soon."

"We'll watch for the distraction. He's used one in each of the previous large burglaries. He will cause chaos somewhere other than the museum."

She sipped her tea. "Hmm. Not an easy prospect in a city this size. There's always some chaos going on. Let's say, however, we identify the distraction and rush to the scene. What can we do to stop it? Crevier will give us nothing. We can't stop a freighter on our own."

Tagget tapped a finger on the invitations. "And these tell me he wants us there. I wouldn't put it past the man to lay some deadly trap for us."

"Agreed. We need help."

Evan stabbed his cigarette into the ashtray and rose from his seat. "Well, then, let's go out and get it."

· · · ~~~ · · ·

Vi flung herself onto the sofa, heaving a frustrated sigh. A whole day of work and she had nothing to show for it. She'd visited three different police stations, all outside Crevier's jurisdiction. They'd laughed at her. Two of the three hadn't even been willing to so much as glance at her thick stack of evidence.

The security at the Louvre hadn't been much better. The man who had talked to her had rambled on about all the heightened measures they'd implemented since l'Exploiteur had delivered his threats. Not a single one would be useful against an airship.

The only good thing Violet could say about the day was that Evan hadn't yet had a chance to hire bodyguards. If he'd had similar bad luck, they would need to develop an entirely new plan of action.

She ordered dinner, then paced the room as she waited for both Evan and the food to arrive.

If they were to win, they had to take control of the situation. They'd have to lure Wechsler into a trap. But how? Violet paced and thought and paced some more until an idea began to form. A big prize. An even bigger spectacle. A show that even "The Greatest Thief in History" couldn't resist.

The door opened and Evan entered. His pinched frown dissolved when he saw her. "Violet, my blossom, how did you fare today?" He walked over and gave her a kiss on the cheek.

"Badly. You?"

He sighed. "Everyone thinks me mad. Despite the previous thefts, they refuse to believe the *Winged Victory* could be stolen. Not a single one of my contacts in the French government was willing to provide us with resources or manpower, even when I offered to pay. The Belgian authorities did at least seem willing to consider an investigation of Wechsler. If it happens, though, it's likely to take weeks at best, since they can't simply break into his castle the way we did. Everything else was similarly hopeless." He held his thumb and index finger about an inch apart. "I was this close to hiring a crew of pirates to storm Wechsler's freighter and capture him."

"*Don't* do that," Violet warned. "I have a plan."

"Oh?"

A knock at the door announced the arrival of their dinner, and they settled on the sofa with their meal.

"Tell me everything," Evan insisted, spearing a small potato with his fork and brandishing it. "How do you plan to stop Wechsler?"

"I don't."

Dark eyebrows arched. "You're ceding the *Winged Victory* to him? What then?"

"We go on the offensive. We lay a trap. Lure him in with an even bigger prize."

"What bigger prize could there be than stealing the *Nike* from the Daru Staircase?" Amusement sparked in Evan's eyes. "Unless he means to build a floating city and sail away with La Tour Eiffel."

Violet grinned. She loved this part of her plan. "Stealing a newly-discovered masterpiece from its debut display where it will be guarded by the greatest security system ever devised—a triumph of manpower and technology working in congress to make the gallery impervious to theft by any means."

"Appeal to his ego? I like it. After all his boasting, he will have to respond. I wonder, however, how you plan to acquire a newly-discovered masterpiece." Evan's smirk said he knew exactly what she planned.

"Oh, I heard a rumor that someone has found a previously unknown de Heem vanitas."

Tagget set down his fork and took a sip of his wine. "I'm paying you a substantial sum of money for that painting. You expect me to simply give it up for public auction?"

"To date we have no written contract and no agreed-upon price. The painting is mine to do with as I please."

"I have ten thousand dollars set aside that says otherwise."

Violet sucked in a breath. Ten thousand dollars. With no haggling, so it had to be an opening bid. He expected to pay more. Even without driving the price up, it was enough money to turn her exhibition into the show of a lifetime, especially with thousands more in emeralds sitting in her jewelry box. It was also enough to escape and start fresh. With that kind of cash, she could travel to London or to America and set herself up in a new studio. She would have time to establish herself without having to worry about where her next meal was coming from. Any sensible woman would finish the painting, take the money, and skip town.

Somewhere along the line, Violet had lost all good sense.

She had never taken on a commission she couldn't complete. This would not become the first. She would see this through and bring l'Exploiteur to justice. For herself and for the art world she loved.

"Save the ten thousand for the auction. I told Mrs. Gaillard you intend to purchase the painting as a wedding gift."

His eyebrows arched. "It will cost me quite a bit more than ten thousand at an auction, if you can make people believe it's genuine."

"I can and I will."

"How, if I may ask? You must have some way to make your brand new oil painting look old."

"Ah." Violet relaxed in her seat and gave him an impish grin. She took a bite of her excellent chicken, chewing slowly, waiting to reply until Evan began to shift restlessly.

"I have a secret formula I discovered while I was experimenting with mixing luxene with ink and paint for Lacenaire's card reader," she confessed. "A diluted luxene spray applied to the oil paints will dry them. Only I know the exact concentration. Repeated applications can be used to age a painting to the desired state. It's the reason for the success of my Vérité works. Your de Heem will look the part."

"Fabulous! I look forward to paying a fortune for it."

She chuckled, then quickly sobered. "We will need to call in your favor from Lacenaire, though. We can't advertise the painting as genuine unless its provenance is beyond doubt. He, or someone in his employ, can create a credible history and provide us the documentation to support it."

"He has done this for your work before, I take it."

"Yes. Customers who know better pay for it. Those who are too stingy have their forgeries unmasked quickly."

Evan stroked his beard thoughtfully. "So, if I understand your plan correctly, you intend to put on a grand gallery showing and auction, with the Vérité de Heem as the pièce de résistance. But instead of using the painting to show off how besotted I am with my fiancée…" He put just enough emphasis on the word that Violet winced. "You will use it as bait."

"Correct."

"You advertise as wildly as our adversary has, and make a spectacle of the security. Done right, you could even imply that Monsieur l'Exploiteur is a coward if he doesn't make an attempt."

"An excellent detail I hadn't considered. He strikes me as the sort who would take offense at the slightest insult."

"How old is he, I wonder?" Tagget mused. "His boastfulness and petulance suggest a young man, but some never grow out of such behaviors."

"He's older than you, I expect. Middle-aged, I thought."

"Middle-aged can mean anything, depending on how long one expects to live. Many would consider me such, I imagine."

Vi frowned at him, trying to guess his exact age. Anything above thirty seemed plausible. "I don't even know how old you are."

"I turned thirty-five the day we visited Wechsler's castle."

She started. And he hadn't said a word? They, both of them, needed to work on their communication skills.

"Happy belated birthday. I'm sorry we missed the chance to toast to your health."

He shrugged. "We all grow older. I find the marking of years rather insignificant."

"When you have a brother who is a mere two months your elder, birthdays become a point of contention. We are both twenty-seven, but he thinks himself years beyond me in wisdom and experience. His letters are full of advice."

"Bad advice?"

"He's never been more than twenty miles from Melbourne. Also, he's a banker now, so he's forever talking about money."

"I'd like to meet your family."

Her heart thudded. That was the sort of thing one said to one's real fiancée. Didn't Tagget realize she couldn't just walk into her father's house and say, "Hello, everyone. Allow me to introduce the rich American I'm sleeping with." Maybe he didn't. He had no experience with families.

"Would you like to take a trip to Australia once we have tidied up everything here?" Evan asked. "You miss your siblings, if I'm correct?"

"We have a great deal of tidying to do before I can contemplate trips of any variety," Vi said primly.

This had to stop. She couldn't take all this talk of the future. He acted as though he saw no end to their relationship.

Maybe he doesn't…

She quickly shut down that ridiculous train of thought.

"My apologies." Tagget waved a hand lazily. "We've gotten off track. I know finishing this job means a great deal to you. Please, proceed with your plan. How do we catch Wechsler once he's taken the bait?"

"I'm still working on that. In part, it will depend on the trap we lay. Where is the hole in our supposedly impenetrable security? I need your help with that aspect. Your company will, naturally, be supplying the machines."

"Right now I can get you automatic cameras and an array of listening devices. More than that will require some improvisation on the part of my engineers. I'm not in the security business. Teletics and small machines."

"Guard dragons?"

"We don't make them, but we can fake some easily enough."

"Good. Most guard dragons are useless, anyway, but people find them impressive."

"Hmm." Tagget's lips pursed. "We'll throw a proximity sensor in that ridiculous owl. It will fly around screaming if anyone gets too close."

"I can arrange for someone to set it off deliberately. It'll make a good show for the audience. Perhaps one of the crew would be willing?"

"I think they'll jump at the chance to help you."

"They're good people."

"Yes." An odd, pensive expression crossed his face.

"And you'll help me?"

"To the best of my ability. What do you need me to do besides supplying machines?"

Violet grimaced. "I need a loan to help pay for it all. Or the money for the de Heem up front. If you can arrange a location, I'll talk to Lacenaire about the paperwork, and recruit artists to display their works. Can you contribute some art for display? Good pieces?" A thought occurred to her. "Wechsler is known as a collector, correct? We should invite him to show off some of his own pieces."

Tagget laughed so hard he coughed. "God, Violet, you are diabolically brilliant! I can think of no better way to taunt the man."

She beamed at the praise. "It's no less than he deserves. Can you begin first thing tomorrow? I want to hold this event in about three weeks, and I have arrangements to make and a painting to finish. I plan to rise early and get right to work."

"Then I will bother you no further with my questions so we can turn in early tonight." He set aside his plate and rose from his seat. "I need to make a phone call or two before bed. Shall I send Harrison or Walton to accompany you when you leave in the morning, or do you want a stealthier escort?"

"Evan…"

His expression was stony. "I'm not letting you go without protection. Especially to visit Lacenaire."

"Send one of the crew. But only if you promise not to go out alone, either. And take your sword-cane."

He smirked at her. "Yes, dear."

She rolled her eyes and watched him cross the room to the desk. "Oh, and Evan?"

"Yes?"

"I never properly apologized for promoting the false engagement without consulting you. I'm very sorry. You must encounter fortune hunters on a regular basis, and I didn't take that into account or spare enough thought for your feelings on the matter. I think we should maintain the fiction through the end of the art show, after which I'll leave it up to you how you wish to dissolve our association."

He stared at her for a long moment, his expression unreadable. From this distance she couldn't make out the emotions in his eyes.

"I will give the matter some consideration," he said cooly, then spun and sat at the desk, reaching for the telephone.

Violet looked down at her half-eaten dinner. She no longer had any appetite.

30

EVAN WAVED HARRISON AND FLYNNE over to the workbench in his warehouse workshop. He'd finished his tedious telephone calls for the day—with excellent results—and was eager to begin a more satisfying task: thwarting the backstabbing, blackmailing Inspector Crevier.

"First, a demonstration." Evan set the necessary supplies on the metal-topped workbench. One small black cube with a single switch and one vial of glowing green luxene fuel. Both seemingly innocuous, until used together. Once, he'd intended to use them to disable motorcars at will. These days, he wondered why he'd ever bothered with such a scheme.

Evan nudged the emitter closer to the vial, ensuring his demonstration would work even on the lowest setting. The jug in his cabinet no longer bore the Dynalux label, but it held about a quarter of the remaining supply of the altered luxene. No sense risking destroying it all.

He turned the switch on the emitter one click to the right. The device began to rumble, the noise pitched so low as to be nearly inaudible. Evan took a few steps back.

The green liquid began to bubble. Seconds later, the vial burst, leaving scattered droplets of flame as the remaining luxene burnt itself out.

"Holy wow," Flynne gasped.

Evan shut down the emitter, smiling. He lit a cigarette on the dying flames, just for fun.

"I'd heard there was a problem with the Dynalux fuel," the engineer continued. "A fire hazard or something. Never thought it would be like that. That can't have been more than a quarter teaspoon."

"My personal stash is more volatile than most," Evan replied.

"I thought the remaining supply was destroyed when you shut down the company."

Harrison chuckled behind him. "Then you don't know Mite too well. Luxene's too rare and valuable. He wouldn't waste millions of dollars of fuel."

Flynne's blue eyes opened wide. "You're not still selling the tainted fuel, are you?"

"I am, in fact," Evan replied, seeing no good reason to lie. "Under a new name."

The boy looked stricken. "Pure-Lux."

"Yes."

"So all that advertising about the clarity and the filtration system, presenting itself as the safe alternative to Dynalux, and it's the same fuel?"

"It's been cleansed. It won't explode."

Flynne's expression hardened. "You're deceiving people."

Evan shrugged. "That's how good advertising works."

"I put that fuel in Mrs. Chatsworth!"

"Good. It's probably the best fuel available."

"But…" Flynne cradled the dragon protectively. "You're certain?"

"No, I'm not certain. I've done no personal experimentation on the fuel quality as compared to other brands. But I can tell you the new filtration system is built to exacting standards and is so superior I have yet to recoup the cost." When the boy didn't look convinced, Evan added, "I also use Pure-Lux in the dragon that sits at Miss Dayton's bedside."

"Oh." Flynne relaxed. "But you're cheating people, in a way."

"That's business for you."

"How can you stand it?"

"I don't actually..." Evan halted mid sentence. Something told him saying he didn't like people very much might hurt the boy's feelings. "It's something you learn when you run a business. Not everyone is suited to it. And I'm no charlatan. My products are worth the price." The memory of Violet and the Ready-Cam flashed through his mind. "If they're not, I fix them."

Flynne relaxed a bit. "Oh, well, that's good."

"Tagget Industries was built on reworked and improved products. People can say what they like about me, but I strive to produce the best technology possible. I play the part of a businessman, but deep down I'm an engineer like you."

He'd almost forgotten that, until Violet had reminded him, with her questions about what he was building and her admiration of his sketches. She'd made him reflect on why he always fled here to his workshop to relax, and he'd found his answer: it was what he loved. In the workshop he could be himself.

Harrison nodded, smiling in a way Evan couldn't identify but that sparked some ancient memory just beyond retrieval. For an instant, he was Mite the rat catcher, gazing up in wonder at Gabe the operator—the kindest of the older boys—who went home at night to that mystical thing called a family, and was paid with more than pennies.

Evan shook his head, trying to bring himself back to reality.

"She's good for you," Harrison said, as if he could read Evan's thoughts.

"She's exceptional. That's why we're going to help her."

Evan gestured at the crate in the center of the room. "Pick out a few dragons each. Whatever you think will cause a stir."

Harrison plucked a miniature elephant from the box, dangling it from a hind leg. "Any idea what these are intended to do?"

"None whatsoever. I asked to borrow a crate of dragons. They look like our high-end line. Each unique, but not custom. I can't imagine they're much use other than to run around and make noise."

Evan turned back to the workbench and wiped away the remains of the shattered vial. He filled several larger bottles with the unstable luxene and tucked them into an inside pocket. The emitter went into one outside pocket, several small tools into the other.

"I'm ready, if you two are."

"We aren't going to hurt these, are we?" Flynne asked. His squirrel was up on his shoulder again, and he held an armload of dragons. "They're adorable."

"No worries. When we're done, we'll put them right back in that box and send them back to the factory for shipment."

"You'll sell used dragons?"

Evan bit his lower lip. For Christ's sake, the kid was worried about hurting machines and whether some frivolous customer might buy a dragon that once ran about on the street for a few minutes? It was a good thing he had a job on Dauntless, because he was too soft-hearted to handle anything else.

"Let's go," Evan snapped, certain if he addressed Flynne's question, he would wind up with an engineer who hated him.

Harrison fell in step beside him. "Are you sure about this plan? The amount of luxene you have stashed on your person is much more than you need to cause a distraction and grab some papers."

"Some distractions are larger than others."

"And all papers are flammable," Harrison murmured.

"Imagine that."

"I won't tell you what to do, but Miss Dayton won't be happy if you get yourself in trouble with the law."

Evan waved a hand. "Miss Dayton is concerned I might get rid of Crevier in a more permanent way. I expect her to be rather happy with mere arson."

Flynne came up alongside him. "Mr. Tagget, sir? This is going to be something I can't tell my mother about, isn't it?"

Evan paused and looked into the young man's bright eyes. "Correct. Are you still willing to help me?"

"For Miss Violet?"

"Yes."

Flynne's jaw set. He nodded.

"Good lad."

The trio walked through town to the police station, drawing little attention despite the numerous dragons. They approached the building from the rear, where Evan stopped for a last briefing.

"I anticipate needing perhaps ten minutes. Give the signal when Crevier is away from his office. When you hear the first explosion, it's time to get out. Leave the dragons if they don't respond."

"They'll respond," Flynne said. Evan liked the determined glint in his eye. The boy had grit. Throw him out into the world for a time, and he might lose that tenderness after all.

"Damn," he muttered where only Harrison could hear him. "I'm going to ruin the kid, aren't I?"

"He'll be all right. I'll watch him. You just take care of you."

"Isn't that what I always do?"

The pilot grinned. "Most times. Come on, Flynne," he said louder. "Let's go see the look on that brute's face when his jail becomes a menagerie."

Evan waited until they disappeared around the corner, then shimmied up a pipe to the second floor. His stomach churned knowing he was doing this in broad daylight, but it had to be when Crevier would least expect it.

Thank God no one ever bothered to look up as they wandered down these streets. Of course, if they did, they would see a man in a brownish, tweedy suit and a revolting straw hat. The entire world knew Evan Tagget would never wear something so plebeian.

He inched across a narrow sill to the window where he'd broken out before. As expected, the repairs had been hasty. Evan also had better tools now than a lone screwdriver. He would be inside in minutes. He pressed his ear to the glass and listened for chaos.

It wasn't long before he began to pick out shouts and pounding footsteps. Evan grabbed his slicer and set to work. The iron bars sheared like butter under the flame of the luxene-powered device. There would be no need to remove the entire frame, as he had done before. Leaving most of the grill in place also gave him something to hang on to.

A shrill whistle from inside cut through the cacophony. His signal—Crevier was out of the way. Evan tossed aside the broken bars and smashed through the window.

Crevier's office lay at the end of the hall. The inspector wasn't a complete fool and he had locked the door, but the slicer made short work of the lock. The tool sputtered and died just as the door swung open. Running it at full power consumed the luxene much too fast.

Evan turned to his sturdy screwdriver to tackle the locked drawers and file cabinets in the office, prying them open with minimal effort. Crevier was a tidy, organized man—the first thing Evan had ever liked about him. At the back of the bottom drawer, he found a thick stack of papers labeled with the name Vérité. He pulled the file out, tucked it under his arm, and dropped a bottle of luxene into the drawer. The remaining bottles, save one, he scattered in other drawers around the room. For extra insurance, he struck a match, lit a cigarette, and then dropped both onto the carpet. While the flames spread, he switched on the emitter to full power and stood in the doorway, waiting and listening to the noise downstairs. Angry shouts were mixed with laughter and cheers. The denizens of the downstairs cells were enjoying the show.

The bottle of luxene in his hand had grown so hot Evan had to dangle it from his fingertips. Time to go. He chucked the bottle toward the stairs. Moments later, everything began to explode.

Downstairs, Flynne roared, "Halt!" in English. It would be interesting to discover how well the voice controls worked on these models. Evan hurried back to the window, climbed to the ground, and walked several blocks before hailing a cab.

One hour later, he lounged in front of the fireplace in his hotel lobby, dressed in his usual attire and sipping an excellent cognac. Harrison and Flynne sat nearby, nursing their own well-earned drinks.

Evan crumpled another page of Violet's file and tossed it into the flames. Even if Crevier was able to put out the fire or recover something from his ruined office, he'd have nothing left to hold over her.

"Our terrible French made it all the better," Flynne enthused. "Or worse, I suppose, from their perspective. Trying to explain that you think you found a cache of stolen dragons when you don't know the word for 'stolen' is remarkably awkward."

"Shouting, 'take man dragons no good,' in a panicked voice was an entirely rational solution," Harrison said dryly.

Evan almost choked on his drink. "I'm glad you were there to play the straight man to Flynne's jester. I may have snapped."

"You would have taken charge and explained everything in calm, perfect French, and there would have been no chaos at all," Flynne replied. "It would've ruined the whole plan. But you're a man of business, and you know how to delegate."

Evan tossed another page into the fire. "It took me years to learn how. The first two times I tried to start my own business, I failed spectacularly." He frowned down at the next page of Violet's file. "Well, this is interesting. This record is all about the painting that hangs in Lacenaire's office. Seems it wasn't a commission. Brilliant woman! Even at seventeen, she was clever enough to get her art noticed and her name in the papers. There's a clipping." He held out the bit of newsprint for the others to see. "Uncovered due to suspicious provenance, but noteworthy for its attention to detail and high level of skill."

"Uncovered?" Flynne asked.

Evan grinned at him. "Didn't you know Miss Dayton is a master forger?"

"She, uh, failed to mention that. I knew she had legal trouble, but..." Flynne's face turned red. "I assumed she ran an unlicensed brothel or something."

This time Evan did choke on his cognac. Between his coughing and Harrison's barrel-chested laughter, half the patrons in the lobby turned to stare at them.

"She's good at being in charge," Flynne apologized. "I suppose it was fanciful, but I imagined a salon where beautiful lady artist-courtesans would sing naughty songs and sketch lurid nudes before they entertained their gentlemen callers."

"I love it," Evan laughed. "I'll put up the money to start the place, but you can take a cut of the profits for the idea."

"I would absolutely not be able to tell my mother about that!"

"We need to include male 'artesans,' also," Evan continued, the idea dancing around in his mind. "Poets, in particular. Everyone loves beautiful poets, but they're really not good for much else."

"My mother would have an apoplexy. I think we'd better not. Besides, what would Miss Violet say?"

Evan's brows twitched in amusement. "I expect she'd find it a delightful idea."

Flynne made a skeptical sniffing noise.

"Though I imagine she would warn me not to avail myself of the charms of the ladies and gents we employed. As if anyone could sway me from her side."

Evan tossed a handful of boring police notes into the fire, looking for more newspaper articles. He thought he might save a few to show Violet. She might enjoy reminiscing, and she would certainly enjoy burning evidence.

He had begun to complain to his companions about all the fools insisting on referring to Vérité as "he," when a magnificent female voice bellowed, "Evan Tagget, are you out of your bloody mind?"

He glanced over his shoulder, taking in Violet's flushed skin and her flashing eyes. Walton hurried after her, looking winded.

Evan beamed at his lady love. "Ah, my ambrosial fruit, come join us. We were just discussing the possibility of a new business venture."

Flynne hopped up from his seat and bowed to her. "Lovely to see you, Miss Violet. I should be getting back to work. You can have the idea for free, Mr. Tagget. I'd rather stay an engineer."

Violet regarded Evan with suspicion. "Business venture?"

"A specialty brothel. Very high-class, incorporating multiple facets of creativity and culture. Staffed by the most highly skilled of artists."

She nodded sagely. "Definitely out of your bloody mind. What's all the paper?"

"Fascinating reading material and fuel for the bonfire in celebration of your freedom."

A dazzling smile broke across her face. She plopped in the chair Flynne had vacated. "Excellent. Pass me some. I shall enjoy watching the leaping flames while I scold you."

31

Violet took another sip of her after-dinner drink. Made from port and pure Belgian chocolate, it was rich, thick, and sinfully delicious. Tagget had specially requested it. He knew what she liked.

"So," she began, "while you were busy taking stupid chances and committing crimes, I recruited a dozen artists to sell their works and three more patrons to contribute pieces for display."

Evan wore his casual smirk. His posture was relaxed, with his drink in one hand and an unlit cigarette in the other. Hair curled across his forehead.

"Committing crimes? I can't imagine where you would come up with so ridiculous a notion."

Their secluded corner table in his hotel restaurant was ideal for private conversation, but he was posturing anyway. It didn't matter. She knew what he'd done. The moment she'd caught wind that there had been a commotion and fire at the police station, she'd known who to blame. She was pleased he'd destroyed the evidence against her—and that he hadn't murdered Crevier—but his methods...

"Really, Evan, in broad daylight? The unmitigated arrogance!"

He lit his cigarette on a candle. "I believe we already had this conversation, madam, and I would prefer not to repeat it. Tell me about your recruiting."

"Twelve artists. Good ones, though most aren't well known. They're my friends from the artists' commune where I lived when I first came to Paris. I've been planning this for years with them in mind. The chance to sell at a high-profile exhibition is a chance at greatness. I will easily double our numbers by week's end, and I promise only to include artists with real talent. I did have to turn down one gentleman who splotches colors onto his canvas to satisfy his yearning for the bohemian life, when in truth he ought to return to his job as an accountant back home in England."

Evan chuckled. "Poor bastard."

"Don't give him your pity. He asked me three times to pose nude for his series of Greek Muses paintings—the third time *after* I informed him of our engagement."

"I can't blame the man for wishing to see you in the altogether."

Violet gave Evan an impish smile. "Also, he didn't have any idea who you were."

"Ah! The wretch. A failing not to be forgiven."

"He even had the temerity to tell me not to worry because he would be certain to 'enhance' my bosom in the final work."

"Wretch!" Tagget exclaimed, this time without humor. "How dare he?"

"Well, he won't be exhibiting, and he'll soon run out of money, so he's not worth fretting over."

"I trust none of the dozen you selected have behaved so abominably?"

He looked unamused when Violet laughed. "None have told me I needed enhancing, but three or four of them at least, have asked me to pose. Artists are always in need of new models. I would feel hideous if none of them had asked."

"I'm not certain I approve of your profession."

"I don't approve of yours at all, so we're even."

Evan stabbed his cigarette into the ashtray and scowled at his drink. "I should have ordered something stronger."

Violet sipped her chocolate and smiled. "You will never best me in cards. I can read your every emotion in those dazzling eyes. You are at least as amused as you are irritated."

He grunted. "Tell me about the patrons."

"Two voracious collectors who have purchased from me in the past. They will display some of their pieces in exchange for a zero percent commission on anything they choose to purchase."

"Acceptable. The Société can do without its cut on a handful of works. I thought you said there was a third patron?"

"This is the best of all. I had a lengthy conversation with Lacenaire. He has agreed to provide us the necessary papers."

Tagget nodded his understanding.

"In addition, he will contribute to the show. It so happens he has saved a full half-dozen of Vérité's works from destruction, as well as a number of other forgeries. We have decided to reserve a special corner for their display. We will put out informational signs and pamphlets to promote discussion. We are calling it 'Forgeries: Their Purpose, Value, and Artistic Merit.'"

"Now who's arrogant?" Evan chortled. "Shameless self-promotion, my floweret. And for nothing but pride, as you can't claim ownership. Best of all, you have the gall to display them beside one purported to be a genuine masterpiece!" He wiped away a tear of mirth. "You, Violet Dayton, are the finest woman ever to walk this earth."

Her stomach lurched. His spontaneous, non-florid compliments cut her to the quick. How would she ever manage to throw off their sham of an engagement when he said such things? The words rang with sincerity, and she was certain he believed them. Whether they would continue to hold true was another matter entirely.

Tagget refilled her tiny chocolate cup and pushed the little tray of biscuits toward her, then surprised her by sampling one himself.

"In return for your delightful update, I will tell you that I have secured a location for our event. I could only book a three-week showing, having made arrangements on such short notice, and our opening gala will occur—most unfashionably—on a Tuesday, but I believe the venue to be beyond reproach."

Three weeks? Violet would have been happy with one. She'd promised no more to Sophie and the other artists from the commune. She leaned forward, eager to hear the rest, but Evan sat silently, nibbling on his sweet.

"Where, for heaven's sake? Stop taunting me."

"Les Grandes Serres de la Ville de Paris."

Her jaw dropped. "No."

"I swear."

"Oh, Evan!" Violet had to stop herself lunging across the table to kiss him. "How did you ever... No. It's you. If you want it, you find a way."

"This wasn't difficult. I actually am affiliated with the Société des Arts. The other members were pleasantly surprised I wished to arrange an event, and amused, I believe, when they learned it coincided with my engagement to an artist. I had to promise them not to promote your work disproportionately. Of course, you have gone and undone all that with your Vérité exhibit."

Vi laughed in delight. "It's beyond what I could ever have imagined. To have the same location as the Salon des Indépendants! I attended this spring. Henri Matisse exhibited a stunning piece."

"I know. I saw it."

"Did you? It makes me wonder if we were there at the same time. It's funny to think we might have walked right by one another or even stood side-by-side with no idea what the future had in store for us."

"Impossible. Had I caught so much as a glimpse of you, I would have stopped everything and demanded to make your acquaintance."

"Don't be ridiculous."

Evan fixed her with a searing gaze. "I'm entirely serious. The moment I laid eyes on you, I knew you were extraordinary."

"Amazing. I knew the same about you." She paused for dramatic effect. "Except it was 'extraordinarily,' and followed by the word 'conceited.'"

"You will not get a rise out of me, my blossom of beauteous perfection. I, too, can read your wicked eyes. Teasing me is one of your great pleasures. I wish you to indulge yourself with frequency and enthusiasm. And speaking of indulging, shall we retire to our suite that we might engage in great pleasures of a different sort?"

"After I finish my chocolate."

"Of course."

Tagget picked up another biscuit and took a slow, deliberate bite, making little noises of pleasure as he chewed.

"Now who is teasing whom? You can't possibly be enjoying your food that much."

He dunked the cookie into his chocolate. "I'm trying to learn from your example, my sweet." He licked the warm, thick liquid from the dessert with a single smooth stroke of his tongue.

Violet shivered.

"Take care not to spill on yourself," he said, repeating the sensuous gesture. "I don't know how we might remove the molten confection from your skin."

She dipped a finger into her cup, then lifted it to his lips. "Oops."

Evan sucked every drop of chocolate from her finger, the heat of his mouth warming more than just the skin it touched.

Vi downed the last of her drink. "Upstairs. Now."

"I am yours to command, my luscious bud."

"Oh, are you? Then pillows on the floor it is." She took his hand and they headed for the steam lift.

Tagget somehow managed to move rapidly without losing any of his polish, tucking her arm under his own and nodding to several people as he passed. It was the most elegant, hasty departure she could imagine.

The moment the lift doors closed behind them, they were in each other's arms, lips hungering for a taste.

"I could kiss you forever," Evan vowed.

"Do it."

His mouth covered hers, and his hand settled at the small of her back, steadying her against the slight sway of the rising lift. Violet rocked into him, kissing harder, hungering for more. Evan seemed content to take his time. His tongue stroked hers in lazy circles, mimicking the unhurried ascent of the elevator. She groaned.

Violet was considering pushing him down onto the bench at the back of the small chamber, when a thunderous crack rent the air. The lift shuddered, tossing its occupants against the ironwork wall. A second later the hotel quaked beneath the force of another explosion, breaking the lovers apart and flinging Violet to the floor. Lights flickered madly. The lift ground to a halt and the chamber went dark.

"Fucking son of a whore," Tagget cursed, in the thick accent of a New York street urchin.

"Evan, really!" Violet responded automatically. Her minister father had objected to even words like "dratted" and "blast" in his home. She'd moved well beyond that, uttering the occasional "damn" herself, but certain words still made her ears burn.

Evan swore again, adding a "goddamn" to the string of expletives.

Violet rose to her feet, bracing herself against the wall with one hand, while she groped for him with the other.

"The distraction?" she asked.

"L'Exploiteur, undoubtedly," Evan grunted. He sounded in pain. Her hand brushed him, but he eluded her grasp.

"Evan?"

"I'm fine." She heard a rustle of fabric and a sharp intake of breath. "Take one step to the left."

She moved aside.

"Your other left."

"That's my right. I'm facing you."

"Just move."

She scurried in the other direction. His dim outline made its way past her to the wall. Metal scraped metal.

"What are you doing?"

"Getting us out of here, if I can find the damned…" Something popped. "Latch."

The elevator door groaned open. They were between floors. The yellow glow of lamplight filtered under the door of the nearest floor, just above eye level. Evan climbed up to the ceiling, wincing in pain. With the added illumination, she could see he was hanging on with just one arm.

"You are not okay."

"I'm fine."

He put one foot to the outside door and kicked. It didn't budge. A fat, wet droplet splashed on Violet's arm. She wiped it off with a finger and held it to the light. A red streak gleamed on her skin. Tagget dropped to the floor, his breathing labored.

"Give me a moment."

She grabbed him and pushed him down onto the bench. "You're bleeding. Sit."

"It's nothing."

"Don't move."

Violet ran her hands over the walls until she found suitable handholds in the wrought iron. She hoisted herself up until she had a firm grasp on a section of ceiling. She slipped her feet from their holds and swung herself like a pendulum, using the weight of her body to place a solid kick to the door. It shuddered, but didn't open.

Sweat made her hands slippery. The scent of smoke reached her nostrils. She cursed. They needed out now. She swung harder, bending her knees, and extending at the last moment for maximum force. The door gave way. Her fingers lost their grip, and she toppled into Tagget's arms.

"I told you not to move," she scolded.

"Go. The hotel is on fire."

Vi scrambled up and out the opening, turning back to help him, but he refused assistance, and climbed after her with minimal noises of pain.

Smoke had already infiltrated the hall. Violet had always found the gas lamps unpleasant, and not romantic as they were meant to be, but with all the electric lights out, she thanked God for them. Tagget came up beside her. The right sleeve of his jacket was badly torn, and blood stained the white shirt beneath. He clamped his hand over the wound.

"Down the stairs," he ordered. "Quickly."

Violet stared straight ahead of them, at the entrance to their suite. Smoke curled from beneath the door. Her heart hammered. Most of her possessions were replaceable, but there was one she had unthinkingly left behind. She raced over and slammed her palm onto the sensor. The brilliant, luxene-powered design slid smoothly open.

"Thank you, thank you, thank you," she gasped.

She tore into the smoky room, covering her mouth and nose. Evan ran after her, shouting her name.

"Go downstairs!" she called. "I'll catch up!"

"No! Violet!" She heard him crash into something and tumble to the floor.

"Get out, Evan! For God's sake!"

Her jewelry box sat where she had left it, just inside the bedroom door, atop a chest of drawers. She snatched it up and spun around. Evan had clambered to his feet, his silly, fire-breathing dragon making circles around his legs. He shoved it toward the door and it scampered out of the suite. Vi grabbed his hand and they ran for the stairs, the dragon trotting alongside.

"Are you out of your mind?" Tagget demanded. "That room could have been on fire. What if you had lost your way in the smoke?"

"Shut up and run."

"I can't run."

He kept pace with her, despite his protestation, but by the time they reached the safety of the street he was wheezing. He doubled over, bracing himself with hands on knees, gasping for breath. Violet helped him to the ground and out of his jacket, inspecting the laceration on his arm. It looked painful, but wasn't as deep as she had feared. With her little knife, she cut away his sleeve and used the remnants to bandage him.

"Thank you."

She kissed his brow. "Any other injuries?"

"No."

"Mr. Tagget, sir!" One of his staff knelt beside him. "Do you need a doctor?"

"I'm fine. Has the fire brigade been notified?"

"They're on their way, and we've evacuated all guests. You were among the last. We were concerned."

"We were stuck in the lift." He eyed Violet's jewelry box. "And Miss Dayton felt the need to rescue something."

"Is there anything we can do for you?"

"Hail a cab. I'm going to my workshop. Call me there with updates. I want to know the instant the fire is out, and then I want to know the damage assessment."

"Yes, sir." The man hopped up and rushed off to do his duty.

"I suppose we have no hope of saving the *Winged Victory*," Violet sighed. She hated leaving Wechsler to his crime, though she'd known they couldn't stop this.

"No," Evan agreed. "He attacked us here and it'll be worse if we go after him. But your plan is sound. Let him have this. We will fight another day."

Yes, they would. And right now the most important thing was to stay safe and make certain Evan didn't exacerbate his injury. When the cab pulled up, she took his arm to assist him up and into the vehicle.

He shook her off. "For God's sake, woman, I'm not an invalid."

His breathing had returned to normal, so she let him alone. "I'm glad of it. I'm sure you would be an impossible patient."

Violet followed him into the cab, and when the door had closed behind them, she lifted the lid of her jewelry box. Her copper bracelet sat atop the rest of the jewels. She caressed it with a single finger, feeling the dimples left by the hammer and the bulges where the sections had been welded together.

Evan rubbed his temple, grimacing. "I can't believe you went after that box. What were you thinking? I can buy you more emeralds. For the love of God, Violet, I'm not going to leave you to scrape by on the cash you can get from pawning your baubles!"

Tears of anguish welled in her eyes. That's what he thought of her? That it was all about the money?

"Devil take the emeralds," she spat. "This was all I wanted." She slapped the bracelet onto her wrist and thrust her arm at him.

"That?" He stared at her in disbelief. "You would risk yourself for a bit of junk?"

Junk. The word was like a punch to the gut. The bracelet was the only thing aside from the shells tucked into her cleavage that meant anything to her, and he termed it junk? The tears began to flow.

Tagget sprang across the carriage to her side. "Darling, don't cry. God, what an ordeal we've suffered tonight. I'm sorry for adding to your distress. You, of course, may treasure any trinket you like." He tucked a stray hair behind her ear. "In the future, however, please leave it behind. I can make you a replacement. Better yet, I can have a real jewelry smith make you one. Then it won't be scratched and asymmetrical, and so on."

Violet squirmed from his arms and moved into his vacated seat. "You don't understand."

"You like to see something old and worthless transformed into something beautiful. It's your artistic nature."

"No. I mean, yes, I do, but that's not the point. You made this just for me."

He frowned at her, still not understanding. "So I can make you another one. I should make you another one. A better one. That was a prototype, and as such is worth little except for determining where improvements can be made."

"It's beyond worth," she vowed. "It's priceless!"

"Everything has a price, my flower."

"Not true." Tears streamed down her cheeks. *Not me. You can't put a price on me.*

She couldn't say it aloud. She knew he wouldn't believe her, and she couldn't bear to hear him say so. In his world, everything was bought and sold, including people. They were just things, perhaps nicer than most, but still things that you went out and got if you wanted one. He had survived and thrived in that world, but it had damaged some part of him beyond repair.

Violet clutched her jewelry box to her chest. Perhaps if she held it tight enough it would prevent the shattered pieces of her heart spilling out.

Tagget moved to her side once more. "No more arguing. This isn't the time. I'm sorry, love."

"Don't call me that."

He flinched.

"You don't love me," Vi said.

"I do."

"Obsession isn't love, Tagget." She hammered on the roof of the cab. "Stop right here!"

"Violet, please. It's not a lie."

"I can't do this anymore." She pushed the door open and leapt out before the vehicle even came to a complete stop. She raced down the street, dodging pedestrians and other automobiles. Left to handle the fare and unable to run for any distance, Tagget had no chance of catching her. She ran all the way to the warehouse and locked herself in her studio, dragging a bookcase in front of the door, since she was certain he had another key.

Standing in the middle of the room was her fainting couch, cleaned and polished, reupholstered in a soft cloth of rich purple. A note sat upon it.

I hope you like it. If not, I can buy you a new one. -Evan

Violet threw herself upon the couch and wept.

32

Evan hadn't eaten a proper meal in two days. He was out of cigarettes, and he had resorted to guzzling brandy straight from the bottle. This last wasn't strictly necessary. He had perfectly serviceable glassware in the workshop, but sipping politely from a crystal snifter wouldn't convey the depth of his torment.

He lay on his back on the floor, the bottle in his hand, staring at the ceiling and listening for any sounds from the studio next door.

He could hear nothing, which meant Violet was painting. Sometimes she walked around, arranging her space. She moved her canvases to get the best natural light. He had even heard her moving furniture yesterday. But now she was quiet, focused on the art. If he listened long enough, he might hear a soft mumble. At times, she talked to herself.

A sound strategy for winning her back eluded him. He had tried handwritten notes, impassioned pleas, even pounding on the door and shouting. She wouldn't answer him. Her single message contained everything she intended to say.

The note was burned into his mind. He could recite it backwards. He knew each stroke of the pen and the smeary splotches where her tears had fallen. He recited it aloud for the thirty-seventh time, softly so as not to interrupt her art.

"Dear Evan. I have decided it is for the best if we are to remain apart. It has become clear to me that we are incompatible, and it's better to face that now than to let things linger. We will attend the exhibition as previously discussed, and then I will depart to begin a new life. Feel free to slander me or forgive me as your reputation and social standing dictates. You have my deepest apologies for any pain I have inflicted. It was never intended. I am confident you will make a full recovery. Sincerely, Violet."

Incompatible.

That single word tore at his heart. How could she believe so evident a falsehood? Never in his life had he met anyone with whom he was more compatible. Certainly they argued, but it was impassioned arguing that made him think and consider her side. And when their feelings and thoughts were in accord, it was glorious. She gave him a new perspective, new ideas. She brought him light and joy. He'd tried to do the same for her, yet somehow he had failed.

Evan took a swig of the brandy—quality stuff, though he preferred the authentic cognac. Regardless, it did nothing to quiet the pangs in his stomach or his craving for a smoke. Nor did it give him any new ideas.

A polite knock sounded at the door. He'd stationed guards outside to chase away any visitors—in particular to protect Violet from Wechler's goons or police harassment. Between the fire at the police station and the latest theft, Crevier would be hopping mad. Hopefully he would be too busy to seek revenge, but Evan wasn't taking any chances.

"I'm not receiving visitors," he called.

"It's Walton, boss," came the reply.

Evan sat up. "Have you brought cigarettes?"

"Yes."

Evan scrambled to his feet and waved Walton inside. The basket the chef carried smelled divine.

Walton shut the door behind himself and handed the basket over. "Brought you some lunch."

Evan yanked off the cloth to inspect the contents. A stew, still steaming, bread, cheese, an apple, and a bottle of Merlot.

"Boss, you look terrible," Walton blurted.

"Of course I look terrible. I'm engaging in a bout of drunken self-pity."

"You don't sound drunk."

"I'm not. I only have the one bottle of brandy, and I've been nursing it for two days. The wine will help. Where are the cigarettes?"

Walton spread his hands helplessly. "I don't have any. I only said that so you would let me in. Miss Dayton is worried you're not eating."

"I fail to see how it's any concern of hers."

"She loves you, boss."

Hope burbled up inside Evan, but he shoved it ruthlessly back down. "That seems doubtful, as she is no longer speaking to me."

Walton shrugged. "You probably said something stupid."

"When did you all decide it was acceptable to be so insolent?"

Walton's mouth curved upward. "When we saw how much you like it when Miss Dayton talks sass to you. Eat your lunch. I'll bring dinner this evening. If you need anything else, you just telephone the airfield. We aren't doing anything but sitting on the ship, waiting for news."

"Send someone around with cigarettes."

"Sure thing, boss." He turned to open the door.

"Walton?"

The chef paused, glancing back at Evan. "Yeah?"

"What would you do if Dahlia said she was leaving you? Permanently."

"Dunno." He pursed his lips in thought. "Not sure there's anything I could do. She decides things for herself. Guess I'd just keep on loving her and trying to deserve her."

"No drunken self-pity?"

Walton chuckled. "Oh, there'd be some of that. I've got my eye on a nice bottle in your wine cellar."

"Put a label on it. You can drink it on your wedding day."

"Thanks, boss. Enjoy your lunch, okay?"

Evan waved him out the door. "Yes, yes, I'll eat the damned food."

The lunch had a near-miraculous rejuvenating effect. Evan felt even better after he washed, went for a haircut and shave, and stopped at the tailor to pick up a brand-new suit. His guards—a pair of hotel doormen—snapped to attention as he approached the warehouse door.

"Good afternoon, sir. No visitors to report. The guard at the far entrance says Miss Dayton went out for a walk but is back in her studio, and your dirigible man stopped by again with your mail."

He handed Evan a stack of papers and—mercifully—a pack of cigarettes.

"Any word on the hotel?" Evan inquired.

"Still assessing the structural damage. One builder says we can't reopen until we rebuild the whole thing. The other two say he's a cheat who just wants the contract. They're saying it doesn't look too bad except for the top floor."

"Thank you."

"Thank *you*, sir, for giving us a job while it's closed."

"You're welcome. I wish I had temporary jobs for all the staff."

Evan pondered the words as he walked inside. He had uttered such platitudes in the past, because it was expected of him, but this time he meant what he said. It infuriated him that his loyal, hard-working employees risked losing their livelihoods because of a vengeful scoundrel. He would make sure they all continued to receive pay unless it was determined the hotel could not reopen. He had a phone call to make.

And quite a bit of other work, based on the size of the stack of mail. It seemed the time for wallowing was past.

· · · ⚔ · · ·

Staying busy made all the difference. Unable to keep his mind off of Violet, Evan focused his attention on the art show. He called, sent letters and telegrams, and went for dinner with anyone who might be of use. Ads went into newspapers, leaflets, and posters. His factories set to work churning out security devices, and he gathered the most comprehensive security team Paris had ever seen. He took particular delight in going over Crevier's head when contacting the police for assistance.

Each evening, Evan wrote a brief note detailing his progress and had it delivered to Violet. He kept the notes short and businesslike. She responded in kind.

Between his dedication to the exhibition and a new secret project for Violet, the days passed more rapidly than he could have imagined. By the morning of the opening gala, he was certain the exhibition would be a smashing success, and he believed the odds of bringing l'Exploiteur to justice better than even.

His single remaining trouble was Violet herself. Evan didn't know how to talk to her. He didn't know how to repair their relationship. At times a sickening dread clamped itself around his heart, telling him the rift might be irreparable.

He'd tried half a dozen times to write a letter to Eden, starting and stopping, adding, crossing out, trying to convey all that had happened and beg her advice. It was hopeless. He couldn't send a ten page missive. She had her own concerns, and his telegraph people had better things to do.

The door to Violet's studio mocked him. Whether he was ready or not, today he needed to pass through it and face her.

First, though, he needed to fortify himself. He went to lunch on Dauntless.

"You look tense, Mite," Harrison said. "Walton says you've been working like a man possessed."

"It's nothing I haven't done before."

"Hmm."

How did the man manage to convey so much in a single syllable? Acknowledgement, skepticism, disapproval, probably more that Evan was missing. He motioned for the pilot to follow him.

"Come have a drink with me, Harrison."

"It would be a pleasure. No more than a glass, though. I'm flying tonight."

Evan nodded and led the way downstairs. When they were seated in his cabin sipping his best cognac, he asked, "Can we be friends, Harrison?"

The pilot chuckled. "Aren't we already?"

"I have no idea," Evan admitted. "I find the entire concept baffles me. Eden tells me friends care for one another and enjoy spending time together. She didn't explain how one acquires them."

Harrison's chuckle turned into a rumbling laugh. "You don't acquire them, lad, you earn them."

"Earn them how?"

"By being the sort of person they can care for and enjoy spending time with. Sometimes it sneaks up on you."

"Hmm." Evan stroked his goatee. "Eden befriended me when I'd been nothing but horrible."

"She must have seen something in you. Maybe something you didn't notice yourself."

"I love her."

"Good."

"I didn't always. I thought I did, but it was no more than an obsession."

With the repetition of Violet's words came clarity. Evan

knew what love was. He'd known it since the day he was born. The memories had long since faded, but the feelings remained. A soft touch. A tight embrace. Whispered words, lulling him to sleep. Laughter. Smiles. The knowledge that he was safe. That he belonged.

But he'd been deprived of love for so long the idea of it had become hazy, and made all the more indistinct by the affections and lusts of his adult appetites. He knew it now, though. Lived it with every breath, every beat of his heart. That deep, overpowering connection with another human being, that time, distance, and even death could not obliterate.

He loved Violet for a million little reasons, and would continue to do so whether she believed him or not. His experience with love was admittedly minimal. It was no wonder she doubted him. But he would prove himself to her. Somehow.

A wry smile touched his lips. "I'm not hopeless. I can be taught."

"I never doubted it."

Harrison again favored Evan with that smile he couldn't quite place, the one that made him feel like a little boy. There was laughter in that smile, and pride, and maybe, oddly, a bit of love.

Paternal.

The word hit him like a thunderbolt.

"My father used to smile at me like that," Evan said, with absolute certainty.

"I know."

Evan reeled. "You do?"

"You told me so. You said he taught you maths." The pilot's fond smile broadened. "I'm the baby of my family, but one day I met this boy who was sweet and smart and a bit shy. He asked me many questions and told me many things. It was like having my own little brother."

"I don't remember." Evan remembered Harrison from the

factory and knew they'd talked when the supervisors weren't in sight, but could recall no conversations. No specifics.

"You were very young."

"I don't remember anything." A flood of pain washed over Evan. He took a big swallow of his drink, but didn't change the subject. "I don't remember my father's voice or his face. Do I look like him? Or do I favor my mother? What did she teach me? Was it she who taught me my letters? I remember crying for her. But nothing else. Just an empty hole, where they should be. All I..." He choked up, his eyes growing moist. "All I know is they loved me."

"Isn't that what really matters?"

Evan pulled out a handkerchief and wiped his eyes. "I suppose it is." He levered himself up out of his chair. "I should be going. I need to see Violet about this evening."

"Before you go..." Harrison's usually confident expression turned suddenly uncertain. "I could use a bit of advice, myself."

Evan quirked an eyebrow. "Oh?"

"There's this lady, and—"

"Parker," Evan concluded immediately. Of course. He'd been distracted by Violet the night of the opera, but looking back, Harrison had been extremely attentive to Parker that entire evening. And when the group had split up, the two of them had gone off alone together. "She's a fabulous woman. You two will make genius children."

Harrison dragged a hand over his closely-shaven hair. "I'm seventeen years older than her. You don't think that's a problem?"

Evan looked straight into his friend's eyes. "Does *she* think it's a problem?"

"She doesn't seem to."

"Then it's not a problem. Do whatever pleases her. Give her the world."

"The way you would do for Miss Dayton," Harrison said soberly.

Evan's throat tightened. "I would walk through hell for her."

Harrison nodded. "Thank you." He rose from his seat. "I should go get the ship ready."

Evan extended his hand. "Thank you for the conversation."

"You're welcome, Evan."

Harrison grasped Evan's hand, but instead of shaking, pulled him into a tight embrace. When he let go, Evan stumbled backwards, flustered, his cheeks burning.

"Someone ought to have hugged you years ago," Harrison said. "Now you go talk to your lady, little brother."

"I will."

It wasn't until Evan was halfway back to the workshop that he realized he'd taken orders from an employee.

33

VIOLET'S PULSE RACED. Her palms began to sweat.

Deep breaths. Straighten up.

For heaven's sake, it was a knock on the door, not a marauding army. She checked that all her paintings were properly covered, pushed the bookcase away from the door, then smoothed out her skirt and took a seat on the couch.

"Come in!"

Evan strode through the door, looking crisp and clean and perfect, wearing a smile of genuine pleasure. Her heart leapt into her throat.

"Violet." He stopped and stared at her for several seconds. "You take my breath away, my beautiful blossom."

"What do you want, Tagget? I thought all arrangements for the exhibition were finished."

"I was hoping to see your dress for the gala. I would like us to match."

"It's purple."

"Naturally. But what shade? I can't show up with a lavender pocket square if you are in plum."

He was playacting. He had a handkerchief and waistcoat made from the same fabric as the dress. Madame Rochette had shown them off when Vi had gone in for her final fitting.

He had to know she would know that. He'd probably seen the dress already.

Violet decided to play along. "It's a dark purple, with buckles down the front of the bodice. Fitted to the knees and then flaring out. The sleeves flare also. It's both stunning and elegant."

"I can't wait to see you in it."

"I will give you only a tiny peek."

He smirked. "Such a tease."

No. No flirting. Vi stood up and turned away from him, leading him to the corner she had curtained off as a temporary closet. She gave him a glimpse of the dress, then shooed him toward the door.

"If that's all, you can be on your way. I need to see these paintings safely delivered. I believe I'm the last artist to drop off my work. The de Heem, of course, will be moved separately, under guard."

"May I see them?" He took a step toward the wrapped canvases.

"No!"

Tagget recoiled at her outburst.

"Not until this evening," she said, her voice calmer. "It's to be a surprise."

"I see." His eyes narrowed in suspicion and he followed her gaze. Violet tore her eyes from the painting too late. He could see it meant something to her.

"I'm still considering which paintings to exhibit."

Still considering whether to exhibit *that* painting. She had poured her heart into it these last weeks. It had been her refuge, the antidote to her grief, her way of moving on. She considered it some of the best work she'd ever done, and she wanted people to see it. She wanted Evan to see it. Putting it up for sale, however, filled her with dread. Could she bear to part with something so personal?

"I'd like to see them all," Tagget said. "You've been working so hard. Even from the other room, I could tell. I know little of your art besides the forgeries. I'm wild with curiosity to see the true art of Mademoiselle d'Aubergine."

Violet gave a careless shrug. "You'll just be disappointed with that attitude."

He walked right up to her, eyes never leaving hers, infiltrating her personal space until he was so close she could feel his breath.

"Nothing you do can disappoint me."

Her heart pounded. A shiver raced through her.

Back away, Violet, said her sensible inner voice. *Tell him to go away. Tell him you don't want this, that you're done with this.*

As if she could utter such a blatant lie.

Three weeks hadn't been enough. Not when she could hear Evan's every movement next door. Not when she painted like a woman possessed while he played her unwitting muse. She would never get over him until she'd put distance between them. A long, long distance.

Violet seized hold of his coat and kissed him so frantically he stumbled backward. Her hands clenched on his lapels, holding him up and pushing him where she wanted to go.

Once more. Just once more.

That damned sensible voice tried to butt in, but she was committed. Her body yearned for him and her heart ached for him. She was going to have him one final time, and only an act of God could stop her.

Violet shoved Evan toward the couch, and he went willingly, tugging at the ties of her bodice. She pushed him down and straddled his legs, yanking up her skirt and fumbling with the fastenings on his trousers.

This was insane. This was stupid. Everything would hurt all over again. She hadn't even been brewing her contraceptive tea. She didn't care. She'd take the heartache. She'd even take a baby if she got that unlucky. She needed this. She needed one last blistering memory of how desperately she wanted him.

"Violet, God," he moaned against her mouth.

She shifted, taking him inside of her, riding hard and fast while his hands splayed over her breasts and then delved between their bodies to tease her clit. She swallowed every moan and noise he made, kissing him to last forever.

The climax took her hard. She gasped, shuddered, her head thrown back, his name a dying plea on her lips.

Evan cradled her against his chest. "Vi, my love, you are everything."

His use of her pet name shocked her back to reality. She scrambled off him, adjusting her drawers and her skirts, tying her bodice with shaky fingers.

"You need to go. I have paintings to see to."

He looked up at her, a mix of confusion and hurt in his eyes. He wanted to cuddle. She didn't dare.

"I'll see you tonight," she said. "We'll put on a show for our guests and the police, and then we can be done."

He rose from the couch, his impassive mask falling over his face as he buttoned up his trousers. "Until tonight then." He bowed formally and vanished into his workshop.

Violet sank onto the couch, legs trembling, heart pounding. *Generations have lived and loved on this couch.*

Now she was among them. When she left the country, the couch was going with her.

· · · ~~ · · ·

Violet and Evan met just outside the gallery, walking a circle around the towering, barrel-vaulted greenhouse to survey the security before entering. Police swarmed the area. Lacenaire and his ilk would have some fun in other areas of Paris tonight, Violet suspected.

She ran her hand over a small metal box affixed to one of the windows. "This thing is your new, highly sophisticated technology?"

"Preventing a break-in from above is tricky in a building

that is all iron and glass," Evan explained. "These boxes detect tremors, should anything strike the glass. Best of all, they send a signal, one to the other. Even the smallest breach of the structure will sound alarms everywhere."

"They are connected without wires?"

"Yes. Very simple, as such things go—signal out, signal in, line of sight only. But wireless teletics are the new thing, and this will be the largest demonstration of their use by far." Evan favored her with a smug smile. "Those who snatched up bargain stock after the spying fiasco will soon be lording it over those who sold."

"The arrogant industrialist. Using my exhibition for personal gain."

Vi knew she shouldn't tease him, but the words came out before she thought them through. He grinned at her and twitched his eyebrows.

"I'm as much an opportunist as you are, my dear. Besides, you never did pay me for my assistance."

"Pity you never thought to draw up a contract."

"Maybe I did that on purpose. Maybe I knew the moment we met that the greatest reward was to be yours to command."

Her heart lurched.

Still smiling, Evan took her arm and steered her toward the entrance. Violet glanced up at the dirigibles patrolling the skies, shaking off the turbulence caused by his passionate words.

"Everything looks in place," she observed.

"It is."

"And the backup plan, if all goes awry?"

"*When* all goes awry," Evan corrected.

"So optimistic."

"Every project carries the possibility of failure." He gave her a wry smile. "Some more than others. Are you ready to mingle?"

Violet called upon her best card-playing face. "Yes. Let's do this."

Evan nodded and escorted her inside, wrapped in his slick, charming armor. They looked the happy couple they claimed to be. Only the tension in his muscles and the wisp of uncertainty in his eyes betrayed him. No one but Violet was likely to notice anything so subtle.

The guests had only begun to arrive, but several prominent members of the Société des Arts waited to greet the hosts just inside the entrance.

"Good to see you, Tagget," a bald, moustachioed man greeted Evan. "This is quite the show you've pulled together in a short time."

Evan shook the man's hand. "It was all Miss Dayton's doing," he said, with pride in his voice. "She has planned an exhibition for the ages. All I did was provide a location and the security. I'm pleased to see a crowd is gathering. I believe the artists will do well here and will earn the Société a nice commission. I plan to bid on a few pieces myself."

"Excellent. May I request an introduction to your enterprising lady friend? I heard a rumor you were contemplating marriage, but that doesn't sound like you at all."

"Rumors can occasionally carry something of the truth. This is my fiancée, Miss Violet Dayton. Not only did Miss Dayton organize this affair, but she is herself an artist and is exhibiting several of her pieces."

"A pleasure to meet you," the man said to Violet. "What do you have to show us today? Sculpture? Painting? Do you belong to any particular movement?"

He sounded bored. Violet assumed he was asking only out of deference to Tagget. She smiled at him. "I'm a painter by trade. Oils, primarily, but I have worked in other media. Over the years I have played with many styles on the way to developing my own. While I'm not part of any movement, my works have something of an impressionist ambiance, often with trompe-l'œil details that I present in stark contrast to their muted surroundings."

"That sounds delightful," exclaimed a nearby guest. He rushed over to her. "Miss Dayton, is it? You must tell me more and show me some of your work. You have a charming accent, but I cannot place it. Where do you hail from? Does your homeland influence your work? Tell me everything."

Violet glanced at Evan. His eyes were alight with laughter. "Please excuse me, darling," she said. "The duties of an artist, you know."

"But of course." He kissed her hand and left her to her new admirer.

Within minutes, Violet had all but forgotten the circumstances surrounding the exhibition. Her dream had come to life, and she luxuriated in it. She chatted happily about her art with a number of interested visitors, eventually falling into a lengthy discussion with a female patron about the artistic merits of and possible motivations behind the Vérité forgeries. When the woman echoed Tagget's words calling Vérité arrogant, Violet almost succumbed to gales of laughter.

"This is fabulous, chérie!" Sophie's voice rang through the hall.

Vi turned to give her friend a quick hug. "Thank you. I'm so happy with it."

"I knew you would put on a show to remember. And I cannot thank you enough for the publicity you have brought to our hardworking artists."

"No thanks are necessary. I owe all of you so much. You were my first friends in Paris, and I will forever be grateful that you gave me a safe space I could turn to if I ever had need."

Sophie's eyebrows waggled mischievously. "You won't have need any longer. I hear you are to marry your millionaire."

Violet flinched, her cheeks burning. "Er, we do have an understanding." There. No outright lying.

"You must introduce me eventually. But first, let us walk."

The two women linked arms and set out through the gallery to mingle with friends and visitors. Violet surveyed the art, greeted guests, laughed with other artists, and answered any and every question about both her work and the exhibition. Through it all, she was Violet Dayton of Australia. No false French name. No cryptic pseudonym.

Her dress was of a color and style she had selected, and she wore it with sturdy boots underneath and no hat. She had done up her hair in a bun skewered with paintbrushes, with several artful curls falling from it. Her only accessories were her mother's shells dangling from a ribbon around her neck and the copper bracelet encircling her wrist.

This was freedom. Freedom to be herself, to display her talents and make her living in the way she wanted. Violet was dizzy with the joy of it.

There were people at the exhibition who criticized her art. A few even criticized her. None of their words could defeat the smiles and the praise from those who saw her worth. After a decade of copying the styles of others without any possibility of claiming the work as her own, she had at last stepped out into the open. She would always enjoy the challenge of creating a master forgery, but from now on her first priority would be to herself.

Only now were her plans for a new life all that they could be—a life not away from her past, but away from her own insecurities. Old Violet had been resilient, but new Violet was more confident, more determined, and happier.

And new Violet wanted to share her joy. She needed to find Tagget. He deserved thanks for everything he'd done to assist her. Their time together was running short. She couldn't resist the longing to seize all she could of it.

She found Evan still trapped near the entrance, talking business with yet another wealthy guest. He beamed at her as she approached, and she could see his relief in the relaxing of his shoulders. He made an excuse to his companion and walked Violet outside for some fresh air.

"You have saved me, my accomplished artiste. Why everyone wishes to talk contracts and finance at an art exhibition is beyond me."

"Isn't that what they talk about at the opera?"

"Yes, but I can escape to my box when the performance begins. Here, it seems they think they can monopolize my time for hours. I was on the verge of telling that man to take his telephone lines and go to the devil."

"Which would be bad, I assume?"

"Very. His company installs telephone and telegraph cables. I can't expand the network with no one to build the infrastructure."

"I'm happy to have saved you from such a fate. Would you like to see my paintings? I'm curious what you will think of them."

His eyes lit up. "Absolutely! But before we go in, I have something for you. I meant to give it to you earlier, but all the security checks and preparations distracted me." He dug something out of his pocket. "I couldn't stop thinking about you during these past weeks. I made a second bracelet to pair with the original. I doubt it looks quite the same, but I hope you like it."

Violet took the bracelet and slipped it onto her bare wrist, comparing the two side by side. "They look lovely together, thank you."

Her heart began to pound. *Maybe this can work. Maybe you don't have to leave him.*

The other voice—the pragmatic one—scoffed at her.

"And I have this," Tagget added. "Similar, but different."

He placed a metal heart into her palm. The piece was made from assorted scrap fused together, and dangled from a simple bronze chain. Scarred with scratches and hammer marks, but polished to gleaming, it took her breath away.

"It opens up. It should be the right size to hold your bits of shell. This should protect them better than a piece of ribbon."

Tears welled in Violet's eyes. Her fingers closed around the locket.

"If you don't like it—"

"Stop." Violet cut him off. "Don't say it. Don't ever say that."

"I—"

"No! Just don't. How can you not understand?" She stared down at the heart in her hand. "How can you make something like this and still not understand?"

"You could explain it to me, perhaps?"

"I've tried! But everything is dollars and cents to you. This for that. Buy and sell. I can't be with you if I'm just a high-priced bauble."

"I didn't make that to buy you. If it were a bribe, I would gift something highly valuable—"

Violet fled into the exhibit hall before he could say anything more. It had been too much to hope for. He loved her as much as he was able. So close, and yet terribly, agonizingly far. It might have been enough for old Violet, but new Violet knew she deserved better. She needed someone who could grasp and appreciate her true worth. She couldn't live knowing she had settled for almost.

She found herself a secluded corner to rest in while she composed herself. Wechsler needed to hurry up and break in. She wanted this over with tonight. Tomorrow, she was packing her things.

34

Evan made no attempt to chase Violet. It would do no good, in any event. Everything he said to her was wrong.

He needed to stop giving her gifts.

It went against everything he was. He adored giving gifts. The smiles on the faces of the recipients when they received a special surprise were like rays of sunshine after a storm. He had far more money than he could ever spend on himself, so why not put it to use? Lavishing presents on his lovers and admirers spread happiness, which was too often lacking in his life. He clung to it. He suspected he needed it more than they did.

He wandered into the gallery, brushing off business associates with vague comments about attending to his hosting duties. The forgeries exhibit was stupendous. The care and pride Violet took in her work was evident in every brush stroke. The paragraph in her pamphlet decrying the practice of burning forgeries was Violet to the core. Yes, she said, they weren't what they claimed, but they were real art, products of hard work that deserved to be valued. She saw beauty and worth where others didn't. Evan liked that about her, even though her choices of what to cherish often baffled him.

With pride of place, the fake de Heem had drawn a crowd.

Many were praising its beauty, though one irritable old man complained it was, "not the Dutchman's best work." Virginia Gaillard was among the admirers, clutching the leash of a tiny horse-dragon and urging her husband to make an offer for the painting. Hadn't Violet told her Evan was buying it as a wedding gift?

Damn. Vi had probably told Mrs. Gaillard to bid the piece higher. Brilliant, devious, delightful woman. Evan would have to pay a ridiculous sum for his own commission. He adored her all the more for it.

"The symbolism in this work fascinates me," commented a man to Evan's left. Evan glanced up at him—the same young art lover who earlier had gushed over Violet and her style. "Much of it is as you would expect for a vanitas painting."

"The reflection in the shiny cup is a mirror, for narcissism," Evan said. "The overflowing jewels mean avarice."

"Quite. The book is a symbol of knowledge, usually meant to indicate how weak our own human knowledge is. The spilling fruits are similar to the jewels, though many, such as the cherries, also carry a connotation of lust. That half an apple, for instance, is a reference to female sexual organs."

Evan's brows rose. "Is it? Interesting. I've always been fond of apples."

The man coughed awkwardly. "Yes. Well, it's all very standard for this sort of painting. The flowers, though, intrigue me. They aren't what one would expect."

"Enlighten me. I'm not familiar with the language of flowers."

"The rose, of course, is love, and the white dittany passion. Those don't surprise me. But then here are blue violets. Faithfulness. Intertwined with them are clematis, indicative of ingenuity, or mental beauty. The abundant snowdrops represent hope. Where all else is vice, the flowers seem to speak of virtues. It makes me wonder if they held other meanings for the artist."

"No. They mean just what you say."

The young man gave Evan a questioning look. "Monsieur Tagget, you speak as if you know the mind of the artist."

"I wouldn't presume that," he laughed. But he did know enough of Violet to understand that she wouldn't like the dour mood of a vanitas. She had added her own optimistic twist. It delighted him.

He gave the young man a firm handshake. "Thank you for your learned insight into this piece. I must excuse myself, now. I need to add my name to the bidding. I intend to purchase it." It would cost him well over ten thousand. Violet was a genius.

Evan tracked down Monsieur Favreau, whose big, black book recorded all bids and sales for any Société auction. Gaillard had indeed put in a bid on the de Heem, which Evan cheerily topped. Favreau marked the numbers with relish.

"This will fetch a fine price. I don't know where you dredged it up, Tagget, but I'm glad you did!"

"How is my fiancée faring, if I might ask? Has she sold anything? I haven't yet even glimpsed her art. She's been hiding her canvases in order to surprise me."

Favreau seized his arm. "Oh, you must come look, then! She has real talent."

"Of course she has real talent. Why else would she be exhibiting?"

Favreau looked sheepish. "There was some faction—small faction, mind you—who felt you were only catering to her whims. Proven very wrong, of course. Come, see. Several of her pieces have garnered attention, but one in particular is causing a stir."

Curious, Evan followed the man past several artists to the area where Violet's work was displayed. A sign reading, "*My Australia: a portrait series*, 1899-1905, by Violet Dayton," had been affixed to the wall beside the first piece.

That first painting caught Evan's eye immediately: a girl on the beach, the purple flower in her hair and matching ribbons on her dress bright and crisp against the soft, filmy background. With her suntanned skin and gold-streaked dark hair, she brought to mind a young Violet. The next painting over was similar, featuring a pale, freckled boy with reddish hair standing in a grassy landscape. The series contained a dozen paintings in total, children of all shapes, sizes, and colors, each lovingly rendered over a different piece of the Australian landscape.

"Stunning," Evan breathed. He'd seen her sketches, and the Vérité pieces, but those hadn't prepared him for this art that was pure Violet. Her love for the places and people of her homeland shone in each careful brushstroke. "Beautiful subject matter, excellent composition. The pops of color are especially striking, and the balance between the crisp details and evocative backdrops is without parallel."

Favreau chuckled. "You sound like an art critic, Mr. Tagget."

"I have nothing critical to say. I am in awe of her talents."

"As are many of us. Come. She has one additional piece that everyone is calling her finest work. Look here."

"Here" was blocked by several tall men, and Evan had to worm his way around them to see the painting. Stylistically similar to her other portraits, it employed a neutral-toned, impressionistic background around a single figure, with small areas of brighter color. This boy and his setting, however, set Evan reeling.

For several stunned seconds, he gaped at the painting in disbelief. In the midst of the rusty ruins of decaying machines stood a young boy, dressed all in black. He gazed out from the canvas in defiance, heedless of the soot smeared across his face and his frayed and torn clothing. The entire painting was in tones of black, brown, and gray, but for two spots: the boy's green eyes, dancing with darker flecks, and the bouquet of violets clutched to his chest.

"Christ Almighty," Evan swore.

He understood.

This fluttering of his heart, this trembling of his hands, *this* was the reason Violet had run to rescue her bracelet. Why she'd been so hurt when he'd offered to replace it with something new, something "better." There was nothing better.

The greatest masters in the history of art could replicate this painting and it would be worth nothing. Violet herself could surely find some flaw in it, and make a new copy, one that was as near to perfect as she could render it. Evan would happily hand it off to any stranger who wanted it.

But *this* painting, this mere thing, had transcended itself. Evan knew, without a doubt, she had crafted it for him. Out of passion. Out of love. It blazed with her inner fire. It was utterly, completely priceless.

He remembered the way he'd felt as he created that bracelet for her. Smiling. Thinking of her. Knowing she'd like that he'd fashioned something out of his pretty bits of scrap. No wonder she treasured it. It wasn't only a bracelet. It was a little work of love. And this was her reply.

He stepped closer, taking in every detail, every brushstroke, every subtle change in light and shadow. The boy was beautiful and emotional. The way his fingers clenched around the bouquet of violets brought tears to Evan's eyes.

I will hold her forever.

Violet's heart was laid bare in the painting, and Evan adored it beyond all reason. He would give his entire fortune for it and then pick himself up off the street and keep earning more, because it would never be enough. Even the heart she had stolen right out of his chest wouldn't be enough. Nothing he could give would ever equal it, because nothing could equal her. She was untouchable. Beyond worth.

"Isn't it something?" Favreau remarked. "Deeply emotional. Sad, yet not without hope. The flowers are so bright and crisp, and the boy looks…"

Evan blinked rapidly to clear away his tears. "Arrogant."

"I was going to say stalwart."

"What did she name this piece?" Evan stepped aside to peer at the card that listed Violet's name and the title. "*Dauntless.*" He laughed. "God, what a woman! Put my name in that book of yours. I'm buying this."

"You have considerable competition," Favreau informed him. "There have been several offers, and the current bid stands at two thousand guineas. That is something near to ten thousand of your American dollars, if I do the arithmetic correctly. I'm confident we can sell it for twice that by the end of the event."

"Fifty thousand dollars," Evan said, without hesitation.

Favreau gaped at him for several seconds. "Fifty? Gracious. I will notify the other bidders and see if any would like to top that."

No. Never. No one was buying this painting but him. Evan stared Favreau down with the same searing gaze as the boy in the painting. "One hundred thousand, and there will be no other bidders."

"Yes, sir." He made a note in his book. "I will see that it is marked as sold."

"You do that."

Evan turned away, scanning the hall for any sign of Violet. He owed her an apology, a kiss, and an impassioned declaration of his undying affection, and he meant to give all three as soon as possible.

"Armand, I adore this painting of the girl on the beach," Mrs. Gaillard gushed, waving at the image of the girl who looked like Violet. "Please, would you make an offer for it? I would so love to be able to show everyone who visits what an accomplished artist my friend is."

"Gracious, madame, how many paintings do you need?" Despite his protestation, the perfumier sounded resigned.

"Oh, Mr. Tagget will outbid us on everything, I'm certain. Won't you, Mr. Tagget?"

"Not on that particular piece. I'm very fond of it, but I have my eye on another of Miss Dayton's paintings. Please purchase that one for yourself. I would love to see it go to a good home." Evan would discourage others from bidding on that particular painting. It belonged in the hands of a friend.

"Perfect!" Mrs. Gaillard exclaimed. "And you must come and visit it. It will be just right in the drawing room, and I would love to have Miss Dayton to tea. She does have tea in the afternoons, doesn't she? Are Australians British? Sometimes it's vexing, being an American. I never know who likes what."

"You make the effort to please, and that's what counts," Evan replied, meaning it. To think, he actually felt something akin to affection for a flighty girl like Virginia Gaillard. It was all Violet's doing.

Mrs. Gaillard blushed exactly the right amount of pink to make her cheeks glow. "You are too kind, Mr. Ta—"

She let out a shriek as a tremor shook the floor. Sounds of cracking and splintering echoed off the high ceilings. Evan flipped open his watch. Nine twenty-six. L'Exploiteur hadn't wasted any time.

"Please, excuse me," he mumbled and rushed toward the de Heem exhibit. His apologies and confessions would have to wait.

He arrived just in time to see the tip of a giant drill disappear down a gaping hole in the floor. A pair of masked men tore past him, ripped the painting from the wall, and followed the device down into the hole. Their suits, Evan noted, were well-tailored and of the latest style. Henchmen, posing as guests right beneath their noses. They had forgone a rigid guest list for the gala for precisely that reason.

Alarms wailed with the breach in security. Dragons screamed and raced about the room. The guests were in an uproar. A pair of guards—more members of Evan's hotel staff—made to follow the crooks down the hole, but Evan interposed himself between them and their quarry.

"No. Don't."

"But, sir…"

Another tremor shook the building. A cloud of dust rose from the hole.

"He has collapsed it behind himself," Evan explained. "But no matter, there are police awaiting him on the other side. If you gentlemen would be so kind as to calm the guests and help restore order?"

Calming guests was a specialty of any good hotel, and his employees sprang into action.

Violet appeared at his side. "I saw it from a distance." She stared down at the ruined floor. "It was more violent than I expected. They've gone down a tunnel?"

"Yes, and while there should be police watching the Champs-Élysées metro stop for any underground activity, I suspect their numbers may be lacking."

"If Crevier's men are there, they'll do nothing at all. He's so vindictive he'd rather see us fail than do his job."

Evan nodded.

"So, plan B, then?"

He took her hand. "Come, my perfect, purple bloom. Our ship awaits."

35

Wind yanked strands of hair from Violet's coiffure as Dauntless coursed through the air. She tied the scarf tighter around her head and leaned over the prow to get a look at Wechsler's freighter. It was a smaller ship than he'd used previously, an express, built for speed.

Evan stepped up beside her, making a futile attempt to smooth down his hair against the rush of the wind.

"Can you breathe well enough?" she asked.

"My chest is a bit tight," he admitted, "but it's not unbearable. I'd prefer we not go higher, if possible." He lifted a pair of binoculars and adjusted the focus.

"He's fast," Vi fretted.

"We won't lose him," Evan said confidently. "This ship was designed by the finest airship crafter in America, and I would pit this crew against any in the world."

Violet clutched the rail. "I don't trust him not to do something mad."

"Neither do I. He will suspect that it was a trap. Either he'll be prepared and have some maneuver of his own planned, or he'll panic and make rash decisions."

"Both are bad. You were right, though, to think he would head for Belgium."

"It's the closest border, and his homeland. It's a logical place to escape to safety. Unless, as you fear, he does something unpredictable."

Violet fought back a sigh. "Until then, we wait and watch."

Evan slipped an arm around her waist. "Yes. Does it bother you, as a self-sufficient person, to stand here and do nothing while the crew works diligently?"

"You know it does. You feel the same."

"To a lesser degree. I've been delegating tasks to employees for years. One grows accustomed to it. Until you began ordering me about, you only had yourself."

"I never meant to order you about."

He chuckled. "I adore it when you order me about."

A small smile tugged at Violet's mouth. "You also like to argue with my orders."

"Naturally. Rumor has it I'm a conceited jackass."

"Some of the time."

"And the rest?"

Their eyes met. He wore an odd expression, part hopeful, part nervous. Almost pleading with her, but for what she couldn't determine.

"Sometimes you're a curious, excitable little boy," she explained, "eager to learn something new or to play with your mechanical toys. Sometimes you're a mad inventor, so enthralled with your work that you forget everything. Sometimes you're the perfect lover, generous, sweet, and overflowing with passion." She paused, because he wouldn't stop staring at her with that vulnerable look in his eyes, as if he would be either elated or devastated depending on her answer. "And on very rare occasions, I simply don't know what to make of you."

His arm tightened around her waist. "I need you to believe that I love you."

"Tagget." Violet stepped away from him, trying to infuse her voice with a tone of warning, without being harsh. She wouldn't have this conversation again.

"I'm still coming to understand how much," he persisted. "But it's no lie. No delusion."

She fixed her gaze on the distant freighter. "This isn't the time."

"It's never the time, with you. Either you don't wish to listen to what I say, or you will say nothing yourself. What are you afraid of?"

Her hands clenched on the rail. He was too close to the mark.

"The moments when you have opened up have been glorious," he said. "Why will you no longer do so?"

He moved to stand beside her, gripping the rail as she had done, his knuckles white with tension. He stared off into the distance, his moonlit profile the exquisite, cold perfection of a Greek marble.

"Or do you not love me?" The flat tone couldn't conceal his anguish.

"Evan, enough. Have you forgotten we're busy chasing down a master criminal?"

"I suppose I've done little to deserve you," he continued, heedless. "I'm a rather wretched, selfish sort of person, and you are—"

"Also wretched and selfish." She gripped his arm and turned him to face her. "So selfish, in fact, that I'm going to walk away if you don't shut your mouth. I do not want to talk about this right now."

His eyes met hers again, sad, but defiant. The look of the boy in her painting. "Then when?"

"Never."

His expression turned to ice. "Very well, madam. I take your point. I will be down below. Send someone to fetch me if anything happens."

Violet stared into the distance, determined not to turn and betray her feelings.

Tagget took one step, then stopped, speaking as if to

himself, just loud enough to be heard over the rush of the wind. "I've seen your painting, Violet. I know you have a heart of fire. What I don't understand is why you keep it so resolutely closed off."

His footsteps echoed on the deck until he slipped down the hatch. Violet's eyes stared, unseeing, in the direction of Wechsler's ship.

"I have no choice," she whispered. Closing off was her only protection. He, of all people, ought to understand that.

She kicked at the decking in irritation. Of course he understood. He was goading her. Evan Tagget didn't give up, he only changed tactics. Well, he would have to learn that Violet Dayton didn't give up, either. Her life of freedom awaited, and she'd be damned if she was going to live it as Tagget's discarded-fiancée-turned-mistress. She would settle for nothing but the best, and if that made her selfish, so be it. No one was perfect.

She returned her focus to tonight's mission. Waiting. Watching. Melancholy, yet resolute.

· · · ~~ · · ·

"Ships on the horizon!"

Violet's head jerked at Dahlia's cry. She'd been all but falling asleep on her feet. She steadied herself with one hand, and tried to spot the ships out past the dot that was the freighter.

"A dozen at least," Dahlia called. "We've hit the blockade. Flynne, what's behind?"

Violet looked toward the engineer. He lowered his binoculars, the bulbous, low-light filters glinting in the moonlight.

"Six or seven French ships to our rear. They're no more than dots, winking in and out."

"There will be more." This from Tagget, who stood just below the bridge, holding his own pair of field glasses.

Violet hadn't heard him return to the deck. Maybe she

had been asleep. She wandered away from the prow to join the others.

"Cutting our speed," Harrison said. "All prepare for sharp maneuvers, in case he turns around. Mite, you tell us if you want faster, slower, or anything else. This is your plan."

"This is Violet's plan," Evan corrected. "I'm merely paying for it."

Dahlia handed her binoculars off to Walton and scampered up to the bridge beside Harrison, running her fingers over the instrument panel. "Everything's looking good."

Violet stopped beside Tagget. He nodded in greeting, but didn't smile. He'd donned a pair of goggles, pulling them down as she approached to hide his eyes from her. Smart man. Exasperating man. He offered her the binoculars, and she took a better look at the ships ahead of them.

"This is where I become entirely uncertain about my plan." Vi shifted a bit and rolled her shoulders, stiff from standing at the rail too long. "He'll be sandwiched between the Belgian and French air guard, and then what? I can't make a good guess as to what he'll do. All we can do is improvise. This is why I don't do plans. They never go as you want them to."

Evan laughed. "You don't do plans? You are forever making plans, my sweet flower, and you do it to perfection. Your creativity and ability to adapt make the plans flexible. Coming upon an unexpected difficulty doesn't make the plan a bad one. You may trust me. I love plans. You've seen the stacks of schematics in my workshop."

She shook her head. "Three weeks of arranging and executing with no clear idea how it's going to end. Doesn't it make you nervous?"

"No. I trust this crew and I trust you. Obviously, I trust myself. We will do what needs to be done." He emphasized his words with a slash of his cane. She could see no purpose to holding it other than to give him the look of a debonair man secretly wishing to be a pirate.

"Perhaps we can fly right up beside him and you can slice holes in his balloon with your sword."

"We only need to pull within shouting distance. You can slice holes in anything with your sharp tongue."

Violet had to fight the quirk at the corner of her mouth. She wished she could see the teasing gleam in his eyes.

"Freighter coming around," Walton called. "Belgian ships moving this way."

"We're a good half mile past the border," said Dahlia. "They can push him right up to us. Flynne, any update?"

"French ships coming up fast, but they won't be here in time to encircle him."

"With this wind, he'll come hard aport the moment he spies them," the navigator surmised. "It will be his best chance to flee. We'll have to cut him off."

"Engines are ready for it," Parker shouted.

Violet looked at Tagget. "You and I wait and watch?"

"Yes."

"Do you really need those silly goggles?"

"I like them. They keep the wind from stinging my eyes."

He was laughing at her, she was certain, behind those dark lenses and his matter-of-fact tone. Absurdly, it made her like him better.

"You should try a pair," he suggested. "Purple, of course, with some artsy swirls on the band. Not that it would hide the cute little pout your bottom lip makes when you're annoyed with me."

A laugh of her own bubbled in her throat, and she had to bite the aforementioned lower lip to keep that laugh from bursting forth.

He offered his arm. "Would you do me the pleasure of accompanying me to the bow, Miss Dayton?"

"Trying to charm me to distraction now?"

"Is it working?"

It was. The familiar flirtations took just enough of her

attention to ease the nervous butterflies in her stomach. She tried not to think about the likelihood of his proximity causing butterflies of excitement instead.

"Of course not. But I would like a good look with the binoculars."

Tagget walked her across the deck and up the step to the raised viewing platform at the front of the ship. "Be my guest. I don't wish to deny you any pleasure."

The fact that he said it without any hint of a leer made it infinitely more seductive. Vi released his arm and lifted the field glasses, maintaining her resolve. She adjusted the focus, and jumped when the freighter came into her field of view.

"My God, he's headed straight for us, and at speed."

"Yes, I can see his sidelights. He knows we're faster and more maneuverable. He thinks he can keep his course and force us to move by virtue of his size."

"He'll change that plan the moment he spies the French ships." She scanned the horizon. "Gracious, those Belgian ships are fast."

"Interceptors. There's a fellow in Brussels who manufactures them. All the European navies start with his basic design."

"They're going to catch Wechsler before he reaches the border."

Tagget leaned as far out on the rail as she had ever seen. "Do you think so? May I look?" He shoved the goggles up, mussing his perfect hair. He rested his cane on the rail and trained the binoculars on the approaching fleet. "I think you're right. We'd better tell the crew to expect him to panic at any moment."

Dauntless began a sharp turn to starboard.

"I think they already know."

"Heading back to France!" Dahlia called. "They're pinching in on him. We'll clear out and watch the border."

A sharp rumble cut through the air, a sound almost like approaching thunder, but on a cloudless night.

"Oh, shit," Tagget blurted.

He passed Violet the binoculars, and she snatched them up. Wechsler's ship hurtled through the air, at a speed unlike anything she'd seen from a dirigible. An orange glow flickered at the rear of the freighter.

Another crack split the night, this one more familiar. Several more followed the first in rapid succession.

"Cannons!" Violet's hands tightened on the field glasses. She searched for muzzle flashes, her ears straining to decipher the direction of the shots. Dauntless had nearly come about, diminishing her field of view to a narrow strip. "But from where? Who is shooting at whom?"

"How the fuck should I know?" Tagget shouted. "Parker! Get those engines to full power! Get us the hell out of here!"

There was genuine fear in his eyes. His right hand held his cane in a death grip. Violet took hold of his left, their fingers interlocking.

"If he does ram us," Evan said, "there's an escape glider beneath us. Just give a yank on the handle at the end of the platform and it will pop out."

"It won't come to that. He's not that mad."

Another round of cannon fire erupted, louder than before.

"Or if we're disabled by a hit from a cannon."

"Evan." She squeezed his hand. "We'll be okay."

"*You* will. I'll make certain of it."

She had no time to criticize his fatalistic tones. A cannonball struck Dauntless a glancing blow. The ship lurched, and it was all Violet could do to keep hold of Tagget's hand as they struggled to remain upright. Up on the bridge, the crew shouted aeronautical terms, pulled levers, and turned dials. Dauntless swayed, then plummeted. Violet's stomach turned somersaults. Baby Fern wailed.

"Damned freighter went right over us," Dahlia called, "and think maybe he's figuring to come 'round again. Gauges are wonky. The wake from that crazy engine."

"Hang on," Harrison replied. "Gonna drop again. I won't let him come down on top of us. Parker, Flynne, full on my signal."

Evan leapt from the platform and jerked the handle that freed the escape glider. Metal creaked, and several inches of a curious device sprang free.

"Just being prepared."

He took Violet's hand, and they sat together on the edge of the platform, clinging to one another, helping each other in the only way available to them. As they sat, Violet watched the crew working wildly to steer the ship to safety. The hatred of leaving the work to others hadn't subsided, but those doing it were the most dedicated, competent group she had ever encountered.

"There is no one I would trust more just now than this crew," she vowed.

"Nor I," Evan agreed.

A long silence passed.

"I'm beginning to grow more accustomed to it, but I still don't like this."

"Yes. All the lurching and bouncing does make the stomach queasy."

"I wasn't talking about that."

His fingers pressed hers. "I know."

36

THE FIRST OF WECHSLER'S MINIONS dropped onto the deck without warning, swinging across from the sinking freighter.

Evan sprang to his feet, the cane flying up into his hands. The knob rotated beneath his palm and he drew his sword. In the time it had taken to do so, three more men had boarded his dirigible. He moved to put himself between the attackers and Violet, but she grabbed a fistful of his coat and yanked him backward.

A metal orb some two-and-a-half feet in diameter hurtled through the air where he had stood only an instant before. It crashed to the deck, cracking the planking, and sprouting several mechanical arms that embedded themselves into the wood.

"What in hell?" he blurted.

"Greetings!"

Evan whirled to face the final man to swing aboard. Albrecht Wechsler was an unremarkable man of medium height, with thinning, grayish hair and flat brown eyes. His suit, however, was of exquisite tailoring, and his gold cufflinks and watch fob gleamed. He held Violet's faux de Heem tucked under one arm, thoughtfully wrapped in a tarp.

Evan spared a glance at the dying freighter, slipping past en route to its doom. The men left behind cried out and scurried around in a vain attempt to resurrect her. The scene made his stomach turn.

"This is a lovely ship," Wechsler observed. "Unharmed by the Belgian cannons and fast enough to outrun those French sluggards. Gentlemen, if you would secure her for me?"

The half-dozen ruffians who had arrived with him surveyed Dauntless with avaricious grins on their battered faces. They gave Evan and Violet no more than a cursory glance, then raced for the bridge. Evan ran after them, Violet at his side.

"Get those little girls out of the way first," one of the goons snarled.

Heat flashed in Dahlia's eyes. Wechsler's men were brainless.

Two men headed for her, one making crude remarks, the other complaining about Fern, who continued to fuss. While they pounded up the steps, Dahlia vaulted over the rail, landing softly on her feet, despite the added burden of her child. Evan felt a grin forming. Dahlia Lasher was an airship brat. The men stood no chance.

She took down the nearest thug with a kick to the back of the knees. When he hit the deck, her boot slammed into his head. He didn't rise. The second man rounded on her, only to be hit from behind by Walton's large form. The two men tumbled and wrestled. The thug looked to be losing, until he reached inside his coat and drew a gun.

Dahlia seized the nearest heavy object—one of the deck chairs meant for more relaxing times.

The gun discharged, and Walton grunted in pain.

"Tony!" she shrieked. The chair crashed down on the head of Walton's assailant. Dahlia bellowed at him with every blow. "No. One. Shoots. My. Husband!"

Walton staggered to his feet, catching her arm before she could kill the man. "Baby, I'm okay. Barely scratched me."

They took up positions back-to-back, Dahlia with a chair leg, and Walton with the gun, looking for anyone else who dared challenge them.

Like Dahlia, Parker and Flynne had jumped from the bridge, but their pursuers were quicker to react. The engineers darted in opposite directions, each followed by one of Wechsler's men. Flynne flicked something on Mrs. Chatsworth's behind, and a hatch sprang open, spilling nuts across the ground. The goon slipped and fell. Walton and Dahlia were on him in an instant, disarming him and pinning him down.

Evan, who had yet to prove of any use to his friends, spun to help Parker, whose shorter stride made outrunning her lanky pursuer an impossibility. He had her pinned up against the rail, leering down at her. Her mouth twisted in a vengeful smile, one hand sliding behind her back. The thug leaned in. Her arm flew. He instinctively threw up a hand to deflect the blow, but her slicer had little regard for human flesh. The man howled in pain as the tool severed his fingers.

Evan turned away, feeling queasy. He flexed his right hand, looking at the white scar slashing across his knuckles. He would never escape the horrors of the factory. But he could— and would—pick up and move on.

When he glanced back, Parker had the injured man on the ground and a rope in her hands, trussing him as a farmer might truss a pig destined for slaughter. Up near the bow, Wechsler was cursing his men in a combination of French, German, and what Evan assumed to be Flemish.

Evan's eyes sought Violet. In the chaos, she had slipped from his side. She scampered up the steps to the bridge, where Harrison tussled with the remaining two goons. The pilot had fared well, but now, unable to overwhelm him, one of the men drew a revolver.

Violet was ready for him. She tapped the man on the shoulder, then took a step back. He whirled, then froze, taking her in from head to toe, admiring the exquisite dress that emphasized her breasts and hips, probably imagining himself stripping it away.

"I'll be right with you, beaut—"

She kicked him in the balls. When he doubled over, she knocked the gun away, then kicked him in the ribs for good measure. The remaining goon, recognizing the hopelessness of his situation, leapt from the bridge.

Evan ran up beside Violet, sheathing his sword. His lungs were burning, though he had hardly exerted himself. At least he wasn't wheezing yet.

"You didn't tell me this outfit included fabulous purple ball-kicking boots."

"They seemed practical."

"I'll buy you a pair in every color."

"Sir, they have an escape glider," Wechsler's minion called. He had reached the bow, and was now sliding the contraption free from its storage hole. He dragged it to Wechsler's side. "Activate the device and let's get out of here."

Evan's gaze flicked over the metal ball embedded in his dirigible's deck. God help them if that was what he suspected it was. He took as deep a breath as he could muster and ran back toward the front of the ship, past his dedicated crew who were diligently securing their prisoners.

"Thank you, Maes." Wechsler smiled at his man, then shoved him with such force that he toppled backward over the rail. His dying scream echoed through the night air. "I am afraid you cannot accompany me. I have a painting to carry."

Wechsler pulled a lever on the device. It came off in his hand, and he tossed it, too, over the side.

Evan pulled up a few feet in front of him, drawing his sword once more.

The shipping magnate laughed at him. "You didn't think you could really outsmart me, did you, Tagget? I commend you on a well-executed plan, but you are dealing with a true mastermind."

"It wasn't my plan." Evan was tired of repeating himself. "And it has worked to perfection. You are exposed, cornered, ruined. Now deactivate the mine or I will slit your throat."

Wechsler threw his head back and laughed. From his waistcoat pocket he withdrew a dainty little pistol. "Deactivation is impossible. Enjoy the next few minutes as you try to prove me wrong."

Evan took a step forward, lifting the sword to his enemy's throat. Wechsler aimed his pistol.

"Defiant," he chuckled. "You prefer me to shoot you? Very well. Goodbye, Mr. Tagget. You have been an interesting adversary. I will be leaving with my painting now."

The crack of a gunshot rent the air. For an instant, Evan marveled at the fact that dying didn't seem to hurt, except for the crushing disappointment that he couldn't explain his feelings to Violet. Then Wechsler crumpled.

"I made the plan," Violet retorted. "And that is *my* painting."

37

Violet was a good Australian country girl. She had fired her first gun at age six. She knew how to protect the family livestock from predators. And she damned well wasn't going to let one kill the man she loved.

The revolver she'd taken from Wechsler's goon served her well. It felt good in her hand, and its aim was true. She thought she might keep it.

Her shot had hit Wechsler in his right shoulder, disabling the arm holding the gun. It wasn't a fatal blow, though there was some chance he might bleed out. She found she didn't care.

Evan stood as if in a trance, his sword still hovering in midair. Violet raced to his side, the crew following her. Wechsler's remaining men were all bound, most unconscious.

"What is this thing?" Flynne asked, nudging the clawed metal ball.

Tagget snapped out of his stupor and spun around. "It's an anti-ship mine. When the clockwork runs down, it will explode. This one is large enough to blow the bow off the ship."

"I gave myself about ten minutes to escape," Wechsler croaked. "You're rapidly running out of time, Tagget."

Evan's gaze swept over his crew. His face turned ashen and his sword clattered to the ground. He grabbed for the escape glider, yanking on it in several places. Wings snapped open. Straps and buckles dangled from the frame. It was a terribly small thing for its purpose.

"How many people can that carry?" Violet asked.

Harrison answered from behind her. "Two."

Two? Were there no regulations? No thought for the number of people who might be on board?

Violet whirled to look at the crew. They regarded her with solemn expressions, facing their fate as bravely as they had fought their attackers.

"Every airman knows he may someday go down with the ship," Harrison added. "Those gliders are reliable. You and Mr. Tagget will reach the ground safely."

Parker flung herself at him, her slender arms wrapping about his waist. He stroked her hair and whispered something.

"No." The word squeaked from Violet's throat in a near whisper, a horrified refusal to accept the truth in front of her. No. She was a passenger. A guest. That glider was meant for her. Her heart screamed in agony. She couldn't leave her friends to die.

Behind her, Tagget continued adjusting the glider. "Walton!" he snapped.

The big man didn't respond. He held Dahlia curled against his side, blinking back tears as he bent to kiss the baby.

"Walton!" Tagget repeated. His voice was choked, as if in pain, but fierce nonetheless. "Get the hell over here. I don't have time to waste. Dahlia, strap that baby down tightly. Your family is going for a ride."

Walton's head jerked up. "Boss?"

Violet whirled around. "Evan," she gasped. A new pain stabbed at her. She'd thought him safe. She'd thought for certain he would use the glider and drag her away with him.

"Now, Walton!" Evan shouted.

"Y-yes, sir, but…"

Tagget cut him off with a sharp gesture at the glider.

Dahlia ran to the machine, tugging at the ties that held Fern to her chest.

Tears blurred Violet's vision. How could she have been so willfully ignorant? Over and over she'd fed herself the lie that he didn't understand love. Yet here he was, sacrificing all for love of friends and family.

"Harrison!" Evan bellowed.

"Sir!" The pride and respect in that single crisp syllable made Violet weep all the harder.

"Take her down as quickly as you can without killing us all. Parker, Flynne, I need your tools!"

The engineers sprang to his side, pulling gadgets from their belts. Evan grabbed as many as he could at one time and knelt beside the softly buzzing mine.

"Take Miss Dayton as far away from here as you can get," he commanded. "The wine cellar."

Parker seized one of her arms, Flynne the other. They were both stronger than they looked.

"No!" Violet struggled as they propelled her toward the main hatch. She couldn't leave him. "Evan, no!"

He didn't even flinch, too busy slicing into the infernal machine. He had shut out the world.

"Evan, I—"

She cut herself off. No matter how it hurt, she couldn't disturb him. Slim though his chances were, those precious seconds could mean the difference between survival and finding himself strewn across the deck in pieces. Through tear-clouded eyes, she watched the escape glider vanish over the rail, carrying a loving family to safety.

Violet stumbled down the stairs and sank to the floor of the tiny wine cellar, weeping openly. Her stomach lurched, and her ears popped as the ship hurtled toward the ground, but the discomfort was no more than a faded backdrop to the pain that crushed her heart.

She had never told Evan she loved him. She would never

hold him again, never look into those amazing eyes or hear the sensuous caress of his voice. She'd been too afraid to trust, too afraid to believe he could, and would, love her for all she was. She'd been ready to run away, telling herself she would find someone else to love her that way, never truly believing it would happen. Unable to believe him when he told her it already had.

It took a haze of tears to see clearly. Understanding came too late.

Violet was certain her heart stopped when the explosion rocked the ship. Evan's name burst from her lips in a strangled sob. She leapt for the door. Parker and Flynne let her go, following behind, stoically holding back tears of their own.

Two large chunks of rail near the bow had been obliterated, and frayed bits of rigging flapped in the wind. The mine was now a twisted wreck, half sheared away, with bits of metal strewn across the deck.

Evan lay on his back next to it, in one piece, but unmoving. Harrison knelt beside him, blocking his face and upper chest from view. Violet's feet propelled her toward them, cooperating even as she trembled with terror that she might find his eyes forever closed.

"I knew you had it in you, Mite," Harrison said.

"Had what, stupidity?"

The wheezing, pain-filled voice was the sweetest thing Violet had ever heard. She let out a breath she didn't realize she had been holding, cried his name, and covered the remaining distance in a heartbeat.

"Heroism."

"Every villain is the hero of his own story," Evan rasped.

His eyes were open. Filled with pain, but bright and alive. They widened the moment he saw Violet, and a weak smile touched his lips.

"My bouquet of unfading beauty."

"Evan," she breathed. "Lie still, you're hurt."

The relief she had felt upon finding him alive was cut short by the six-inch metal splinter jutting from his chest. Blood trickled down his left cheek, and his jacket was torn in several other places. The black fabric made it difficult to gauge the extent of the bleeding.

"It's not bad," he said. "Hit the filter." He took several shallow breaths before speaking again. "I told you they saved my life."

Violet wiped his cheek with her handkerchief. The laceration under his eye was superficial, and she doubted it would even scar. She made a quick assessment of the other injuries. The gashes on his arms didn't look dangerous, but the chest wound had her heart racing. She wouldn't lose him.

"Is there a medical kit on this ship?"

"Yes, ma'am," Flynne replied at once.

"Fetch it. Parker, can you run below and bring up a bottle of strong spirits from Mr. Tagget's liquor cabinet?"

"Yes, please," Evan agreed. "Cognac will make everything better."

"You just hold still," Violet scolded. "I need to cut away your clothing to get a good look at this wound." She drew her knife and made a careful slit in his waistcoat.

"This was a brand new suit. I looked dashing. Now I shall have to order another one. And I can't even rail at Wechsler, as he's unconscious."

There was something oddly soothing about Evan's raspy voice, but the pauses to catch his breath and the amount of blood he was losing terrified her. He was overexerting himself.

"Hush."

"I'd hoped to gloat. I deconstructed his mine enough to release much of the pressure and direct the remaining blast horizontally so as not to damage the balloon. It was a brilliant feat of engineering. I also wanted to watch while you taunted him. He is an anti-feminist prick, and I don't think he liked being captured by a woman. Or shot by one."

"Evan, be quiet."

"I won't. You're charming when you scold me."

"You're gasping for breath. Why waste it talking?"

"It..." He winced when she peeled back a section of his shirt. "It distracts from the pain. Parker, my merciful angel, hand me that bottle."

Violet intercepted the bottle before it reached his hand. She uncorked it and poured a small amount over the wound. Evan jerked and let out a yelp of pain and surprise.

"That's my good cognac!"

"It will keep the wound clean. Hold still while I pull out the shard."

Violet wrapped a bit of cloth from his shirt around the metal to keep it from slicing her hand, and gave a firm yank. The sound of metal on metal assaulted her ears, but the jagged piece sprang free from the biomechanics. Blood oozed from the gash.

Violet had no aspirations to join the medical field, but she didn't fear blood, and she knew how to clean and bandage simple wounds. Evan's injury went well beyond her experience, but unless one of the crew miraculously proclaimed to be a doctor, she was the best he had. She would do whatever it took to save him. She poured more cognac over the wound, then tipped a small amount into his mouth.

"I will smell like a lush, but one who knows his brandy."

Violet cleaned the wound as best she could, then began to stitch it closed with a needle and thread from the medical kit. Tagget declined the offer of an opiate, so she handed him the rest of the cognac, hoping it would dull the pain. He took several large gulps.

"I had no idea you knew how to sew," he marveled, trying not to cringe whenever she stabbed him with the needle.

"Of course I know how to sew. I told you, I was once intended to be a governess."

"Ah, yes. I said it would have been a waste. A far, far

greater one than even your insistence on pouring good brandy all over me."

"I'm glad you think so."

"I like you much better as an artist."

"I like me this way, too." She looked up at her friends, who watched her with smiles of admiration. "Harrison, can the ship make it back to Paris?"

"She can limp her way home," he replied.

"Good. I think Mr. Tagget is past the worst of the danger, but I want him to see a real doctor."

"Cambridge," Evan gasped.

"What?"

"I need to see Dr. Hathaway in Cambridge. For a new filter." His eyes drifted to his crew. "But take Miss Dayton and her painting to Paris first. She has an exhibition to run. And we can't fly to England without picking up Walton and Dahlia. Also, I would like those ruffians off my ship." He waved a hand in the direction of the trussed-up goons.

Violet had to force a stern expression. Trust Evan to give orders from flat on his back, with only one working lung. Seeing him act his usual self brought lightness to her soul. He would recover, so long as she kept an eye on him. And she would make sure he was cleared by a doctor in Paris before he went flying off to England without her. Now, though, it was time to get him some peace and quiet.

"Could you three help me carry Mr. Tagget down to his bed? I think he should rest."

"I can walk myself."

Evan began to sit up, but Violet pushed him back to the floor. "Oh, no you don't." She could be as stubborn as he was. She would sit on him if she had to.

Between herself and the crew, they managed to get him tucked into bed with a minimum of cursing. He put on a good show, but Violet could tell he was exhausted, and when the others left the room he sighed and closed his eyes.

"Stay with me?" The question carried a raw vulnerability that stabbed straight to the center of Violet's heart. "Until we reach Paris?"

She climbed onto the bed and curled up at his side, her arm around his waist, her head pillowed on his shoulder. "I'll be right here. Someone needs to keep an eye on you." His body relaxed beneath her, his breathing slowing.

"Thank you for saving my life," he murmured.

"It was only a few stitches."

"No. When you shot Wechsler. I would be dead without you. I don't think anyone has ever defended me unless I paid them to do it. But you—you shot a man for me."

He fell silent. Violet didn't know how to reply, so she said nothing. After several minutes listening to his gentle, steady breaths, she assumed he must be sleeping. She closed her eyes, still too unsettled to sleep, but needing rest nonetheless.

His hand settled over hers, gentle fingers stroking her skin. Not asleep, after all.

"I love you, Violet Dayton."

Vi buried her face against his chest. He smelled of brandy, sweat, and soap, brash and masculine. Her eyes watered, and her throat constricted. She had come so close to losing him.

"Oh, Evan," she sighed. She pressed a kiss to his skin, intimate in a way that transcended the mere sexual. "I love you too."

"Hope… not… dreaming," he mumbled. Seconds later, he lay sound asleep.

38

Three weeks later

DEAR EVAN,

Wow! What an adventure! I'm glad no one but you was seriously hurt. Er, I'm glad they weren't hurt and I'm sorry you were, I mean. But I hope you're doing well. I know your new biomechanics will be exceptional. Dr. Hathaway is the genius who helped create my earpiece, after all. When you're all better, you <u>must</u> bring Violet to visit. I want to meet her so much, and I want to take you to a football game. (You'll survive. You're tougher than you look.)

Your friend,
Eden

"Walton!"

The chef stuck his head through the cabin's doorway. "Yeah, boss?"

Evan pawed through the liquor cabinet, shoving glassware and half-empty bottles aside. "Where are my cigarettes?"

"There are none in there, boss."

"Could you fetch me some from the cargo hold?"

"None there, either."

"What? Why not?"

"We discarded them."

Evan blinked at him, not understanding. "You did what?"

"The doctor said you aren't supposed to smoke for a month, on account of the new filters."

"I was in bed for three weeks, abstemious as a saint. That's close enough. Find me some damned cigarettes." Evan poured himself a very large glass of cognac.

"Can't do that, boss. One month beginning today. He was very specific. We all felt it was important to follow his advice and protect your health, so we removed all the cigarettes from the ship."

"I hate you."

"Yes, sir, I'm sure you do."

Evan sank into a chair with his brandy. "I'm going to go mad."

"We'll be in Paris in time for dinner. We telephoned the hotel before we left, so they'll be ready for you. And Miss Dayton knows you're coming."

"I don't think she wants me."

"Bullshit." Walton cleared his throat. "Er, if you'll pardon my language."

"She needs to be free. She's creative and wild. Independent. Unstoppable. I can't win her with gifts. I can't offer her money. I can't control her and I wouldn't dream of trying. How do you hold on to a woman like that?"

"Love her. Be worthy of her."

Evan stared down into his drink. "That's where I fail utterly."

Walton huffed. "My family begs to differ. You want to tell my little daughter you're unworthy? After what you did for her?"

Evan looked back up, meeting Walton's dark-eyed gaze.

"That night haunts me. Violet very nearly murdered a man for me, and what did I do for her? I gave up her place on the glider to someone else. And if I went back, I'd do it all the same. In that moment, I looked at my crew—my friends—and I saw a beautiful family, full of love and hope. Everything I never had and always longed for. And my heart broke, because I knew I couldn't save her." He tossed back a boorishly large gulp of brandy. "Do you think she thinks I don't love her?"

"No, boss, I don't. I think she adores you."

Evan hopped out of the chair and raked a hand through his hair. "Dammit, there must be at least one cigarette on this ship."

"Sorry."

"Want to sit and get drunk with me?"

Walton chuckled. "Tempting, but I'm still working on the temporary repairs to the ship. Rigging and rails are done, but we only just got the treated deck planks. Had to cut out a big section to unhook the remains of that mine."

"I should have thought of that," Evan lamented. "I knew those thick arms would take too long to cut, but Parker's slicer could have cut through the wood. I could have chucked it overboard."

"The remaining chunk must have weighed a hundred pounds. In one piece I'd guess it was near three hundred. That's more than two of you."

"I could have asked the others for help."

"You did just fine."

Evan crossed the room to the liquor cabinet to fetch the bottle and another glass. "Let's go up top. You can have a glass while you work. I'll drink the rest and bellow orders for you all to ignore."

Walton's bushy brows arched. "You're riding up top? Even without Miss Dayton?"

Evan shrugged. "I can test the new filters."

Evan spent the majority of the flight slightly tipsy. He

wasn't certain it made up for the lack of cigarettes, but it did ease his anxiety. He moved from one crew member to another, talking about anything and everything. For two full hours he played number puzzles with Parker. She knew scores of them, including some she had invented herself. Evan solved everything she threw at him. He would have to be appallingly drunk before the numbers stopped making sense.

"Someday I'll stump you, Mr. Tagget," she vowed, when the game concluded. Evan looked forward to it.

By the time he entered his hotel, his pleasant buzz had worn off, and he was once again humming with nervous energy.

"Do you have any cigarettes?" he asked the concierge.

"No, sir. We received strict orders from your doctor not to allow you to smoke while you adjusted to the new biomechanics."

Evan gritted his teeth. This couldn't go on forever. Someone would be bribable.

"Is Miss Dayton here?"

"Yes, sir. We put her up in a lovely room on the second floor while your suite undergoes repairs. We have a key here for you. Dinner will be ready for you in twenty minutes."

"Thank you."

Evan took the key and ran up the stairs. He wasn't even out of breath when he reached the top. The new filters were phenomenal. He slipped the key into the lock and paused. Should he knock? Should he burst in unannounced and throw himself to the ground in front of her, sobbing his undying love?

No.

The last thing he needed was to look foolish. He unlocked the door, knocked, and entered.

Violet sat at a dressing table, dressed for dinner, adjusting a tiny hat that was a riot of black, white, and gray feathers. She turned slowly, acting calm, but Evan could see the tension in her posture. He glanced down at her boots to gauge the likelihood that he'd be kicked in the balls.

They were cute black ankle boots with chunky heels, tied with delicate silver ribbons. Tough enough for kicking, but only in an emergency. His eyes traveled upward, over a scandalous expanse of bare leg to the black, pinstriped skirt, tight over her hips and thighs, with a little flare just below her knees. To complete the ensemble, a black and white striped underbust corset covered a black, high-necked top. Her arms were bare and she wore fingerless gloves of white lace. She looked smart, sexy, and strong. Perfect Violet.

She stood to greet him. Behind her, propped against the mirror, was a printed photograph—of him.

There he sat, shirtless, his brow furrowed as he concentrated on his work. His scars were visible, and a stray lock of hair fell almost in front of his eyes. He didn't look perfect; he looked human. This was the boy in the painting. This was how Violet saw him. And she'd kept his photo close while they were apart.

Evan's palms began to sweat. She loved him. Rehearsed declarations played in his mind. He only had to find the right moment to explain himself.

"My lovely flower," he began. "As always, I am rendered speechless by your magnificence."

"You're never speechless." Her scolding frown turned into a smile. "You're looking well."

Evan took stock of himself. He liked the new suit, with the silver buttons and trim on the jacket. He'd paired it with his favorite silver and black brocade waistcoat this evening. He and Violet would look good together.

"New clothes," she observed. "Recent haircut and shave."

Evan stroked his short beard. "I'm not certain what I think of that English barber. He told me, with great pride, that this was the same style he recently gave to a friend who is playing the villain in a Shakespeare tragedy."

Violet grinned. "It suits you. I see little difference from your usual look." The smile subsided. "But how are you feeling? You've told me nothing. Was the surgery successful? Have you recovered from your injuries? Are you still sore, or tired, or suffering in any way?"

"Not at all. I'm perfectly well. Better than well, in fact. Improved. I can breathe more easily than at any time in my life."

"Good." She peeled off her gloves and tossed them and the feathery hat onto the dressing table, then walked up to him and planted an impassioned kiss right on his mouth. Her fingers caught fistfuls of his jacket. "Sex. Now."

Evan only cringed once or twice at their mistreatment of their beautiful new outfits. He sank into her wet, hot kiss, reveled in the caress of her soft skin, and danced to her every rhythm, in a union of pure pleasure.

The world outside his bedroom was harsh and puzzling, a never ending cascade of people and ideas, where he toiled with his reason and struggled with his emotions. But here, with this woman, in this wild tangle of lust and love, he was at peace.

· · · ~~ · · ·

Violet set aside the remnants of her dinner and snuggled up against Evan, running a finger over one of his scars.

"The new filters will last fifty years," he told her. "At which point I will either be dead or two-thirds biomechanical. But I'm told no smoking for another month, and I'm dying for a cigarette."

"You poor thing."

He scowled at her lack of sympathy. "Enough about me. Tell me everything that's happened since I've been gone."

"Wechsler is in hospital, under guard. The art is in the process of being retrieved and distributed. The Belgian police have been most helpful. And the French, too. Crevier is in disgrace for allowing l'Exploiteur to escape to his airship. He tried to denounce me as Vérité, but everyone laughed him off. One paper said, 'I could almost believe it, with the talent she has.' I clipped the article out and saved it."

Evan laughed. "Ah, my brilliant bloom! And how was your exhibition?"

Violet grinned. Even now that it had ended, thoughts of the exhibition caused an upwelling of joy inside her. "It was spectacular. The theft was the greatest advertisement we could have devised. We put up ropes around the hole in the floor, and people flocked to take pictures of it. My friends sold many pieces, I received a scathing review from a nasty critic that everyone hates, which only made me feel like a true Paris artist, and I've been asked to organize another show for next year. I'm brainstorming ways to make it even better. We won't have the draw of a master criminal, after all."

"Wonderful!" Evan kissed her cheek. "I'm so proud of you. How much am I out for the de Heem?"

"Quite a bit. I wasn't following the bidding too closely, but once it was back in place offers poured in. I *think* your proxy outbid them all." Vi arched her eyebrows. In truth, she knew the exact amount of his winning bid, but keeping him guessing was more fun. "What I'm most looking forward to is the follow-up in the coming months when we reveal it as a forgery and everyone talks about how much money you wasted."

"You're a wicked woman." His fingers trailed gentle strokes up and down her arm. "I adore you and your painting was worth every penny. Tell me about your own art. How did it sell?"

"Very well. Better than I expected, in fact. I need to get back to work to replenish my inventory."

"I'm glad to hear it."

Vi touched a teasing finger to the tip of Evan's nose. "Best of all, some fool paid one hundred thousand dollars for a single painting. I'm packing up my canvases and painting the world, with that kind of money in my pocket."

"I would have paid more." He sat up abruptly and seized her hand between both of his. "Violet, I've been lying in bed for three weeks, thinking of nothing but what I might possibly say to you, and now that we're here it's all gone out of my head, and I can only think that I will make an ass of myself. I can't even begin to explain the grip you have on my heart. Every time I think I understand it, I discover I've only unearthed one more tiny piece of the truth.

"That painting, though. It made me understand how you see things. Why you treasure what you do. You are in that painting. It oozes from every brushstroke, every detail. Staring at it, I could see right into you, as if I were seeing your heart lying open for me alone. I would have given my entire fortune for it. I would give anything, just for a chance to deserve you.

"I know I'm deeply flawed. I know I have failed you on more than one occasion. I will fail again and again, I'm certain, but I am begging you, from the depths of my soul, to believe that I do love you. You are my world, and you have made me a better man. If you are done with me, if I can be no more than a fling to you, that decision is yours and I will respect it. But you will never leave me. You are lodged so firmly in my heart that nothing and no one can ever take you away from me."

He let out a slow, deep breath. "I ask only that when you leave me you make it quick and direct to spare me as much pain as possible."

Violet's fingers pressed his. "I don't want to leave you, Evan. You may not have understood me, but I didn't understand you either. Not until I watched you give up your place—give up even *my* place—for a sweet, innocent family. I was so wrong to think you didn't know love. Because that was love, Evan. That was perfect, pure, beautiful love, and I…" She wiped away a stray tear. "I was the fool who tried to run from it."

Her hand cupped his cheek. "I said you were bribing me, but you weren't. You express your love differently. You want to give me the most perfect, the most expensive of everything because you believe I deserve the best."

"You do," he vowed.

"We were both mistaken. We're each different. And yet

very much the same." She pulled him against her, and they clung to one another, cheek-to-cheek and heart-to-heart. "And that painting?" she added. "I would have given it to you for free."

"Speaking of giving you the best," Evan murmured a short time later, "while I was recovering, I thought up a better gift for you than jewels or money."

"Oh?"

"I have a number of charities that I routinely support, and I've been working to expand that number, and possibly to start some of my own. And I know you don't wish me to pummel anyone on your behalf."

Violet twisted in his arms to frown at him. "I don't see the connection between the two."

"Word of our engagement has spread like a wildfire. There are people in my business world—an unpleasantly large number, I fear—who believe my choice of bride inappropriate. Instead of pummeling anyone—or hiring goons to do so, as I was laid up—I gave away money. Whenever someone criticized your profession, I made an additional donation to a foundation for the arts. If they had a problem with your lack of social standing, I gave to associations to support low-income workers. After seeing articles lambasting me for my choice of friends, I have supported organizations for the rights of people of color, unwed mothers, and those with disabilities. I am now the largest sponsor of a New York ladies' suffrage organization after a particularly lengthy conversation with a woman-hater. From now on, every time anyone has anything bad to say about you, me, our friends, my employees, or anyone else, I give money in your honor to fight such ignorance and hatred. And I've honestly never found anything more satisfying in my life." He hugged her close. "Except perhaps for losing myself deep inside you."

The kiss they exchanged was soft, gentle, and achingly sweet. "I love you, Evan Tagget," Vi sighed.

"I love you, my priceless Violet. Will you stay with me? Forever?"

"I will. But on my own terms only. I told you from the start I won't be your kept woman. Make the engagement real. Marry me."

"Done. First thing tomorrow. Do you have a suitable dress? Wear anything. Or nothing. I don't care."

"I have a brand new dress from Madame Rochette."

He grinned. "You truly are an excellent planner."

"Actually, I bought it with my own money as a celebration of the success of my exhibition. It wasn't meant to be a wedding dress until Virginia Gaillard walked into the shop while I was having a fitting and started gushing over it."

Evan chuckled. "I think it *was* meant to be a wedding dress and you simply didn't know it."

"Virginia is horrified that I don't have a ring, by the way. I pretended the emeralds were your love token."

"The emeralds are worthless junk, and I have a ring for you."

He scampered from the bed and dug a small box from his jacket pocket. "I like to plan too. I bought this on my way here, at the same store where you found your fainting couch."

Violet tipped the ring into her palm. Five purple stones were arranged in the shape of a flower. One was badly chipped, and a hole gaped in the center where another stone should have been. The metal band had darkened with age. It was as perfect as she could imagine.

"It's not fancy, but it made me think of you."

She beamed down at the ring and slipped it onto her finger. "Aren't you going to offer to buy me something newer and nicer if I don't like it?" she teased.

"No. But I will offer to have it repaired and cleaned."

"I think I'll wear it as it is, for now." She lifted a hand to his cheek. "Things don't have to be perfect to be worth loving."

Evan caught her other hand and placed it over his heart. "Fortunately for me."

"Fortunately for us all." She kissed him again, pushing him down onto his back. "Enough talking. Our wedding night is fast approaching and we're out of practice. No more spending three weeks apart."

He closed his eyes and lost himself in her taste. "Never," he breathed.

39

"I'M NOT PROMISING to obey you!"

Violet peeked out from behind her privacy screen. Evan strode across the cabin toward her, glaring at the paper in his hand.

"Those vows are lovely and traditional," she teased.

"I will call off the wedding, and you know how that will break my heart."

Violet took pity on him and handed him the real vows. He gave her a look of annoyance that didn't reach his eyes.

"Is this a taste of what I can expect from our lifetime of wedded bliss?"

"Planning to flee at the last minute?"

"And let some other man snatch you up? Certainly not." He fluttered the paper. "These are much better. I prefer them to the ones I picked out. You have a better eye for the poetic, unsurprisingly."

"Good. I think we're ready, then." She shooed him toward the door. "Go, so I can dress. I want to surprise you."

"And where am I to prepare?"

A mischievous grin played across her face. "The wine cellar?"

"Excellent idea. I understand bridegrooms often drink themselves silly before marching to their doom."

"Walton put your things in Harrison's cabin."

"Thank you." His face grew soft and serious. "I will see you shortly, my love."

She blew him a kiss.

Violet didn't need long to ready herself. The lavender silk slithered over her skin, clinging to her body and pooling at her feet to cover the soft, matching slippers. She wore no gloves and no hat, only a few flowers in her hair and—as usual—a paintbrush. The heart locket with her shells went around her neck, and the copper bracelets on her wrists. Evan carried her ring until the ceremony. Her finger already felt bare without it.

Up on the deck, her friends awaited her, arrayed in their finest. The airship crew were all present of course, along with Sophie, Amal, a few of the other artists from the commune, and Virginia Gaillard—with her husband and a pet. Everyone looked lovely and happy, and Vi spared them all quick smiles. She tried not to run, tried not to stare, but Evan was there, standing and waiting for her at the bow, and she was drawn to him like iron to a magnet. She hitched up her long skirt and jogged across the deck, her slippers whisper-soft on the wood planks.

"My unparalleled Elysian inflorescence," he breathed.

Violet thought she might melt beneath his adoring gaze. He looked his usual perfect self, all black, but for a tie of the same silk as her dress. Passion radiated from him. She read it in the curve of his lip, his sparkling eyes, his outstretched hand grasping for hers.

"My ridiculous, supercilious, and strangely adorable engineer," she replied.

Their fingers entwined. Their eyes locked. A ritual began. Words were exchanged. The details passed by in a blur, because all that mattered was this joining. The two of them, loving, being loved, knowing in their hearts that this was right. Together in body. Together in mind.

"Under the laws of the sky and by my authority as Captain of this vessel," Harrison intoned, "I pronounce you husband and wife."

Violet wasn't certain who kissed whom, but the instant their lips met she wound her arms around Evan's neck and gave him a good preview of what to expect once they were alone. She had to force herself to pull away before she scandalized everyone.

Her friends clapped and offered the happy couple hugs and congratulations. Walton opened several bottles of champagne and produced trays of hors d'oeuvres and fresh-baked sweets. Violet sipped, nibbled, smiled, and clung to her new husband's arm. She couldn't bring herself to stop touching him. A mad, bubbling happiness flooded her body every time she looked into his eyes. Evan looked mesmerized. An idea floated through her mind for a painting of a man struck by Cupid's arrow.

"Mrs. Tagget!"

Vi started at the use of her new name. Virginia Gaillard rushed over and gave her yet another over-enthusiastic hug.

"This was the most lovely, unique sort of wedding. I'm so happy you invited us. You two will be the talk of the town, and I took many, many photographs."

"Don't sell them too quickly," Evan warned. "You'll want to find the highest bidder."

"Oh, don't be silly! The photos are for you to remember your special day and to share with your children and grandchildren. But the newspapers will want some, I expect."

"Send them as many as you'd like. I want everyone to know how enthralled I am with my darling bride. And, if you would, send a few of the nicer ones to Mrs. Eden Caldwell of 312 State Street in Ann Arbor, Michigan. My one regret is that she can't be here to celebrate. I will see that someone writes down the address for you before you leave."

"Oh, never mind that. I have a spectacular memory, don't I, Armand?"

"Oui, madame. You forget nothing, except perhaps your animals."

"Yes." She looked up. "We will have to fetch my dragon down from the rigging. I suppose that is what I get for ordering one in the style of a monkey."

"A charming creature, I'm sure," Evan replied. He was struggling not to laugh. "Please excuse me, my wife and I would like a moment alone."

"Your wife," Violet said once they reached a quiet spot along the rail. "It's strange to hear it."

"It's strange to say it. But I love the way it feels on my tongue. I shall have to say it often. So, wife, about our honeymoon. I understand you wish to travel the world and paint all that you see."

"You are correct, husband."

"This ship is as much yours as mine now, and the crew, I'm certain, like you better than they like me. Tell them where you want to go, and we shall travel there. However…"

"Yes?" Violet eyed him with suspicion.

"While I was lying in bed adjusting to my new filters, I sent a great many telegrams to various of my employees and business associates. There are parts of the world, you know, that have not yet benefited from the high-quality Tagget Industries telephone and telegraph services. One such place is your homeland of Australia, and these recent arrangements have begun the process of establishing a business foothold there, based out of Melbourne. If at some point we could spend a few weeks there so I might handle certain in-person tasks, it would be most appreciated."

Violet laid a hand over his heart. "Purely for business, of course."

"I'd like to meet your family. And there is one lady, in particular, whom I think we both should meet."

Her heart pounded, and her fingers went automatically to the locket that carried her shells. "My father refuses to tell me where she was or where she might be now."

"You get your tenacity from him?"

"Yes."

"Well, you are a grown woman now. I'm certain you can out-match him. If you're ready?"

Vi took a deep breath. "Yes. I think I am. And where will you be while I do this?"

"Standing behind you, ready to fight the world at your command. Where else?"

Her eyes clouded with tears. "Thank you."

He beamed at her, his own eyes a touch misty. "We will find her. I promise."

"Of course. Evan Tagget always gets what he wants."

He drew her closer and his lips dusted hers. "I got you, didn't I? Despite the many challenges you presented me."

"*I* got *you*, you conceited jackass."

He had the gall to smirk at her. "Truer words have never been spoken. I am as you say." His brows twitched flirtatiously. "And, yet, you like me that way."

She wound her arms around his neck and gazed into those wild green eyes. Sparkling. Teasing. Happy.

"I love you this way."

EPILOGUE

New York City, 1925

EVAN SPUN ACROSS THE FLOOR in the arms of yet another gorgeous woman. Dancing kept him young. He could, and often did, spend hours here, in the dim, smoky hall, his body swaying in time to the sensuous strains.

"Well," the woman murmured. "The Salon des Artistes does appear to live up to its name."

"Indeed," Evan agreed, his eyes roving the collection of fine art on the walls, as his body moved in rhythm to the sounds of some of New York's best musical talent. "It's a popular destination for the creative and eccentric."

What he didn't add was that the club also served as a haven for bootleggers, gamblers, prostitutes, and others of less-than-stellar reputation. The rules were simple. Anyone was welcome. Everyone's business was his own. Those who respected the employees and the other patrons found their money was most welcome. Anyone causing trouble was barred for life, no matter who he or she might be.

The song ended and Evan abandoned his partner for a younger, prettier woman.

"Thanks, Mr. Tagget," the girl said, grinning down at him and launching enthusiastically into the up-tempo dance. She would be his last for a time. His legs were tiring, and he wanted to conserve energy for more rewarding nighttime activities.

A moderately-popular actress who adored scandal and made a nightly habit of propositioning Evan sidled up mid-dance.

"I'll take better care of you than that pretty, young virgin can," she purred.

"I'd rather screw your dance partner," Evan replied casually, partly to chase her off and partly because it was true.

"Would you?" the man with her began. "I might be interested in—"

Evan shooed them both away, as his young companion giggled.

"This place is sensationally scandalous," she enthused.

He resisted the urge to scowl like a disapproving parent. Or like the disapproving godparent he was to the teenager in his arms. The girl had no business here in his notorious speakeasy. But Ava Harrison and Fiona Tagget were inseparable, and Evan spoiled his daughter terribly. When Fiona wanted a night on the town, that's what she got. He just made certain to follow along to supervise her.

When the dance ended, Evan kissed Ava's cheek and executed a formal bow.

"A pleasure, as always, Miss Harrison. Would you care for some refreshments?"

"Yes, please." She scampered over to the bar, Evan trailing behind. "Gin and tonic, please," she said to the bartender, her eyes wide and shining with excitement.

"Er, sorry, miss. Boss said we're not to serve Miss Tagget or any of her friends anything but what's strictly legal. We have root beer, Coca-Cola…"

"I'll have a ginger beer," Ava sighed.

The bartender handed her a bottle, then poured Evan his usual.

"Daddy is such a spoilsport," Fiona complained, taking her friend by the arm.

Evan grinned as he watched the girls walk away, their heads bent together, their voices a conspiratorial whisper. Those two would rule his empire someday.

A whiff of lilac perfume caught his attention, and he turned to greet the loveliest woman in all of New York. She came directly from her studio, judging by the paint on her fingers and the messy knot tying up her hair. Her purple dress was fashionably short and slinky, and she wore heels that made her several inches taller than him.

He greeted her with a kiss. "Vi, my exquisite flower, how have I not yet lost you to a man half my age?"

"Because you're always saying things like that and making me feel special. And who can compare with your sense of style? Come, dance with me."

"I'd hoped any further dancing tonight would be of the horizontal variety."

"Only if you take a turn about the floor with me now."

Evan waved at the musicians, and they segued into one of his favorite tangos. Not as hip as the Charleston, certainly, but smooth, sensual, and just right for taking Violet into his arms—or arm, since he still held his drink in the opposite hand.

"Why did you bring a pair of innocent sixteen-year-old girls to your sordid nightclub?" she murmured, her lips pressed to his ear.

"It's *our* beautiful nightclub, and I couldn't very well let them go by themselves."

"You think Fiona would have snuck out?"

"She's your daughter," Evan reasoned.

"Mmm. And did you drag our son along on this adventure as well?"

"Certainly not! This is no place for a ten-year-old boy. He stayed behind on the dirigible."

"Alone? Our brilliant, excitable child who as yet lacks all common sense?"

"He's not alone. Some of the Walton girls are there."

"Terribly reassuring. We may not have a ship when we get home."

They spun to avoid one of the security dragons that wandered the hall. The creatures kept near the walls unless activated. Now they had come out to alert the patrons, red lights pulsing on their backs.

"Your pig is flashing."

"Perfect. The girls will get to see how we handle a raid."

The musicians didn't miss a beat, and Evan and Violet continued dancing. Over at the bar, the bartender had flipped the hidden switch, and the entire bar area was descending smoothly into the floor. Guests with drinks stashed them in cubbyholes before wooden panels slid down to cover them, blending in with the rest of the wall.

"Officer Jameson!" Violet greeted the policeman who led the group of law enforcement personnel into the room a minute later. "How good to see you again."

He nodded to her. "Mrs. Tagget. Routine checkup. We've been hearing rumors about this place again."

"Shocking. As you can see, Evan and I brought our daughter and her friend here tonight." She gestured at Fiona and Ava, who waved back. "Certainly we wouldn't allow them near any illegal goings-on."

"Right." He looked at Evan. "What's that you're drinking?"

"Cognac. Perfectly aged. Smooth and crisp. Imported from France."

"Smuggled from France."

"An ugly word. Would you like to have a glass with me? You're welcome to come visit us on Undaunted at any time.

We'll fly her up before we drink, of course. The laws of the skies, and all that."

"I ought to arrest you."

"But you won't," Violet said, "because it would be a waste of all of our time. I certainly hope you have better things to do than inconvenience people having a nice evening."

"Frankly, Mrs. Tagget, I keep hoping they'll move me to a different post, but right now my job is shutting down speakeasies."

"Well, aside from my personal indulgence, we are perfectly clean." Evan waved a hand. "Feel free to look around."

Jameson glanced around the room, then down at one of the pig-dragons. "Curious creature. What's it for?"

"Atmosphere. Tiny dragons are once again all the rage in Europe, you know."

"Right. You folks have a good night." He tipped his hat and led his men out.

Fiona rushed over to her parents. "That was nothing! Where were the guns? The pounding on walls to find the hidden chambers? The smashing of things? He didn't even make you pour out your drink!"

"I pay good money not to have those things happen in my establishment," Evan replied. "You'll understand when you become more invested in the business."

"It was terribly disappointing. Can we go to a different club tomorrow? One where they will shout and overturn tables searching for stashes of bathtub gin?"

"Absolutely not. In fact, I think it's time we all went home for the night." He ushered the ladies toward the exit. "We need to see if your brother has dismantled the ship in our absence and reconstructed it as some Art Deco masterpiece."

"You just want to go to bed so you and Mother can have noisy sex."

"Fiona!"

"It's true. Fern Walton says it sounds like you enjoy it, so that's good, I suppose. She also says her parents are worse."

Evan took his wife's arm. "I suppose I brought this upon myself when we decided to have children."

Violet pressed up against him, letting him feel the curve of her hip through her thin dress. "Yes, you did. I blame you for all their faults."

"Naturally."

"Ugh. So flirty," Fiona grumbled. "You'd think they would get too old for that." She took Ava's hand and the two girls hurried out the door and down the street to talk apart from the adults.

"You'll understand someday, my love," Violet laughed.

"Ha!" Evan snorted. "I doubt I'll ever see anyone good enough to deserve her."

"Remember, darling, they don't have to be perfect. Just perfect for her."

Evan put his arm around his wife's waist, loving the feel of her, the scent of her, and the taste of her that he would have in a few short minutes. "Like I hope to be for you."

"You are. You always will be."

Evan's heart swelled with a joy that had grown familiar, yet had lost none of its thrill with the passing of the years. He paused right there, in the middle of a New York City street, and kissed the love of his life.

THE END

ABOUT THE AUTHOR

AWARD-WINNING AUTHOR CATHERINE STEIN believes that everyone deserves love and that Happily Ever After has the power to help, to heal, and to comfort. She writes sassy, sexy romance set during the Victorian and Edwardian eras. Her stories are full of action, adventure, magic, and fantastic technologies.

Catherine lives in Michigan with her husband and three rambunctious girls. She loves steampunk and Oxford commas, and can often be found dressed in Renaissance festival clothing, drinking copious amounts of tea.

· · · ⚙ · · ·

Visit Catherine online at
www.catsteinbooks.com
and join her VIP mailing list for a free short story.

Follow her on Twitter @catsteinbooks,
or like her page on Facebook @catsteinbooks.

ALSO BY CATHERINE STEIN

Potions and Passions

The Earl on the Train - Book 0.5

How to Seduce a Spy - Book 1

Not a Mourning Person - Book 2

Once a Rake, Always a Rogue - Book 3

Sass and Steam

Love is in the Airship - Book 0.5

A Shot to the Heart - Book 0.75

Eden's Voice - Book 1

What Are You Doing New Year's Eve? - A Holiday Novella - Book 1.5

Other Books

The Scoundrel's New Con

Mating Habits

Available at your favorite online retailer.
www.catsteinbooks.com